I0684981

The Nettle Wits

The Legend of the Girl With No Knickers

Susan Doyle

The Nettle Wits

Published by Sugilite Publishing, United Kingdom

ISBN: 978-1-7392827-2-1

CONTENTS

Part One – Dreams

Part Two – Nightmares

You may also enjoy Susan's first book:

The Runt and the Ladybird.
ISBN 978-17392827-0-7
Publisher -- Sugilite Publishing
A reality-fantasy following the over-protected Conscience of
The Almighty, as she finally learns about the most important
thing in the whole World -- herself. Se *is* the World.

Part One

DREAMS

CHAPTER 1
THE ARCHAEOLOGISTS

"Wallow in your dreams, but stand to attention in your nightmares."

The north-east of Ireland, 2015

It was a glorious September day as I hid with my sister in the crack between the doorsteps. We were covertly watching a group of teenage schoolchildren as they worked with their teacher and an archaeologist from the Queen's University Belfast, and their mission was to prove an ancient myth.

You see, the area around here, known locally as Snake Farm, is reputed to be have been the centre of an industrial revolution some two thousand years ago. It has also been referred to by some as the catalyst for the unification of Ireland, but very few believe. It's all myth, apparently.

"What do you think they're looking for?" My sister cuddled into me as we watched the towering humans digging and searching. "If they want to know about the history, just ask us."

"Don't be silly. We're not allowed to have any contact with them. They're humans, they'd just squash us. Nobody's ever talked to humans, so don't even think it." I tutted at my sister's naivety. "Anyway, they'd never believe anything we told them, they already know everything. That's what Old Murphy always says."

We watched a little longer, then the group stopped for a sandwich and drink, and sat around the camp fire. The archaeologist spouted off some more about the myth being a myth, as they'd found nothing except a couple bits of pottery, and he made his assessment in that the farm was only ever a 'farmers' hovel'. Then one of the boys put his hand in the air.

"Sir," the fourteen-year-old human boy hesitated, then bravely stated, "my grandad says that even if we don't find anything, the legend is still true, because he was told it. Just because we can't see something doesn't mean it never existed." He breathed in and waited for the wrath of the expert, but the archaeologist just smiled, so the boy continued. "And he says that the leprechaun that told the legend to him, would never lie."

At that point the archaeologist burst out laughing, and the rest of the group laughed with him. Clearly they didn't believe in leprechauns.

My sister pulled hard into me as we both giggled with the humans, but eventually calmed, and she whispered into my ear, "That's good, ain't it? They don't believe in us."

"To be sure, never seen us, so we don't exist. Just like the boy says, like the myth of Snake Farm, we're make believe, fairytale, and so long as that never changes, they'll never destroy us." I noted that the boy's grandad seemed to have had some contact with a leprechaun, and the rest of them just treated him as a nutter.

The site was just a little way inland, on the edge of the moors which extended as far as the Mourne Mountains, and on the other side was the Irish Sea, although the sea was not visible from the site. The moors rolled on as far as the eye could see, just heathland and old stone walls, broken up by the white of a few sheep. Wilderness, backed by the misty shapes of the mountains. It certainly didn't look like a site of thriving industry, so the boy who believed the legend of Snake Farm stood alone amongst the group of investigators, and I felt a little sad for him. It can be a lonely life for a believer.

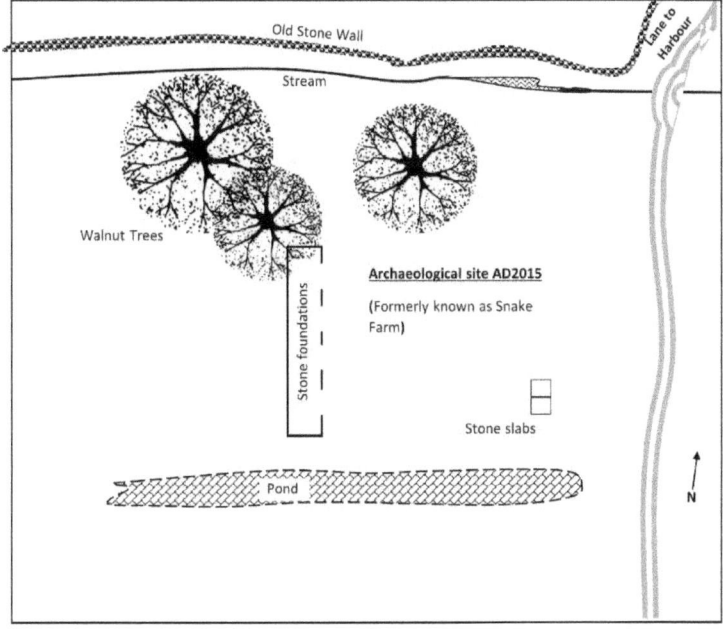

CHAPTER 2
THE LEPRECHAUNS

Modern-day leprechauns (aka lupracáns or leipreacháns) are just a joke. Nobody seems to know whether they are a foot tall or four feet tall, wear red or wear green, with a pointed hat or a stupid hat, make a living as a cobbler or as a thief, in fact they're just a derogatory incarnation of an Irishman. The likes of Disney have done to the leprechauns what Coca Cola did to Father Christmas when they created his image for the Coke adverts. So, leprechauns are just myth, make-believe, commercial effigies aimed at the un-broken imaginations of children, that's all.

But hang on a minute! Who says they're not real? Ok, the modern depiction of a leprechaun is pretty bloody childish, but hundreds of years ago somebody first put their myth into writing, with the earliest known example describing how Fergus mac Léti, the King of Ulster, was captured by leprechauns whilst asleep and dragged to the sea. That was in Mediaeval times, hundreds of years ago, and the idea of leprechauns way back then was not influenced by Disney, but by myth, and what is myth? Very often it is an adaptation of the long-forgotten truth, and what is truth? Very often it is akin to belief. So, a true story is one you can believe in, myth or otherwise.

Now, the truth! Not everybody has forgotten the truth regarding leprechauns, and so I'm gonna tell you a true story of one of the early tribes of leprechauns and their naïve plight to survive the immigrants, the climate change, and the human expansionistic exploits, dating from around two thousand years ago.

I can almost feel you thinking, 'how would he know?', so,

5

in case you haven't already sussed me, I'll tell you how I know when all others purely guess, and I'll say this only once. "I am a leprechaun." And that is not myth.

So, I'd like to tell the true story of the leprechauns of Snake Farm, north-eastern Ireland, very distant relatives of mine.

Two-thousand years ago, there lived a particular species of leprechaun, scientifically known as Leprechaunus Nettlewitticus, and they had developed a dependence on Moors caterpillars, which themselves had developed a dependence on the Irish Stinger Nettle, which they themselves were dependent on the human farmers leaving them alone. So, a perfect, but uncertain, civilisation lived for hundreds of years in the Irish Nettle forest at Snake Farm, behind the pigsties.

Like myself and my sister, our forebears didn't need too much room to live, just a decent sized nettle forest, because they were only about ten millimeters tall (less than half an inch) and the Moors caterpillars which they farmed were only a little bigger. So, they lived out their splendid existence in the Irish Nettle forest, behind the pigsties at Snake Farm, for hundreds of years. They were the Nettle Wits.

The Nettle Wits had beautiful, rich, nettle-green complexions with brilliant-red lips, and wore bright red jerkins and pyjamas, but contrary to 'Disney' belief, they never wore a hat. They were, and still are, a handsome species of leprechaun and this is just a part of their very long story. So, is it legend or myth? Well, I call it history!

CHAPTER 3
THE PHILOSOPHY OF LIFE

About two thousand years ago, in the year AD 69.

On the school platform, The South Hold.

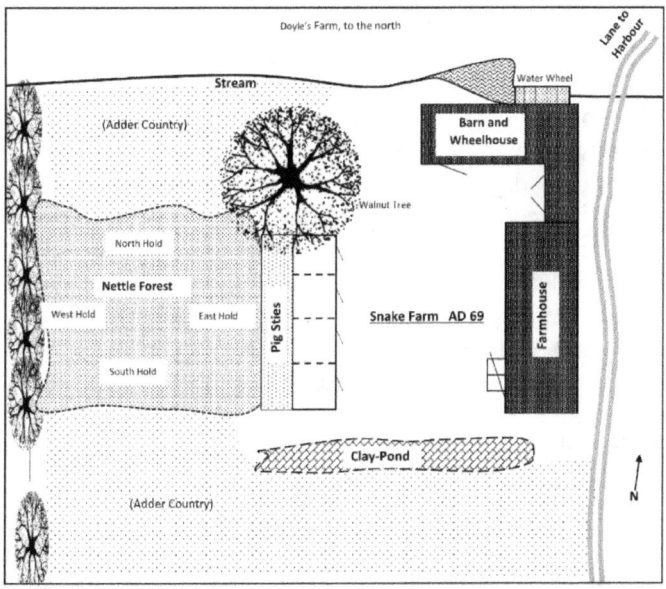

The education of the young Nettle Wits was the responsibility of selected elders, each Hold had its own school, and the education of the South Hold youngsters was, on that day, the responsibility of Mr Murphy Who Knows a Lot Cos He's Old.

Most of life's necessities were learned by doing and being

involved, a very practical approach, but the Nettle Wits were proud storytellers and so history, legend and philosophy were important in their culture, so much so that going to school had been made compulsory. Mr Murphy Who Knows a Lot Cos He's Old understood the importance of learning but never lost sight of the importance of fun, especially to a young leprechaun. He was very informal.

Leprechauns do not read and write, everything being spoken or drawn, with hieroglyphics being their only form of permanent record, so talking and laughing played a heavy role in their make-up. Nettle Wits were no exception as far as leprechauns go, and so Mr Murphy Who Knows a Lot Cos He's Old built his lessons around history, legend and philosophy, not necessarily in that order, and, of course, the drawing of hieroglyphics.

On this day philosophy was on the timetable. The old teacher paced around the platform, looking over the edge at the world below, and was wary of what was the other side of the dock-leaf which divided the platform in two. He looked at his attentive class as they sat cross legged, all nine of them.

"Right, children, today we're learning about philosophy. Can anybody remind me what philosophy is?" He waited, then looked at Stephen. "You, Stephen, tell me what philosophy is. Or if you'd rather, give me an example of a philosophical question."

Stephen, about eleven years old and in the middle of the age range, thought carefully. One thing that they learned at school was to always 'think before you speak', and he did just that for several minutes. The class was very patient. Then he waved his head about and, "It's not really a question, but my dad said that he knew him, they went to school together, and that his sister was a right one. Edna O'Sophical, that's what Phil's sister's name was, and a *right* one, to be sure."

The teacher ummed below his breath but bit his tongue as the rest of his class sniggered into their hands. He looked around for further input from the pupils. One of the older girls obliged.

After a nod from her teacher's green head she confidently added, "That's *definitely* not a question, but I do know one. Now, if Edna O'Sophical was the right one, then who was the left one? I think that's a Phil O'Sophical question." She started to giggle as she looked around for support, but none came. They were all a bit nervous of how their teacher would respond.

After a short silence and a glare, Mr Murphy Who Knows a Lot Cos He's Old made his own contribution. He threw a salted-moors-meat sandwich at her!

"Sandwich fight!" The entire class erupted and emptied their dinner-boxes across the room and the lesson turned into bedlam. What a row and what a mess. It was brilliant! It was what young leprechauns were made for.

Sadly, all good things have to end. Mr Daniels Who Turned Grey by the Time He was Eighteen appeared from the other side of the partition and stood glaring at the children, who instantly froze.

"What the....?" he shouted.

The headmaster stood beside Mr Murphy Who Knows a Lot Cos He's Old, spreading fear amongst the children. He was a frightening figure with his off-green complexion, wild dirty-grey hair and dimply skin, and had a fearsome reputation. The children sank back into their sitting positions.

"What the Hell's this row?" He scanned the classroom, eventually settling on the teacher, Mr Murphy Who Knows a Lot Cos He's Old. "Well?" he bellowed.

Mr Murphy Who Knows a Lot Cos He's Old looked sheepishly at his boss, Mr Daniels Who Turned Grey by the Time He was Eighteen, and thought carefully, just as he had always taught his pupils to do.

Now, I don't know about you, but I'm finding this Nettle Wit thing, about adult tribal names, bloody hard work, to be sure. You see, since time began the Nettle Wits have had this thing about giving every adult male, at the time of leaving school, a tribal name based on his attributes. When a boy leaves school and becomes a man, the other adults can put forward suggestions for a tribal name, to be used for the rest of his life, and the short-list is made by the members of the top table, with the final decision being made by the chief. Now Murphy was a bright child, with a mind which was older than his years, and so he was honoured with the name Murphy Who Knows a Lot Cos He's Old. When it came to Daniels there was a lot of umming and ahhing, because he was never a popular child and a bit of a bully, so the first proposal of Daniels Who Couldn't Do So He Taught was considered too restricting on his career, especially if he was to leave teaching, and the other name proposed, Daniels Who Couldn't Earn Respect So He Demanded It, was considered too offensive, so they settled on Daniels Who Turned Grey by the Time He was Eighteen. This process of naming applies to every male as they leave school.

All very pretty, but very hard work, particularly when you're telling a story, so I am going to do as the children are allowed to do and show no respect. In that I mean we will, whenever possible, refer to the adults by their *informal* names. In class that day were Old Murphy and Hairy Daniels. Isn't that a lot easier?

So, getting back to the story....

Old Murphy looked back at Hairy Daniels, then back to his class, who he addressed. "I think, children, that Mr Daniels Who Turned Grey by the Time He was Eighteen has something to say." He stood back and left the headmaster to it.

"Yes indeed!" he bellowed. "Thank you Mr Murphy Who Knows a Lot Cos He's Old, I do have something to say. I am the headmaster, I am in charge, and I do not approve of the methods used by this man to teach young leprechauns. I do *not* approve of laughter and joviality in the classroom, so if it doesn't stop I'll have no choice but to relieve Mr Murphy

Who Knows a Lot Cos He's Old of his duties and do the job myself. Well? Would you want *me* teaching you?"

His greyness radiated around the class, and he didn't have to say any more. He sidled off behind the dock-leaf partition.

"Right, he's gone. Please keep it down, else you'll have him teaching you and I don't think you'd like that." Old Murphy frowned. "Where were we?" He looked at Dana. "Can you help me, Dana? Remind me and the younger ones what we were on before that rude interruption."

"Sandwich fight, Sir." Dana, sitting beside her twin brother, was one of the older ones who often helped Old Murphy out. "But we can't throw sandwiches, so we need to get back to the philosophy. We were on Edna O'Sophical being a right one, but who's a left one?"

"Oh yes, I remember. Now, Tommy, can you give us a more sensible philosophical question?"

Tommy, Dana's twin brother and a handsome lad at that, stood up to address the class. "Right, a stupid human-type question. What came first, the chicken or the egg?" He sat down.

Old Murphy clapped his hands. "Yes, a stupid human-type question, one which has had humans dumb-founded for millions of years, but one which our science department worked out in a jiffy. But then *we're* not stupid humans. And, interestingly, our scientists have recently proven the answer by logicisation. You see, The Almighty Gayla would have known that an egg can't hatch unless it's under a broody hen, so She would have first created the hen, so that when She created the egg, it could be incubated under the hen. Blatantly obvious, but not to the humans."

One of the girls asked if any of this was relevant to the Nettle Wits.

"No. Not at all. We don't eat chickens or their eggs. We eat Moors caterpillars. As you all know, the entire World revolves around the Moors caterpillars. Without them we would all die. They feed us, clothe us and control us, and when Gayla, The Almighty, made life on earth She would have first made the Moors caterpillar before even considering anything else. Even the seasons were designed around the Moors caterpillar. The spring is for the butterfly to lay her eggs, the summer is for the eggs to hatch into the caterpillar, the autumn is for the caterpillar to turn into the chrysalis, and the winter is for sleeping. Then it all starts again, and is a never-ending cycle of life; our life. So, class, we know for certain that the very first thing to be created on earth was the lifecycle of the Moors caterpillar, then the seasons."

He paced around the classroom before continuing. "And the big question? What came first, the butterfly, the egg, the caterpillar or the chrysalis? Well, it's generally accepted that the answer to that is that it doesn't matter, because the eggs don't need to be incubated. So, there's the philosophical answer, 'It doesn't matter'."

But Dana was not entirely happy with that. "Our dad says you don't always teach us the complete picture."

Dana and Tommy's dad was a very important member of society and ran the Defence Regiment. He was named O'Kief Who Fights Adders and Lives, and was a legend in his own lifetime, as was the shillelagh which he wielded. Nobody was really sure quite what was so special about the shillelagh, but it was acknowledged as such throughout the tribe.

Perhaps to diffuse the attack by Dana, Old Murphy asked, "So, what's so special about his shillelagh? Looks like a shillelagh to me."

Tommy bit and jumped to his feet. "Dad's shillelagh might look quite ordinary, but it has special spirit which protects the tribe." Perhaps to diffuse the attack by Old Murphy he stressed, "Back to the philosophy!" Dana pulled his hand, so he sat down and calmed a little. "What came first? Dad says you teach us about what the scientists tell you, but he says it's all too shallow. He says that the Almighty would *never* have created the Moors caterpillar life cycle first, because the caterpillars don't need a mother to incubate them, but they do need the Irish Stinger Nettle to feed them, so She would have first created the Stinger Nettle. Obvious! The World revolves around the Irish Stinger Nettle, not the caterpillar." He looked down at his lap and huffed.

Old Murphy grinned in respect for the young man. "That's why, one day you'll be a great leader. Like father like son." He then nodded several times. "Yes, one day Tommy O'Kief, you'll rule the World!"

CHAPTER 4
LEGEND

Mr O'Kief Who Fights Adders and Lives, otherwise known as Jim, looked sternly at Dana and Tommy who sat opposite. He was about to say grace, but was interrupted.

"Dad, Old Murphy said I'd one day rule the World. He said it again today." Tommy frowned. "That's not a nice thing to say, is it?"

Jim sighed. "I don't know. What's a ruler, anyway? We don't have them, never have had. We have an elected chief, but we self-rule, and there's no such thing as a ruler of the World. He's just winding you up."

Dana jumped in. "Gayla! She rules the World!"

"Yeah, she created it and everything, and sends us weather and life and things, and luck and fortune. Yeah, suppose she rules the World. But Old Murphy can't be suggesting that you'll be God, so, why don't you ask him?"

"But the legends…." Tommy looked at Dana. "The Legend of Seamus Mac Notti, who couldn't hold onto his power by kindness, and so had to bully and imprison and threaten, and in the end they all hated him so much that they pegged him out on the beach for the crabs to eat, and…."

"Stop!" Mrs O'Kief, Mary, waved her finger at her twins and reminded them, "It's time to eat. Stop this stupid talk of ruling, it was just a mis-placed compliment from Murphy, so forget it." She had a sarcastic raising of the eyebrows. "He could've been kind by saying 'One day Tommy O'Kief, you'll be a lazy beggar,' couldn't he? So forget it. Now, we eat." She forced a smile towards Tommy and Dana. "Now, quiet while your dad says grace."

Jim thanked Mary, rolled his broad, green shoulders and

the muscles rippled. With his dark eyes commanding attention he began.

"May the Lord be thanked for this meal, which is reward for our commitment to Her. We vow to eat every bit and not waste any. Amen."

"Amen." "Amen." "Amen."

They all got stuck into their meal which was the usual winter diet of salted Moors soup with dried chrysalis-skin dippers. It was just beginning to warm up for the spring so they could soon look forward to fresh meat from the new hatchings, and simply couldn't wait after such a long winter.

The sacred act of eating was soon over, and they relaxed.

Jim sighed. "Be glad when this bloody winter's over. Tired of salted meat, but mustn't complain too loud, in case She's listening."

They sat thinking, and Tommy forced himself to forget about Old Murphy's word. All they could hear was the soothing song of the cock robin. Then Jim quietly spoke. "Talking of legends, did you know that I'm a legend amongst us Nettle Wits?"

Dana feigned a yawn and put her hand in front of her mouth. "You told us last spring, and the spring before that, and the one before that."

"Then it's time I told you again. You might've forgotten some of it." He stood up and walked over to their bed, under which he kept the special shillelagh. He placed the weapon on the table for all to admire. "This club is the O'Kief Shillelagh, famous for its defence of our tribe. We must be proud to be the holders of it, and one day, Tommy, you'll need to use it. The O'Kief Shillelagh." He held it above his head and swung it round. Tommy studied the jet-black weapon, thick at one end with a club, tapering down to a comfortable handle, and as long as his dad's shoulders were wide.

Jim lowered it back onto the table. "Right, we're now beginning to see the first signs of spring and will soon be moving into the new growth and preparing for the new herds of caterpillar. The cycle is soon to restart. Spring, warmth from the sun, new injection of life. What does that mean, Son?" He looked Tommy in the eye. "Well?"

"Fresh food. Hard work. Happy times." Tommy grinned, as if he knew what was coming next.

"And all that means travelling across open ground, to the new growth. What does that mean, across open ground, between old and new growth, in the springtime? What does that mean to all of us, *especially* to the Defence Regiment in springtime?"

Still grinning, Tommy answered, "Danger. Lots of danger from the babies. Those small enough to eat a leprechaun, and still no sense when it comes to our vile smell and taste. Adders. Newborn, baby adders that come out with the spring sunshine. Danger!"

"Well done, Son. And don't you ever forget it. Some of the other families forget, and some have paid the price. I'll tell you a story, of a time when you two were tiny."

Dana again feigned a yawn. "Heard it before."

Mary tutted and waved her finger. "It's that time of year, coming up for the Spring Holi, and your dad has to practice his story on us three. So just sit and listen."

Jim grinned. "I know it's the same every year, but this year I want your help. I want you to tell me what you think, and how I can improve it. You're getting to that age where you can be involved. So…. just listen." Once he was satisfied that he had his children's full attention, he tensed his bulging arm-muscles and began. "We'd moved across and were on our way up a new nettle growth when the lookouts howled. Suddenly the howl was being passed around the entire forest, like a pack of wolves warning of danger. We all hurried to a safe height and the howling ceased, but I noticed the little O'Sullivan girl standing down on the ground, seemingly unaware of the danger. Suddenly the howling started again, but she never moved. She was rooted to the spot, and then I noticed why. Right in front of her was a baby adder, neck coiled back and ready to strike. The girl was the perfect size for that tiny snake's mouth, and she must've known it, as she was frozen solid with fear. Then, as the snake began its strike, I dropped from my bough and landed on top of the snake's head and a desperate struggle ensued. It wrapped its coils around me and turned its head to take *me* as its dinner, and the mouth gaped wide, fangs dripping with stinking, white venom and my whole life sped past my eyes as I prepared to meet The Almighty. But as my life sped past, I never saw my death, so I knew it wasn't my time, so, I drew my trusty shillelagh and thrust it forward. As the snake struck, the shillelagh wedged between its upper and lower jaws, then stayed there, lodging its mouth open. The club held tight, and the dumb creature panicked, letting go its grip on me, and I was able to grab the girl. We escaped up the nearest nettle trunk, and the....tribe....roared!"

With a massive grin he leaned back and nodded. "And that's why you have to remember the dangers of spring. I won't always be there to save you."

Mary was so proud of her husband, rightly so, as were his two children, but Jim had taught his children well. Although they admired everything about their dad, they had been taught to comment, criticise, put right and even scold their father when he made a prat of himself. So Dana was not at all nervous to question her dad's story.

"Every year you add something to the story. Isn't that dishonest? And is that why you haven't added anything this year?"

Jim was pleased. "You noticed lasts year's! The fangs dripping with stinking, white venom. Good, hey? But I see your point. When I fought the adder, I can't remember *anything* clearly. So, it could have happened, and who wants to hear a simple statement of fact when listening to legend? It's all about belief. So long as it's based around fact, then it's true and our tribe lives on its legends and want them to be true. So long as they want to believe them, then they will. All we have to do is make them enjoyable enough to want to hear again, and again, and again." He flexed his solid muscles and held his head high. "But I haven't added anything this year, not because it's dishonest, but because I can't think of anything."

"But…." Dana thought carefully. "But why do we need to keep creating legends, and then building them up to be bigger and bigger? Haven't we already got enough? Like that stupid one about Seamus Mac Notti."

"It might seem that way, but a legend only lasts for so long before it gets forgotten, so we need to create new ones to replace them. You know my dream."

They had heard Jim's dream, the one where every legend and piece of history would be written in stone, on a giant wall, never to be forgotten. They respected their dad for even having a dream; it keeps a balanced mind, so long as one always keeps sight of reality.

Tommy observed, "So, legend is history, flowered up to keep the interest alive. That makes a lot of sense. And you want to flower it up a bit more for this year's Holi?"

Jim nodded. "Yes. The history is made, now we need to build the legend into an unforgettable experience for the tribe. But I'm out of ideas. Will you help me?." He grinned as he pointed Tommy in the face. "Are you up for it?"

Tommy had been accused of being the one who would rule the World. Ridiculous. But he was to be a story-teller, like his dad, so, with his wild, youthful imagination, he set to work building his own reputation, and his father's legend which would one day be passed onto him. "Well, for a start, you could change the 'dropping from the bough' to 'leaping from the bough'. Make it sound like you meant it, even if it was an accident. Some people claim that you slipped and fell onto the snake. True or not, that's not what people want to hear. Then there's this silly thing about the legendary shillelagh. What's so legendary about it? It's just a shillelagh, and it's not even the one that you fought the adder with. That one went off in the adder's mouth! So, why is the shillelagh so special? What's it got, that other shillelaghs haven't got? Well?"

Poor Jim had no idea how to answer.

"So, Dad, before the others start to question the truth behind the shillelagh, lets make some truth up. You can build it onto the end of your story at the Holi. Ready?"

Jim looked at Mary with such pride. "That's what Old Murphy really means. Our boy'll be a great leader, one day, to be sure."

Tommy took a deep breath, then reached over to feel the handle end of the 'special' shillelagh. It never felt any different to any other, so, let's make it different. His dad had taught him well. "Right, this is an almost new shillelagh, but it's still very, very special. That's where we're at."

He stood up and paced around the table. "You said that you went off, after the girl was safely up the nettles, to try to find your old shillelagh. That's the history, now for the legend."

He sat down opposite his dad. "I'm telling it in your shoes. So, after I left the girl safe with her parents, I sped off into the thick to retrieve my shillelagh. After a good run I got sight of the baby snake, making its way back into the adder country, slightly westward towards the blackthorn hedge. I managed to keep track of it, but was wary about approaching, as I no longer had a weapon to use in my defence, and so I followed it all the way out of the forest, into the grassland, and finally to a clearing on the edge of the hedge. I was stopped in my tracks! There, right in front of me, sunning herself in the clearing, was the mother adder, coiled and towering high above me. She looked at me with unblinking eyes. 'What do you want?' she hissed, 'This is adder country. Go home.' So I showed her the respect that such a wise old set of eyes deserved. I asked, 'Will you let me pass, please? I'm looking for my shillelagh, and I think it came this way.'

She moved her head toward me and flicked her tongue. 'It did. I watched one of my children slide past with it in her mouth. She spat it out over there. It's broken.' She nodded towards the hedge. 'I'll allow you to pass, but first tell me why she had your shillelagh in her mouth.' So I explained that she was trying to eat one of our children and I fought her off to save a life, but she hissed and shook her head. 'But you never saved a life. You just saved the girl. My baby had to go and eat a new-born shrew instead. So the life still went, just a different one. By saving the girl, you killed the shrew. Is that justice?' So I asked *her* if she thought it was justice, for the girl to live and the shrew to die, so she hissed at me and flicked her tongue so close to my head that I felt the wind. She looked me hard in the eye and, 'What is justice? In this World there is only one life, and we all borrow a little bit of that life, but eventually have to give it back, for another to borrow. If my baby didn't take the life she would have to surrender her own, through starvation. So, yes, it was justice.' So I asked her if I was wrong to defend the girl, if it caused the death of the baby shrew, and she waved her head and replied, 'If you *hadn't* defended your own kind, that would *not* be justice. You look after yours and I'll look after mine. *That* is justice. I lay here for many hours, looking, never closing my eyes, never sleeping, seeing all, and the only justice I see is the defence of one's own. So go, O'Kief Who Fights Adders and Lives, before I defend my own, and squash you. Go off and defend your own.' But I still hadn't found my shillelagh, so I asked her, 'Could I just find my shillelagh, and then I can be on my way, properly equipped to defend my own?' So she hissed and waved her head towards the hedge, towards a small, young blackthorn, and suggested, 'Look over there. But your shillelagh is broken, so take a new one from the thorns of that young tree and treasure the new weapon, as that is a special tree, with knowledge and spirit, and will live on in your shillelagh to look over you and your tribe, and so long as you continue to understand the justice of life, the spirit will stay with you, in the shillelagh. Now go and look after your people.' But I was confused. I had to ask, 'But what if I break my new shillelagh? Won't the spirit die with it?' And I believe that if she could have smiled she would have done. She said with a surprisingly friendly tone, 'The shillelagh is just a lump of wood. The spirit, however, will live on in your shillelagh and protect your people. So, use the shillelagh, bash in posts with it, break stones with it, replace it when it's done, but whatever you do, the spirit will live on in your shillelagh, old or new. The spirit of the O'Kief Shillelagh.' So I went over to the hedge and cut a brand-new club from the thorns of the special tree. The mother snake bid me well, but before I left her presence she warned me, 'What you have in your hand is a lump of wood, but what it has in its heart is the spirit of the Nettle Wits. Take care of the spirit. It's my gift to the people of the nettles, but beware that it only respects true justice.' I left the clearing with the spirit in my hands."

Tommy looked rather pleased with his off-the-cuff story. "Well?"

"Brilliant! Old Murphy's right, you'll one day rule the World." He jumped up and went over to the cupboard and brought out a bottle of nettle wine. "He's also right, that you two aren't children any more. Let's drink to it. To my new legend, sláinte."

"Sláinte agatsa!"

CHAPTER 5
LAWS ARISING FROM THE TAIPING REBELLION

Tommy and Dana were back in the classroom the next day. One of the lessons was about why they had to eat their Moors meat every day, and Old Murphy decided to pass the buck and allow Tommy to tell the story.

"You can make a much better job of it than this old codger. So, the class is yours Tommy."

With his ever-faithful twin by his side Tommy began. "Many generations ago, there was a family called Brady. There was Mr and Mrs Brady and three children, and they were farmers from the West Hold. One day, when the stock needed herding to new grazing trees, Mr Brady never turned up for work, and also the three children never went to school.

"Apart from worrying, not much was done about them going AWOL for the day, and since they were back home that evening, it was all quickly forgotten about.

"Then the following week the family went missing again, but were home that evening, so nobody worried too much. However, they went missing again the very next day, and then again the day after that, and people became concerned. The talk down the pub that night was that they were up to no good.

"So the committee sent Chief Zebedee round to tactfully warn the parents that Nettle Wits have to go to work, and the children have to go to school. It was the law. And just to remind you all, it still is.

"The next day the children were in school, and the teacher addressed the oldest boy, 'Since you've been missing so much lately Taiping, what do you have to say for yourself?'

"The boy stood up and replied, 'Hey man, love you man. Peace be with you man.' The boy, aptly name Taiping, just sat down again and said no more.

"Well, the talk down the pub that night was all about Taiping's rebellious ways and his wanton corruption of our beautiful language. But Chief Zebedee said that the important thing was to find the cause. Find that and the remedy will follow. So the Defence Regiment had the family followed, with the reasoning that they could be in danger. At the break of dawn the family left their platform and were followed out of the forest and through the blackthorn hedge and into the cow meadow, where they set up camp. They were bang in the middle of the poppy patch. The family formed a circle with a large poppy seed-head in the middle and just spent all day licking the seed-head.

"That night at the pub the committee made a unanimous decision that, in order to protect our beautiful language, the licking of poppy seed-heads was illegal. The town crier spent the whole of the next day moving around the forest announcing the new ban on the licking of poppy seed-heads, and after that it was noted by the teacher that Taiping's speech had returned to normal.

"However, the 'back to normal' behaviour of young Taiping didn't last for long and the teacher had to report to the committee that he was again behaving strangely. He had been heard talking to the other children and telling them that the family had been visiting the cow field and sitting around a camp fire, talking to Gayla, The Almighty.

"Although there was no law against talking to The Almighty, the committee considered it unlikely that The Almighty would sit around a campfire when She had the World to run. They thought that Taiping could be making it up, so they again had them followed, with the suspicion that they were still licking the poppy. The tail reported that they never touched a poppy head, but also he never saw Gayla, although they were talking to Her. He also reported that they were avoiding the poppy patch and were instead setting up in the hemp patch. The hemp is used for the making of rope, but the family were actually stripping fibres from the stems and burning them, whilst sitting directly in the smoke. He never saw anything else untoward.

"Chief Zebedee visited the family that night to find out the truth, and he was welcomed by the sweet, pungent smoke of burning joss sticks. The family had made the joss sticks from rolled up hemp leaves, and the family smiled at every opportunity. The Chief was soon feeling heady and happy himself. He had to take the bull by the horns and asked straight out what the hell was going on, and Mr Brady explained that they go to the hemp patch and burn the hemp, and then Gayla visits them for a chat, and gives them guidance. He was very open about it and told the chief that She had told them that they were not to live off the flesh any longer, and they must leave the Moors meat alone. He proudly announce that they had become….vegetarians!

"Within a few weeks of eating no Moors meat they all turned grey and died. The end."

Tommy sat down.

Old Murphy stood at the head of the class and scanned the children, before asking, "So, what can we learn from this true story? It was thoughtfully told by Tommy, with no added adornments, and I think the story is clear, so what is it? What lesson must we take from it?"

Jane fiddled with her fingers and then bravely stood up. "We mustn't talk like hippies."

"Yes, that's a good one. Our language is sacred, and important. But what else? Brian?"

He was a bit older and so could see a little deeper. "Well, Sir, we must always remember just how dangerous it is to leave the forest. All sorts of dangers, including temptation."

"Exactly! And the dangers in this case were associated with the Devil himself, who entrapped them into a life of drug abuse. It was after this sad episode that the recreational use of hemp and poppy were made illegal, referred to as The Laws Arising from The Taiping Rebellion. Always remember that when temptation calls."

Old Murphy paced around the room before continuing. "But the most important lesson from this unfortunate story? If we were to not eat our Moors meat? Loss of colour, then death. We must always eat our Moors meat, or else…."

The children were frowning and tutting and grumbling under their breaths. Then Sean asked, "So, what's banned? What about skipping ropes, which are made from hemp?"

"Hemp itself isn't banned. It's the smoking or eating of hemp and poppy that are illegal. So carry on skipping. The real issue is that the use of drugs leads to other problems, such as not eating your Moors meat, which in turn will cause your early death. You must always eat your Moors meat, or else…."

Tommy wasn't happy about something and so stood up, but Dana pulled his arm and he returned to the ground. Old Murphy cast an appreciative glance towards Dana.

Neither Tommy nor Dana were convinced with some of the tribal beliefs about eating Moors meat. It was only *assumed* that the Brady family died because they never ate their Moors meat, and ever since their deaths everybody has been too frightened to experiment with their diets. But they also appreciated that the tribe remained so strong partly due to the gentle brainwashing of the children. But, of course, it could well be true that without the Moors meat they could all become unhealthy and eventually dead. Tommy wasn't convinced.

It was all a bit of a mystery, one which would have to remain that way for the sake of the tribal togetherness.

CHAPTER 6
MISCHIEVOUS

Tommy and Dana went through the spring quite routinely, with the only memorable moment being when their dad stood to the front at the Spring Holi, supposedly to tell his extended story of the O'Kief Shillelagh, but he instead announced that this year's story would be told by his heir to the role of storyteller, Tommy.

The young man stood tall and hid his nerves well, as he entranced the tribe with the truth behind the shillelagh. He was a knockout and was rightly proud of his input to Nettle Wit legend, despite privately almost crapping himself. The story didn't just strengthen the legend of the O'Kief Shillelagh but added another dimension to their dad. Not only was he O'Kief Who Fights Adders and Lives, but suddenly he was the one who could talk to the adders. The beauty of true belief!

It was a hot day towards the end of the summer when the twins sat taking in the warmth of the sun, nestled in the petals of a dandelion flower. They had taken to discreetly breaking the unwritten rules of the forest, by leaving it, becoming more and more curious about the outside world and so took regular trips along the south wall of the pigsty to watch the humans working in the farmyard. On that day they looked out over the yard towards the house, with the clay-pond to their right. The ducklings were almost ready to take flight and learning about life by poking their noses into everything, but they had learned from an earlier age to stay clear of the Nettle Wits on account of the horrendous smell and taste, as had the adders and grass snakes. Also, the young snakes had grown too big to take any interest in the Wits.

Tommy looked across the dandelion at his sister and suddenly wowed. He had never noticed just how beautiful she was until that moment, with the deep blue sky behind, the deep yellow of the petals, and her radiant nettle-green complexion which was complimented by the red of her lips and tunic. She was like looking into a kaleidoscope. He realised that they were both perched on the fence between childhood and adulthood.

"You know, Dana, you're beautiful. This time next year we'll probably both be married, with children on the way. Need to make the most of this summer."

She grinned. "Married? You got someone in mind?"

He just shook his head. The only girl he had ever known was his sister. "Don't know if there's anyone to compete with you. You got anyone?"

She shook her head, and they never spoke any more on the subject of marriage.

Dana not only had the visual beauty, but also a genuinely tender heart. She loved watching the humans go about their business, and she admired the innocence of the children. However, what happened that day made her realise that some children have a naughty streak and her opinion on their innocence became strained, to put it mildly.

As they relaxed on the flower, the door to the farmhouse opened and out bounced the sheepdog, followed by the little boy of about six, and his sister of about nine. Then the grandad appeared with his woven-rush tool bag. He was the maintenance man and he was to make repairs to the shutters which hung raggedly from the windows. The summer was glorious, perfect weather for preparing for the next winter. It was all about being ready.

"Right, you two, we've got to get this re-hung. You, Boy, stay out my way. Me and your sister'll soon have this done. And leave my tools alone!"

The girl helped Grandad to remove the old leather hinges,

and while they were occupied the boy sneaked up to the tool bag and took the hammer. He hid it in a large tuft of grass.

Grandad went to his bag, hoping to secure the new leather hinge. "Where's my hammer? You had my hammer, you little devil?"

The boy huffed. "I ain't touched it. It was her!" He pointed at his sister.

"Your sister's been helping me all the time! Can't be her. Now, where's my hammer?"

The naughty little boy shook his head and accused, "The leprechauns! They must've taken it. They're *always* taking stuff!"

"The little liar!" Dana jumped up and down on her petal and pointed at the boy. "He took it. We never touch anything that's not ours!" But, of course, Grandad couldn't hear a word from the tiny being. She was seething, but totally ineffectual with her screeching.

The girl and Grandad eventually found the missing hammer.

Tommy just laughed, and the boy had a private giggle, but Dana was not amused. "Why do they always blame the leprechauns when things go missing? It's not fair! We never touch anything, but they always blame us. Always!" She put her head into her knees and had a sulk.

Tommy put his hand over to touch her shoulder. "It doesn't matter. They always do it, and always will. No point in caring."

"There is a point! I thought he was a nice little boy, and now I hate him. He's evil. I'm going over there and tell Grandad the truth, so he can smack him."

"No! He'll just stand on you….you'll be dead, and the boy'll still be a little swine. So I won't let you. And besides, it's not allowed, talking to them, since we don't really exist. Not in their eyes."

He allowed her to sulk it out of her system for a few minutes, then leaned over and whispered something into her ear. "Yes? Up for it?"

Then she rolled onto her back and looked up at him, her red lips slowly turning back into the smile that Tommy so loved to see. "Brilliant idea! Yes, just like Old Murphy always taught us, don't get down, get even." It was loosely agreed. "Yeah, as he says, 'don't get angry, get clever.'"

They wandered off towards the forest. All the way back, during the forty-five-minute walk, Tommy's head churned over his idea of revenge. He only had one little doubt, "But Old Murphy has also taught us that there are many ways to learn, and the hard way isn't always the right one. Wonder what he meant by that?"

Next morning, the family was up with the larks, just as it was getting light. They were always up at dawn, ready for the new day and all the challenges that it might conjure up, and this day was set to be one of personal challenge for the twins; they had Tommy's plan of revenge simmering in their minds. They sat around the breakfast table. Dana needed to know.

"Dad, as a *senior* member of our civilisation, would you agree that when something upsets you, you should do as Old Murphy suggests; don't get down, get even?" She cocked her head.

He grinned at Dana's humble piece of creeping. "Well, Murphy Who Knows a Lot Cos He's Old is your teacher, and he knows best, so yes. But don't forget the bigger picture, like whatever you do you'll learn from it, and let's hope it's not the hard way. Learning the hard way can be pretty painful." He smiled at the two youngsters.

So, they took that as the nod to go on a mission of revenge. They would teach that horrible child at the farm that he shouldn't go slandering the leprechauns, or else.

Tommy was at the age where, almost before he could say Paddy O'Ginty, he would be out of school and in service with his dad in the Defence Regiment, so he took charge of the mission.

He clapped his hands and shouted, "Come on! Got to

complete the mission before the humans get out of bed. Run!"

So they ran their hearts out all the way to the two stone flags which stepped up to the farmhouse door. They stood at the base of the stone doorsteps and suddenly became nervous. They needed to go inside the house. "It's got to be done," whispered Dana, so they climbed the doorstep and warily crept under the door.

The dog! He lay at the door to make sure no intruders entered, but as soon as he smelled the Wits he moved across to the other side of the room, so they climbed onto the stair string and walked quickly up the stairs to the top floor, took a quick recci around and decided that this was the room. It was the bedroom of the girl, perfect. The intruders walked around, and all the time Tommy was searching for something, then he spotted them, so they went under the bed, and they each took the corner of a piece of linen clothing. They pulled with all their might until they had dragged the clothing out onto the landing and, once they had found the target room, they dragged it into that room and left it bundled below that bed. It was the little boy's bed.

"Right, let's get down and wait."

They went back down the stairs, past the wary dog, and under the door. There they found a suitable gap between the two doorstep flags where they could hide out and wait for the action.

It was to be quite a wait before the humans rose from their beds, and during that time the twins reflected on what they had just done, and what could come of it. Suddenly the seeds of doubt were germinating.

The leprechauns had always, since the beginning of time, been blamed when things went missing, always unjustly, but did it ever matter? Of course not! That's what leprechauns meant to humans, somebody to blame so that the case can be closed, and life gotten on with. But perhaps it did matter, and that Tommy and Dana could go down in history for fighting back and be legends, to be hailed at the Spring Holi as those who gave the humans what they deserved. Perhaps. Perhaps not. A little bit of doubt was creeping in. Then he thought about how the leprechauns never did anything wrong, but were blamed for doing wrong all the time, and that this would be different, where they *would* do something wrong, but the humans would *not* blame them for it. Reversal of the norm. They would be worshipped for it! All they had to do was to stick to the plan, and not feel guilty. Nothing could go wrong, could it?

Dana was also feeling nervous about it all. "I know what you're thinking. You're dreaming of being the hero, who goes down in legend for getting our own back on the humans. But dreams are dangerous, Old Murphy's always told us that. He said that dreams can often turn into nightmares."

"Don't be silly. What the hell could go so wrong with our prank? It'll always be a dream, not a nightmare, so stop fretting. We'll be hero worshipped, and even if we're not, then we'll just forget about it. Nightmares?" He huffed.

But she thought about why and how and who. She thought her twin brother was a true leader, but was he ready to lead them into battle with the humans? Was he old enough to make such decisions? Did they really need to do what they were doing? Was it too late to take the clothing back to its correct place in the girl's room? What if the humans had good reason for blaming the leprechauns when things went missing?

"Why?" She sat up straight. "Does anybody know why? Why they blame us? What if they have good reason?"

Tommy frowned. "Bit late to think like that. Yesterday you were all for it, so what's changed?" But he was also feeling a bit guilty about doing what they were doing, although he could not quite understand why. After all, the injustice of being accused of theft has always been there, so why not get their own back from time-to-time? Nevertheless, they were leprechauns, and always liked to understand their actions. "Well, a very long time ago, Old Murphy told us a story which explained it. Remember? No? Ok. He said that when The Almighty made mankind she made several mistakes. One of them was that humans live in fear of taking the blame, and as long as a crime lay unsolved, they were all under suspicion. So, in order to close out those difficult-to-solve thefts, the humans ordained that they could blame the leprechauns, and so stop suspecting, pointing and accusing, and get on with their lives. It was the leprechauns! An easy out, just as the boy did when he was up against it. Old Murphy said it's called The Blame Culture."

He stopped to think for a while. Eventually he frowned deeply and continued. "When I asked him why we don't do anything about it, like get revenge, he told me that I might have to learn the answer the hard way." They both looked into each other's eyes. "What did he mean by that? Wish I hadn't remembered it, now, it's starting to scare me."

Too late for cold feet. The dog suddenly started to scratch at the door to be let out, and the man of the house obliged. The dog shot out and onto the lawn, followed by the boy who rolled around on the grass with man's best friend, then the mum came out with a basket of wet linen and set about hanging it on the line. Then the man of the house and the grandad came out and went over to the pigsties to do whatever they did in the mornings.

"Where's the girl?" Dana stretched her head up to look over the step, and she spotted her fussing at the top of the stairs. Eventually she thundered down the stairs and stood on the doorsteps.

Dana looked up. "Urghhh!" She grabbed Tommy's head and forced it down onto the floor of the crack. "Don't look up, whatever you do, don't look up!" She held his head down in the dirt.

The girl stood right above them, one foot on each slab, and Dana sat hard on her brother's head, to make sure.

"Mum!" The girl screeched. "Mum! Where's my knickers?

I can't find my knickers!"

Mum put her linen down and looked at her. "Wherever you left them. Take another look."

"Ain't there. Bet *he's* took them." She pointed accusingly at the boy who just wrestled with the dog.

Mum picked her linen up. "Have another look. They can't have gone far. Wherever you left them."

Then the boy perked up. "Bet the leprechauns've taken them."

The girl huffed, turned, and went back indoors, and the light returned for the Wits.

Dana relaxed. "Phew, that was close." She allowed Tommy to get up out of the dirt. "That was close."

"What was that for? You got dirt all in my ear, what's your problem? I'm nearly a man, you know."

"Had to, cos I love you. She had no knickers on! You could've gone blind if you saw that. *Horrible.* Mum's told me about the dangers of boys growing up and thinking they're men and then going blind, looking at *those* sorts of things."

Then the light faded, and the girl was back. Dana jumped, but stopped before she shoved his head down, and allowed him to look up.

"Mum! Found my knickers."

"Where? Where you left them?"

"No way." She smirked. "They were under his bed! He took them. Bet he's been wearing them, the dirty little tyke." She pointed at the boy. "He took them!"

The mother momentarily froze, then the anger boiled, and she flew at the boy. "You devil! What've I told you about wearing your sister's knickers? You're gonna get my hand. Come here you…."

But the boy was too quick for her and ducked the lunging hand, taking flight across the yard. She took chase but could not quite reach him before he got to the walnut tree and scrambled up like a squirrel to a safe height and out of reach. He perched on a strong bough, in fear of his life, and contemplated jumping for the pigsty roof, but it was too far away. He desperately clung onto the trunk. He was cornered but safely out of his mum's reach.

"Get down her, you little swine." She was seething, and it was clear to the twins that this was not the first time the girl's knickers had gone missing. "I'll sting your hide so hard that you won't sit down for a week!"

The poor boy stuttered, "But it weren't me. Please Mummy. It weren't me." He sniveled. "Must've been the leprechauns. It's always them. Please Mummy."

But she wasn't having any of it. She tried to shake the tree to flush him down, but his hold on the trunk remained firm and she eventually stood back to get a clear look at him.

"You swine! You've gotta come down sometime, and I can wait, I ain't going nowhere." She blew out some bubbles, then calmed down, just a little. "Don't know what's come into you, your sister's knickers, and all you can do is blame the leprechauns. Well you won't get away with this one, they were under your bed. It's always the leprechauns, but not this time. It's *you*. It's just like Mrs Doyle's….? Oh my God. The leprechauns didn't take Mrs Doyle's knickers either, it was you, you dirty little devil. What's the matter with you? What am I gonna do with you, and what'll I say when Mrs Doyle finds out it was you? And your poor dad. He'll never be able to show his face in the pub again. And, oh sweet mother of Jesus, what will Father Patrick say when he finds out? And, and…."

The twins rolled around in the crack in hysterics, and the sister sat down on the step and giggled and giggled, and the mother ranted, and the little boy sobbed and sobbed. They never dreamed it would go so well. Brilliant.

It was time to make their escape. With their sides aching from the laughter they left the crack and set off along the side of the pond, towards the south wall of the pigsty. It was a good thirty minutes of fast walking to reach the corner of the pigsty, during which they endured the ranting of the mother, the giggling of the girl and the weeping of the boy, but by the time they arrived at the sty the battlefield had calmed. Mum had given up her vigil and was working over near the barn with the girl, taking down some woven, woolen cloths from the tender hooks, and the men were still in the pigsties. The only evidence of the battle was the boy. He was still in the tree, and still sobbing his little heart out. He was devastated.

The Wits were no longer laughing. "Will he ever stop crying?" Dana frowned at her brother, who tried to ignore the question.

He changed the mood a little. "Bagsy telling Mum and Dad!"

"No. It was my revenge, so I should tell them. At tea-time."

The storyteller seemed pleased to let her do the telling. "All right. I'll get plenty of chance to tell it when I'm an adult."

As they walked along the south wall of the pigsty they could still hear the boy weeping, all the way from the other end of the building.

CHAPTER 7
THE HARD WAY

That evening the O'Kief family sat up at the tea-table, with Jim and Mary sitting opposite the twins.

Dana was fidgety with excitement, and Tommy excited but somewhat muted. Dana was to tell their parents their proud story of revenge.

However, the sacred act of eating had to take first priority, so the twins would need to contain their pride a little longer, until the time was right. They would then reveal their heroic exploits which culminated in an historic success, the enemy being totally humiliated. The good name of the leprechauns upheld.

Before the meal of fresh Moors meat and nettle soup, Jim had to thank the Lord.

"Dear Lord. We thank Thee for the meat on our plates and the soup in our bowls, and vow not to waste any. And we thank Thee Lord for the spirit of forgiveness and tolerance which you have bestowed on our kind. Amen."

"Amen." "Amen." "Amen."

Dana kicked Tommy under the table. She had noticed the bit about forgiveness and tolerance, but he nodded and smiled, suggesting that she was overthinking things. The Wits often used the act of grace to remind each other of their values. But it did hit the spot and she was quite put off from the sacred act of eating.

As Mary put her empty plate aside, she looked sternly at Dana. "I hope you were listening to your father's grace."

Oh no. Dana almost turned from bright green to red as flushes of guilt raced through her veins.

"We vow not to waste any! Now eat up or you'll be

turning grey. I don't want the other women saying I don't feed you properly." She tutted and Jim grinned.

Dana put her head down and ate. Why was she so nervous? They were heroes, having taught the humans a valuable lesson, not just the boy, but they were all going to suffer, apart from the girl who had a great laugh over it. 'Pull yourself together', she told herself, 'it was just an innocent prank.'

Once she had cleared her plate she was ready.

Jim started the after-dinner conversation. "Right you two, where've you been all day? Not misbehaving, I hope."

Tommy. "Went out of the forest again. Went to the farmyard and watched the people, and Dana's got a lovely story to tell." He looked sideways at her sweating face.

But before Dana could say anything, Jim put his finger in the air. "Love to hear it, Dana, but we've got one for a change. You've missed a really strange day in the forest. Really strange. But I think Mum can tell it better." He passed it to Mary.

"Yes, it's been a day to remember. It all started early morning, and it crept right through the forest from one end to the other. Everybody was so upset that nobody could work all morning, just sit and listen and wonder, and some even cried." She put her hand across to Dana's. "If you'd been here, you would have cried, a sensitive girl like you. Anyway, there was this little boy who was stuck up in the walnut tree and sobbed and sobbed his heart out, and everybody was so upset and wondering what on earth the poor little mite could have done to deserve that. Nobody deserves to be so upset for so long. And that's why Dad put it in his grace, because we can never understand why humans have to keep hurting each other the way they do. Thank God we're not that way. Thank God. We thank Thee Gayla for our gentle ways." She smiled in her own gentle way.

The twins were sitting up straight, but their hearts were under the table, flat on the floor.

Dana was dumb-struck, and Tommy knew that he had been feeling so guilty for a reason: he *was* guilty. How could they live with themselves? They were Nettle Wits, with values bestowed on them by The Almighty. They had failed their kind.

Mary broke the chilling silence. "So Dana, what's your story? We're ready now. Give us something to cheer us. I always like happy stories."

Dana was stuck. She cleared her throat, mumbled under her breath, then "I'm not in the mood for my story. Another day. But Tommy has something to tell. He's the storyteller's apprentice, he can do it."

Poor Tommy felt a little dumped on, but he kept his wits about him. His dad had taught him well regarding self-defense, and about how to get out of a sticky situation honourably, without resorting to lies. "Well, me and Dana are going on a mission tomorrow, straight after our work. We're going to the farmyard to find out if that little boy is all right. We feel for him, and want to bring good news back about his fortunes. We feel deeply for the boy." He stopped for thought. "One day, in class, I asked Murphy Who Knows a Lot Cos He's Old why us Nettle Wits don't seek revenge for the lies the humans tell about us, and he told me that I would learn the answer as I grow up. I think I grew up today."

Jim smiled. "Yes. It's sometimes called the hard way. And, in case he never told you, if the hard way doesn't sink in, it only ever gets harder. I hope you understand that, son."

CHAPTER 8
THE TREE OF LIGHT

The following morning the O'Kiefs were, as always, up at the crack of dawn. The warmth of the sun crept into the forest as the golden globe rose above the pigsty, shedding new life across the Nettle Wits' world.

Tommy and Dana had very loosely made plans to go on their fact-finding mission, driven by guilt, in an attempt to learn about the fate of their victim but their plans were put on hold. Jim stood in the centre of their platform and gave out the day's orders.

"Right, Dana, you're in with your mum. She's got a whole pile of work to do on winter clothing. Tommy, you're out with us men. It's that time when the farmers need to split the herds."

The Wits had learned the *very* hard way that they had to think about feeding the tribe next year, as well as this year, ensuring that the future breeding stock of Moors butterflies are protected. You see, many generations before, their farming practices were less developed, and one year they almost starved to death. They had a fire in the forest which destroyed the herd in the East Hold, but they still had enough meat in the other Holds to feed the tribe. However, they ate all the herds, and left nothing to breed the following season, so they starved the following year, many families dying, and it took a whole generation to get the stock back to the full strength. So, they now put aside one fifth of the herd for breeding-stock, and it doesn't matter what happens, that breeding stock is preserved for breeding and cannot be eaten. They call it sustainable farming.

As the men of the families moved towards the agreed

assembly spot, Jim took the opportunity to educate Tommy.

"You see, all four Holds are different, with different shade and different challenges and produce different amounts of meat each year, but the Central Corale, smack in the middle of the forest, has all the good aspects. So, that is where the most important herd is kept, the breeding stock, in the Central Corale. It's our future."

They arrived at the meeting area. All the men from the South Hold families were there, and one of the farmers stood at the front to issue instruction.

He spoke loudly and clearly. "The Committee has set the useable stock numbers for the South Hold at twenty-plus-ten-twenties *(six hundred)*. Once we've set aside those, the rest will be herded right over into the Central Corale for breeding. Jim's team will stay with the meat stock to stop them following, while us farmers drive the breeding stock to the Centre. All happy with that? Then let's get working."

The team spread out and began the rounding up of the moors caterpillars, which lived high in the canopy of the nettle forest where the leaves were young, succulent and full of sugar, and the trees were close enough together to be able to move from tree-to-tree across the broad leaves.

Mr Jones Who Could do Maths was the man in charge of counting in the caterpillars, and eventually he announced, "Twenty-plus-ten-twenties! That's the food stock."

The group-leader stood to the front of the team and spoke. "That was very quick. Now, we have to round up all the rest and drive them into the Central Corale. We're all experienced drovers, so hopefully we'll be done before sundown. Let's get going!"

Jim and Tommy, along with two other men, were left with the food herd to ensure they stayed put while the drovers were at work. It was not going to be hard, since Moors caterpillars are slow moving, and don't ever go anywhere unless driven, or run out of food. "So, let's just relax and enjoy the sun," was Jim's orders to his small team. He laid back across a leaf and grinned at Tommy. "Waiting for the others to get the breeders moved. That's all we have to do, and keep an eye on this lot. But they won't go anywhere fast."

All three of the men laid back on their selected leaves. Tommy was disappointed, he was a teenager, and boredom would soon set in. He watched the caterpillars munching. He watched them moving to the next leaf, and munching, then moving over and munching. *So boring.*

"What can I do, Dad?"

Jim grinned at him, understanding his son's itchy pants. "If you can't sit still, get up onto the highest tree and watch the drovers. You'll see them moving through the canopy, as just slight movement of the trees, but if you see anything that doesn't look right, give us a shout. If in doubt, shout."

That appealed more to Tommy than sitting around in the sun, so he found the highest tree in the area and climbed to the growing-tip. It was so beautiful. He could see right across the canopy of the nettle forest, with the blackthorn hedge away to his left, bordering the West Hold, and the pigsty to the right, which defined the edge of the East Hold. Straight ahead of him was the expanse of the North Hold, beyond which he could see the scrub and rough-land of the northern adder country. It all rolled out like a green, carpeted paradise, and it all seemed so enormous. He realised just how big the forest was, and knew that there were many people in the other Holds which he had never even met before. He suddenly had a hankering to get out and about with Dana, a lot more often. That fleeting mention of marriage while on the dandelion had given him a little prick in the heart. He thought to himself, 'Yes, there must be some lovely people over there, and there, and even there. Lovely, pretty girls.'

But his dreaming was shattered as he looked to his right, towards the north-east corner, and there it was. The walnut tree. *The* walnut tree, the *boy's* walnut tree. He was instantly fretting about their cruel trick on the poor little boy. He had been fretting all night, as Dana had been, and he had not expected it to be thrown in his face whilst out at work, and he found himself in a cold sweat.

He tried to divert his thoughts by scanning the South Hold for the movements of the drovers, and he located them, to his left, and away from the sightline of the tree. It allowed him to concentrate his mind on something else. The team were causing a sway of the trees as they moved across, just below the canopy and out of sight, but he knew it must them, then he noticed another set of movements beyond them in the West Hold. All the Holds were moving the stock that day, so he scanned the entire forest canopy and located all four of the teams, and he thought about his job, not the boy.

"Dad! I've located all four of the teams!"

Jim acknowledged and went back to chatting with his comrades.

Tommy whispered, 'What will they do to us when they find out it was us?' He spoke as if Dana was there with him. 'Whatever they do, we deserve. We've bought shame on the tribe, behaving so spitefully, and we deserve to be punished. But I'm sure they won't do much to us, we'll be all right. So stop worrying.' He was telling himself, but he wasn't convincing himself. 'I think we might upset Mum and Dad, though. I think we've let them down. They've bought us up so well, and what do we do? Bring shame on the family, that's what. A couple of spoiled brats who need a good spanking.'

Then he looked across at the tree. The boy was no longer in it; he'd gone. 'What happened to you, boy? Did you fall asleep and fall to your death? Did they get you down, and beat you so hard that you can't sit for a week? Did they take you and sell you into slavery in Great Britain? Did they hang you? Did they….?' He suddenly felt a tear develop. The poor boy, what had happened to him? He realised that he shouldn't be worrying at all about his and Dana's punishment, he should be worrying about the fate of the poor boy, the one they tricked into a life of suffering, a life ruined because of a stupid, self-centred gripe about a harmless human tradition. He felt himself talking to the tree and telling it that it was fine to blame the leprechauns, that was what they were there for, and please pass that message on to the humans, but the tree just ignored him.

To his left a family of goldfinches twittered and sang as they harvested seed from the Scotch Thistle, and that seemed to lighten Tommy's heart, but he was abruptly awoken from his daydreams.

"Woop, woop, woop." It was a call from the North Hold. It was warning call.

"Dad! Quick, Dad! A Warning call!"

Jim and the two men rushed up the tip with Tommy and they all scanned the North. Then the warning call came again, and again. "Woop, woop, woop." It was a hedgehog warning.

"There!" Jim spotted the danger. The trees were thrashing around as the creature pushed its way through the forest, and it was moving in the direction of the drovers in the West. Jim called "Woop, woop, woop!" and repeated three times for good measure, then the creature's movement turned, and it was heading straight at them. "Coming this way! Hold tight!"

Hedgehogs were friends to the Wits, eating snakes and slugs, but were like a herd of bulls stampeding when they went through the forest. Anyone caught unawares would be thrown from their tree and who knows what when they hit the ground.

"Hold tight!" They clung on for dear life as the creature bashed its way through the nettles, grunting and snorting, and suddenly they were being thrashed about as the trees were pushed aside and then sprung back to upright, but it only lasted a few seconds, and it was over. The hedgehog left the southern boundary of the forest and was gone.

After a swift look around to check the others, Jim gave the all clear. "Woop, woop." The signal was passed around the forest. Then after a few seconds, single woops were passed around by each team acknowledging that there were no casualties. Panic over.

"That was fun. Broke up the morning," jested one of the other adults. "Not so funny if you're caught by surprise."

The whole episode was over in no time, and almost forgotten about. It was all quite normal day-to-day activity, not really anything to write home about, but Tommy sort of enjoyed it. For him it was relatively new, to be out in the open forest with the men. He was impressed at how they all just took it in their stride, and it was a lesson to him. He climbed back up to his look-out spot.

Once he had located the four teams, he listened to the goldfinches, who suggested he relax, and so he looked across to the tree for advice. It suddenly looked more stable, a lot wiser, and a great deal more commanding. He thought he could hear the leaves whispering to him, suggesting that 'Yesterday you were a child, now you're a man. Start behaving like one.'

He nodded his answer and thanked the wise old tree for the advice. It spurred him on to make a decision about the boy, and that he and Dana must own up to their mischief, because that was the grown-up thing to do. He was feeling like a man.

CHAPTER 9
OWNING UP

"Dad!" He looked towards Jim, who was admiring a fine specimen of a Moors caterpillar. "What do you think about when you're doing these boring jobs?"

Jim left the fine caterpillar and joined him at the tip. He pointed back down to the caterpillar which munched away just below them. "Isn't that beautiful? Almost as beautiful as Dana." He looked around towards the blackthorn hedge. "We'll soon be getting the sloes in for the wine." He moved his gaze far to the right and back towards the clay-pond. "We'll soon be digging clay and repairing the cold-caves, under the pigsty." He looked all around at the forest-scape. "These are all things to think about when you're on one of these 'boring' jobs. Boring, but safe. The hedgehog was nothing, compared to the dangers in the pond and in the hedge. One day you'll find out just how pleasant these boring jobs are, once you've faced the real dangers of some of the other jobs. You'll find all that out soon, the hard way." He gave Tommy a massive grin.

The young man nodded. "I think you're telling me that I'm growing up, but not to rush at it."

"Yes, well spotted. Take your time to learn and accept what is. So, that's what you need to think about when you come on these boring jobs....everything. The nice things around you, the hard work ahead of you, the dangers to be avoided, and anything that you want to think of, including your dreams and regrets. Is that a good answer?"

"Yeah. As good as I can expect from a philosopher who talks to adders." He leaned forward and gave his dad a big hug.

After about three more hours of driving, the teams passed around the "Woop, woop, wit," which signaled the end of the drive. Jim and the two men shrugged their shoulders, which seemed a rather squibby ending to Tommy, who had expected at *least* a cheer. But never mind, it was probably the grown-up thing to do, play it all down and be cool.

They set off towards home, and the men were deathly quiet, and when Tommy asked Jim if there was anything wrong, he snapped, "Nothing to concern you, son." There was definitely an anti-climax in the air.

And at the tea table, the atmosphere continued. They said the usual grace, ate their food in silence, then Mary eventually cut the thick air with a sharp snap at Jim. "What's wrong? We've been worried ever since we heard the end-of-shift call, all so early. We thought there must have been a disaster, or a major problem. You shouldn't be home until sun-down. Why are you so early?" She was clearly worried.

Jim sighed. "It was just an easy drive. Everything went so smoothly, that's all."

"Don't keep things from me, nor the children! What's wrong? It's been getting earlier and earlier every year, and this year I've seen less butterfly pelts than I've *ever* seen. Why?"

Jim put his hand over and held hers. "Look, let's not worry until we know there's something to worry about. We'll find out more tomorrow. In the meantime, think about what we need to think about, like our two children, here." He looked from Tommy to Dana, then back to Tommy. "These two both seem to have worries of their own bouncing around in their heads. Well?"

Dana nodded and looked at her brother. She spoke directly at him. "I could feel you today. You're right, we have to come clean, and we'll pay the price together. As one."

Jim and Mary never pushed, but just patiently waited as Tommy thought it through.

Eventually, "You know the boy in the tree. Well, we've been worrying about him and what could have happened to him. We've been worrying all night and all day what could have come of him especially as he wasn't there in the tree today. We thought he might have gone to sleep and fell off, breaking all his bones, or his parents could have got him and put him up for adoption, or sold him to the slave traders in Great Britain, or even killed him by thrashing him to death." He paused. "I wish we knew what happened to him." He held Dana's hand.

Jim looked into Mary's eyes, then back to Tommy's. "So? What of it? He's just a human boy, not one of us, and as much as it upset everyone with his crying, he doesn't matter to us, does he. So why are you two so worried about it?"

Dana kicked Tommy to push him, so he confessed. In a very low voice, "No time like the present. Get it over with." He cleared his throat. "We've brought shame to the tribe and to our family. That poor little boy....he suffered because *we* made him suffer. It was all our fault, wasn't even an accident, but a deliberate, spiteful prank, which we're now so ashamed of, and we wish we'd never carried it out. But we did, and we hurt that boy so much...." He sniffed. "Sorry Mum, and Dad, but it was us. We did that to that boy."

Jim sat bolt upright, his green complexion shining, muscles flinching and shoulders slightly rolling. "Yeah, we know."

The twins sat back in their seats and looked at each other in shock. "You know?"

Jim grinned. "Course we do. You're not really meant to leave the forest unaccompanied, so when you do I put a tail on you. For safety reasons. Philips Who Moves With Stealth, my best man. My captain. We knew it was you, even before you got back yesterday."

Tommy hung his head and Dana just shook hers.

Jim continued. "My best man, Captain Philips. He checked out the clay-pond for adders while he was watching you, so it wasn't just about you. But you know you can't go wandering around in the big world without us knowing where you are. So Philips Who Moves With Stealth did his job, as always. My best man."

The twins sat in shock and confusion.

Jim continued. "Anyway, once he'd reported back with his findings, we had a committee meeting to discuss the situation, and work out how to punish you. It never took long to reach a decision. It was proposed and seconded that we should blame the leprechauns. So that's what we did, blamed the leprechauns, in particular Murphy Who Knows a Lot Cos He's Old because he's the leprechaun who should have taught you the right way, and he didn't. He admitted that when you asked him why we don't take revenge he told you you'd learn the answer as you grow up, and that was considered irresponsible for a school-teacher of his calibre. So, on record, it was his fault for not teaching you the answer, which would have been the easy way. There, blame the leprechaun. We did."

The two young ones were stunned. "What, no punishment?"

"Don't be silly. You've been punishing yourselves all day. That's a good start. No, something else you'll learn about when you become adults, is the politics of the committee meeting. The official committee meeting is always closed off with the Chairman proposing a free beer for all those who attended, and once the beer starts to flow, then the *proper* meeting begins, at the bar. This is all normal routine for all committees. Anyway, at the proper meeting, after the official meeting, it was proposed that you get some real punishment. Daniels Who Turned Grey by the Time He was Eighteen proposed that he puts you over his knee and spanks you for a full half hour, but we didn't want him getting back into his pervy ways, so that was never seconded. Philips Who Moves With Stealth wanted to take you on as his apprentices, as he was so impressed with both of you, but Chief O'Hoolihan said that couldn't be done while you were still at school. Then the chief himself proposed that whatever happens to the boy, happens to you two. That was seconded and passed." He smiled with a certain air of authority. "What you gotta say to that?"

Tommy blurted, "But he could've been sold into slavery. What if he has been?"

Very calmly Jim squeezed Mary's hand and replied, "Then you'll be off to Great Britain. I'm sure Queen Boadicea will find a place in her slavery for you both."

Dana, who had been very quiet, asked, "So, what *has* happened to the boy? What's our punishment?"

Jim nodded. "Good question. That was the other bit that was proposed, seconded and passed, after several more pints I must add, that you two find out for yourselves. You tell us what your punishment is."

Mary, who had been very quiet, nodded in agreement. "Whatever he gets, you get. That's fair. And don't think we don't care about you, because we're both so proud of you. You see, Dad was very supportive of your good characters and insisted that you would come clean, so several of the others bet your dad for a couple of pints that you wouldn't admit to it, and you've rewarded our faith in you both; you've come clean. So, Dad's won the bet and can drink for nothing next time he goes to the pub. Well done, both of you."

Jim clapped his hands. "Six pints you've won me. I knew you'd own up eventually. What a team."

Mary tutted. "Men and their beer! But I'm so proud of you, Dana. Philips told us about how you protected your brother when that girl stood over you. No knickers! I hate to think what poor Tommy would be like now if he'd looked up. Probably blinded."

Tommy looked down into his lap and wondered what he might have missed out on. He'll never know. "I could've risked just one eye."

Dana gave him a slap around the head.

Anyway, the subject was closed with the next move being down to the twins to establish their fate. They all helped to clear the tea-table.

Then, as they were settling down for the evening, the forest was awakened to the bellowing of the town crier. "Hear ye! Hear ye! An emergency general meeting in the Corale, at sunup. All to attend."

Jim put his head in his hands and uttered, "Hope it's not what I think."

CHAPTER 10
GET OUT OF OUR FOREST!

The next morning was routinely the same; up with the larks and get back into life. The only difference that morning was that they had been called to an Extraordinary General Meeting, as had all the members of the civilisation.

It was about a half-hour journey to the Central Corale from their platform, moving between trees, high up in the safety of the nettle growth, and as all the Wits from the South Hold left home at the same time, it was like a swarm of red and green heading north to the meeting. There were about seventy Wits in their Hold.

When they reached the meeting arena the entire population was arriving. About three hundred Nettle Wits existed, and it seemed that they all turned up for the mysterious emergency meeting, and the babble of curious leprechauns filled the early morning air. It was still dull, as the sun had risen but not enough to clear the pigsty, so the dampness dripped from the leaves. The arena was just a very small clearing in the forest, with a small platform to one side where the Chief would sit with his committee, close to a very, very important platform which overlooked the clearing: The Centre Point Pub. The Wits surrounded the chief's platform from the comfort of the nettle leaves. It was all set.

Jim left his family and friends high in the overhanging nettles and joined the committee at the table. The top table consisted of the chief and six committee members, made up by Jim and Hairy Daniels, plus four others from the other Holds. The chief was conspicuous in his red, pointed hat, the only member of the tribe who was allowed to wear a hat, a tradition which went back so far that people were no longer aware of its origins.

Before the meeting was opened by the chief, Jones Who Could do Maths announced from the wings that the attendance was 'fifteen twenties and eighteen'. That was a full complement of three hundred and eighteen Wits, the entire population.

"Thank you all for coming at such short notice. I am pleased that everybody was able to come, especially bearing in mind the importance of this meeting. I called this meeting upon the advice of my technical team and the leading farmers, and we have some major issues to discuss." He looked around at the tribe which loomed high in the galleries of nettles. "As we are all aware, we split the herds yesterday. It was a straightforward drive with no accidents and only one near miss, and it was completed in record time. In fact it was completed so early that we were all sat down for our tea at the usual time, *hours* before we would expect. Why? Are the drovers becoming better and faster? Are the caterpillars behaving more accommodatingly? There must be something allowing the drive to be finished earlier and earlier, every year. Well there is! The caterpillars are not there to drive! There are less caterpillars than we've ever known, and disaster threatens!"

He stopped to play with his red hat which was slipping down over his face. The crowd silently waited.

"We have to report that there were hardly any caterpillars moved into the breeding grounds. Hardly any! The least we've *ever known*. Please understand what this means. It means that, if we don't do something about it now, we will be facing famine next year. We'll starve to death! All of us."

The chief was in a panic, which quickly spread. The Wits began to murmur, then the murmur turned into shouting and pointing at the committee, until not a word could be deciphered. It was bedlam.

Jim stood up and held his hands out wide, then shouted several times, "Quiet! Quiet!"

After a few minutes the shouting died down. Jim remained with his hands out wide, and as the shouted abated, he made his voice heard. He bellowed, "Let The Chief speak! Give him a chance!"

They settled into an unhappy but silent audience, although many showed their annoyance by crossing their arms.

Chief O'Hoolihan pointed to the crowd in a circular motion. "You *all* need to listen carefully. We *all* need to work together, and not just shout about it, else we'll not see another season after this one. This is serious, so listen." His words were deliberate, threatening, but not very commanding. He was, essentially, a farmer who had been placed in a position of honour but was now in the hot seat and was expected to lead. He had never had to do that before, and was nervous. "We need to talk about two things: one, our immediate survival; and two, our long-term survival. Are you ready to listen?"

The tribe mumbled and looked at each other, then began nodding and un-crossing their arms.

"Right, that's better. The first thing we must do is to learn to live on smaller rations. The times of plenty are over, for now, and my team have worked out a system of ration-vouchers which will be issued by my department. This is necessary because we need to take one fifth of the food herds to put aside for breeding. It's the only way we can see to ensure future stocks. Tighten our belts today, to give us a tomorrow!"

The Wits mumbled, just a little, but nodded in agreement.

The chief continued, carefully following his pictures which he had drawn out before the meeting. "That way we'll get through until next summer, and still have stock next year. It'll be tight, but if we don't take care now, we'll starve by next spring. Work together, and we'll make it!"

The crowd again began murmuring which slowly escalated into another rant. Three hundred and eighteen leprechauns in red jerkins, and not one could be heard. It was jus a babble of shouts and abuse.

Jim stood up and held his arms out wide. "Quiet! Quiet!" but the crowd continued to vent their discontent with the committee. He picked up the legendary O'Kief Shillelagh and slammed it on the table, and the crack echoed around the arena in the dampness of the morning. He did it again, and the ranting lowered. "Quiet! All of you. Shut….up!"

Instant silence. Jim held his arms in the air, his shillelagh waving from his right hand, and he thanked the crowd. "Thank you! Now if you can all be quiet and give the meeting a chance, we can hear any questions or suggestions." He sat down.

A man from the North Hold stepped forward on his leaf and put his hands in the air.

The Chief acknowledged. "O'Toole Who Has a Lot to Say. Please speak."

O'Toole cleared his throat. He looked around at his 'support' before speaking. "We're farmers. We know that the breeding stocks are too small to provide for the future. We know that we'll have to forsake part of this year's food-stock to protect our future. We know all of this. So….who the hell are you to think you need to tell us? Well? Who?" He looked at Jim. "Well, I'll tell you who you are. You're the Science Department, the Teaching Department, the Philosophy Department, the Farm-Planning Department. That's *who* you are. Now I'll tell you *what* you are. Well?" He looked around the crowd and scowled. "You….are….leaches! That's what you are, a bunch of leaches, draining our hard-earned food stocks. You lot, your families, all you hangers-ons, you're *all leaches*. As we've watched the stocks get smaller, we've seen the leaches get bigger. Now, we can't afford overheads, so, what do you say Tribe? Should we feed them for any longer? No! Go! Get out of the forest and do your schoolwork elsewhere, on someone else's rations. What do you say, Tribe? Are you with me? Get rid of the leaches?"

He looked around at a stunned tribe. The murmuring began.

Tommy and Dana clung onto Mary, but then caught the eye of Jim's captain, Philips Who Moves With Stealth, who nodded towards the top table, and suddenly, as the nods went around, the members of the Defence Regiment began moving to the table. Tommy and Dana left Mary with the neighbours and moved to join the Regiment.

This was a big unknown amongst the Nettle Wits. Never, in their thousands of years in existence, had they ever known serious dissent against each other. The entire Tribe was stunned and a little confused.

Jim nudged the chief who reluctantly stood up. He was a designer of farming calendars, not a real leader. He meekly addressed O'Toole. "What are you saying, O'Toole Who Has a Lot to Say?"

O'Toole stood proud with his family and friends behind him and pointed around the arena. "These people want me to say that we don't want *you*....the intellectuals. We don't want to go hungry just to feed about thirty people who sit in their classrooms all day, eating our food, just to tell us what we already know. That's what I'm saying. Go and sponge off somebody else."

Jim looked around the tribe and could see little commitment from the crowd. He needed to know if the revolt was general, or was it restricted to a small group. He slammed his shillelagh on the table, and it rang through everybody's ears.

"Mr O'Toole. Who is this *we*? You speak about how *we* don't want them, so why don't your accomplices stand up and be counted."

O'Toole waved his hands around him, and his 'accomplices' looked to the ground. None of them had the resolve to start a revolution. They were all farming leprechauns, not revolutionaries. O'Toole was alone.

He pointed at Jim, then at several other members of the

Defence Regiment and with a tinge of begging, "Jim, don't ever think that we would hold it against you. We've always had a Defence Regiment and always will, and you earn your keep. You're one of us...."

"Never!" Jim jumped to his feet. "I'm not one of your anarchists! I was put on this Earth by The Almighty to defend the Tribe, never to forsake it. I....am....the....Tribe! Forever!"

A small cheer went up, mainly from the South and West Holds, but quickly died through nerves. The two men stared at each other across the arena, and everybody froze.

Dana poked Tommy. "Dad's gonna fight. Do something."

So, not knowing what he was going to do, he moved along the line to the top table and put his hand on the chief's shoulder. "May I address the Tribe, Chief O'Hoolihan Who Designed the Farming Calendar?"

The Chief stared him in the face. "You're just a child."

Then the member to the right, Hairy Daniels, waved his mop of greasy grey hair around. "Don't be ridiculous! This lad's as grown up as you are. Let him speak!"

Tommy was elated. Hairy Daniels had shocked him with his confidence and support, and it inflated his ego to bursting-point.

The Chief, "I call Tommy O'Kief Who Has Not Yet Been Named!"

Tommy moved cautiously around to the front of the table, all eyes burning into his pumping chest. He looked at Dana, then at his mum, then at Jim, and they all grinned in support of their loved one. It was his stage!

"Thank you." The tribe were silent, the sun had just risen above the pigsty, and the atmosphere had changed, then Old Murphy caught his eye and gave his spiritual support to 'the one who would rule the World.' "Thank you. Now, I have been raised to believe that I'm part of this tribe, always will be, and would never have it any other way. But look at us!

Two grown men eyeballing each other across the void, goading a fight, and all we need to do is talk." He first looked sideways at his father, then across to O'Toole, and they both nodded their respect. "The tribe seems to have lost sight of its own values, and also of its own history. It has forgotten what we are and where we came from, so I'm going to remind you all. Then you can decide on whether or not to fight. Right? Well, perhaps the Teaching and Philosophy Departments have been slacking of late, so we can partly blame them for allowing us to forget our history, because without remembering who we are, we'll just resolve everything through fights, until not one of us is left standing. We are like a swarm of bees: together we thrive; alone we die. So, let's look at how we got where we are, together."

He stopped for thought; he was making it up as he went. The crowd was respectful, they were lovers of stories and legend and had been brought up never to interrupt a good story, so Tommy just had to make sure it was good enough to hold them.

"Many centuries ago, the Nettle Wits were poor, hungry and struggling. They didn't worry about starving next year, they worried about starving *this* year, *every* year. And they did. Life expectancy was short. The wild caterpillars were small, about one third of what our modern ones are, and the forest not highly productive, and then the winter came. Those who survived the hit-and-miss of the warmer months, suffered long, hungry winters with almost nothing to eat. Then one day, a certain Zebedee noticed that the caterpillars from certain patches of forest were bigger than the others, so, because of his scientific way of thinking, he gave his life over to finding out why. He discovered that in the better patches the nettles had much higher sugar content in their leaves. So the farmers all moved their stocks to the better patches, which were quickly overgrazed and stripped of all foliage. So he made a scientific plan of action. He convinced the farmers not to move the herds to the better patches, but to move the better patches to the herds. They set about a program for propagating the higher sugar-content nettles and replanting the entire forest. So, our forest is a farmed environment, not natural at all. Thanks to the scientific input from Zebedee. The meat output almost *trebled* once the forest was replanted with the nettle variety that we now take for granted. Then, Zebedee and his descendants never stopped looking for improvements. He thought that, if it was the sugar that made the caterpillars bigger, feed them sugar. He set up scientific processes to extract the sugar from the nettles, and succeeded in producing high quality sugar, but they could never get the caterpillars to eat the raw sugar. Failure? Never. The scientists never gave up. They played around with the sugar and managed to produce alcohol, which they experimented with to preserve the meat to last through the winter, but with limited success. So the alcohol was refined for other purposes and is now irreplaceable in the tanning of the butterfly hides and, just as important, for human consumption. That is why we have our wonderful pubs and nightlife. Thanks to the scientists. But it never stopped there. The winter months were still killing many families through starvation, and it wasn't until Zebedee and his team went down the hill to the Docks, that they found the solution to the winter starvation. They struck up a trade deal with the Cockle Wits, which exchanged our alcohol, sugar, and tanned butterfly pelts for their salt, iron tools and pottery, and the deal has flourished ever since. In fact it has grown year-on-year. And *that* was when we stopped dying every winter. We suddenly had salt to preserve the meat with and pottery containers to store it in, all thanks to the never-say-die efforts of the scientists. The farmers and the scientists have always worked successfully together, and that is why the Nettle Wits are now such a successful civilisation. Scientific farming."

He put his hand out and swung full circle. "Look around you. This isn't Gayla's work, it's the work of the scientists and the farmers. Irish Nettles, the improved variety. Moors caterpillars, the giant variety. And look what's caved below the pigsty; quality salted moors meat, the winter-survival variety. Now, tell me that it was all down to the farmers."

He looked across to O'Toole, who was rather impressed.

He needed to close out, so he made his final broadcast. "Well, I know you can't tell me that it was all down to the farmers, because it wasn't. So who was it down to? The farmers, the philosophers, the teachers, the scientists, the planners, the industrialists....? No, the answer is simple. It was down to the *tribe*. We are one, and our entire worldly existence is down to us. We all play our part. The tribe. And that is why I'm the tribe and *always* will be. Now, are you with me?"

The crowd were, by then all standing with their arms un-crossed, smiling. Then almost in unison, like one, they held out their arms in the welcome posture. They were with him. They started cheering.

But he had been taught, as is tradition for their culture, that you don't just walk away from a story-telling session, you had to be relieved by the audience, and since they seemed to want to cheer him for the rest of eternity, he just stood and waited. It seemed like a lifetime, and his mind began to wander. He was suddenly sure that he could feel the chief's eyes cutting into his back, and he began to realise that this was a chief with very little self-confidence, and his position was, at that point in time, under threat from an upstart from the South Hold, named Tommy O'Kief. He began to panic. He had never had an enemy before, and it was never something that he had prepared for, but suddenly he felt that he had one. A powerful one.

He looked sideways to Dana. She would know how to get him out of the limelight, so he begged with his eyes. She took the hint and whispered into her dad's ear.

Jim stepped forward and raised his hands. The cheering mellowed, then stopped. "That was a wonderful reminder about our past and our values. But where does that leave you,

O'Toole Who Has a Lot to Say? Is there anything else, before my son steps down?"

O'Toole stepped forward. "Tommy O'Kief, that was a timely reminder of our values. I think the tribe owes you a debt of gratitude. You'll make a great leader….one day."

Tommy could suddenly feel the chief's eyes spiking him, even sharper, but he knew he could leave the stage after O'Toole's closure, so took one step sideways when….

"But" shouted O'Toole, "before you leave the stage, would you please tell the chief what we need to know from him!" He stepped back with his family.

Poor Tommy. He knew that O'Toole was goading him, but he had to do as asked, else he would never get off that stage. His imaginative creativity was certainly being put to the test.

He turned to the insecure chief. He was about to make him even more insecure. If only he could tell the poor man that he wasn't interested in his job. "Chief O'Hoolihan Who Designed the Farming Calendar. The tribe have been reminded of our past; they all know about the present. Now, what about the future? Are the Science and Planning Departments worn out dogs, who have seen their day, or do you still have a place in the hierarchy." He took in the chief's look of fear. "You've told the tribe about what we already know, now, tell us what we *don't* know. *Why* aren't the caterpillars here? Tell us why it's happening, and we, as a tribe, can ride the storm. Or are you now a lame duck?"

The young man said no more. He walked off the stage.

The chief, a little shaky, stood up and nodded towards Tommy. He was aware that he had been attacked from two sides, O'Toole from one end, and Tommy from the other, but Tommy had never even meant to get involved. He just wanted to stop his father from fighting. But one thing that they had brought to the surface was the tribe's need for strong leadership through what threatened to be a rough ride. The chief bent over and quietly discussed something with

Nostradamus, then beckoned Jim's ear. After a brief discussion he held his hands up.

"As a farmer I can understand the frustrations and concerns. We need to know why. Well, we've been studying trends and statistics for several years now, and the drop in caterpillar numbers has mirrored the rise in *rainfall*. So the Science and Philosophy Departments have been putting together their results, which just need some loose ends tidying. So, we'll make our presentation tomorrow at sun-up. This meeting is adjourned until tomorrow. Please all be here and bring along any useful comments or suggestions. Tomorrow at sun-up."

CHAPTER 11
FATHER PATRICK

The Emergency General Meeting was over but a continuation had been convened for the following morning, and so rationing was put on hold.

The entire tribe of red jerkins and trousers fanned out from the centre of the forest and headed back to their usual routines. Jim, Mary, the twins and their neighbours all headed south.

The children kept quiet, as they do in the company of their parents, but the adults made up for it with a constant babble of yap and nonsense and as they moved across the forest high up in the trees, Tommy and Dana also kept quiet, as did Jim and Mary. They never really felt like treating the meeting as a gossip item; things were far too serious for that. But Jim did keep smiling every time he looked at Tommy. He knew that his son was growing up and promised to be a lot more than a private in the Regiment. Tommy also seemed to know, and it made him very nervous.

Once they had reached their home-platform, Jim finally spoke. "You made a name for yourself today. I hope you're happy with it because I heard them yacking on the way home, away from your ears, and they *all* think you made a name for yourself. A good name, I must add."

Tommy was not sure what he had done, but "And what about enemies? Did I make any enemies?"

Jim frowned as if Tommy had asked a stupid question.

"Because I think I did. Mr O'Toole, and the chief."

"I'm not gonna expand on it, but you never made an enemy of Mr O'Toole, believe you me. And the chief? Well, if he's feeling threatened about his position, then it might make him take it a bit more seriously." He looked sideways at the young man. "You're not after his job, are you?"

Tommy gave him back the frown. *Stupid* question.

"Anyway, you two, just because we're gonna starve and all die by the end of next spring, you still have to be punished. I suggest you get out there and find out what your punishment is, before we have to let Hairy Daniels get his way. And I want to know before I go down the pub tonight, when I'll collect my winnings," he rubbed his hands together and smiled at both Tommy and Dana, "so that the committee can finalise the punishment, whatever it will be."

The twins had not forgotten, but somewhat hoped that the committee and their parents had; no chance, it would take more than a mere famine to err *Jim* off his line of duty, and Jim duly expected his children to show similar commitment to *their* duties. They had to establish their own punishment before that evening.

Once they had reached the south wall of the pigsty, they both felt more talkative. Dana stated, "I was really proud of you earlier. You were so grown up, and you talked up there just as if you were talking in class, with no nerves. So cool. You told our story so well."

"No nerves? You should've looked at my bum pinching up. I was crapping myself." They both had a welcome chuckle. "But I told it so well because it was all truth, not just legend. And besides, you know why I got up there; to stop Dad and O'Toole from fighting. That's the only reason, and I hope I won't have to do it again. Ever." He huffed as they marched towards the farmyard. "I don't like this idea that I'm some sort of leader. That was all down to bloody Old Murphy, and he was only joking."

"Was he?" She grinned directly at him. "You'll lead the Defence Regiment one day. You know that."

"I know. But I don't know if I want to. And besides, I haven't got Dad's muscles."

"Not yet. They'll come with a bit of age. But what you do

need, though, is your own shillelagh."

He had the chance to swing the focus back on her. "And one for you!"

She shook her head, but with little desire. "Not me, I'll be working as a seamstress," and then closed out on that subject.

They reached the start of the clay-pond and took a veer left once at the end of the sty, to give any snakes a wide berth. They were both very alert when out of the forest, for good reason, their lives could depend on it, and it did seem to set them aside from the other youngsters who feared even venturing to the edge of the forest, let alone out of it. They certainly had what most Nettle Wits did not, a wander-lust, a desire to go, to travel and learn, and they had the confidence to do it. They were naturals.

As a group of ducks waddled out of the water and took up temporary residence directly ahead of them, Tommy and Dana veered even more to the left, and eventually found themselves marching directly towards the farmhouse door. Then the light was obscured as the family dog looked down at them, his cold nose almost touching their heads. They never panicked, but stood up proud and offered themselves even closer, and the stink was too much for the dog who decided to go and annoy the ducks instead.

"Ain't it funny how we're not scared of the dog? One snap and we'd be squashed, but we just stepped towards him." Dana was thinking very deeply about everything. "Mind you, being scared of him wouldn't help us. He could squash us however brave or cowardly we are."

They walked further across the yard towards the door. Tommy wondered, "Where d'you think he is? Philips Who Moves With Stealth. Dad must've sent him to tail us, he said he always does. So, wonder where he is."

Just as they were beginning to look around for signs of their stalker, their minds were pulled right back into the task of the moment. The farmer's wife came out of the door. She already had a small barrel placed on the grass, and had brought out a wicker chair, placing it by the barrel. She sat herself down and did some repairs to some garments.

The twins made haste to get to the safety of the crack between the doorstep flags.

After watching from their crack for some time, all they learned was that she was darning. She was alone, so never spoke, so Dana suggested, "We'll have to go inside if she stays there. See if we can learn anything inside." She nervously looked through the gap below the door, but it seemed to be just as quiet inside. "Not gonna learn much like this."

But almost as she spoke, footsteps could be heard from down the side of the house. Somebody was walking from the lane. The sound was very soft, but with a slight slap with each step. The man then appeared from around the corner and had a black cloak and bare feet in sandals which clapped on his foot with every step. It was the Holy man, Father Patrick.

"Eileen. Top of the morning to you. Hope I've found you well."

She greeted him with a certain amount of suspicion, but then went inside and returned with another wicker chair. Once he had sat down, she went back inside and collected a flagon of wine and some wooden mugs and poured them both a good measure.

The Father held his mug up in front of his face and stated, "Here's to a fruitful friendship between us. Never visited you before, but I'm certainly glad I have. You know, this is the finest nettle wine in the World. How on earth do you do it?"

She smiled. "It's all about the nettles, Father. We've tried other nettles, but our patch behind the pigsty is the only one that gives us this strength. That's why we'll never plough them up." Unlike the Nettle Wits, the humans did not have the scientists to establish the reason for the high alcohol content, the very high sugar content of the nettles. They also ran hundreds of years behind the Wits in that they had not yet discovered how to refine the sugar.

The Father politely nodded towards the pigsty. Then he pointed to the tree past the end of the sty. "And what is that tree? Not seen any like it round here."

"No, it's the only one in Ireland. It's a walnut tree, and it was a gift from a sailor, who said it came from a place called the Med. Don't know where that is. My granddad planted it and now we get nuts from it each year."

They were running out of polite conversation. She poured another mug of wine: it would help the conversation flow.

The Father again held his mug up to in front of his nose and stated, "You could sell this, Eileen. It's so powerful. They'd kill for it over on Great Britain. Never tasted anything so fine, must be worth a fortune."

Tommy and Dana were taking it all in, but straining to hear everything, so they moved out of the safety of the crack and climbed into a dandelion flower, much closer.

The Father continued. "It's now been over sixty years since the birth of our saviour, Jesus Christ. I've been pleased with people's uptake of his spirit into the community, and you're no exception. You and your family are always an important part of my congregation. We must support each other, and take lesson from Jesus, and forgive others for their sins, as they forgive us. Do you understand what I'm saying?"

"Of course, I'm not totally illiterate. You want me to forgive my boy. Well, if that's all you've come for, you're too late. I forgave him as soon as he came down the tree, sobbing his heart out. I don't need you to tell me how to love my children."

"Exactly, you don't. I wouldn't try to, he's just a boy and still with no sense, and you know that, so all I'm saying is that you shouldn't punish him too hard, and I can tell you why. But where is he, by the way?"

"He's safe. This morning the Doyle's boys went down to the tar-pit, then over to the wicker-man to get some goose feathers, and it was the wicker-man who shot round and warned us, so Fergal and my dad have taken both the children to my brother's. They're safe. They can stay there for a week or so, until the fighting calms. So, if all you want to do is preach forgiveness, go and preach elsewhere because we always forgive our own. Now, we've got a fight to prepare for, with those neighbours of ours. We'll all *die* before they tar and feather my little boy." She leaned down below her chair and pulled out her knotty old shillelagh. "I might be a woman, but I'll die defending my children."

The twins were sweating. What had they really caused with their thoughtless prank?

"Calm down, Eileen. You're not the only one I've preached forgiveness to today. The situation has already been diffused, so please stay calm. I've already been round to see Mrs Doyle today, immediately before coming here. But, before we go into that, tell me exactly what the boy did. Please."

She nodded, then filled both their mugs again. "Well, her sister couldn't find her knickers, but on a second look she found them, under *his* bed. So I had a go and chased him up the tree, and I lost it. But, after I'd come in, Fergal came back and got him out the tree, and I'd calmed down by then. He sobbed his heart out, swearing that he never touched her knickers, any of them. Anyway, when we worked out about Doyle's knickers, Fergal remembered that him, Dad and both the children were all day down in the woods, collecting oak dust for the beans. He couldn't have taken her knickers." She sniffed. "He's a good boy, just mischievous. I miss him already. God help me for doubting him."

Father Patrick reached over and took Eileen's hand. "And God *will* help you." He smiled like a saint. "So, all is forgiven with the boy, and the boy has learned the hard way about his sister's knickers. All good. Now, the other problem, the Doyles. Now, this is where your faith in your old Father, here, starts to pay off. As I said, I've been to visit Mrs Doyle, before coming here, and I managed to use some Godly influence to calm the waters."

Several years earlier Father Patrick had arrived in Ireland to spread the word of the Lord and the new saviour, Jesus Christ. There he found a land of mixed religions as well as a wide range of inconsistent understandings of justice. It usually boiled down to 'I'm bigger than you, so you're guilty'. He constantly found himself in the middle of bitter disputes. Luckily he had spent years travelling abroad, mainly in Gaul, and had learned that you can often buy justice with a package aimed at 'saving face'. This was one such occasion where his Worldly experience could be the saviour, and save face.

"As I sat with Mrs Doyle, drinking her nettle tea, not a scratch on your nettle wine I must add to be sure, her three boys were down at the peat cuttings, and on their way back she had reminded them to pick up the tar. She said that some of it was for the barn, and the rest would go with the goose feathers. I told her that the brutal act of tarring and feathering was frowned upon by the church, but she just growled at me. When I mentioned that the boy could be scarred for life, once the skin had eventually shed along with the tar, and she never growled, but looked to the floor. Then when I told her that Jesus would not look kindly on her for such an unjust attack on a little boy, she looked to the floor *and* shook her head. Then when I told her that there is a way out to save face for both sides, she almost began begging. From growling to begging in not many minutes. The power of persuasion." He tapped his finger on the side of his nose. "You see, I *know* who took her knickers. So, next Sunday in church, she'll apologise publicly to you, and I expect you to take the apology with grace, like a good Christian. Can you do that?"

She jumped, a little surprised at the question. "Of course I will! Why wouldn't I, if we can get a peaceful end to this fighting talk? Of course I will, but why should she apologise? She'll look like a firkin idiot to the rest of the village."

"Yes, and she's prepared to take that chance, and I've promised to smooth the waters with a word from the pulpit.

You see, she knows that your boy didn't take the knickers, and she's *always* known. She never believed that your boy took them, but when the opportunity arose for her to pass the blame and the embarrassment onto somebody else, she jumped at it. She blamed your boy in order to protect her own family's reputation. You see, last week the two old spinsters from the hill spoke to me after the congregation and told me that they had caught somebody trying to steal their knickers off their line and wondered if I could have a quiet word with the family. They never wanted the man punished, they just sent him packing with a flea in his ear and have now left it to me to help the old man who is rapidly becoming senile. The old man, a pillar of society, was old…. man…. Doyle." He sighed. "Mrs Doyle confirmed that she had found her stolen knickers, in old man Doyle's bedroom. Her own father was stealing knickers from people's lines, and she was tearing her hair out to know what to do with him, then the opportunity came to blame your boy. Now, whatever she decides to do with her father, she must make sure your boy is cleared of any suspicion and I gave her a bit of a kick to do the right thing. It wouldn't be the first time people have tried to renegue on one of my deals, so I looked to my Satan in me and threatened her with exposure through the pulpit if she let me down. She won't. A bit of blackmail always works, to be sure. When forgiveness fails, blackmail usually works. She's got a choice."

Eileen was pleased and began to relax. "That was naughty, using the example of Satan. What if God is listening?"

"You know, Eileen, Satan was once The Lord's favourite angel, until he got too big for his own shoes and God sent him packing to roam the Earth to and fro. So, he can't be all bad."

"But…." she took a swig of her wine. "But somebody took the knickers. If it weren't my boy, and she wants to keep her dad out of it, who took them?"

"That's the other thing I promised if she cleared your boy's name, that I would announce from the pulpit that it has been proved beyond all reasonable doubt that they were taken by....the *leprechauns*! Case closed."

Dana almost fell off her petal, but this time not through anger, through hysterical laughter, and her and Tommy rolled around the dandelion in stiches. What a wonderful result, and what a profound lesson in life. "It's what the leprechauns exist for, and I'm so proud to be one."

They calmed down and thought about the outcome. Tommy meandered, "Could've been tarred and feathered. D'you think the tribe would've done it to us?"

Dana shook her head and watched the two humans drinking yet more wine. "We'll never know. But the boy's been sent to his relatives in the other village. We ain't got any relatives to be sent to, so I think we'll be all clear. A happy ending all round, don't you think?"

But their attention was grabbed as they heard people along the side of the house. They could see around the corner enough to see five big, burley Irish boys moving their way, all with their shillelaghs to hand, swinging and threatening. As Eileen and the Father heard the same, they both jumped up and pulled out their own weapons.

"We're gonna get trod on!" They made a dash towards the safety of the doorsteps and made the crack just as the men rounded the corner. They were safe, but what about Eileen and the Father?

"God!" Eileen shouted, "Don't creep up on us like that, you could've been crowned!" She and the Father breathed out and put their weapons on the barrel. It was the man of the house with her brother and three cousins. They had come to fight the Doyles! "This is Father Patrick. I'll get some more wine while he explains what he's sorted."

The twins made their escape across the yard and towards home. During the long walk they lamented over just how close they had come to starting a bloody, totally unnecessary war between the humans, and just how lucky they had all been for the cunning of the holy man, Father Patrick. He had averted a very nasty situation with his sly use of the church's young power, and maybe one day he would receive his just rewards. He could be a saint.

"You know, Tommy, we've been very lucky. It all could have gone very wrong for everybody, and it was only the cunning of that Christian holy man that saved all out necks. But it's worth mentioning it to Old Murphy, that he *should* have told us why we don't take revenge. The hard way is not always the best way to learn. Not just us that can get hurt."

"Perhaps Old Murphy doesn't know all the answers. He could never have known what would happen if we pranked that boy, nobody could have known, so how could he teach us?"

Dana smiled. "Yeah, you're right. If he'd told us, we would never have believed it. Anyway, I was so proud in the end to be one of the leprechauns that get blamed. They *do* have good reasons, and it's so weird that they don't know we even exist, but they still believe in us enough to use us when it suits. Weird. It's like blind faith." As they reached the edge of the forest she poked Tommy on the arm. "Anyway, it could've been a lot, lot worse." She just grinned.

"Yeah, if they had to fight."

"No, not that. Just think how bad it could've been, if you'd looked up. You could be blind now."

"Shut up! That's only a myth. Wouldn't have done any harm, I'm sure."

"Are you? Are you *sure?*" She was laughing under her breath. "Are you prepared to take the chance, look up next time and see….that? Well, would you take that chance? I bet nobody's ever tested the theory."

"And they never will, because we've learned our lesson and won't be hiding any girls' knickers in the near future, to be sure." They giggled as they entered the forest. "Come on, need to tell Dad what our punishment is."

CHAPTER 12
NEW WEAPONS

It had been a long and hungry day, all in all, with the early start at the meeting, then the long trek to the farmhouse. They were ready for their food.

As they sat at the table, "Bagsie I tell about the punishment," begged Dana. "Please."

"Okay. But keep it short and sweet. Don't think they need to know about the fight that the father avoided."

Jim said grace. "May the Lord be thanked for this meal, all be it of smaller rations, and we thank our beloved Creator for making us different from the humans. Amen."

"Amen." "Amen." "Amen."

Mary quietly informed the twins that the rationing had begun early. "There's plenty of fruit preserve and pickles and mushrooms. Meat must never be wasted as it's going to be short this winter."

They silently performed the sacred act of eating. There were slices of toadstool laid out to fill the stomach in the absence of the larger caterpillar steaks. It was the start of harder times.

The plates were all licked clean, so they were able to relax.

Mary opened the usual family discussion. "This is normal from now on. So long as we all eat some meat we should stay healthy. We'll survive and not get Brady's disease."

The twins looked at each other, as if to say 'now'. Dana fiddled with her fingers and prepared her words, wishing to be careful not to talk their punishment up too much, but at the same time, being honest.

She nodded to her dad. "Dad, the boy was alright in the end. We found out what his punishment was."

Jim put his hand over and held her arm. "You don't need to go through it all. Phillips Who Moves with Stealth, he got back well before you. He filled us in down the pub. Your punishment's been agreed." He grinned. "Don't look so surprised. You know, we keep an eye on anyone who leaves the forest for everyone's safety. The tribe never feels comfortable when any of us leave our home."

The twins sighed. Tommy almost asked Jim a question, but thought better of it. Instead, he asked, "Do you want to know about the other things we learned about humans and their Father?"

Jim shook his head. "No need. Phillips always does a thorough job, he told us everything." He stood up very deliberately and collected some items from under his bed. "While Phillips looked out for you, I went with some of the tannery ladies to collect toadstools for their brown dye and, while there, your mum made the quivers. I cut the clubs."

Lying on the table in front of them were two elongated carrying pouches with straps to hang over their shoulders, and poking out the ends were sharp pieces of black wood. Dana had a grin from one ear to the other as she pulled one of the pouches to her.

"Are these for us?" she shyly asked. She held the pointed end of the wood and drew it from the quiver. It was a blackthorn spine. The shaft was jet black with a heel of wood left on one end and a sharp point at the other.

The twins beamed with pride. They had topped a memorable day off with the presentation of their very own shillelaghs.

"All you have to do," Dad said, "is to make them part of you. Shape the heel into the club, then mould the thin end to your own hand. They'll be like an extension to your arm."

The youngsters played with the weapons and drooled. Jim fetched his own shillelagh from below his bed and laid it on the table. "Oil to a shine and balance it to you. That's all you have to do. Just like this, the legendary O'Kief Shillelagh."

The weapon shone like jet.

Mary reminded them that, "You have till the end of winter to make your mind up. You could still be garment makers if you wish." She had a grin which showed that she knew she would be making garments alone next year. But she would always support their choices.

Tommy suddenly sat back. "What about our punishment?"

Jim calmly told the two, "You'll find that out tomorrow."

As they readied to finish their meal-time, the crier swung through the village.

"Hear-ye, hear-ye! General meeting at sun-up. Central corral. Everyone to attend!"

CHAPTER 13
THE SPEECH

The next morning, the tribe was assembled in the central corral. The chief stood at the centre of the top table and held his hands out, and the entire worldly population of Nettle Wits stood to attention in anticipation of a speech of deliverance. They were expecting.

"Thank you for coming to this continuation of yesterday's meeting. We will be answering some of the questions relating to why this is happening." The sun was up, but not yet clearing the roof of the pigsty, so the air hung damp. Two young children whimpered. He continued, "I believe we have arrived at some answers which will point us in the right direction, and if any of you have anything else to add, we'll be pleased to hear it at the end of the announcements. As you all know we're facing a famine. If we ignore the threats we'll certainly starve. So, after many meetings and statisticalisation procedures, we have some answers. We have tried to follow recognised processes of logicisation but logic does not always satisfy our needs for direction. We have therefore depended heavily on the input from the philosophers. Anyway, see what you think."

He looked around the tribe. They were not readable, and the mood was shrouded in uncertainty. They were not in the mood for empty bullshit.

He turned to his right and held his hand out. "I call Nostradamus Who Sees Tomorrow."

He sat down and Nostradamus slowly got to his feet. "Thank you. Thank you all. We, in the science department, have assembled data from many years of study in order to arrive at these conclusions, and some is a little subjective to opinion. But it's what we have." He held some drawings in front of him. "I'll give it to you straight.

"The foundation of the problem.

"We are Nettle Wits. We've evolved around a diet of Moorish caterpillars and in an environment which is driven by the Irish Stinger Nettle. We know from our studies that the Irish Stinger Nettle is no ordinary stinger nettle. Unlike the Common Nettle, the Irish variety is very high in sugar and Iodine and, as far as we know, only grows in our own managed forest and in two other mixed wild forests on the other side of the Doyle's farm.

"Then there are the Moorish, or Moors, caterpillars which we rely on for food. Without their meat, we quickly lose our colour, go down with all sorts of ailments, then die. The Moors caterpillars, without the Irish Stinger Nettle to feed them, they never gain enough weight to be able to turn into pupa. They just die. They cannot live on the Common Nettle for very long.

"So without the Irish Nettles, the caterpillars die out. And without the caterpillars, the Nettle Wits die out. We are all dependent upon each other. So, what's happening?

"What we do know from many years of study is that the rains in spring and summer are getting heavier. It's becoming wetter and wetter, has been doing so for many years now. As the rains become heavier, the moisture-loving Common Nettles have been encroaching on our arid-loving Irish Nettles, and we've all had to work harder each year to protect the forest from reverting back to a wild habitat. The Irish Nettles do not thrive easily in wet conditions.

"On top of that, the spring rains have become more damaging each year. Increasing numbers of butterflies have been swamped and drowned as they emerge, dying before they've been able to breed, leaving reduced numbers of eggs to spawn the season's stock. Some of those losses have been made up for by the visiting wild butterflies from the Doyles farm, but this year, they never came. Not a single wild butterfly was recorded this year.

"So that's where we are. Reduced domestic herds and no wild herds. It all spells famine."

The crowd began to fidget. Responding to the silence, Nostradamus jumped in before they were lost.

"That's not a great summing up, is it? So let's consider the ways forward. Ireland seems to be getting wetter each year, a weather phenomenon to which we've given the name of climate change. It's happening and it looks like it could carry on happening, but why? What's causing the climate change, and can we do anything about it? I pass you over to Daniels Who Turned Grey by the Time He was Eighteen"

He sat down and up stood Hairy Daniels.

"Scary! Doesn't sound good to me, but like all phenomenons we have to live with it or die with it." Hairy Daniels was not the man to argue with. His ragged grey hair flowed around his dull-green head as he swung to survey the crowd. "And you'd better listen well! Don't think you can simply blame our beloved creator, The Almighty, because She's no leprechaun, She might not take kindly to being blamed. She might just stop sending the rain and instead send fire." He huffed. "You've been warned!"

As Hairy Daniels sat down with a clump, the chief rose. The crowd was shocked and silent.

"Well, that told us. It's now back to the science department to come up with some answers. Back to Nostradamus Who Sees Tomorrow."

Nostradamus stood up and laid out another set of drawings to prompt him. He cleared his throat. "Yes, thank you, philosophers. I must confirm to the tribe that we scientists *do* heed the warning laid down by Daniels Who Turned Grey by the Time He was Eighteen, and our conclusions in no way deliberately lay blame on our beloved creator.

"Yesterday we all congregated in the pub and spent all

day working through a set of questions. Now, each question could be answered logically with a 'yes' or a 'no', and eventually we ended up down the line of questioning which answered 'yes' every time. The whole group of outstanding minds eventually agreed that there could only be one logical answer.

"The process of logicisation never lies, and there is no doubt in our findings. The climate change is being caused by…. the *Romans*!"

He opened his arms in the welcome gesture, awaiting the applause. Not a dickie bird. Total silence apart from the goldfinches on the thistle heads.

It seemed like a lifetime as he awaited some kind of response then, just as the sun began reaching past the pigsty roof, he asked, "Any questions?"

The tribe mumbled, then a woman from the West stepped forward. She held her head high as she politely asked, "What's Romans?"

Nostradamus nodded his head several times. Then thought a bit. Then raised his finger. "Yes, Romans. I'd better pass that one over to our in-House foreign affairs expert. I call Murphy Who Knows a Lot Cos He's Old."

He sat down and up stood the teacher, Old Murphy.

"*Romans*!" He said it with emphasis. "I'll give them their full name, Roman navvies. Now, I've had longstanding communications with our friends, the Cockle Wits down by the docks. They make it their business to listen to what the sailors talk about and are the most knowledgeable people in the lands about what's happening in the wider world. It seems that for the past twenty years, the Roman navvies have been carrying out a major programme of road-building, stretching for thousands of miles across Great Britain, and their roads are quite monumental. They are not like the mud roads outside the front of the farmhouse, but are constructed of solid stone bases, with substantial, metalled surfaces and built to last forever. They are impressive. And that's what the

Roman navvies are doing in Great Britain."

He stopped to check his own drawings which lay on the table in front of him. He then continued. "The real issue with the Roman navvies is that their roads are so substantial that the weight of the stone, which has been relocated to build them, is causing the world to tip on its axis. Great Britain in the east is now lower than us, and the rains to the west of us are being tipped towards us. They are rolling downhill towards us and causing the heavy rains. The world is no longer flat but dipping from west down to east, with us in the middle. It has been caused by the weight of the Roman navvies' roads. The clouds now roll *downhill* from the west and saturate our once-dry Ireland."

He paused, but seemed to decide that he had finished, so he sat down.

The crowd began to grumble. The buzz of discontent began to spread through the ranks until Nostradamus stood up and raised his hands.

He shouted, "Quiet, quiet! I still have important summaries to announce." He waited a few seconds and the crowd settled. "Right. As a think-tank, we have formulated three possible outcomes. Here we go, so listen carefully.

"One. The Roman navvies will eventually finish their work and the world will settle back to its proper flat position. The rain will return to normal. This will take several years.

"Two. It's believed that there cannot possibly be an unlimited supply of rain clouds in the west. So, they'll eventually run out. The rains will stop coming from the west. This could take several years.

"Three. The protesters in Great Britain will win the day and stop the road-building programme. Our hopes are pinned on one group from Anglia, Queen Boadicea and the Iceni tribe. They are working hard to stop the Roman navvies, but even if they succeed, we'll still have to wait for the world to go back flat again. This could take several years."

He shook his head, then sat down, leaving the stage to

the chief.

The chief did not really know what to say, so he improvised. He asked if anybody had anything to say or ask.

O'Toole Who Has a Lot to Say stood forward. "Nostradamus, you're not being very clear. May I propose that our preferred spokesman tells us all what it means in plain language. No big words. May I call young Tommy O'Kief?"

The chief nodded towards Tommy, who was on a leaf with Dana, Mary and their neighbours.

Dana poked him. "It's you. They want you."

Poor Tommy looked across to his dad, who nodded his approval, then smiled. It seems he had no choice, the tribe had chosen him. He stood forward. He coughed, put his hand up to his shoulder, where his new shillelagh hung and thought, 'they want me'. He felt the pump of adrenaline through his heart as he delivered his youthful exuberance to the crowd.

"Friends, wits, and countrymen, lend me your faith. The science and philosophy departments have spent a long time trying to say, 'it's going to rain for years, get used to it'. So let's be Nettle Wits and grab the bull by the horns. Not just live with it, but *use* it. Use it to make a better world for us. Make it work for us."

He stopped for thought, then inspiration arrived. 'Use the faith, belief and our beloved creator' was what came to him. It was like a vision from heaven. 'Use what we have, belief.' His mind went back to the previous day when Father Patrick saved the day for the humans, and he was inspired.

"We were put on the World by The Almighty, all equal. She sent each tribe off to make a life from this varying land, and we came here. Like the Cockle Wits at the coast, we made the land our own and changed it to what it is today, a managed plantation which has evolved, and we've evolved with it, and now believe that we'll all die without it. Well, I don't believe that is true. This is not a natural environment, it is a farm, home to *domestic* creatures and feeding a developed tribe of leprechauns. The forest, the Irish Nettles and the Nettle Wits have evolved into what we are today. None of this is original nor natural, all changed to suit our needs. All unnatural. Looks like we need to carry on changing as we always have been. Changing, evolving, and controlling.

"The Roman navvies are not destroying our world, just changing it. It has never stopped changing and *will* never stop changing, so we must not just change with it, but take control of the changes and make them work for us, as we always have done. Can we still do it? Do we still have what it takes? I say 'yes'.

"We have belief. We have faith. We are the children of Gayla. We will thrive. It's all up to us. Gayla gave us *her* intelligence, *her* imagination, *her* industry, *her* belief, and *her* understanding, and she left us with a message with which to live by. I'll remind you of her mighty words, which were:

"Boredom is the mother of invention, but desperation is its wayward uncle.

"And I believe that Uncle Desperation is about to make a long overdue visit, and we must welcome him with open arms and embrace him as we would our beloved." He paused, then, "Please believe me; we will emerge *better* and *stronger*. Believe!"

He looked around at the auditorium, full of gaping Wits, and without the tribe's permission he stepped back with Dana.

As soon as they all realised that he had finished, the auditorium erupted. With arms open and shouting, the tribe was alive with new enthusiasm for the future. It went on for many minutes.

Once it had begun to fade, the chief stood up and raised his hands. "Now, it's up to us. We will change with the world and be a better nation for it."

They reconvened the meeting for two weeks' time, asking for ideas, inventions, inspiration, and anything which could

help them to take control of their future.
    Meeting adjourned.

CHAPTER 14
BIG PLANS

The reconvened emergency general meeting was over, but the tribe were to meet again in exactly two weeks from today to put forward ideas, options and inspiration.

On the migration back to their home Holds, Tommy could feel the eyes and the gossip burning into his back, as he moved silently through the canopy. He was feeling very conspicuous.

"They'll soon forget you," Dana jested. Tommy thanked her for her support.

When they arrived home, Jim finally spoke. "You two. Just because the tribe is going to starve next year, you don't get away with no punishment, remember? The boy?"

Mary threw together a quick meal of dried Moors skin and nettle soup and they sat down to eat. Dana noticed that she had put extra portions on hers and Tommy's plates.

Jim said grace. "May the Almighty be thanked for this food, and we vow to not waste any. And we ask the beloved Creator to watch over our children as they venture yonder. Amen".

"Amen." "Amen." "Amen."

The twins respected the mealtime silence as they wondered what on earth Jim must have been thanking Gayla for, but the meal was soon over, plates licked clean, and Jim broke the ice.

"It's been agreed. Your punishment was agreed last night in the pub. As per the boy." He paused to study twins' faces. "Surprised? Shouldn't be. The boy was sent away."

Dana stressed. "Not as punishment, the good of the family and for his own good."

"Exactly! Now this looks like punishment and all those at the pub see it that way. But I don't. There is a little teeny-weeny bit of punishment, but, in reality, it's a whacking great lump of reward. You've both earned this honour."

The twins looked at each other and raised their eyebrows. It was beginning to feel interesting.

Jim continued. "My best man has been given the job of surveying and reporting on the two forests at the other side of the Doyle's farm, and when asked to select two capable people to accompany him, he selected you two without hesitation. Very few of our people like leaving the forest, but you two love it, and he says that you both handle yourselves very well when out on your jaunts. You're both totally aware, you instinctively watch each others backs, you both understand the dangers as well as the beauties, and you are fit, keen and intelligent. What a reference he's given you. So, I agreed that you could go, and the committee agreed."

Tommy meekly asked. "Is he to look after us?"

"No, he's to command you. As soon as I shake your hands, you'll be drafted temporarily into the Defence Regiment. I'm your general and Phillips Who Moves With Stealth is your captain. In my absence, he's your boss. Never forget that."

Phillips Who Moves With Stealth was to take command of the two recruits and take them on a dangerous mission. The twins were not quite sure whether they should cheer or cry, but to their credits, they held out and behaved impeccably. Jim, sorry, General O'Kief, shook both their hands and they were in, privates in the Defence Regiment.

Mary collected two beautiful red backpacks and explained, "Inside is food, wine, rope and the standard toolkit. It's just basic equipment, but it's now part of you, so look after it all and it could keep you alive. Your quivers will hang neatly beside the bags, across your shoulders." She grinned at Dana. "You look so beautiful. Everyone loves a squaddie."

"Rules!" Jim laid his hands out onto the table. "You know the rules of the forest. Well, they don't exist out in the world. Your commanding officer is the law and you abide his law at all times. If in doubt, you ask. Names: The Regiment doesn't use ranks nor tribal names, so Captain Phillips Who Moves With Stealth, is to you, Phillips, and you, as his subordinates, are Tommy and Dana. Simple as that. Make sure you abide by it at all times. Discipline is what'll keep you together and in one piece."

Mary and Jim gave both the children a tight hug as Phillips moved across the approaching nettles, and all four had a little tear.

Mary reminded them, "We trust Phillips to look after you both, and we trust you both to look after Phillips. You're all the same team, so look after each other."

As the young captain collected the new recruits Mary handed each of them a little red, peaked cap. "Don't put them on until out of the forest, else you might upset the chief." She hugged both her children and, "If you don't make it back, we'll see you in the Waiting Room."

The three adventurers left the safety of the forest, seen off by Mary and Jim and the mother and father of Phillips. The nettle-green squaddies looked quite stunning in their red clothes, red backpacks, green shillelagh quivers, and little red caps. A tiny army on the march.

Phillips was not a big man, not much taller than the twins but with more developed muscles and was a bit older than them. He said he was twenty-one and rather shyly told Dana that he still lived with his parents. Something for her to consider, perhaps?

The red caps were made by Mary at the request of Phillips, who explained that in the forest only the chief could wear a hat, but out here they could do whatever was sensible. He explained that some birds would mistake the green heads for an insect or seed and peck at it, possibly doing a bit of damage to one's brain. The bird would always leave alone once they got the taste, but by then the damage would be done.

They left the forest from the north-east corner and took the route of the blackthorn hedge northwards, past the adder country, and after about three hours found themselves fronted by the boundary stream. The other side was the Doyle's farm, and an unknown world.

They looked back beneath the low boughs of the blackthorns and could no longer see the forest, but the top of the pigsty and walnut tree were still in view.

"We've made good time," said Phillips. He retrieved a map from his backpack and the three of them studied their planned route. "We're going straight north. Looks like two fields of pasture, with a pond across the middle of the first field. It'll be slow going through the pasture, and we've got to move around this pond, somehow. Once we're over this stream, we need to find a campsite. It'll be well into the evening."

They looked down at the water which was moving very rapidly. It was going to be a dangerous crossing.

After scouting for a relatively open part of the bank, they made the crossing with the help of a long, dry piece of grass which acted as a bailey bridge. The only scare was when a loud 'plop' came from upstream, but it was just a friendly water rat.

As they reached the top of the opposite bank, a celebratory cheer went up, then Phillips ordered, "Leave the grass and rope where it is. Hopefully it'll all still be in place for us when we come back. We've got plenty of rope." They were soon at the top of the bank.

The team was on uncharted land and their only guide was the map which had been made up by a man who was accidentally picked up by a crow and dropped when the bird realised the taste. He had roughed out what he had seen from the sky, but it was really just his fleeting memory from way up in the claws of the crow. It was never seen as an accurate route planner, just a rough guide.

The route ahead was through open pasture, which, to a tiny leprechaun, was an extensive, solid jungle, but what stood out was a large thistle which the sheep seemed not to eat, so Tommy suggested that they could set up camp in the heights of the thistle, if they could get there before dark. They should then be able to see the pond from above the grass level.

Phillips agreed, and after a couple of hours of struggling through the thick grassland, they made it, and set up camp high up in the plant.

Phillips looked around them. "This is a good viewing point. We can see all the landmarks from here, the entire field, and look, can just see the top of our walnut tree, and the farmhouse chimney." He spent some time surveying the visible world, all the time referencing the map, then making updates. "Part of our mission is to get this map into a reliable document, one on which we can believe in the future. This one has loads of errors and the scale is all over the place." He beckoned his soldiers over. "Look, this is where we are. On this map, we're in the middle of a pond! It's almost a work of fiction."

They began to wonder if the forests were really where the map showed. Phillips spent some time updating what they had already learned, then, "Look, this is where the forests are shown, the other side of the next field, two to three days away. If anything happens to me, you need to maintain the mission as well as turn this map into a reliable chart. Also, this'll get you back home so long as it's updated."

He put the map away in his backpack.

The tiny army had been travelling for several hours without a break, so they were hungry. The officer ordered, "We need to eat."

They each had their backpacks in front of them as Tommy observed, "They look quite well packed. Any Idea what's in them? Never got chance to look before we left home."

Dana nodded. "I know there's some rope in the big document pocket. I used one of mine at the stream, one roll left."

Phillips half laughed. "Get to know these and get to love them out here." He opened the flap of his pack. "Two main compartments this side are for your tools. This side is for drinks. You'll have a skin of wine." He pulled it out, then returned it. "That's gotta last you the entire mission. Drink it all too quick and you'll go without wine for the rest of the trip." He pulled out the water skin. "This will last you a good day and you must remember to fill it from the dew on the leaves every morning, else you'll go very thirsty, and we can only go for a couple days before dying of thirst. Never forget that. Now, in this very small skin is pure alcohol, for cleaning wounds and, watered down, can be used to preserve any specimens we wish to take back with us. And....if we desperate...." He dug deep. "And look at these." He held up three medium sized water skins with open tops, but these were different from the other skins. They were totally transparent. "Have you ever seen anything like these?"

They were clear, waterproof bags, possibly for use preserving or storing samples to be taken back to the farmers and scientists.

"This is the sort of thing that we do as a tribe. We invent, create, develop, just for the fun, so your speech earlier was so relevant." He smiled. "My mum is part of the tanning workshop. They made all the pelts for our clothes, these bags and our bedding, and now they're experimenting with this clever material. The Cockle Wits have already put in a massive order for this material, as part of our annual deal, and the trade deal with the Cockles is getting more and more important each year, to both tribes They have serious uses planned for it."

Dana asked. "How's it made? She felt the texture of the bag from her pack. "They're not like the butterfly skins, haven't got that velvety feel."

"No. Remember the dens we used to make as children, totally see-through, but dry out and fall apart after a couple of days, and that's what this is, Wood Ant wings, but specially treated and tanned. Brilliant!"

In a utopian civilization with everybody fed and watered, boredom quickly sets in. From a very early age the Nettle Wit children triumph over Mother Boredom by inventing things, just for the fun of it, and it becomes a habit which remains with them right through life. So, the adults work and go down the pub, and then triumph over Mother Boredom by inventing, just as they'd done since they were knee-high.

A couple of years back, when the annual trade deal was completed down at the docks, the Cockle Wits gave Old Murphy a flagon of very light oil, and they called it crab oil. Murphy's friend, Weaver, asked if they could find a use for it because they had an almost endless supply of the oil, so, ever since, it has given the adult Nettle Wits great pleasure in trying to invent uses for it. One of the uses was for waterproofing and subtling pelts, particularly the wings of Wood Ants and the even finer Mayfly. It produced material which stayed subtle, never dried out to a crisp, and was totally waterproof. It was also see-through.

The tribe could find little use for the clear, waterproof material, but thoroughly enjoyed inventing it! However, when Old Murphy showed it to his Cockle Wit friend, they put in an order for dozens of pelts, to be delivered with the annual trade deal. That annual delivery was due in a few weeks time.

Captain Phillips continued. "Doesn't look like much, a water bag which can you see through. We've got them as a trial for collecting specimens in, but we're also trialing the process in a more useful way." He nodded towards Dana. "You're a garment maker, done a lot with your mum. What do we do if it rains tonight, and we can't get cover below the leaves?"

She thought carefully. "Well, normally we would cover up with a butterfly blanket. But one of those would barely fold small enough to go into these backpacks, so, I suppose out here we'll get cold and wet."

Phillips smiled his approval. "Correct! Now, out here, cold and wet could mean pneumonia and death." He grinned at the doubting twins. "If you feel in the right-hand side of your documents pouch you'll find a rolled-up survival blanket. Made of mayfly wings, it's been treated in the same way as the ant wings, but it's so fine that it rolls up into almost nothing. Your life, in just one of your hands."

The twins took out the tiny rolls and examined them, but never opened them. They really did make travel safer, allowing the other space to be filled with other essentials such as food, drink and tools.

The captain proudly said, "We'll invent our way through this, Tommy, just as you predicted in your speech. And this is just one example of a useless invention, with a positive use. You're so right, we can invent our way through this climate-change!"

The three slept comfortably without the need for the mayfly blankets.

Once they'd filled their water bottles from the morning dew, Captain Phillips called the team over to the edge of the leaf. The sun was just rising over the horizon. "Before we do anything else, we must get our bearings. I've updated the map but we're not gonna use it right now. Dana, where's east?"

Dana pouted as if she was being drilled by a schoolteacher. She pointed to where the sun rose, and then pointed out north and south without even having to think.

"Well done. We're going north and must keep on a straight line with the walnut tree behind us, south, and that eared tree ahead of us, north. If we stray off that line, we could be in trouble, and when we go through the thick growth, it's easy to end up walking in circles, so we must constantly monitor our four directions and adjust our course as needed. Happy with that?"

They were, so the captain told them to keep watch while he went down the thistle, to collect some slices of a mushroom which he had spotted. They would eat before setting off north, and any food collected would help to make their rations last.

While Phillips was collecting the mushrooms, Dana observed, "He's like a schoolteacher, so intense. I bet Dad has given him orders. I bet we're not just here to keep him company."

They eventually set off, but only reached halfway down the thistle before Phillips called them to a halt. He pointed east, towards the boundary hedge and the gate. The sheep, goats and the two large wolfhounds waited.

"Sheep and goats are waiting for the farmer to feed them. That'll give us a free run for a bit where we won't risk being trodden on. Now, look north, where the grass is moving about. That's a hedgehog. It's moving north and I bet it has a regular run which we can follow. It'll give us a pathway."

They moved to the ground and found a hedgehog run. Deep into the meadow-growth, they followed the run northwards. Not only did it give a clear passage through the thick meadow, but also relative safety from baby snakes. The snakes stayed well clear of hedgehogs who would eat them as soon as look at them, but they just needed to be wary of the hedgehog coming through and standing on them.

The run was like a highway with side roads joining from both directions, some big and used by the hedgehogs and some smaller used by mice and shrews. It was surprisingly busy. None of the other road users bothered the Wits as they all had acute senses of smell and thus gave them a wide berth.

"Do we really smell that bad?" Dana asked. "Funny how we don't notice us."

It was their main defence against the many hungry predators which roamed the world. They smelled so bad that even the pygmy shrew, which is probably the most voracious carnivore in the whole World, would take one sniff and then run. It was a good job, as the shrew, not much larger than the Wits themselves, had to eat more than double its own weight each day just to stay alive, and hence would tackle anything which they thought they could overpower, apart from a Nettle Wit.

Now, the ecology of the British Isles was different in the year 69. The untamed woodlands and moors which surrounded the farms would be home to herds of deer, which would be followed and hunted by wolves and humans, and the humans would be hunted down by the wolves and bears, and the humans would employ large dogs to warn the larger predators away from themselves and their livestock, and the humans would become expert bowmen, to hunt food and protect their families from the large animals. Then the humans would hunt each other and take the land and enslave their enemy, and so on. It was a world of dog-eat-dog, where the main object in life was to remain in that life, still alive.

Down at the Wit level, it was no different. As they marched along the hedgehog run the world around them fought for their very existence. The meadow was a veritable labyrinth of small runs, and they were used by the thousands of voles, and the hundreds of other creatures which lived on the voles. Stoats patrolled the lofty grasses above the runs while weasels, with their elongated bodies, moved through the runs like hairy snakes with legs. And they were all just looking to eat anything which shared the runs with them. Anything except for the rancid Wits.

At all levels of life, life has to feed life and has always been the case. A very simple model, and very constant, never changing.

However, in the finer detail of the cycle, things do change. They never stop changing. They never will stop changing. It's called evolution, and it affects every level of that cycle, apart from, of course, the power of the sun.

Tommy, Dana and Phillips spent many hours marching,

and as a reward, had many hours of philosophical thought time, time to consider life, death and the world. They didn't waste that thought time, and it made the trek pass by very quickly, but thinking philosophy was never going to keep them alive. Their minds wandered!

"Look out!" screeched Phillips.

Out from a side run, shot a vole, desperate to escape a weasel which flew after it. The three Wits were knocked flying!

As they picked themselves up and brushed themselves down, they sighed with relief. They pulled together for a huddle.

Dana gasped, "That was a shock. None of us saw it coming, thinking too much about other things, weren't we?" They had been travelling for some hours and were getting tired, with their heads wandering and leaving themselves vulnerable. "Should've seen that weasel coming."

Phillips peered along the tunnel hoping to see something. "We need to find a tall plant to climb, check out our position and direction. We can't afford to wander off our course."

They moved ahead with a fresh alertness, and after about an hour found a tall sheep's parsley, which they ascended, to where they could see unobstructed across the meadow.

The first thing to consider was their safety. Way over to the west, their left, by the layered hedge, was a herd of small deer with some young. They were grazing peacefully. To the east, their right, around the farm gate, was the mixed herd of sheep and goats. Then around the herd wandered the farmer's two wolfhounds, tall and powerful, while two farmers were building what looked like a bonfire.

"Getting ready for something, don't know what."

They thought that it was all far enough away not to bother them. They checked their bearings. They had remained almost perfectly on the south-north line and had made good distance, thanks to the hedgehogs, and were about three quarters across the field. Straight ahead of them was an old tree stump, just before the hedge.

"If we can get there today, we can make camp on or under that stump, and it's tall enough to give us a vantage point." After about two hours and several climbs to check their position, they arrived at the stump, and were soon sitting on the edge watching life go by.

Looking back, the stately thistle which had given them shelter for the night, was almost out of sight, and their walnut tree was becoming smaller as they moved north. Probably another hour and they would have been at the hedge bordering the north of the field. They would do that short section in the morning.

Phillips pointed to the east. "The farmers are building fires." The bonfire, which they noted earlier, was not a bonfire, but a stack of wood to feed four smaller fires which they had made around the herd, or flock. They were lighting them. The deer over to the west? Well, they were trespassing on the farmer's field, but all the farmer could do was protect his animals. You see, wherever the deer go, the wolves will follow, and a baby goat is easier for the wolves to take than a baby deer, so the farmer has to protect his goats and sheep using the fires and his dogs. "They'll be there all night. Be there until the deer move on."

You may well be thinking that the wolves would just take the easy option and catch a few rabbits, but in the year 69 there were no rabbits in Ireland, they hadn't yet been introduced.

The stump was well aged with oyster toadstools growing on the top, offering some protection from the rain and from possible air attacks from the Owls. They put their backpacks under the toadstools.

After a period of quiet recovery, Phillips got the military show back on the agenda. The sky was clouded over with little indication of exactly where the sun was, so he walked slowly around the stump, carefully peering over the edge, and eventually stopped. He pointed north, towards the eared tree.

"This confirms that we're still moving north."

Tree moss, unlike most plants, loves to live in the shade, the north facing edge.

Phillips explained that one of the most likely causes of death, apart from being squashed, would be to get lost and never finding their way home, soon running out of their rations of Moors meat and pickled skins. "We have rations for nine days, after that, we would become undernourished, weak and eventually succumb. Without the Moors meat, we would quickly die from Brady's disease."

Tommy and Dana were quiet, allowing their commanding officer to talk. They had been told that out here the law was the officer, but were also told, if in doubt, ask.

Tommy just had to ask. "How do we know that we'd die if we went a few days without the meat?"

"We just know. Everybody knows, but just in case you've got any ideas, we'll have one portion of our rations each day, and that is an order. Don't get any stupid ideas about experimenting, because if you put our mission at risk, you'll be on a charge."

The voice of authority. The two privates quietly acknowledged.

Phillips relaxed. "I'm starving, talking about rations. We need to eat."

He said Grace and they all respected tradition by eating in silence. Phillips had kept some of the mushroom from the morning, so they each had a piece to top up their rations. They were very bitter, but edible.

Dana nervously asked, "What did you mean 'on a charge'? If we're put on a charge for anything, like you mentioned earlier, what would our punishment be?"

Philips stayed calm as he thought. He nodded towards the east, the Doyle's farmhouse. "We're not like them, the humans. We don't have real punishment, so we don't know until the time comes. I don't know the answer."

Dana calmly continued, "Has anybody ever been

punished? I know this is our punishment, but it's not, is it? We're here to do whatever. But it's not punishment." She studied the captain's face. "So why are we here, because it's not punishment, is it?" She waited for a reply. "My dad would never accept lies, so tell us the truth, as Dad would expect. Why are we here?"

Tommy struggled to keep a straight face as his sister began to show some of the determined venom which he knew she had, but Phillips never grinned. Then he held his hands up. "Alright, I'll tell you what my orders are. But never forget I'm still the captain. Your dad has made that quite clear. I.... am.... the.... captain."

The twins nodded in agreement.

"Well, your dad has given me very specific instructions. I suppose you knowing what they are will help me to administer them, so, here goes." He adjusted his seat position and cleared his throat. "The mission is to locate the wild nettle forests, survey them, learn about them, and learn about the world. It's all about options." He stood up and looked around the field as he thought. "Now, I was asked to go because I'm young, intelligent and part of the inner circle. I'm a trusted member of that circle, a secretive group, who all have similar beliefs."

He sat down and tried to relax. "The circle has been meeting for many generations, in fact, ever since we opened the first pub. The small selective group meet over a pint or two each week and publicly discuss the weather, our children's education, the quality of the beer, but privately discuss the state of our civilization and its direction. We all believe that we follow our dreams, but plan for our nightmares. You...." He pointed his finger straight at Tommy. "You have spoken publicly about our favourite uncle calling, Uncle Desperation, and we believe you're right. The shit will be hitting very soon, as you told the tribe, and they all believe you, but they won't do much about it unless led. We're like a nest of ants, we all blindly follow, so it's absolutely important for the one that we follow, well, that he knows the way." He raised his eyebrows at Tommy.

Tommy jumped up. "I never planned on anything, but to stop Dad fighting! O'Toole was meddling for a fight and Dad was up for it. That's why I stood up, O'Toole wanted a fight, and we don't fight!"

"No, we don't fight, not yet, but there's always a first time, I'll give you that. But that's not what O'Toole was looking for, he was just doing his job. It was just a job. He led the tribe to select you as their chosen hero. You obliged." Phillips held his finger up to stop Tommy objecting. "He set you up, you bit and then showed the tribe what you're made of. You showed them, showed us, what we were already suspecting." He smiled at Tommy, then Dana. "O'Toole's an important member of our circle, a valuable and respected member. He's got what the rest of us ain't got, a real gob."

Tommy had been led into a position of esteem, admired by the Nettle Wits, but he felt ashamed of being used so easily.

After a few seconds out to sulk, "Where does that leave me? Am I to be some sort of revolutionary, used by the circle to achieve their covert ambitions? Has this 'Inner Circle' set me up as a conspirator?"

Phillips shook his head. "No, it's not like that. Your dad would never do anything like that to you. But you are truly admired by the tribe, and you've given them something to look forward to, an escape route, or a saviour. The thing is, Chief O'Hoolihan, well they'll all follow him at the moment because he doesn't need to lead them anywhere. But when the famine really hits, he'll be as lost as the rest of them. They'll look to you. We're certain of that."

Dana stood up and took Tommy by the hand. She led him to the edge of the stump, and they both looked down into the thick grass, hand in hand. She whispered, "You're their saviour, like that bloody Father Patrick who spoke of Jesus." She looked sideways into his face. "Can we do it? Or should we just jump?"

Tommy giggled. "After three."

She pulled into him. "That's why I love you so much. Not just my brother, my stupid brother." They stood for a while, then she suggested, "Let's finish off with Phillips. Loose ends."

They returned to sit in front of their captain.

Dana, the self-appointed spokeswoman to the Saviour, asked. "Well, you haven't answered my original question, just like a typical bloody politician. So, why are we here?"

Phillips nodded towards home. "Your dad instructed me to teach you everything I know and to learn from you everything you know. He said to return home with information on the wild forests, and as a team. That was his main reason for you coming, for us to become a team. He was thinking of the future and looking for some insurance. That's us. We all have what the others don't, that wanderlust, no fear of the outside world. He wants us to be a team." He stood up and held his hands out in the welcome stance. "We are all the same, all privates or all captains. That's what he wants."

Dana, the spokesman, held her hands out, then lowered her head. "We accept the situation. We'll teach you, you teach us, but as equals." Once she had pledged her part, "But you need to tell us the truth, now. We're partners, so, why are we here? We could become a team in the forest, so, Mr. Equal, why are we here." She stood proud, facing him. "And no more bullshit!"

Phillips just sat and thought.

Many minutes passed with nothing being said by the three, then the twins followed their captain's stare over to the west, where the sun was dropping, where the land gently fell away downhill as far as the eye could see, backed by the feint silhouettes of the Mourne Mountains. They looked at the endless expanse of wild land.

At last, Phillips spoke. "Do you ever wonder what's out

there?" He pointed. "All over there. Do you ever wonder what's really out there, in the big world?"

Dana turned her nose up. "What's that got to do with it? I asked why. Why are we really here? And all I've got from you is the start of some philosophical crap. I want to talk about reality!" She huffed.

"Alright, keep your hair on. But do you wonder what's out there? Ever?"

She glared at him and was about to tear into him until Tommy grabbed her hand. He almost whispered, "He ain't picking on you, he's testing you, so give him a chance." He squeezed her hand. "Honesty! Answer him with honesty."

She looked Phillip's hard in the face, and with a raise of the hand, she calmly replied, "Of course, all the time. Don't we all?"

"No. Haven't you ever noticed how you do, but no one else does? There are four families who do wonder, the rest of the tribe just dread the thought of ever finding out. That's why you're here, because you're different. You're like us. You don't simply wonder, you actually want to find out. You can see beyond the pigsty. You can see as far as the horizon, and you wonder." He pointed towards the sun. "You want to know what's over there, not just here, don't you. And you're not afraid to go and look. You're not like the others, you want to know."

The twins held hands as if it was them and him. Dana threw down the gauntlet. She jumped to her feet and stood directly between the two men, but she faced Phillips.

"Are you accusing us of something? Crimes against the state? Treason? Treachery? Dishonesty? Disloyalty?" She glared at him. "If you are, get to the point. Now!"

The beautiful, green, young lady raised a hand to her shillelagh. She was serious.

Phillips fidgeted on his backside, but never raised his hand to his weapon. He looked from one to the other and back again, then coughed.

"Please sit down, please. We never fight. Let's not start now, please."

She looked around to Tommy who, quite nervously tapped the ground beside him, and she sat down cross-legged, but with her knees up high, ready to jump. She nodded. "You'd better explain yourself, and it'd better be good."

He agreed, "I'll do my best."

He sat bolt upright. "Not sure where to start. Yes, start with me. That'll make you feel more relaxed, amongst friends.

"About five years ago I started in my role in the Defence Regiment straight from school. As my father and his father did, and all our fathers before that. I tagged along on some routine patrols which seemed to be there just to make work, then after four days of boredom, I was collected for a special duty.

"The duty took me out of the forest. I was so excited, not afraid, not reluctant, just excited. It wasn't much, I surveyed the wild hemp patch, making sure it was safe for the rope makers to harvest the hemp. The annual excursion out of the forest for the rope makers, and it frightened them so much that some children chose other trades just to avoid it, to never have to go out into that dangerous, fearful world beyond the forest. Fear of the world beyond. Inbred and yet unexplainable.

"My superior officer kept testing me to make sure I had no fear of the world, and he sat me down. He asked me, 'Do you often wonder what's out there? Out there, beyond. Or are you afraid to wonder?' I was wary of telling him the truth, just as you were, but after a bit of reassurance from him I answered. 'Of course, all the time, don't we all?' And he responded by telling me, 'No. Haven't you ever noticed how you do and nobody else does?' Exactly the same as our conversation a few moments ago. That day I was sitting where you are now, and my commanding officer was sitting right here where I am now. He was your dad, General O'Kief, the top man."

He went on to explain how he had been born into a cast of more than just the Defence Regiment. He was one of a small group which had another role in life. "Now I've been asked, ordered, to explain the same to you two."

Tommy and Dana were becoming wary of what he was about to tell them.

Dana asked, "Is this thing illegal?"

"No. Your dad's part of it, and your mum, and your family has been there from the beginning, founding members, just like my family, and it's not illegal, just secretive and exclusive. And you two were born into it, part of your breeding." He stopped to study their mood. "We all have to find out at your age, and nobody has ever refused to be part of it. I've no idea what would happen if you were to refuse. No idea."

He stood up and stared into the wilderness. "Look at that copse over there, a bunch of trees, standing alone and surrounded by nothing but peat bog. It's a world of its own. It has entire communities living there which never leave the copse, some have been there for so long that they have evolved to rely entirely on their copse, could even be unique species. Now, burn the trees down or cut them down and what happens to those species and communities? Move out and live in the peat bog? No, they all die. Like millions of species, cultures and civilizations before them, they become extinct, then forgotten about. Gone, forever.

"Now look over there." He pointed to our walnut tree. "The Nettle Forest is no different. Its inhabitants, us, are the same. When our forest goes, the entire civilization goes. Extinct. That's us, the Nettle Wits." He sat down, legs crossed. "Now, tell me this. What do all these vulnerable groups have in common?"

Dana obliged. "They all live in a limited environment."

"Correct. What else?"

She thought. "They all live as a tribe. Do they all live one common life like ants or bees?"

"Yes, and like Nettle Wits, no individualism, but as one body working in clockwork consistency. But what else? What? What could be the final downfall for all those civilizations?"

Tommy. "They're all successful and content."

"Exactly! And that leads to their biggest common failing -- complacency. They've got everything they need, never having to do anything that they haven't always done, and their lives are perfect. Utopia. And that means they all will fail at some point because they will never plan for change. Major change, like their forests or copses being cut down, will kill them all. None of them have planned for change. So, when it happens, they'll all become extinct, incapable of survival outside of their utopian world. That's us, the Nettle Wits."

The twins were not new to philosophical talk, it was one of the main school subjects for young Wits. So, they nodded their heads and suggested he carry on.

Phillips returned the nod, then continued. "We have a perfect civilization. We have everything we need, all the time, with no worries, no need to move on, no greed, no unachievable ambitions, no crime. And so it goes on. The perfect world, the Nettle Wits' world. Couldn't be any more perfect.

"Many, many years ago, when we first developed the processes for making the alcohol from the sugar in the nettles, the tribe began opening the pubs in order to make the alcohol available to all, and to bring us together in social groups. The pub quickly became the centre of our communal lives. Work hard all day and then relax in the pub. What else could any of us need? We never need to dream of better things, there aren't any. We never need to develop better things, there's nothing else we need. Perfect.

"And when that very first pub opened, The Centre Point, a small group, who had grown up together, began meeting in the pub each week to get beered up. It was all beer-driven conversation that covered just about everything under the sun, putting entire worlds to rights and analysing the very roots of the universe to the finest detail, then all forgotten about by the next day. The weekly get-together, by the group, went on for some time, then one week it changed.

"One of the group members, Mr. Zebedee, asked, 'Does anyone remember last week's conversation?' They all replied, 'Of course not. We never do.' And Zebedee stated, 'I do, and it's worried me ever since. The conversation was about what we do if things go wrong, if the utopian paradise turns to purgatory, what would we do?'

"For weeks, the subject occupied the group before they came to the conclusion that the answer, although not totally clear, was that we would all die together, the entire tribe.

"The group came to a realisation that the tribe was sitting in a perfect world which catered for everything they could ever want, but becoming so tightly dependent upon the nettles, Moors and salt, that if the ice broke, there would be no way out. The tribe had forgotten how to swim.

"At the next annual general meeting, the question was put to the tribe. Almost down to the last man, the tribe insisted it would never happen, so it was against the interest of the tribe to even think about it. The tribe, as a democratic unit, insisted that raising such questions would cause seeds of doubt to grow and those seeds could quickly fester into discontent, and a breakdown of the spirit of the tribe. Any such talk was banned by referendum. Everyone in the tribe voted in favour of the ban, except for our group of drinkers.

"For the next three-hundred years, our families and their descendants have met on a weekly basis to discuss the question. They're still meeting each week and making plans for survival. Thankfully, those plans have never been tested and the tribe continues to live in its utopian paradise. We all hope that it'll continue that way forever, but if it does ever happen, we'll have given a lot of time and thought about the survival of our tribe."

Tommy and Dana sat motionless. Dana still had her knees up ready for action but seemed a little more relaxed.

After a while, Tommy realised that Phillips had finished, so he asked. "So, who are these people who meet with our parents? Apart from us, who else?"

"Your family the O'Kiefs, my family The Phillips, the Murphys and the O'Tooles, just our four families. The Zebedees died out, as you know, he never had children, so there's just our four families, as has been for three-hundred years. The Centre Society. The CS."

Tommy scoffed. "Yeah, the CS. People snigger and whisper, then laugh when they hear about the CS. It's a joke. I've heard Dad say many times that sober talk is cheap since beer is free. Three-hundred years of beer talk. So what? It's a drinking club, that's all, a weekly drinking club."

Although it was getting dark, they could still make out each others facial expressions. Phillips's expression was one of achievement, contentment.

"That's really good. That's exactly what we want the tribe to believe. That's really good to hear."

Dana suggested they settle down and continue while walking in the morning. Phillips, however, had a little more to say.

"So, you're part of a secret society, which is a joke to others but very serious in its very existence. We have a motto. Wallow in your dreams, but stand to attention in your nightmares. We all believe that we have a duty to the tribe, preparing to stand to attention. Somebody has to do it."

CHAPTER 15
THE DESERT

It was getting get dark, so, while there was still some light, they found their sleeping spots below the toadstools, being sure to push their backpacks right back into the cover. The three then walked slowly around the perimeter of the stump, looking out at the dimming wild world.

Dana observed, "This is a very hostile world."

To the west, the deer were tightly bunched, forming a communal defence against the wolves which lurked nearby. To the east, the four fires blazed and the two wolfhounds lay in front of one of them. With the two farmers seated in some lambing chairs which protected them from the cold evening breeze, they all watched and waited for the wolves.

As the sun went down in the west and the silhouetted deer became part of the night, the wolves began howling. They were talking to each other, discussing tactics and laying down plans, and the two dogs barked.

Phillips said quietly. "Wolves, wild dogs. But if you ever hear barking, you know that the humans are close by because only the tame dogs bark." He shrugged his shoulders. "Wonder why?"

They sat for some time with their feet hanging over the edge of the stump, but Dana's sharp eyes caught something coming towards them. "Don't move," she whispered.

It was the ghostly white shape of a barn owl, floating silently above their heads.

Life just went on around them, everything fighting for survival, trying hard to turn that piece of life into this piece of life, to keep the cycle of life moving, some being the hunters, some the hunted, and some stuck right in the middle. It wasn't surprising that the tribe feared leaving the relative safety of the forest.

Just as they were thinking about getting to bed, something began screaming, then began crying like a baby and the dogs flew from their fires. The crying baby stopped, then started again and the dogs began growling at something, and they could be heard in the dark getting aggressive and the baby still cried. Then the crying stopped as one of the farmers ran over, then he shouted to his partner, "Just a leveret! Stoat got him."

It all settled down again and, once they were settled in their beds, they cut their minds off from the struggle for life.

The three soldiers awoke as soon as the sun reached the horizon to the east. It was damp.

They had all considered the new command situation overnight, as well as the lesson on their heritage, so Tommy decided to start as he meant to carry on.

"Now, we're all one team, equal to each other, but somebody needs to be the lead. Captain Phillips has been given this mission, so Captain Phillips needs to lead it. As he did yesterday."

They all agreed.

After filling their water bottles and snacking on pieces of the oyster mushroom, Captain Phillips gave the order to move out.

They climbed down and set off towards the eared tree. The warring armies from the big World were still holed up each side of the field, allowing a fairly clear route towards the north, but the general bustle of life in the burrows still rolled on.

The hedgehogs just plundered through, the voles, shrews and weasels battled it out, and the Wits watched each other's backs, and it seemed that life could just be a monstrous, endless battle for survival. It must all be worth it.

After a couple of hours of hard marching, they reached the hedge. Would the next world, the next field, be any different from this one?

They climbed the layered hedge right to the top. Just along to their right, a lone holly tree had been allowed to grow above the hedge. That would be their southern marker in case the walnut tree became out of sight.

Phillips pulled the map out.

"The forests are thought to be the other side of this second field, due north, ahead of us."

They climbed as high as they could to see across the field. The pond that showed on the map was there, but in the wrong field. It was bang in the middle of this second field, with rushes standing high around its margins. Phillips made some notes on the map, moving the pond from the first field into the second.

The pond seemed to be part of an otherwise invisible boundary, cutting the field into two. The closest half was meadowland, with many tall thistles and parsley, as if it had not been grazed recently. The far half was just a brown crop, but they could not make out what crop was. They also noted that they could see no nettle forests.

"Probably just too far to be seen from here. We need to get higher." Dana nodded towards a branch nearby which had escaped the layering and was growing higher than the rest.

They climbed along and ascended the vantage point. They could still only see a brown crop. Behind the crop was the boundary hedge, which even from that distance clearly stood against the wilderness.

Dana took Phillips' hand. "Don't get down. We just can't see them, that's all."

Tommy sensed the need for moral support. "Yeah, they'll be there, just the other side of that hedge. On the edge of the wilderness."

Phillips snapped out of it. "Good point. Only one way to find out. Get over there."

Tommy noticed how Phillips hung on to Dana's hand,

even after he had snapped out of his disappointment, and he noticed that she did not pull her hand away very quickly.

"Come on, you two." He just snapped them into action. "Got a bloody long walk across that field. Several hours, at least."

The two broke away from the handhold and looked immediately away from each other.

Tommy was right. It was a bloody long, hard walk and the hedgehog run took them off the north line, to the west, so, they had to fight through the thick undergrowth to get back en-route and then push their way north, with regular climbs. They managed to keep on track, but it was tough going.

At last, at about mid afternoon, they broke out of the thick meadow growth and stood staring at another alien environment. It was almost unbelievable; they'd never seen anything like it. Traditionally, the farms in that area were pastural, keeping sheep for their wool and meat, and goats for their milk and cheese, with a few cows for milk. But this half of the field had been ploughed and tilled, and the crop was now cut down and ready for gathering.

It was flax. The Irish people had begun producing linen, so flax had become a good money crop, supplying the linen industry with the strong strands from which the linen and canvas is woven.

This field had been cut and left to dry in rows, and ready to be collected.

The three Wits stood in awe. They were looking at an impenetrable wall of dry flax, towering way above them, and could see no way through. They could see nothing but brown, dry vegetation which was piled up even higher than their own Irish Nettles would stand. It looked, from their very low perspectives, like an impassable mass of stems and shriveled leaves.

"Wow." Dana was a little scared, but also impressed. "This entire field is laid waste."

After some umming and aahing, they took a walk to the east to see what they could work out. A little way along, the pile of flax dropped off and they realised that they were now standing between two rows, and could see right along the aisle to the hedge at the other end of the field. It was relatively clear, and although the weeds had begun to grow back, was easily navigated with their tiny legs. It was like a giant hedgehog run.

However, before setting off across the flax-field, they decided that they should take some new bearings on their exact position. They found a stately thistle and climbed to the top and it was high enough to see clearly over the rows of flax.

Looking ahead, they could see evermore clearly the eared tree. Looking back, they could see the holly tree as part of the last boundary hedge. They could no longer see the walnut tree. It was a sobering reminder that they were far from home, about one and a half kilometers, and alone, just the three of them. Their only link to their beloved forest was their memory.

"This is it," stressed Tommy. "Out of sight, but not out of my mind. Just remember, we have each other now, but not a lot else."

It was a frightening moment of realisation for the three adventurers.

After a long rest period of contemplation, Tommy addressed his colleagues. "It doesn't look good, does it? No sign of wild forests, long way from home, and on our own. What should we do? Doesn't look good."

Phillips sighed. "It looks like the forests aren't there. We could go onto the edge of the farm, see if there's anything in the wilderness. Or we could turn back, face the prospect of failure."

They all sat in the thistle and considered their options.

Dana suggested. "Carry on to that headland. That's what was planned, so see what's the other side of that hedge. That way, we've succeeded in our mission to find out and learn. That's all we can do."

It was disappointing, but she was right. If the forests are not there, they at least need to confirm it by reaching their destination and updating the map.

"We can't turn back. We've got orders." She clapped her hands. "Come on, team. A good march and we can be there before dark."

Phillips nodded to Tommy, then looked hard at Dana. It was a little more than a look of agreement, more like admiration. Understandably, she was a beautiful young Wit. Tommy looked on as an interested brother.

They set out on the walk to the other side of the flax.

Determined to keep their spirits up, they marched hard for four hours and eventually reached the end, scrambled up the small, mounded bank, and up to the layered Hawthorne hedge. As they sat high up, they looked north. It was just wilderness, peatbogs broken up by groups of small alder and oak, and it was noticeable how there were no nettle forests, just heather and thick grasses mixed in with a multitude of natural flowers. Quite beautiful, wild, inviting, but no nettles, no forests, just heathland, peat bogs, tar pits, and spinnies and small woodlands. That was all.

Dana solemnly made her statement. "They've gone."

The farmers had cut down the wild nettle forests and claimed the land for arable farming, for flax. That's what it looked like.

"What've they done?" Dana seemed the only one willing to speak. "Look what they've done. They've taken a wild home to thousands of creatures, moles, voles, weasels, ants, everything, and made this. A field of crops and nothing else. Where have all the living creatures gone? No cover, no runs, no highway. It's like a desert, almost dead."

The three sat a bit longer without talking. It was depressing, but it's not natural for a Wit to get depressed. Tommy jumped up and held his hands out in the welcome stance. He forced a smile and swung around full circle.

"This is the World and we're part of it, and it's not all bad, look. Look all around, we can see three different environments, all in one. Behind us is the wilderness with thickets, bare patches, trees, bit of everything, but not perfect for everything. Then here, we have two man made environments, the livestock meadows, full of life, and this flax field, which is low in life. They're both man-made ecologies, both unnatural, and they're no different to our Wit-made environment. When the flax was growing, it must have been just like our nettle forest, that is, a single-species plantation which harbours a limited amount of life. So, before we start cursing the humans, let's first remember what *we* are and what *we've* done." He clapped his hands, then sat down.

Slowly, Phillips and Dana began smiling. The chosen one, the storyteller, was doing his bit and inspiring his followers to be realistic about life and to be optimistically philosophical about what, where, when, why, how, and who. The blues lifted and their spirit returned.

Phillips clapped. "Good speech." He laughed and grabbed hold of Dana's hand, and there was no objection from her. "You know what, Dana? My uncle said that Tommy will rule the World one day with his bolstering speeches. I'm starting to agree with him!".

"Oh yeah, what does your uncle know? Who is he?"

"He's your teacher, Old Murphy, my mum's brother."

They sat hand-in-hand while the bemused Tommy climbed along the hedge in search of a platform to use as a camp.

CHAPTER 16
TOPSY TURVY

Tommy found a suitable camping area, with a flat surface, on top of one of the large side bows. There was leafy cover above and below them.

Dinner was eaten, their rations suddenly seeming more important than ever. The Moors caterpillar, no longer living wild in wild nettle forest by the north field, and no longer the great hope that they had searched for.

"This is an historic day," Tommy said, thoughtfully. "If we can't find any more of the Irish Nettles, then the Moors butterfly becomes extinct, what will we do?"

As they sat in a circle of three, legs crossed and empty plates in front of them, Dana responded. "What we'll do is die of Brady's disease. We'll all die of Brady's disease, the entire population of Nettle Wits, supposedly." She spoke very matter of fact. "Unless we do something about it, take control."

They drank some of their wines.

"Let's celebrate." Tommy looked at the other two. "We found our destination. No ones ever been here before us, so, let's celebrate. Dana's right, we'll take control of the situation, but first celebrate getting here. Well?"

Phillips was still in his captain's mode. "First get some food for the morning. Then we can celebrate."

Tommy stated, "Food? Moors caterpillars? They've all gone, ploughed in for flax, so what food can we eat?"

They all sat thinking, but as Phillips had been voted to carry on leading, he felt compelled to answer that. "We can eat anything that agrees with us, so long as we get our daily ration of Moors meat. For those essential nutrients. We've used three portions of our nine, so should be back before they run out, so we can eat what else we want in reason. So long as it agrees with us."

Then Dana observed, "After nine days. On the tenth day, we'll start going grey. When the Moors meat runs out, we'll all turn grey. Is that really true? We've all heard the stories of the Brady's, but is it really true?"

Phillips was a little older than the twins and a little more wary of the establishment. He looked around in case someone was listening.

"No-one here. Just us, so you can talk with your team." Dana was slowly becoming the alpha bitch.

So, the captain relaxed. "Well, that's what we all believe. And we know that we'll lose our colour, but it's not just that is it? We'll lose our health and our lives. We all know that."

She smiled. She knew that Phillips was speaking very half-heartedly, so, "Never been proved." The twins had always been taught by their mum and dad to think outside the box. Question the beliefs, the legends, the superstition, the traditions, the outdated caste systems, and consider things realistically and logically. "We know we'll lose our colour but never been proved about dying. We could eat hawk moth caterpillars, and we'll slowly change to whatever colour they give us, but never been proved about dying from no Moors meat. Never."

Phillips did not bite, but calmly replied. "No, never been proven."

Nettle wits are a colony of bodies which normally behave like one body, like ants. Dissent was very rare and any questioning of things such as dieting was only ever raised by the scientists, and the team was in an area where they had never been, in more ways than one.

Dana suggested, "Let's try it. Find another caterpillar and eat it. See what colour we go."

Tommy stood up. "You're not going to do anything stupid. Not out here. If we do get sick, we could be in real danger out here. No, we'll think about it and try it out back home."

"Unless we run out of Moors meat." She nodded. "Yeah, we'll go with that. Try it back home, unless we *have* to try it out here. Agreed?"

The team nodded in agreement.

Phillips grinned at Dana and caught her eye-to-eye. "If we do have to try another meat and turn purple, will you still fancy me?"

She jumped to her feet and stomped over to him. "What, fancy you? What makes you think I fancy you now?"

Phillips was a little shocked, but a lot embarrassed. He went the colour of his lips and made his apologies, then went to find some food for the next day, for breakfast.

Tommy said, chuckling at his sister, "His green face went bright red. Do you fancy him as much as he fancies you?"

After a couple of deep breaths, she began smiling, then sat down beside him. They had a cuddle.

"Jealous?"

He shook his head gently. "Of course. You're my sister. Never been anyone else. Just you and me."

"Well, you shouldn't be jealous. We're nearly sixteen. Mum and Dad married at sixteen. It'll happen to both of us soon. You mustn't be jealous of me."

"You are of me! You may remember, just a few days ago in the doorstep, you sat on my head to stop me seeing that girl's thing-me. You know, her honka-ma-donk. You were jealous!"

"Never was! Anyway, that was different." She was grinning. "I was worried about you going blind, that's all."

They both had a dirty laugh over their private thoughts.

Phillips returned with three blackberry balls for the next morning and sat down, looking sheepishly at the twins. "Sorry, shouldn't have said that, sorry."

Dana uncharacteristically turned almost as red as Phillips had earlier. She said nothing.

Tommy, however, did have something to say. He stood upright and proud, directly between Dana and Phillips, then made his statement of intent. "We're out here on duty. While we're out here on duty, I feel that I have a duty of my own in the absence of our mum and dad. I don't know if there are any rules on this subject, but since we are the rules while out of the forest, I'm going to make one of my own, and if I need to, I'll apply it to the best of my ability. Do what you want when returned to the forest, but while out here on duty it's not right for a captain to play with his privates."

Dana burst out laughing. "You'll go blind!"

Suddenly the boys were laughing and giggling with her.

Once they had cooled, they decided to have that toast and celebration which they had earlier agreed on.

"To us, the future of the civilised world. The Wits will live forever. Sláinte."

"Sláinte agatsa."

Tommy had made his point, while very subtly pulling the team together.

The next morning started with a bang, and a crash, and a whoop and a bark.

It was just getting light, the sun not quite over the eastern horizon when the three were awoken. They jumped up and moved to the edge of the bough to survey the disturbance.

In the half light they watched four men and two dogs moving along the perimeter of the field, hitting things with long poles or staffs and shouting out whooping sounds. The men all carried burning torches, and had bows across their backs, while the dogs darted about, poking their noses into the hedge and barking.

They were to begin the collection of the dried flax, before the rains could spoil their crop, but before they could, they had to make sure the wolves had moved on with the deer. The entire perimeter of the field was beaten out by the men and dogs.

"Wonder what they're doing?" whispered Dana. "Getting

rid of the wolves? But why?"

They watched the men and dogs flush out the entire perimeter of the field and, when the check was over, the men hung around with their dogs at the far gate, almost directly opposite the Wits.

They looked around at the wilderness as the sun rose. It ran away from them to the north and west, and seemed to drop slowly downhill for as far as the eye could see. The peat bog was broken up by oak and alder copses, and damp air hung over the bog, misting any clear view of the open ground.

The team climbed higher into the Hawthorne hedge once the mist had cleared and did a more thorough scan of the area for nettles. There were nettles, but only the taller, hairier, Common Nettles. No Irish Nettles to be seen.

Dana reminded the others, "We can't go without making sure of the natural forests. They're not here, but we've already found that the map is wrong. They could be over at the top end of the field, in the West."

Phillips nodded. "You're right, Dana, we must do what we came to do, not just find the forests, but record what's out here." He looked to the West. "And you're right, it could be over that side of the field. Can't see from here. But why would the map show it here, if it's over there? Is it worth going all the way over there? We could take the safe option, and set off home."

"Hang on, you two. You sound like you're almost giving up and clutching at straws. We've got six day's rations, loads of time, so no rushing home!" Tommy stood up tall and looked over to the pond. It was long and thin, creating the border between much of the two halves of the field. It was big enough to be seen clearly. "Get that map out!" he ordered. He and Dana had never really looked at the map in detail.

"Yes, Sir." Phillips smiled as he retrieved the map and laid it out in front of them. "What you thinking?"

Tommy looked again at the pond, the other side of the flax, and was in the northern field, this field. He then looked at the map. Phillips had put a light cross through the original pond, in the south field, and lightly marked out the actual position. It was exactly opposite where it was originally. Also, the tiny arrow in the top left corner had always been considered the north marker. Then the wavy lines which were drawn on the east and south boundaries were always thought to mean other farmland. A lot of assumptions and a lot of questions developing in Tommy's head.

He quietly observed, "According to historic legend, he fell into that pond and it saved his life. So, the pond was there and it's big enough to be seen from up there and he would never have forgotten it. It saved his life, so it was there, but not where the map shows. Then what happened?"

A little puzzled, Phillips said. "Well, he survived the fall and wandered for days. He had no food, and just like the rest of us, believed that he could only eat Moors meat or be poisoned. But quite miraculously, he found his way back to the forest, almost dead and delirious, but once he'd recovered, the philosophy lot helped him to draw this map from his memory of what he saw."

Tommy nodded. "And he would've got a good look from out there. A birds-eye view, from the claws of a crow. So why is the map so wrong? Why are things in the wrong place? And if he fell into a pond so close to our home, why did he take all that time to get home?"

Phillips replied, "Because he was delirious and his memory was affected, probably went around in circles."

Tommy thought about the answer for a while as he studied the map. Carefully he suggested, "The pond shows as being in the first field, exactly *opposite* where it really is. I don't think he got it wrong. Now, do you know the history of this map?"

"Well, drawn about two-hundred years ago. Since then, it's been hanging in the Philosophy Department. But it's never been considered reliable, just an indication. We bought it out as a last straw, and to accurately update it, and it's all been wrong so far."

Tommy shook his head. "Wrong? I don't think so!"

They all studied the map. Yes, the legends and markings had always been a bit of a mystery.

Tommy continued, "The Philosophy Department moves each year, with the new crop of nettles, as we all have to, so it's been rehung about two hundred times."

He took hold of the map, still open, and stood up. "Stay where you are." He moved forward, swung round so that he was facing the other two, then placed the map down. He moved round and took up his same position between them.

"Bloody idiots!" He began laughing. "All these years. Look, the little arrow. Isn't the north pointer, it's pointing at our home in the south, our forest! And the wavey lines are now in the north and the west. They must indicate *wilderness*. And look, the pond is now in the correct place, in the north field and…."

He jumped up. "For up to two-hundred years the bloody map has been hanging upside down! It now all makes sense! The map is accurate!"

He danced around a bit, then came back down to the others. "So, we are here in the north-east. Now, looking south-west, diagonally across the field, we see the pond exactly in the right place, and look, the bottom left of the map in the south-west corner, *the nettle forests*! They're not here. Never were. They're in the opposite corner of the map, right over where the deer herd was." He again jumped up. "Upside down, all the bloody time! And look, we've wasted three days getting here."

As the realisation sank in that the nettle forests had not been ploughed into the ground, they danced. It was a happy moment for the adventurers as they began to believe that the extinction of the wild Moors butterflies may not be as imminent as they once thought. Hope was still alive.

But the celebrations were cut short. Dogs began barking as humans of all ages began moving into the flax field. The three Wits laid on their stomachs and watched.

The Doyles had called upon their neighbours to help collect the flax, which had dried sufficiently and was ready to go to the linen works, and the work needed to be done quickly before any rain fell. Even Eileen and her family were there, clearly having made peace with the Doyles thanks to Father Patrick.

There were three handcarts, each with a team which loaded the card and pulled it to the eastern headland for transporting to the works. The transport which took the flax away consisted of two horses, each pulling a cart with poles standing up along the sides, and were parked on the eastern headland.

"Look at those." Dana was impressed. "They must be horses. Never seen any creature so big!"

The human teams worked hard and efficiently, but it was still to take at least a day, maybe two, to sheaf and collect all the materials on the field. It soon became clear that this would be a major problem for the Wits.

The farmers and their neighbours would be working all over the field for the next two days, with dogs running, children playing and carts rolling. Death from squashing, everywhere they looked.

"If we have to go," observed Phillips, "we should take the shortest route. That's straight across to the far corner of the map, south-west. That direction. Diagonal. But we'd be squashed, almost certainly."

Dana, "And we'd never get over the pond, that's if we don't get squashed on the way or after. And there could still be young grass snakes, which would eat us. We'd be risking our lives with every step. It'd be suicidal to go that way."

Just as they were looking towards the pond, an elderly woman, probably the famous Mrs. Doyle with no knickers to wear, shouted at the children to stay clear of the tar pit. That made their minds up; the pond was bad, but the tar pit was a no-go area for just about all small creatures, including Nettle Wits.

Dana confirmed, "We'll need to stay well clear of the pond and tar, and take the north, then west, perimeters, all the way down to the wild forest. No choice, go round the perimeter. The long way round."

They all agreed. The problem, though, was their supplies. Taking the north/west hedges would take at least five days, maybe more, and they would still need to survey the forests and then get home before their remaining rations were up. They would have to go straight home.

"We'll have to go home, then plan another trip. It only looks about a day or so to go direct from our forest to the wild ones. So close to home and yet we've never even visited them."

So, the general consensus was to go home, but even their route home was overrun by humans and handcarts. They needed to take time out to consider their options.

But Tommy, as usual, was thinking outside the box and considered his dad's teaching. "Dad says if you can't avoid it, use it."

"All good advice, Dad, but not necessarily much help right at the moment! And it's a pretty dangerous philosophy." Dana said no more.

They watched the industry.

As Tommy lay out on a bough, thinking about their predicament, a handcart came towards him along the headland, over which their bough hung. It was moving from the west end of the field to the haywains on the east headland. It passed directly below their vantage point.

"Quick, hurry!" Tommy jumped up. "Get your backpacks on, now."

They grabbed their bags and pulled them on, along with their shillelaghs. Tommy led them to an overhanging branch which reached right out and over the headland. As the cart was unloaded onto the haywain he told his colleagues that they'll drop onto the empty cart when it passed below and ride all the way up to the west headland. "Ready?"

It was all too rushed to even question, so they hung onto the branch and waited as the cart approached, and silently prayed to Gayla. The wait for it to reach them seemed like a lifetime and the adrenaline flowed.

The handcart approached. The empty boards bounced and rattled ever closer, and as they hung beneath the branch the farmers hair almost brushed their feet. Then, "Now!"

They dropped, crashed and rolled, and they had landed on the empty cart, but it bounced them all over, not allowing them to get hold of anything. They rattled closer and closer to the edge, and disaster loomed.

Then it all stopped. The cart pulled to a halt and the three Wits scrambled to get hold of some loose flax which had not been cleared. They pulled into each other.

Tommy ordered, "If we go, we all go. Can't get split up, so hang onto each other."

The farmer had stopped for a reason. The Wits pulled themselves into the depression between two boards as the sun was momentarily hidden from them by three children being lifted onto the cart. The children settled down, giggling and jigging with excitement.

"Hang on and mind your bums! This might be a little hairy." The farmer laughed as the children grasped the side poles and braced themselves. "We're off!"

The journey resumed. The farmer, wary of the children, set off at a slightly slower pace, but fast enough to throw the little people into the air with every bump, and the screaming and giggling went on for several minutes as they moved along the headland.

The Wits watched out of the back and marveled at the speed at which they flew, sweeping along the headland, and had never travelled so fast, never even dreamed of it. At least five miles per hour. Unbelievable!

Dana said, "Be ready to jump as soon as we stop at the end. If we hang about, we could be in real trouble. Could even end up back over the wrong side."

They, like the children, were beginning to feel the bumps as they approached the corner of the field, but before they arrived, the farmer shouted, "Hang on, going round!"

Instead of stopping at the corner, the cart did a ninety-degree turn, almost on the spot, throwing the noisy children sideways along with the Wits. The children screamed with joy. Then they realised that they were heading south along the west headland, going much further towards their destination than they had expected.

After several minutes moving south, the cart pulled to a halt and they made their escape, dropping into the grass and scrambling through the undergrowth to the safety of the bank, lay exhausted a little way up the slope, safe from the feet and the wheels.

The three recovered quickly, and hurriedly moved into the hedge and climbed to about four feet in the layered boughs. They needed to establish their new position.

From a suitable vantage point, they watched. The farmer had manoeuvred the cart, and while he was away unloading, they had bundled up and tied the flax into sheafs, which they were already piling high into the cart for its next trip. There was clearly a rush to get cleared before the rains.

The children jumped around the farmer wanting to play some more, but he gently sent them away from the work area. "But don't go near the tar pit, I mean it."

Lying on their bellies, high in the hedge, Dana very thoughtfully said, "Eileen and Father Patrick made the Doyles boys sound like evil. Like monsters with curly ram's horns and fire coming from their nostrils. He's nothing like that, the children all love him." But he still would have tarred and feathered Eileen's boy!

They slowly began to realise how far they had travelled in just a few minutes. The north-east corner, where they spent the night, was so far away, it was almost alien to them. They were now at the halfway point along the west boundary of the field, where the flax ended and the un-grazed meadow began. About three days of walking, in about five minutes!

"That was the most dangerous, irresponsible, childish, compulsive thing we've ever done." She just grinned.

Phillips nodded. "Yeah, fantastic. What a trip!"

The sort of thrill they'd never have enjoyed in the forest!

But the ride of a lifetime had already saved them at *least* three days of walking, as well as bypassed the risk of being squashed, making the round trip to the Southwest corner very achievable, with six days of rations still remaining. They just needed to get to the southern perimeter of the north field by the end of that day, and the day was still early, so no real challenge.

CHAPTER 17
LOST FORESTS

While Phillips updated the map, the right way up, with pictorial notes and legends, Dana watched the farmers in their work, and the children in their play. She looked at Phillips and wondered what he would be like around children. But she soon snapped out of it.

She and climbed down the hedge and across the small headland to collect three flax seeds. They went into her backpack. She also found a piece of flax that had been run over by the cartwheels, exposing the fibrous threads which went to make the Irish Linen. She pulled several lengths away from the stem and rolled them up for samples. It was strong, long and fine, much better than their hemp rope. All those samples would go back to the forest for analysis.

Tommy had made note of their directions and landmarks and the team needed to set off towards the south, but he wasn't ready. He gathered the tiny team together.

"We're about to enter the thick growth of the meadow, and head south. It took nearly a day to cover this distance on our journey out, and it was dangerous. We're in the hedge, in the trees, where we live. Why the hell would we leave the hedge to struggle and risk our lives in the meadow. Leave it for the voles and weasels. We live in trees. Come on!" He deliberately began moving along the hedge, towards the south. "Your uncle" Tommy said with a bit of a jest, "always says there's a hard way to learn. He was right."

They stayed in the hedge and moved comfortably across the canopy, and after just six hours were nearing the southwest corner of the north field. There they made camp.

They could see the deer. Then they spotted the wolf pack,

which was never far away from the deer.

Just along the hedge which divided the two fields, a lone holly tree stood which had been allowed to grow up above the layered hedge. They climbed to tree and could see both fields in their entirety.

The farmers began to pack up, although they had not quite cleared the crop, and two of the men were moving around the perimeter with the dogs. Before they reached the Wits, one stopped to cut a white giant puffball and put it into a sack to take home. He left the ripe ones and the small ones.

"Get a bit of that for our breakfast." suggested Phillips. "Young puffball, lovely with a blackberry broken over it."

All the Humans were gone, leaving the field for the usual inhabitants to play. The sounds of the evening were amplified by the Wits' sensitive ears, and they could even hear the sheep and goats in the south field.

"It's quite beautiful here, isn't it." Tommy was enjoying the evening. "The day creatures are preparing for bed, as the night lovers awaken." It was like a busy factory at shift change over. "It's not so bad away from the forest. Not so bad."

They looked around and realised that the 'desert' that they had found was almost covered in life, as the flocks of small finches and sparrows made plenty of the seeds left behind by the farmers.

"You know what?" Phillip stated, "There's so much room for life out here, even for us. Every square yard is like a miniature reserve, packed with plants, insects, animals and birds, and different environments. So many opportunities. We could live here."

They lay on the bough, about twelve feet up, and watched. Even at that height, the leaves of the holy were home to all sorts of caterpillars, beetles and spiders, all feeding from, and into, the cycle of life.

Phillips continued. "All we would need is food."

Dana added, "And alcohol, and butterfly pelts, and sugar

and salt."

"But it would just need reinventing, or remanufacturing."

All sounded too easy to Tommy, who was keeping quiet about it, continuing his scan for the wild forests. "Look! Diagonal across the field. It's our Walnut Tree." He could just see the top of it. "You know, by going around the perimeter and using the hedge, we're only about two, maybe three, days away from our home. All so close. Why don't we ever come out from our tiny forest? This is right on our doorstep, and this world could be our oyster, with hidden pearls around every corner."

Dana said, "Take a lot longer than that across the meadow. We should avoid going below the grass, it's so dangerous, exhausting, and so, so slow." She sighed. "We're learning."

Tommy suggested, "The point is, we could all live here, us three. It's close enough to home to live here for a bit to get to know it and develop some products. Live in the forest and out here. It's much closer than just a dream. It's right here."

Perhaps Dana was being cautious, or perhaps she was just being the devil's advocate to motivate their thoughts, but whatever, she was intelligent enough to understand the importance of debate. She questioned their thoughts.

"Why? Why live out here when we've got the forest? It's still there, despite the stupid ideas about the Roman navvies tilting the world. We'll still be there for years."

The boys waved their heads in agreement but still chewed the cud.

She suggested, "Finish our recci from up here, then get down and set up camp. Sun's going. We can talk some more after eating."

Phillips went down to find the puffballs, then they ate their Moors meat rations and enjoyed some wine.

The sun was almost gone as they relaxed after their food.

Dana began the conversation. "You two thought I was

being negative back at the holly, but someone's got to take the other side." She looked at the other two. "So, why? Why do we need to move from the forest?"

Tommy was the first to respond. "We're not saying we have to, just if we do, we could move out here, that's all. And we could do it while still in the forest. An exploratory stay."

"That's not what I asked. I asked why."

He sighed. "Well, the nettles are struggling, aren't they? Look, it gets harder each year to keep Common Nettles down and the rain is killing many of the butterflies before they can breed. And something is happening in the wild forest because no butterflies are coming from there anymore. So, the Irish Nettles are dying. Could be years yet, but they're losing out to the Common Nettle, and to the climate change. That's what it looks like is happening."

He looked at Phillips for support, but Phillips sat back and thought hard, then looked out over the wilderness.

Many minutes passed with nothing being said by the three. The twins followed their captain's stare over to the west, where the sun was dropping, where the land gently fell away downhill as far as the eye could see, backed by the feint silhouettes of the Mourne Mountains. They looked at the endless expanse of wild land.

They decided that it was time to rest.

It rained overnight. The gossamer-thin sleeping drapes came into action for the first time. They were outstanding.

In the morning Dana joked, "The tribe's not all bad at development. These covers are unbelievable and fold up to nothing. We never stop inventing as a tribe, even if it's just to stave off boredom."

"Nice idea, the tribe. But the tribe wouldn't allow these to be done until we convinced them that the Defence Regiment needed them."

"Which is true. No?"

"No, we've never needed them until now. Unless we leave the forest overnight, then we'll never need them again. But mum and my sister were allowed to make these in the tannery, and they have secretly made about four hundred. They're stashed in the caves under the pigsty. So, if we all have to move from the forest in the future there's one for every member of the tribe. They'll save a lot of lives, especially the children." A wry smile. "The tribe's too regimented for its own good, sometimes. Thank God for the CS."

The twins were quietly realising what The Centre Society was all about, not just drinking beer.

As soon as they had eaten the slices of puffball, which they squeezed blackberry juice over, Dana took her notepad and made detailed drawings of the plants and their environment. The puff balls were the very first entry into her compendium of edible plants. She was getting the bug about planning for disasters.

The rain had stopped a bit before sunrise, which woke the World up with a lot of promise. The sun broke through the layered hedges and life seemed to kick start as the sheep and goats began calling the farmers for their breakfast. The wolfhounds walked round on their perimeter checks with two of the farmers.

The three green soldiers moved along the dividing hedge, then set out on the long journey south, towards the legendary wild nettle forests. The going was good along the hedge, and at that time of the morning they met several other users of the highway; mice, small birds, an adult grass snake, and hundreds of butterflies and moths, plus two dogs. They also passed the peat diggings which the Doyles managed. It was a different world from the underground runs of the meadow. An attractive world.

By about midday, they estimated they were halfway along the west boundary, then the south boundary was lot clearer, and it was fronted by a stream, the one which they had to cross on the first day. Yes, their forest was only half a diagonal field away and their walnut tree was much closer than they had expected. About one and a half days walk and they would be home!

"Look, so close." Dana grinned. "We could pop home at anytime."

"Homesick?" asked Phillips.

She looked down. "Not really. More like Mum and Dad sick. Miss them." She fidgeted with her jerkin, then took her hat off. "What's your name?"

He smiled and looked out towards the distant deer herd. Then he asked, "Why? You know my name, Captain Phillips. So why?"

She suddenly felt embarrassed for asking him. She looked out towards the south-west corner. "I think I can see nettles."

The two men stretched up to look south. They raised their eyebrows, and Tommy exclaimed, "I think you're right. Look like nettles, right colour."

Captain Phillips made an unexpected woop and then settled down. "I think they're nettles. You know what this means, Dana."

She shook her head, still grinning.

"We might only be one and a half days away from Mum and Dad, but I don't think we'll be home for at least three days. We've got work to do. Surveying."

"But not yet!" Tommy swung his backpack off and pulled out his wine bag and leather cup. "First we've got to celebrate."

They all poured some wine and stood with their cup raised.

"You toast," ordered Dana to Tommy.

"Right. Here's to The Centre Society, adventurers, pioneers, explorers, here's to us. Sláinte."

"Sláinte agatsa."

The spirits were high and the motivation strong as the wine went down like nectar.

They decided that there is no time like the present to tackle the final leg of their pilgrimage, so they packed the wine away and set off. The adrenaline which the sight of the nettles had raised gave them determination, and their youth gave them the power. They surged onward toward the wild nettle forests.

CHAPTER 18
BELIEF

The regiment arrived at the edge of the wild nettle forest at about teatime. They had put everything into the last stretch and were tired, so they plonked down on a wide bow and stared across the corner of the field, the earlier excitement no longer evident.

After a period of thoughtfulness, Tommy spoke. "It's not what I expected."

They were about sixty or seventy feet from the south boundary, where the stream ran eastwards towards home. Between them and the boundary corner was a forest of nettles, which extended about twenty yards into the field. The forest also extended west into the wild side, but not very far.

Tommy noted. "It's about the same size as our forest. If you include the bit in the wild. Yeah, about the same size."

They all stared, a little disappointed. Most of the trees in the field side had been flattened by the deer, sheep and goats. It was a bit of a mess, but it was still there and still alive and kicking. The damage by the livestock would have been temporary, with new growth quickly replacing any lost. However, it would face similar damage by the large animals quite regularly. As its name implied, it was a wild forest, but the colour?

Tommy was trying to stay positive. "Nettles always come back from that sort of damage. It would be a real disruption, but not something that couldn't be managed."

They decided to take a break before doing anything else. They made camp.

After the earlier celebration, the mood was sombre, the

state and colour of the nettle forest knocking back their enthusiasm somewhat. But they had arrived at the destination, so Phillips still felt it was worth celebrating.

"Let's have a slap-up meal tonight. Must be plenty of food around of some sort, so let's do it. We've found the forests."

Yeah, they had succeeded in their mission. They had found the forest.

"No thanks to the map reader." Dana punched Phillips on the arm. "Get the map upside down. What an idiot. Wait till we get back to school, Uncle Murphy'll have a good laugh."

Phillips could take it. He nodded and forced a sheepish look of apology before pulling the map from his backpack. "Talking of maps, let's get it updated. At least we know it's good now."

They laid the map out in front of them. The three knelt over the document with Phillips in the middle, pencil at the ready, and Dana began laughing.

"Look, that's the south boundary." She pointed to the hedge and ditch, just at the other side of the wild forest, that led down to their very own blackthorn hedge. They were only about one day away from home "And other side of the boundary, not on the map, is Eileen's little cow field. Where we get the hemp from. It's right there. We could get over the stream and that hedge takes us all the way to our blackthorn hedge. Unbelievable. One day's walk and climb, and we're home, and we never even knew this forest was here. And it's just a day from our home!"

They all sat and contemplated just how their civilization had cut itself off from everything around it. They had isolated themselves for hundreds of years, but that was part of their success. Dana summarised, "Single-minded, focused, stable, and supremely successful. The model culture which wants for nothing. Until...."

Tommy was the first to respond to Dana's little speech. "Why? Why haven't we ever questioned anything? We've lived in a little bubble, cut off from the world. Why?"

Captain Phillips was in the seat. He was the elder and had been ordered by General O'Kief to mentor his twins. "Because.... That's why. Just because. And that's been the key to the absolute success of the tribe. We do and we have, because. No questions asked, and that is why the perfect culture and utopian lifestyle never changes. Dreams create nightmares. We all know that. So, keep your dreams to a minimum, longing only for it all to continue. Don't dream. Don't fret. Don't wish. Don't aspire. No, we do because we are one, and our lives are so ideal. Don't do anything to spoil it. Things fester quickly. Things like 'the grass is greener over there.' 'I want more than I need.' Or 'I could be better than this?' All those type of things spawn discontent, then dreaming, then greed, then competition and individualism. Then the individuals worry more about their own needs than those of the tribe. Then the tribe breaks down. Then the tribe starves. That's how the tribe works. Always has worked that way."

He stopped to test the ground. "We're just like a hive of bees. Nobody tells them what to do or when to do it. They just do it and live happy lives."

Tommy shook his head and smiled. "Not quite like us, is it? When it matters, the bees have the queen. She's the one they follow. But we don't have a queen, we have O'Hoolihan." The thought of the chief made them all smile.

"You're right." Phillips stood up to think. "You were at the last two emergency meetings. Who was in charge? Who do you reckon? Who ran those meetings?"

Dana stood up with Phillips, while Tommy fidgeted on his bum. She frowned a bit then, "It looked to me like somebody's hand was stuffed up the chief's back and working him like a puppet. Nostradamus or Daniels seem the most likely."

"Well spotted. Tommy?"

He nodded. "Yeah, I did wonder myself. Are we right?"

"Sort of, but I must remind you that right now you're on active duty and not at school. Learn to answer the question that's been asked. I didn't ask who was running our chief. I asked who was running the meeting. So be careful with questions. Make sure you know what's being asked." He sat down, probably to look a bit the less of a commanding officer.

He continued. "Now. Who was running those meetings? Well, the catalyst of the moment was O'Toole, and he was very competently supported by the hero of the moment, your dad, General O'Kief. They drove the meeting, looking after the brakes and throttle, but the one steering? That was you. Your youthful, naive, unrehearsed presentation took the whole tribe to a renewed communal spirit. They all love you. So, who ran the two meetings? The CS. We did, mainly O'Toole, your dad and you, Tommy O'Kief."

That was a bit of a shocker for the twins.

Phillips grinned like a cat at them and took a deep breath. "The tribe worries about you, that in itself is support. They got quite uptight about the punishment for your treatment of that poor little boy and tried to stop you being sent on this mission. They all accepted that you should be punished, but on this mission, you could be lost. We convinced them that you would be safe and so they warily allowed it. But they weren't worried about me, a little bit about Dana, but you." He pointed at Tommy. "You they worried about! They'll be worrying about you right now. You're special. They believe in you."

The two sat staring at the captain, then Tommy slammed down his hand. "Is that why you were trying to recruit us?"

"No, never. Nobody's ever been recruited into the CS. Like all Nettle Wits, you're born into your role. From the day you were born, you were born into this CS, from day one you have been fully paid-up, lifelong members. I don't need to recruit you, just help you."

This was becoming a little bit deeper than the twins have

been used to. They were members of a secret cult, not totally to their surprise, they always had inklings that Mum and Dad did a bit more than drink at the Centerpoint, but this thing about the tribe seeing Tommy in some special way? What does it all mean and why?

Suddenly Dana jumps to her feet, then stepped forward to stand in front of Phillips. "Why is Tommy special? He is to me and Mum and Dad, but the tribe? Tell us why, it's scaring us both."

"Because he stood up in front of the entire civilization and impressed them all with a beautiful speech which pulled the tribe together, with our history and some beautiful analysis, like Mr. Desperation, the favourite wayward uncle, and the mother of invention, boredom. They were all surprised. No, not surprised, moved, stirred, hooked, anything but surprised."

"I only did it to protect Dad. Stop him fighting O'Toole. I didn't know O'Toole was a friend."

"Of course not. But that made it all the more impressive. So defensive, of not only the tribe but your own kin. It was just what they expected of you, ever since the Spring Holi this year." Phillips raised his eyebrows. "Don't you remember the Holi, your first turn in a storyteller's seat? All the others told their stories of the golden days, the good old days, when our civilisation grew from the ashes and how the gallant scientists and philosophers saw our future in the nettles. All good bolstering stuff. Then you got up there and you turned heads. You told about the modern legends, not just prattle on about the olden days of yore. You told about now! You made legend and you gave them new hope. The legend of the O'Kief Shillelagh. Not just a piece of wood, the holder of the spirit of the Nettle Wits. New legend, new hope, new horizons. And now they have something concrete to look up to, something real, The O'Kief Shillelagh. Our very own icon in the flesh. Legend in his own lifetime. The real thing, held by the man who not only fights snakes, but now even talks to them. The man to follow, a man to believe in, a real man."

"But that should make them look up to Dad, not me."

"They've always looked up to your dad. But now they have his right-hand man. They have one to follow, one to guide them. They all believe in you, Tommy O'Kief. The man who would rule the World. Weird but true."

Tommy got up and stomped around then came back to hold Dana by the hand and asked. "Anyone could have said what I said? They don't need to believe in me."

"But not anybody said it. You did. And I'll tell you why they believe in you. Because they *want* to. You're their choice. They've been waiting for a long time, and here you are. A bit like that human Jesus Christ."

Tommy held Dana, his own spirit, and willed her to lead him. She did just that, as always.

"Now, Captain Phillips,"

The captain sat down, wary of the young leprechaun. She was never an easy face to read.

"Now I'll tell you what we're gonna do right now," She held her arms out in the welcome stance. "eat! We'll celebrate with a slap-up meal, right now." She began laughing, grabbed Tommy and hugged the breath out of him. "Celebrate!"

They all relaxed.

Was this how Jesus Christ felt when he found out he was special, all a bit of a damp squid?

CHAPTER 19
ROOTS

As the twins had grown up, their mental kindred had become ever stronger, and Tommy had become the talker and Dana the thinker. What she tended to think, he tended to say, which often gave him the label of trouble. They both enjoyed the partnership, which was not surprising for twins. She would sit back and control while he would step forward and take the accolade, a perfect union of minds, and genetic Nettle Wit behaviour. The bitch always drives!

She ordered that Phillips would go north, Tommy downwards, and she south, so, like obedient little boys, they donned their backpacks and shillelaghs and set off to harvest a celebratory meal.

After about twenty minutes, Phillips returned with some blackberry balls and a sample bag of nectar. Then Tommy climbed back up the hedge with the heads of two fairy toadstools and some tender wild oats seeds. They sat high in the bough and waited for Dana's return.

"Your sister's a really deep, dark woman. She's a job to read sometimes."

"I don't have any trouble. But I've known her longer than you."

They both laughed, then looked south.

Tommy said, "Hope she's alright. Shouldn't really go off alone like that. None of us should."

Phillips had a small chuckle. "I think she's taken charge. She's good at making decisions."

"Is that a problem with you? A girl in charge?"

"Not really, it's natural. No, not at all, the bitch is always head, and she's probably better at being in charge than me.

I'm happy for her to lead, make decisions, most of the time."

They sat waiting. As they did, they looked westward into the wilds. The sun was still quite high above the horizon, and in the far distance the herd of deer were silhouetted in the light. It was rather romantic. The birds were beginning their dusk chorus and an inquisitive hedgy-bet sat on a twig close to them.

Tommy put his hand up to it. "Hello Hedgy, what you knowing? Where you been and where you going?"

The bird never answered him.

"Peewit. Peewit."

"That was Dana!" Tommy jumped up. "She wants us to go." He acknowledged with a single peewit.

They set off along the hedge and soon reached the edge of the nettle forest. They looked down from their elevated route along the edge. It was their first detailed view of the wild forest. They never said a word.

Tommy called for Dana's position. "Peewit."

He heard a reply, just ahead of them, and within minutes they had located her. She forced a big smile as they approached each other.

"What you smiling at?" droned Phillips.

"And what you droning about?" was her response. "We're celebrating. Eating our faces full and celebrating, so no moaning, right?" She greeted them both with a welcome gesture, "No moaning or grizzling. We're gonna have that slap up meal. Now, what've we got?"

The boys pulled themselves together and found a good, wide bough to camp on. They presented their contributions.

Phillips proudly laid out the slices of puffball which he had kept from the previous day, then the blackberry balls, then his salted Moors meat, and proudly held up his sample bag. "You've never tried this! I squeezed it from the flowers of some dead nettles. It's pure nectar. Might be good on our salted meat, sweeten it up." Could even sweeten their moods up.

Tommy retrieved his offering. "My Moors meat, some sweet young oat nuts and these toadstools. They smell so good, like walnuts, and no acid taste. Could be one for your compendium." He forced a smile at Dana.

Her turn. "Well, I'm not gonna get down tonight, we're celebrating, so I've got these lovely red honeysuckle berries. Not sure how they taste. We'll soon find out. My other offering needs picking up with your help."

"What about your salted Moors meat? Got much left?"

"Yeah, same as you. But look. She moved along the bow and leaned out against the side. "Look.". She pointed down to the nettle forest. "Look, what do you see?"

The boys leaned over with her and stared. Tommy felt he had to say, although he did not want to dampen their party mood. "I can see a forest of strong growing, but trampled, Common Nettles. Just Comment Nettles. No Irish Nettles. None of our nettles. That's what I can see."

She waved her head and pointed. "Look harder. Down there. Swamped and strangled by the Common Nettles. Look."

It was what was left of an Irish Nettle. It was almost finished, pushed from existence by the more powerful immigrants, Common Nettles.

Phillips tried to keep up their good composure. He laughed as he spoke. "I don't really fancy nettle soup, but you can. I'll have toadstools and syrup."

"I don't fancy nettle soup, but look just below the growing tip. I'm having Moors meat. *Fresh* Moors meat! Come on, I can't get it on my own."

There was a real, but tiny, Moors caterpillar hanging onto the Irish Nettle. They rushed down the hedge and located that lonely nettle and within no time at all, had butchered the caterpillar and were humping it back up the hedge. They stuffed on the fresh meat and then topped up with toadstool and puffball, then a final course of oat nuts in blackberry and honeysuckle juice. It was all washed down with a few cups of nettle wine. The feast took them right into the darkness of night, and they certainly slept well on full stomachs and intoxicated heads.

They needed the sleep. Despite achieving their tribal goal of locating the forest, their initial assessment of the situation was not good. They had only seen a small part of the wild forest, but early indications were that the Common Nettle had beaten the indigenous species, their staple habitat, the Irish Nettle.

Despite the misleading name, Common Nettles were not common in Ireland until after the birth of Jesus Christ and a little before the marauding visits of the Romans, and were not native to the Emerald Isle. Nobody knows where or why, but they were like Eileen's walnut tree, introduced. It may have been accidental, and once the east coast of Ireland began enjoying wetter weather, the imports took hold. They were unstoppable, and the native Irish Nettles never stood a chance. Dominant immigrants and climate change. The poor indigenous species was doomed.

They all knew, deep down, that it was no good blaming the Common Nettles, nor the Roman navvies, nor the trampling livestock. No, they knew better, and in their hearts they believed without doubt that it was all down to The Almighty, Gayla, The Creator. When she made the Irish Nettle, she forgot to give them that essential ingredient needed for survival, a competitive nature, so the Irish Nettles just rolled over and surrendered to their intruding cousins. Mother Nature always wins, and loses, and sometimes draws. There was nothing the tiny Nettle Wits could do but pray to Her.

They woke early, as the sun rose in the east, and as the farmers arrived to feed their animals, the sheep and goats joining in with the dawn chorus.

"Today we need to prepare a report for the committee."

They were very professional about it. They were soldiers of the Defence Regiment and without a single complaint they began the systematic survey of the forest. They kept their opinions and dreams to themselves, just doing their tribal duty of assessing why the wild butterflies no longer came to the forest. It was obvious why they had died out, but they still had to complete the survey, just in case.

Most of the work could be done from the vantage of the layered hedges, so they were able to complete the work by evening, by which time they were very tired and a little despondent.

"Nothing left but three small, dying patches." Phillips was very matter of fact about it. "And they are on their last legs, and we've found just eight stunted caterpillars."

Dana noted, "And those eight are tiny. Not much more in total than one of our farmed ones. Not even worth sending a team out to collect, unless we become really desperate."

Phillips continued. "So, a report needs to be honest but not cause panic and not take the tribe's focus off our foundations, Moors farming. We've survived since the beginning of time by all being single minded, look after the Moors and everything else would look after itself." He stood up and paced. "If we do let our focus blur, our forests will be like this one, dead."

The regimental report was agreed.

"Now we could talk about our other work. The Centre Society."

Before they did, they ate. The three almost bloated on the fresh Moor's meat, which was butchered the previous day, and enjoyed some fairy toadstool and oat nuts, topped with a mix of berry and dead nettle syrup. The lot was washed down with the last of their wine.

"We could be in trouble," whispered Tommy. "Plenty of meat, enough for a couple of weeks, but no wine. What we gonna do?"

That essentially made the decision for them. The thought of sitting down to tomorrow's tea with no alcohol was unbearable.

"Whatever we do, we're going home tomorrow." Phillips gave the command.

"Yeah, but which way?" Dana scoffed with a big grin. "Go your way, it'll take six days. The Phillips longcut. I've heard of shortcuts, but....."

"Okay, but it wasn't me that hung the bloody map upside down two-hundred years ago. Not all my fault." He laughed with Dana. "And I've marked the map so it doesn't happen again. I've got a new hieroglyphic. It's a sun with the corona extended to a point on top and to make sure it's up the right way, I'll put a happy face on it. Put it in the east where the sun rises. I've called it Dana." He grinned at the pretty girl. "After your pretty face."

Tommy noticed a little bit of chat-up in Phillips's talk. He was never jealous, not of his sister, but he was protective.

He stated. "Good job the wine's all gone; you could get out of hand. I might have to try my shillelagh."

"Shut up!" Dana snapped. "It's only a bit of fun. Don't get all manly on me or I might have to try *my* shillelagh. And Phillips, don't forget that captains don't play with their privates. It's rude."

"And send you blind, apparently." He took it all in good faith. "And we're not on duty now, so I'm not a captain, just an equal CS member. All equal right now."

The mood was becoming more relaxed. Tommy kept quiet as he normally did when the play started, but Dana was always ready to lighten the load.

"So, equal CS member, when you gonna introduce yourself?" She stood up and held her hands towards her brother. "This is Tommy, my darling brother, and I'm Dana, the one who got all the pretty genes." She chuckled very playfully. "And you are? Name? Who the hell are you? Come on, if you're going to call me Dana off-duty, like my intimate name, my personal name Dana, what do I call you Mr. equal?" She poked her head towards him and grinned in his face.

He nodded nervously. "Alright, but promise not to laugh."

"No promises!"

Right. "It's.... Aaron."

Tommy stirred from his spectator role and joined in. He started laughing and whooping, then, "Aaron? What the hell sort of name is that? Foreign?"

Poor Aaron looked at his feet. "Not my fault. I didn't choose it, so just leave it. It's my name."

"Okay keep your 'air on." He laughed loudly, then kicked down his foot on the bough. "Hey, Sis, what do you call a right tit with 'air on? It's.... Phillips!" Dana joined him in the hilarity while Aaron just kept quiet. But he did smile.

Once the piss-take calmed, Dana spoke with a gentler touch. "It's a nice name, Aaron."

Then Tommy, "Yeah. Sorry. Just had to be done this once. All over with now. Friends?" He stood up and stepped to Aaron, offering his hand, and they shook meaningfully. Tommy began to feel that Aaron Phillips was a good man and could, perhaps, be a close friend, not just a fellow member of some crank secret society. He was so relaxed that he let his own defence down and admitted, "When me and Dana came out, Dad was drunk and named her Dana and me Tomikins. Luckily, Mum wasn't drunk and overruled him."

The sun was getting close to the western horizon.

Aaron suggested. "Early start tomorrow, and we'll be home for teatime."

Dana slowly waved to head in thought. "What if we stayed here for a bit longer? We've got enough fresh meat for a couple of weeks. We could really study our options properly by living them. Actually learn from experience. Proper experience."

They all sat deep in thought for about five minutes. The idea was exciting and fitted in with all the ideals of the CS but broke the spiritual ideals of the tribe.

They all agreed that the only way, was to actually do it,

but the immediate problem was alcohol.

She admitted, "But I don't want to go without the alcohol. Our daily alcohol is too important to give up without a fight, to be sure."

Aaron, "One of the important studies that the CS did a hundred or so years ago, was kicked out without ceremony by the tribe. Now, dead nettles are considered a serious hazard with strong, fibrous roots that can compete better than our Irish Nettles and they harbour large numbers of cuckoo spit, covered in them. So, any ideas associated with dead nettles were branded as both dangerous and totally unnecessary. Anyway, we recorded what we found from the studies, then shelved the project." He reached into his backpack and pulled out a sample bag, almost full of syrup.

"This is interesting, dead-nettle syrup. It's officially banned, through the tribe's self-imposed hurdles, but we convinced them that we needed some of this syrup for the Regiment's work. That's the only way we get left alone to develop new products, by claiming that the Defence Regiment needs it. And the stuff inside this bag, as you know, is delicious as a sweet sauce. It's also perfect for preserving fruit and meat, and it can be easily distilled into alcohol. That alcohol gives us our beers and wines, our tannery materials, our pickling vinegar and medical supplies, and we trade the alcohol with the Cockle Wits for our salt and metal goods." He waved the clear bag around. "This amount of sugar would have taken a whole industry to produce from the Irish Nettles, but this bag-load took me a couple of minutes to squeeze from the dead nettle flowers. But we're not allowed to collect it or use it. No arguments, just no."

Dana raised her eyebrows. "So, nearly all our needs can come from dead nettles, apart from the Moors meat and Moors butterfly pelts. That's amazing."

"So, we believe that life could go on outside of our beautiful forest. We just need meat and clothing. Clothing is easy, use other butterfly pelts, any butterfly, their wings are all similar. Meat? Well, we mustn't forget the Brady's."

Tommy had made little contribution, although he was taking it all in and his brain was turning over like tumbleweed. "You know, we should do it."

Dana, "I hope you've thought this through, whatever it is."

He had a saucy grin. "I'm not talking about you two setting up home out here. No, not just you, but a few of us, bringing out wine to last us long enough to start distilling the dead nettle syrup, and enough salted meat, just to get us going, and take it from there. Try a new culture, right here in these beautiful hedges."

They were quite moved by the thought of living in the open, away from the confines of the forest.

Aaron agreed. "It is beautiful here, so open and free."

It was agreed to sleep on it, think some more on the way home, then maybe discuss it with the other CS members.

Before they shutdown beneath their tanned blankets Dana privately watched Aaron arrange his bed, and wondered.

The next morning was another bright one, day number seven of their expedition and probably their final day away from their families.

There was no activity in the distant north field, the flax harvest being completed the previous day, but the sheep and goats called frantically for their hay. The three Wits watched them hustle and bustle, while eating a good breakfast of fresh meat and syrup. The syrup was a fine, sweet luxury, but banned by the tribe. However, Phillips would be taking his sample with him, for scientific purposes of course.

They were already close to the corner and close to the south boundary, which was a loose hedge fronted by the stream. They studied their options for crossing the flowing water. As they did a big nose pushed into them, almost knocking them off the bough, but luckily, it withdrew as soon as it got the vile smell of Nettle Wits. It was one of the wolfhounds.

Moving along the boundary by the stream were four humans and their two wolfhounds. As the dogs went to and fro about their business the four people talked. They were two of the Doyles boys, including the one who pulled the handcart, then Eileen and Father Patrick. The Wits stayed put while the humans passed around the corner of the field. They were talking about flax, and one of the Doyles was saying how well they were paid for the crop. Then Eileen asked Father Patrick about an idea he had had about her wine and its quality, and Father Patrick spoke of the Tuatha, who were the local royalty, and how it would be a good gesture, but it would need to be sorted within about one week. Father Patrick said, with a tongue in his cheek, "Good job your boy took the girl's knickers, otherwise I would never have known about the wine. God certainly works in mysterious way."

As they passed the Wits, one of the boys became agitated when Father Patrick mentioned the Saviour, and he stressed how the local people already had their own Gods, as did the Tuatha, so he should be careful with his preaching. His tone was aggressive.

Then they were gone, leaving the Wits to wonder what it was all about, and the mention of the boy taking his sister's knickers gave Tommy and Dana a poke in the heart. Guilt or regrets?

Dana whispered, "Mustn't read too much into it."

A hard walk and climb along the hedge, which was not layered and so a little slower, and they found themselves standing at the north-west corner of their forest. They were tired and hungry but cheerful. Home at last.

It was with mixed feelings that they parted, Phillips going to his family in the West Hold and the twins working their way right across to the South Hold.

Part Two

NIGHTMARES

CHAPTER 20
DEATH TO THE COMMONERS

The twins worked their way across to their home platform with stealth, not wanting any fuss from the tribe until they had reunited with their family, and besides, it was teatime, in between work and pub, so the forest was quiet with most people at home eating.

Neither the Phillips nor the O'Kiefs spoke about the trip as the families ate, their rations topped up with the remainder of the fresh meat from the wild forest and the surprise packs of unusual samples from the hedges.

They were all relieved to be back together with their families and amongst their tribe as part of a much bigger thing, but all three adventurers had restless nights dreaming of the other world; no nightmares, just pleasant dreams. It was a strange lesson that they learned that night, about the stability and long term success of their culture. Dreams and aspirations are very dangerous creatures, ravenous carnivores, which can devour contentment and breed discontent. They can often be the hidden enemy within. They can turn into nightmares.

As children, Tommy and Dana had shared each other's fears and had always sought solace by cuddling tightly, so, early that morning, Dana sneaked over to Tommy's bed and climbed into his arms for a cuddle.

"I'm scared," she whispered. They lay quietly for a while. Then she said in his ear, "I think I know what you're thinking. I think you're thinking the same is what I'm thinking."

He grinned and confirmed, "Yeah, I'm scared about something."

Dana took on the lead part. "Yeah, all three of us. I'm so scared." She came close to tears but took three deep breaths for bravery. "I love Mum and Dad so much, I do, honest, but I don't want to be here. I want to go back. I've never felt so happy as I was when we were in the hedge. So free, so open, so varied. All the different foods, all those interactions, the distant wilderness, the farmers, everything. I miss it after only one night. How can I ever forget it? The grass is so much greener over there." She pulled into him harder. "Cuddle me. Help me."

They lay for several minutes, then Tommy quietly confessed, "I've been awake half the night thinking about all this. You know, nobody has ever worked out what Brady's diseases is. I have. I know what it is and it's not about not eating Moors meat. That's just one of the effects *caused* by Brady's disease. And you know, I think we have Brady's disease; addiction, mind changing addiction. Theirs was the poppy and hemp, ours is the outside world. We're addicted to that world, and we've got to go back to it. And like you, I'm so scared."

After a quiet few minutes they were pulled out of the nightmare. "What's this?" It was Mum standing over them. "This is not you, you haven't done this for years. Are you worried about something?"

They both climbed out of the bed and Dana carefully said,

"Mum, we need to speak to Aaron urgently."

Mary put two and two together and made nineteen, as mothers do. "Aaron? You got something to tell me?" She looked gleamingly into Dana's eyes, then raised her eyebrows at Tommy.

"Not now, Mum. Captain Phillips. We need to speak to *Captain Phillips* before anybody else does."

Jim wandered over and Dana said the same to him. He could tell that she was serious, so he called a few whoops from the front of their platform, and after a very short time the General's messenger arrived at their home.

Jim ordered, "I need to speak to Captain Phillips. It's an emergency. Tell him not to speak to anybody on the way. Just get here now. And once he's on his way here, stop at the crier's place. Tell him to be here in a couple of hours."

The messenger went.

Tommy explained to his parents that they needed to finalise the tribe record urgently before they speak to anybody about anything. Jim and Mary seemed to understand. They all sat at the table without a single awkward question, nor comment. The only thing really said was for General O'Kief to remind the two privates that, if it is regarding tribe business then, he is General and Phillips is Captain. The twins understood.

When Phillips arrived, Jim welcomed him formally and invited him to the table with the other regimental members. Mary took the opportunity to move to the other end of the platform to carry out some stitching work.

General O'Kief started the meeting. "I've called you over, Captain Phillips, because your two privates feel that they have serious issues to discuss regarding your mission. I believe Dana is speaking on their behalf. I'll stay out of it, unless I need to intervene." He nodded to the captain then held his hand towards Dana to proceed.

She cleared her throat, smiled at her captain and held tightly onto Tommy's hand. "We've had a bad night and we need to discuss it."

Phillips nodded. "Same here, but carry on, please."

"Well, the only time anybody leaves the forest for more than a few hours, is to go down the hill into the town by the sea, to Hell, each year to trade with the Cockle Wits. Everybody hates it. They all hate it so much that they all pray never to have to leave the forest again. Then, there's the threat of Brady's disease, if they can't get Moors caterpillar meat. And so, everybody is single minded about preserving the Nettle Wits' way of life. It's perfect. Same routine day in, day out, forever. Everyone is happy, so happy that they believe that if something happened to our forest, we'd all die!" She breathed deeply. "But the docks downhill aren't the world. We've seen the real world, and it's beautiful. Unbelievably beautiful.

"And not only that, we know what Brady's disease is. It's addiction, physical or mental, but it's an addiction which takes over the mind. It makes you want more of what you haven't got, and worst of all, it destroys the clockwork mechanism which drives the industry of the entire tribe. You suddenly want more or different or better, and discontentment thrives."

Jim was taking it all in, but keeping quiet.

After a hug from Tommy, she continued. "Me and Tommy, well, we think we've got Brady's disease. We're addicted or spoiled, depending on how you look at it, and all night we've wrestled with ourselves. We're addicted." A deep, deep breath. "We think we've got to go back."

Jim nodded to Phillips, silently permitting him to talk.

He took the nod. "I don't know if I should be saying this in front of General O'Kief, but.... so do I. I didn't sleep all night. I'm ashamed to say that I began wishing that we'd just stayed out there. This is beautiful, this life of plenty, safety, comrade-ship, but there's more in life, so much more."

Jim raised his eyebrows. He wasn't expecting that. He asked, "Is this about the big world?" He looked between

Dana and Phillips. "Or is it about you two?"

Tommy was ready for that. "No! And even if it is about those two, then they don't need to leave the forest to be together, do they! They can do that here." He hesitated, "If they want to be together, then they have my blessing. Aaron is a good man." He spent a few seconds smiling at his sister. "But it's not about that. I want to go back as much as they do. We've all.... got.... the.... disease. And if you'd been out there, and you Mum, I know you're listening, you'd want to go back, same as we do. You would be affected by that yearning, obsessed, and as a result you'd become dissatisfied with your monotonous, but stable, existence." He thought for a few seconds, "Just like the Bradys."

Mary took it upon herself to join them at the table and the others never objected. She looked worried.

Jim asked in his capacity as their father, "Where does this leave us? Would you really leave this life? It is, as you said, perfect. It's the result of hundreds of years of perfecting, honing it into Utopia. Would you really leave it?"

Dana looked Aaron in the eye, then smiled at Tommy. "Probably not, but I'll suffer for the rest of my life wondering. I don't think I'll ever have our forest properly in my heart, not as an idealistic dream. My dreams will probably be out there, in the hedges. My old, blinkered dream of being a soldier in the forest has been overpowered by the beautiful world, the one just a day away from where we sit. Yes, I'll suffer for my dreams, but I'll never leave you two."

Tommy said, "Don't think we're about to runaway, Dad, but that commitment to the tribe's needs might be affected. Blindly following the farming calendar and routines and drudgery year-in year-out is not going to be easy. The dream of the hedges is not going to go away. That beautiful green grass over the other side is not going to stop eating at my aspirations for a long time, maybe never." He shook his head. "I'll have to live with it. We all will."

Both his comrades nodded in agreement. Dana asked,

"But could the rest of the tribe grin and bear it? How much damage would be done to everybody's way of life, and our future, if the entire tribe was to become diseased? Dissatisfied with their lot, and dreaming of better. Commitment is what has made this life of ours, not dreams, not ambitions, nor individual aspirations for the better life. It could destroy the Nettle Wits even quicker than the Roman navvies and climate change."

Aaron nodded in agreement, looked at his hieroglyphs in front of him, and tutted.

Jim asked him, "Is this about you, or the tribe? Because I'm concerned. You've all got serious reservations about certain things, like your own sudden longing to be elsewhere, not living this life in the forest. Just tell me now, as I've got the crier coming round soon, and I need to tell him to inform the tribe about progress. Should we have a general meeting, for you to share your findings? Should I call the meeting?" He looked to Captain Phillips, his own right hand man. "Are you ready to present to the tribe?"

"Well, I thought hard about this and with my team's agreement, I'd like to do it. I'll tell them about the wild nettle forests, and how the Irish Nettles have lost the battle with the Common Nettles, and how as a consequence, there are no more wild Moors butterflies. All we have left is our own managed forest and livestock. That's all they need to know. That's why we went, so that's what we should be reporting. The bare facts, no? Then, once I've given them the basics, I thought that Tommy could give one of his spiritual, bolstering speeches to bring the Wits back up from the floor." He looked at Tommy, who seemed a tiny bit nervous. "If you can read my hieroglyphs, I've got some good stuff you could include. Yes?"

Tommy reluctantly nodded and squeezed Dana's hand for support.

Jim slapped the table. "I don't feel totally convinced, but I'll back it all the way. Whatever we do, the tribe must maintain its communal spirit, focused on what we have and how we keep it. The community must be conserved! Now, all the other business, like the beauty and excitement, and potential attractiveness in case of a meltdown here, and the worldly alternatives, need to be private. We can't afford to start a panic, nor a dreamworld free-for-all. We'll discuss those issues on Saturday in the Centre Point. And remember, walls have ears."

So when the town crier arrived, Jim was ready with his message. "General meeting at six PM today, in the Central Corral." The message was delivered to the entire forest.

Everybody turned up at six o'clock and the top table included Captain Phillips, the guest speaker. The sun was still fairly high.

The members were respectfully silent as Captain Phillips explained how they had read the map upside down, adding about four days onto the journey, and the Wits were lifted a little with some playful piss-taking of the Philosophy Department. He then explained how the wild Irish Nettles were as good as gone, as well as the wild Moors butterflies, and any hope of the wild stocks boosting their farming stocks was probably gone forever.

The meeting was dire, with the Science Department suggesting that they could have told them that, but the meeting brushed their criticism aside and showed great appreciation for the three adventurers and their brave efforts. If nothing else, a serious effort was made by the three soldiers, risking life and limb, to confirm what had previously just been scientific theories.

Then, as the murmuring began to overwhelm the meeting, O'Toole Who Has a Lot to Say stood forward and hushed the crowd. He held his hands out high.

"Perhaps we could hear some words from young Tommy O'Kief. Tommy, would you talk to us?"

The Wits all nodded, then held their hands out in the welcome stance. Tommy stepped up to the top table.

"Thank you for the invite." He respectfully bowed his head to O'Toole, then swung around to include all the members, including the top table. "Thank you. As you know, we've been away for seven days and nights. Things that we never knew existed are out there and we found ourselves overwhelmed by the absolute size and endlessness of the outside world. We never stopped dreaming of home, and now that we're here, we're reminded of just why we're so fortunate. Family, friends, community spirit, security and safe surroundings, things which have not just turned up here by luck. No, it's not by luck that the Nettle Wits manage such ideal surroundings. No, not luck, but hard work. Single mindedness, skills, learning, innovation, imagination, all those things and many more. But the one that puts our civilization out there with all the very best, is our communal commitment and spirit. Alone, we are leprechauns, together we are the Nettle Wits! The one and only Nettle Wits!" He held his hands up as the crowd cheered and waited for it to slow.

"Yes, we're one, always have been one, and the important thing is that we *will* always be one. We all enjoyed the stories told at the Spring Holly, they're our blood, they feed fire through our veins and pump pride into our hearts, but right now we need to concentrate on other legends, ones which haven't even been written yet. Yes, we need to lay aside our past and think about that future and make legends for future generations to look back at and admire. Our own future is in our own hands. We will be what we achieve, and what we do today will mould our tomorrow. Today is tomorrow's past and tomorrow's legend. Today we start the rest of our future and we, the Nettle Wits will thrive."

He stopped and looked around the meeting, at their smiles, and at the top table, and at his friends and family. Just as the crowd began to shout, he returned, his arms held high, and the babble respectfully died. It was suddenly silent.

He took the biggest breath, then. "War! Yes, war! We're

about to enter into a period of conflict never before suffered by so few, a war against a monster which spreads through the lands, devouring all in its path and striving onwards towards World domination. But we will never surrender! The Common Nettle will find an impenetrable wall around our forest, never to weaken, never to submit to the onslaught of the marauding beast. We will fight them on all fronts and forever become stronger, and we will win."

The crowd was silent, then, as Tommy raised his hands, they screamed. They roared in collective support of the very spirit, the Wits. They were one, never to surrender to anybody.

After a heart wrenching display of solidarity from the tribe, the chief stood up and the crowd allowed him to speak. He looked to each of his sides, at his committee of scientists and philosophers, then gently said, "Talk is cheap."

A shocked tribe just stared at their chief, who, with just three little words, had soured his support from his people. They all crossed their arms in shame.

A member from the North hold stood forward. "If talk was so cheap, then you'd be better at it. Get back to your calendars."

Many cheered in support of the insult to the chief, but others were shocked. Two women started shouting at the man from the north before Jim stepped forward and stood right in front of the top table.

He held his arms up and the tribe responded. Instant silence. "Tribesmen, listen to us. Every time we have a meeting, we turn against one another. The chief never meant any disrespect for Tommy. And Tommy never meant to challenge the chief in anyway." He looked at the chief. "That's correct, yes?" The chief nervously nodded. "So let's give the chief the respect of listening to what he has to say." He stepped back to the side of the table.

The chief was momentarily tongue-tied. He coughed, then fiddled with some notes, then slowly stood up. "I'm sorry if my words were taken as an insult." He looked sideways towards Tommy. "What I meant was....I meant that talk is cheap, like most of life's best bits. Yes, quality can't be measured by price, so, young Tommy O'Kief, you're a good speaker. Thank you for again pulling us together. But now the talk is done, what next?" He was quietly challenging Tommy, clearly through his own feeling of inadequacy. "Do you have any answers? What about the Roman navvies? The rains?"

Tommy stood up and had a few seconds of eye contact with Dana, which inspired him. "The Roman navvies! The tilting World caused by the roadbuilding Romans. Yes, I do have some answers. I know it's only my belief, but the Science and Philosophy Departments must be told. Not everything can be answered by the application of logic, or processes of logicisation. Yes and no are too simple to explain certain things. So, I need to report some findings from our expedition. A few days ago I was with my sister and Captain Phillips, way over there," he pointed to the north-west. "Way over there in the big world and believe you me, it's big, it is so big that you can't even see the end of it. And we stood high up in the hedge and looked out. We looked west. It just rolled on-and-on, gently downhill, the wildlands seemingly never to end, further than the eye could see, and I watched the clouds roll towards us from the west. And I thought of the Romans and then realised immediately that no one is as big as the World. The Romans can't affect the World, nor can any other mortal. Mere mortals are themselves controlled by the World, not the other way round. And I wondered if I could be wrong and that the Roman navvies are not so insignificant, and that they may be big enough to tilt such an enormous World.

"So I watched some more, I thought some more, and after a great deal of soul searching I remembered the most important thing in life. I remembered what I am as I stood on the alder bush. I remembered that I am a child of Gayla,

The Almighty Creator, our mother, and I remembered her power over all life in the World. And I realised just how insulting it must seem to the Creator, the maker of everything, for me to believe that anything as trivial as the Roman Empire could ever affect her beautiful World. And as I thought further, I wondered if I could be wrong and the scientists right, but as I watched the clouds rolling towards me I finally understood that the World had *not* tilted on its axis. Can't have done! The clouds were not rolling downhill from the west, they were rolling *uphill* from the West. Coming towards us *up....hill!* Then I knew that the only power capable of such a feat was our Gayla, The Almighty Creator."

He paused for thought and looked at Dana for inspiration. Before the attentive crowd could loosen, he resumed.

"Once I knew the truth, that the rain clouds were being sent by Gayla, I only wondered yet more, and began asking myself why she would punish her children with rain. Why would she work so hard to push those clouds uphill, just to punish us? What had we done so wrong, to deserve that? So in desperation, I asked one of the clouds why. We all know that clouds can rumble and flash lightning, but that doesn't mean they can't talk, because I heard them ask me, 'Why on Earth would you want us to stop?' So I thought hard about the question. Knowing that whatever I told the cloud would be heard by Gayla, I thought about what would happen if the clouds never came. And I imagined in my mind how everything would shrivel, it would all die of thirst, then all turn to dust. I imagined how this beautiful Emerald Island would be nothing but a lifeless desert without the rains. That was when I learned the truth. Gayla is not punishing us, She is rewarding us! The rains are life and the rains are a gift from Gayla, a sign of her love for her children. So, I asked the cloud to ensure that they always came with the rain, forever, and the cloud promised that they would, and then told me that we must learn to use whatever the Almighty was generous enough to send us, and be thankful. We thank the Lord."

The crowd was mesmerised.

"So whenever we eat, we must always remember to thank the Almighty for her generous gift of rain. It's then up to us to live with it."

He looked around at the reassured faces and settled on Dana's. He took an enormous breath, then held his chest and arms out to the tribe.

"So, thank the Almighty! In the meantime.... death to the Common Nettle!"

CHAPTER 21
NEW ROLES

The meeting closed on a resounding vote of support for the war, the chants of death to the Commoners shrilling through the forest as the Wits headed home.

While the sun dropped behind the blackthorn hedge, Jim stood with Mary in their platform. He called. "Tommy." The young man moved across to face his mum and dad, followed by Dana. "That took everyone by surprise, especially me and your mum. Where did that come from?" He looked from Tommy to Dana.

The twins pulled into each other and smiled at their parents. It was a satisfied smile. "You know, we surprised ourselves, that feeling when the entire tribe rose up against the enemy. It wasn't them that chanted, nor them that jelled as one spirit. No, not them, us. We came together today. We all realised who we are, including me and Dana, and probably Captain Phillips. This is where we belong, with our family and friends." He squeezed Dana. "I think even that's not quite right. I really mean that this is *what* we belong, with our tribe. Where the tribe is, and what the tribe is, is where we belong and what we are. Together."

Mum shook her head. "Weren't just them you were convincing, were it. So I take it you'll be staying?"

Dana answered. "Wherever the tribe goes, we go. It's us, the Wits." She suddenly held her green brother. "We can't go back to hedges, can we? Not now, we have all these followers, the entire tribe. I don't think we can ever desert them. Wouldn't be us."

Jim lumped his big hand on Tommy's shoulder. "No, it wouldn't be fair. They belong here and they thrive here. All the seeds of doubt, which thoughts of the outside world would fertilise, need to be left dormant. And don't forget you're now active members of the CS. I'm sure you've learned what that means. In a nutshell, insurance against disaster, not the insemination of the seeds of doubt." He looked them both hard in the eyes. "You'll now be at the weekly drinking sessions, from this Saturday, and that's when we talk about the alternatives, never outside that meeting with non members. Remember that always." His voice was commanding, laying down the law, "Understand?"

The twins changed that week. Last week they were school children, this week, adults, and they're not just ordinary adults, but ones that matter.

I know what you're thinking, everybody matters, and you are right to think that, but sometimes people shine in particular circumstances. They stand out in the crowd and this was one such circumstance. They definitely mattered.

After Tommy's first two speeches, all the talk was about him, how well he could put things into words, how confidently he stood up in front of the crowd, how poetic, how his storytelling was heavenly, how he always helped Old Murphy with the younger children, how he would make a good teacher.

But this time it was different. It was all about his message, how the Common Nettle had to be defeated and the rain had to be loved and lived with. This time, his speech really mattered. The tribe had woken up to the reality of life, through Tommy's mythical message.

It was the day after the meeting and the O'Kiefs were up with the lark, along with the rest of the forest and activity seemed to contaminate life. It had been done that way every morning since the birth of leprechaun-kind. The cock Robin shrilled his melody from the pigsty roof, goldfinches competed for the best thistle heads, a family of ten long-tailed tits performed through the blackthorn hedge like a team of trapeze artists, and the sounds of whoop and hey-up echoed from the forest as the drovers moved their livestock. Even the grass snakes and adders were out taking in the warmth from the morning sun.

General O'Kief summoned his two new recruits. He stood watching from their platform and could see a small herd of caterpillars being moved to new pastures.

"Right. You've been in the regiment for nine days today. You won't be going back to school." He stood watching the forest with his back to the twins. "Until Captain Phillips works out your details you can survey the entire perimeter of the forest. That'll keep you busy for a few days."

Dana asked. "What we looking for?"

"Everything. Report back each day. I want to know exactly what you see, and take a leaf out of Captain Phillips's book; make sure you're only seen when you want to be seen."

It was part of Jim's training for his new staff, keep them busy. It also felt like a game to the two trainees, so they happily donned their backpacks and shillelaghs and set out towards the southern edge.

They moved through the upper canopy of the nettle trees and after about half an hour were at the edge of the forest. First thing was to find a tall nettle from which they could see right over the forest and right along the perimeters to the east and west. As they perched in the very tip of the nettle, they smiled.

Dana noted. "This suddenly takes me back to the hedge. Not so high, but open and free." She scanned the space around her. "Suppose we'll one day get it out of our system. Hope so."

"Don't forget it too soon. I know they're dangerous, but memories are nice to have, especially good ones."

The best way to forget temporarily is to think of something else. They looked along the edge of the forest to the east, towards the pigsty and farmyard. Then towards the west, where it runs down to the blackthorn hedge. Tommy pointed out some nettles that lay out and into the adder country. They had been broken down by something large, such as a human or a farm animal. That type of damage was common and always pulled back up again. They couldn't see anything worth reporting, then they looked across the forest canopy towards the north-east corner, and the walnut tree. The nuts were filling out, almost ready for Eileen to harvest. They looked all around.

"Would we see any more by moving along?" Asked Dana. "Can't just stay here all day. Could move nearer to the blackthorns and find another viewing point."

Tommy nodded. "Could move all the way to the blackthorns and become Hedge Wits again. Get right up and see the entire forest. Could even see what's on the pigsty roof. Never seen up there, have we?"

"Nah, not allowed, remember? Not allowed to climb above the height of the nettles."

"Why?"

Dana hunched shoulders. "Dunno. Probably a control thing. One of our rules designed just to control us. Rules for rules sake."

They pondered on the subject. It seemed that many of their rules were there for the sake of control. They frowned at each other.

Then Dana asked. "Do you know if we should be looking *into* the forest or *out* of the forest? Reporting on the forest or on the outside world?"

They both thought for a while about that, then Dana said, "I think it's up to us. Yeah, I don't think there's a job for us. I think we're just being employed because we need a job." They both thought for a while. "Yeah, just think about it. Mum doesn't need me. Their team is massive. So is the farmer's team and the forester's and the butcher's and the tanner's. You know, I think most people are working hard on work that doesn't even need to be done. Have you ever known anyone not to have a job?"

Tommy shook his head. "Everyone has a job. It's our culture. Everyone works. Yeah, twelve twenties adults doing about three twenties jobs. As they say, idle hands make mischievous minds. That could mean that we can write our own job descriptions, make a couple of new rolls just for us, one that nobody else does. We could scout the outside world, keep an eye on what's going on around the forest, as opposed to in it. We're perfect for that, a couple of wanderers."

"Brilliant!" Dana was impressed. "That's why I love you. Not just a pretty brother's face."

Tommy suddenly raised his head, then looked at her and asked, "Phillips, Aaron. Do you like him? You know, like like him, not just like him?"

"Shut up." She suddenly dropped her voice and talked like a ventriloquist. "Don't talk like that. You know what he does? I bet he's tailing us right now."

They both looked around and kept quiet. It was a fact that part of Captain Phillips's work was to tail people and keep an eye on anyone venturing outside the forest. "He probably wrote his own job description, one to suit an adventurer."

Tommy whispered, "Let's leave the forest and see if it gets back to Dad. That way we'll know. Let's go down to the end of the pigsty and see what's going on in the yard." He raised his voice. "To the end of the pigsty!"

So they climbed to the ground and headed east, towards the farm. At the corner of the forest they looked as far as they could along the back wall of the sty. It was wet all along, as far as they could see, and the nettles close to it were visibly dying due to root rot. Something to report. They then carried on as far as the front of the sty, just before reaching the start of the pond. The slow walk took them nearly an hour. They found a sheep's parsley to climb. "No young grass snakes by the pond. Something to report." And as they were outside the forest, they donned their red caps.

"Look." Dana pointed across the yard towards the barn.

"Father Patrick and one of the Doyles."

They were with Eileen and discussing business. The twins could not clearly hear the conversation, but it was apparent that they were discussing the land each side of the forest where the adders and grass snakes lived. They pointed here and there and a couple of times raised their voices. They seemed to be arguing over a deal of some sort. Or some prices. Then Father Patrick left via the side path, by the house.

"Look," Dana stood high in the parsley. "he's got some nettle plants in his hand."

Father Patrick was gone, then Eileen went into the house and returned with two cups and a flagon of wine. They shook hands over a drink. The deal had been agreed.

"Wonder what that was about?" Dana frowned. "Wonder if it has anything to do with that talk in the field the other day. About flax. About a deal with the Father?"

Dana felt a prick in her heart as she remembered him joking about how the girls nickers had thrown them together. A prick of guilt? She shrugged her shoulders and pulled herself together.

The two soldiers decided to get back to the forest. They moved along the edge, using stealth and youth to conceal their presents from the workers, as per their dad's instruction.

Once home, just before tea time, General O'Kief sat with them at the table for the report. It was agreed that Dana would present it.

"Well, we spent some time viewing the southern perimeter from the top of the canopy and noted some nettle plants had been pushed down into the rough. Couldn't really tell, but the surrounding vegetation looked like it had been trodden down by humans. Don't think it was farm animals." She had a think. "We then went east and noted all along the sty's back wall and it was dark and wet, and the plants close to the wet were dying of root rot. The water must be dangerously close to going into the storage caves. Then," She stopped and looked Tommy in the face. "We thought about moving to the west and finding a viewing spot high up in the blackthorn hedge but Tommy remembered that we can't go above nettle-height. Or might've been me that remembered."

Tommy quietly asked. "Why not?"

So Jim replied, "Old rules. Goes back hundreds of years when some Wits were attacked in the trees by a migrating flock of wagtails. No one got hurt, but they made the rule just in case. And besides, nobody needs to go higher than the nettles."

Dana wasn't surprised. "We've been at work for one day and learning quickly. Anyway, we didn't go up the hedge." She looked down at her notebook, which was slowly filling with pictures and hieroglyphics about life. "Has Captain Phillips decided on our details yet?" She hesitated. "Have you spoken to him today?"

"Yes, you only just missed him. He's been in the north hold all day with the rope makers."

She was happy that he wasn't trailing them, so she took a bit of a chance with the general. "We wondered if he was watching us, like he was before."

"Not allowed to stalk fellow Defence members, nor investigate other members of the Regiment. Internal principles. So, whatever you do is up to you, do it privately, but you won't be followed. But, big but, you don't do anything that you can't tell me, or else. Got that?" He laid his hand onto the table rather aggressively. "Take that as a warning."

They both stored that safely away in their databanks. Dana then relaxed.

"Well, we didn't just go to the end of the forest, we went right along the side of the pigsty, as far as the pond. There we studied the near-bank and all the baby grass snakes have grown to a safe size. Good news. But while there, we studied the farmers. We don't know exactly what they're planning but it looks like Eileen is doing some business with the Doyles and Father Patrick. I don't know if you know these people. They run all this land round here. Now, when we were out in the meadows we watched them harvest a field full of flax. It's stuff that they make cloth and rope with and it's really good. I brought some back for the CS to look at. I'll show you at the next meeting.

"And they've grown so much of it, a whole big field, bigger than Eileen's cow field, and they talked about it to Eileen and Father Patrick. Then today they talked about it again and shook on a deal. Then Father Patrick went, carrying some of our Irish Nettles." She and Tommy looked at each other. "We ought to find out what's happening."

Jim put his hand to his chin and scratched. "Well, we've never worried about what the human farmers do. They've always left us alone. They don't even know we're here."

"But it looks like they're going into different things, the flax. They said in the field about how much it's worth, you know, they use stuff called money, that sort of talk."

Tommy said, "We don't have a job, so why not make us responsible for finding out what's happening outside the forest? It could affect what's happening inside the forest. Makes sense?"

"Well, that is a new position and you two are perfectly qualified. A couple of nosy adventurers. Perfectly qualified. However, I don't know if the tribe would approve. We stay in the forest, this is where we live and nothing else matters."

Tommy snapped. "You don't think that, surely?"

"No, but the tribe does." He chewed the cud. "But leave it with me. Got things going on tonight, so I'll sleep on it. On the new roles, I'll let you know tomorrow. I need to think about it, and need to get used to you being adults, all of a sudden."

For millions of years, many civilised cultures have differentiated between children and adults. All kinds of privileges are earned by reaching adulthood, and all civilizations seem to have different ideas as to when one turns adult. In reality, biologically, it takes years to move from childhood to adulthood, but because of the way cultures work, they all have to set a trigger which suddenly turns a boy into a man or a girl into a lady. That switch between the two chapters is, for the Nettle Wits, when one leaves school.

For Tommy and Dana that was today. They had never even given it a thought.

Jim made it quite clear that work ended at teatime and Mary jested, "That's until after the second pint." The Grace was said by Jim that night, thanking Gayla for the generous rains she bestowed on the Emerald Isle. Unbeknown to them, so did the rest of the tribe, showing just how powerful the word of the young storyteller really was. He had come of age, in more ways than one.

So, why does it matter about coming of age? Lots of reasons. Benefits include; no more school; go to work everyday; can vote; can get married and have children; have an entitlement to one's own home; can leave home; can get an adult name like Dana Who Saved her Brother's Eyesight; can shoulder responsibility; can be held to account; and many, many more.

Then of course, there are the downsides with the coming age. They include: no more school; have to work every day; expected to vote; can get married and have children; have to take on your own home; have to leave home; can get an adult name like Dana Who Denied her Brother's First Look; have to shoulder responsibility; will be held to account; and many, many more.

It is totally understandable that the twins had almost gone through their coming without even giving it a second thought. But however you look at it, there is, in every civilization, one thing that everyone remembers about their coming of age, right up until the day they die.

Jim laid both his hands on the table as if to get up, but paused and asked. "Well, you coming?"

Yeah, you've got it. The most important thing about the

coming of age, you're allowed in the pub.

So, they all scurried around to clear the tea things, then set off down the nettles towards the pub. Tommy and Dana were on their first time-out with the grownups, in the grownups' playground, where they suddenly expected to experience the real joy of adulthood.

The Nettle Wits were one of the oldest civilizations in the World and one of the most successful, partly because their culture and politics all blended into one, and as of that very day the twins were voting members, as brand new grownups. They were part of the only truly communist society ever known, where everybody is equal, and they would be running the tribe along with all the other adults. They would be making decisions of state regarding policy, laws, directions and anything else, along with all the other adults. They would be enjoying the rewards of life in whatever form they come in, just like all the other adults. In fact, the Nettle Wits enjoyed pure communism to the point where they had forgotten that there could ever be any other type of communism, and they have proven, to anyone who may be interested, that communism can work without the need for fascist control over the populace. They are proof that communism does not have to be fascism. People really can be equal.

This equality even extended to respect for their elders. The Wits don't respect their elders for being old. Why would they? If you get old, you're lucky, there's nothing clever about it, just lucky. So Murphy's tribal name, Murphy Who Knows a Lot Cos He's Old, does not actually mean that he's old, but that he knows a lot because he's been Tommy's age for a lot longer than Tommy has. Hope that makes sense.

Anyway, Jim and Mary always used their local during the week, the Southerner, and promised the twins that they'd have a nice quiet drink, allowing them chance to get settled. Get to know the bar staff and other locals, and just relax over a few pints.

What they had not bargained for was the snowballing effect of Tommy's rousing speech. You see, Chief O'Hoolihan had been rather taken aback by the experience and caught between admiration and fear for the young man, so decided to use the Southerner in the hope that he might get to know Tommy a little better, off the record. Then, all the farmers heard that the chief would be using the Southerner, so they all decided to join him, with the view to getting their new ideas into the next calendar. New ideas? All prompted by Tommy's rousing speech. Then all the industrialists who rely on materials from the farmers for their new ideas, prompted by Tommy's rousing speech, wanted to agree new time scales and volumes with the farmers, so followed them to the Southerner. By the time Jim and his family arrived, the place was heaving. So much for a quiet night.

All those people had not turned up for Tommy and Dana, they had turned up *because* of Tommy and Dana. But despite that, it quickly turned into a coming of age party. The business flowed, the arrangements jelled, the updates rolled out and most importantly, the beer poured. It was a new experience for the twins, happy times. By the end of the evening, they were all pissed.

Overall, it was a successful night. The twins had a night to remember, something to take with them through life, to remind them of their first day as grownups, and the rest of the tribe did their bit to make the night one to remember.

One thing that Dana learned was that her heroine, her mum, was not always right. She said that work ended at teatime, until after the second beer, but on that occasion it resumed after the very *first* one. By the time they had fought their way to the bar for their first drinks, work had taken over. However, it never spoiled the night for Tommy and Dana, but introduced them to the new chapter in their lives, in the vane in which it should carry on. They made full use of the new status, that of being the same age as every other adult, and soon learned to stand their ground.

The chief took the opportunity to infiltrate the O'Kief circle, quickly indicating that he was a little concerned about Tommy threatening his position as The Chief, but Dana solidly stood their ground. She informed him *very* publicly that he was a master at design and his farming calendar would never be undervalued by the tribe. And besides, Tommy was not interested in the leader's position, as he already had the best job in the forest, that of Regimental Offsite Scout, and when the chief took a sigh of relief and nodded in agreement, unwittingly authorising the role of Regimental Offsite Scout, Jim silently admired her powers of persuasion. He proudly accepted that his daughter was more than capable of twisting everybody around her little finger, including him.

The chief not only went home feeling more secure but also with a wealth of new procedures and activities for inclusion in the latest farming calendar update. The twins went home as the acknowledged Regimental Offsite Scouts.

The Science Department had worked with the farmers to estimate that the wild caterpillars, due to their small size, only made up about ten percent of total meat production. This could be made up simply by creating a new team to move all newly laid eggs away from the perimeter of the forest before the scavenging ants could collect them.

The tanners had come up with a design for a temporary rain shield that could be placed over the chrysali at the time of hatching, to prevent the emerging butterflies from being drowned before they had fully developed. The new clear leather, made from flying ant wings and crab oil, was an ideal material.

Then a small group had begun designing a system of drainage dykes to protect the plants and caves close to the pigsty.

But the most important thing that came out that night was the contagious disease which was spreading through the camp like wildfire. That rampant, uncontrollable enthusiasm, that spirit and belief, yes, it was being fired up by alcohol, but even with the hangovers the next morning, the tribe was on the type of roll which had not been experienced for many generations. They all went about their business chanting, "We will survive."

CHAPTER 22
THE COCK OF COCK ROBINS

The next morning, after the tribe had publicly accepted the new roles of Offsite Scouts, Jim sent his two soldiers out on their duties very early. The youngsters easily worked off their hangovers as they moved through the nettles towards the southern perimeter, and they were soon at the top of the highest nettle. The sun was just rising over the pigsty.

"You were a bit off with Phillips last night. Everything alright?"

"Yeah, but Mum put me off. She's too pushy, like she wants to get rid of me. She made me feel pressured, so I kept out of his way."

They surveyed the forest edge, east and west, then made a fine scan of the adder country. It was just meadowland with access through a gate in the blackthorns to Eileen's cow field where her four milking cows lived. They watched the daughter walk through to the cows with her yoke across her shoulders and two buckets hanging each side.

"The girl'll be back soon with her milk." Dana swung in the nettle head, backward and forth, to see more of the farmhouse, past the sty. "Some noise going on in the yard. Should we investigate?"

They both agreed that their new roles required it. So they climbed down, donned their red hats, and left the forest. Half an hour later, they were on the corner of the sty, with the yard and farmhouse ahead, and the pond ahead and to the right.

To their left were the four gates into the pigsties. The man of the house was busy feeding the pigs, all of whom had piglets which screamed and chortled as they competed for their food, and Eileen was removing some cheese from the lever-press with the help of the little boy. It was a hive of activity. Once Eileen and her son had put the cheese into the barn, they placed a large log out on the yard, then brought out armfuls of woolen cloth which had been soaked in ammonia. The ammonia was a concoction of pig manure and human urine, and it disinfected and softened the wool cloth in readiness for fulling, which involved the soaked cloth being bundled, folded, then placed on the log, then beaten continuously for some time to bring out the woolly effect of the cloth. It was then hung to dry on rows of tender hooks on the front of the barn. A quality, full, woolen cloth would result.

In the first century AD, the human Ireland was ruled by about ninety separate dynasties called Tuatha. Each Tuatha was essentially a Kingdom with the head of each dynasty governing, owning, taxing, policing and setting laws. Ireland was made up of about ninety different countries.

The Tuatha local to the Nettle Wits was quite a powerful dynasty, governing its lands efficiently and with strong trading relations with the other countries. The people living there were safe and reasonably prosperous, so long as they paid their taxes.

Like most of the farmers in Ireland, Eileen and the Doyles were tenant farmers paying duty to their kings who resided further south, along the coast. Their homage was paid to the state in the form of goods and was collected regularly by the Tuatha military, a small group of foot soldiers dressed in dull, green tunics, with swords hanging and all carrying pikes. They didn't only collect debts and taxes, but also offered protection from the neighbouring Tuathas, who would go out on plundering expeditions from time to time. They also pulled their handcarts around with goods which they exchanged with the farmers and so provided an essential supply chain, over and above the local markets. The Tuatha was pretty much self-sufficient. However, more and more ships were visiting the quay downhill to trade with the local farms and businesses. As always, things never stopped changing.

It was a hard but fair life, up on the heights. Each farm tended to be specialists in some form of goods which ensured that income was quite evenly distributed amongst them all. The Doyles made most of their living from sheep, goats and cut peat, but more recently had joined the local boom industry which was producing Irish linen from the farmers' flax crops.

Eileen's small farm made its main income from rearing pigs and fulling the locally woven wool. Eileen was a highly skilled trades person when it came to fluffing up the woolen cloth, taking work in from many of the weavers, producing an end product of soft, water-and-windproof woolen cloth which was sought after, along with the local linen and canvas, by the visiting long ships. Mr Fuller and the grandfather, if not plying their other trade of wattle and daub repairs, had big plans for the fulling, by making use of the flowing stream which passed between theirs and the Doyle's farms, and had spent years designing an automated hammer, with which to full the cloth. The hammer would be powered by a water wheel, hopefully giving them additional capacity to take in the entire output from the area's weavers.

Of course, everything else available had to be used to sustain their lives, and they also, like the Wits, had a comprehensive farming calendar. The year was occupied by essential work activities, which included some lesser known money making tricks, such as collecting the alder flowers in February to be sold to the linen factory. The flowers were used to create the green dye for the soldiers' tunics. Almost every month there would be mushrooms and fungi to be collected for eating fresh or dried, or for medicinal purposes, and even snail collection from the stream was a monthly chore. They made the rennet from snails, which was then used to separate the curd from the whey when making the cheese. Everything was used or traded, and the farmers never stopped looking for more.

Tommy and Dana found a large dandelion flower to sit in as they watched the activity. They could see that the humans were well organised, each having specific duties to perform for the benefit of the tribe. Their tribe extended outside the family as far as the Tuatha itself, and geographically as far south as the Mourne Mountains. Their immediate responsibilities, however, mainly focused on their own farm.

"They're very similar to us, you know. They all have a place in their society and have to work to put into the kitty." Dana was being very philosophical about life. "I think we have a lot in common. Only difference is size. They could just stand on us and we're gone."

Tommy wasn't so sure about the similarities. "I think that if we went out into the world and made use of everything, not just a forest, then we'd be more like them. They're traders of everything. They also plunder and steal. We only do one trade a year, with the Cockle Wits. And we don't plunder and steal!"

They watched and thought. They both had strong imaginations, extending their minds way beyond the confines of the nettle forest, and they could not help but to extend it out into the wider picture, the hedges. They were going to take a long time to get over their longing.

Dana observed. "They don't worry about climate change, they just seem to invent or improve to get round it. More rain, more water in the streams, so, a water wheel. If it's there, use it." She pointed to the roof of the farmhouse. "Last summer, that was a mess. It was straw and dried grass. Now, they've got reeds from the wilderness. Rains more, so make a better roof. That's exactly what we need to do, just keep up with it. They don't worry about climate change."

"Know what?" Tommy frowned as he thought. "Let's make a deal. I won't ever mention climate change again, if you don't. I'm sick of hearing it. The climate will always change and there's nothing we can do except live with it. Do like the humans, and use it."

She grinned at him and pulled over to cuddle her brother.

He whispered, "Hope Phillips is not watching. We're on duty."

"Don't care. They can send us away on punishment again, if we're really lucky." She laughed before moving her head away from his shoulder. "Anyway, he's not allowed to stalk us, we're part of the Regiment."

Just then, the farm dog poked his nose at them before bounding over to the boy, by the barn, followed by the girl with her milk buckets on her yoke. Then Mr Fuller joined them by the barn and Grandad came from the house with breakfast. It was some bread and jam.

Grandad asked, "When's that priest coming? The shady bible-basher." He spat on the ground.

Eileen took a deep breath. "Should be here by now, with Sean Doyle. Hopefully coming soon, we've got some big decisions to make."

They all sat down on the log by the barn in front of the woolen cloth which was stretched over the tender-hooks to flatten and dry, along the face of the barn. Eileen stretched the cloth on the tender hooks to dry, because it would shrink otherwise, and they were paid by the square foot.

Then, just as they had all finished their bread, Father Patrick, Sean Doyle and another man walked around the corner of the house.

The father introduced the other man to Mr Fuller and Eileen, as Captain Garibaldi from Gaul, and he was a trader who had been given permission from the Tuatha to trade goods with the local farmers and businesses. His ship was docked down in the village.

The captain, dressed very smartly in a rare light-blue jacket, disappeared into the barn with Mr Fuller and Grandad, being shown the partly built water wheel and mechanical fulling machine, while Eileen spoke quietly to Sean Doyle. They both pointed to the adder country, first to the south of the forest and right back to the lane, then to the north, and after some nodding, shook hands.

When the captain returned with the two men, Eileen rushed into the house and returned with some cups and a flagon of her wine. All five adults had a cup of the wine and drank it slowly, as if judging its flavour and bouquet, paying particular attention to what the captain thought. He held his arms out and declared his love for the wine. It was some of Eileen's nettle wine, Irish Nettle wine.

Eileen pointed over past the pigsty, then the captain went to the corner of the house and beckoned his men from the lane. The men came into the farmyard with boxes full of metal hand tools. They looked like good quality and as soon as Mr Fuller, Grandad and Eileen handled some of them, they all shook the hand of the dark-faced captain. The deal was done.

Father Patrick held his cup up to toast, "Sláinte! God moves in mysterious ways. If the boy had never taken the girl's knickers, we'd never have been thrown together. Here's to a prosperous relationship!"

The twins suddenly felt a shot of guilt rush through their spines.

Then Sean Doyle snarled at the Father before pointing around the farm and said "Flax." and they all held their cups high and toasted the changes.

Tommy and Dana looked and listened, and mentally noted the Father's mention of the girl's knickers. They were seeing a different side to humans, the side which makes them so much different to the Wits, their greed and endless desire to have more and better and bigger. They were witnessing the devastating result of those differences. It was climate change, but this was a different climate change, one that strikes fast and cuts deep, and leaves no life untouched. This was 'economic climate change', the worst kind.

Tommy suddenly jumped to his feet. Realisation had hit. "Quick, we've got to warn everyone! Come on!"

They set off at a sprint, back towards the forest to warn the Wits. They knew exactly what was going to happen, trade with the captain from Gaul, who loved the wine, and the tribe had to be ready for anything.

The twins ran their hearts out, and which took them almost an hour earlier, took less than ten minutes, and they never slowed as they climbed the first big nettle that they came to, their green brows beaded with sweat.

"Woop woop woop!" Tommy shrieked out the warning as they climbed. "Woop woop woop."

By the time they reached the top, the warning whoops were being relayed across the forest, and within no time the entire forest was on danger alert.

They watched from the tip of the nettle right across to the opposite northwest corner, as the warning was being relayed around the forest.

Nothing happened. They waited, but nothing.

"What've we done?" Dana suddenly worried. "We'll be in big trouble."

"No. If we hadn't warned and something had happened...."

Then, almost on top of them, stood the captain and Eileen. They scrambled down the nettle and across the canopy, away from the humans.

The captain asked. "All of them?"

Eileen nodded. "Got better use for this space."

The captain pulled up a nettle, roots and all. "We can keep them alive. They *must* be alive."

They shook hands very heartily, then the captain stepped forward. He pushed into the forest, which reached up to his waist, and Eileen followed. The two relative giants shoved their way into the nettles, flattening trees with every step, like a tornado sweeping through, and anything in their way crashed to the ground, Wits scrambling to move aside and trees whipping down and up like catapults.

Centre Point was destroyed as they passed through the Central Corral and they eventually exited from the north perimeter, leaving a line of devastation from one side to the other.

Warning whoops again relayed around the forest as they waited for the ogres to walk back across, but they stood back and surveyed the bed of nettles before turning towards the walnut tree. Eileen walked under the tree and then proudly showed the captain the only walnut tree in Ireland. He joked that the nettles will be the only Irish Nettles in Gaul. They then returned along the north wall of the sty to the yard, to make arrangements.

The immediate panic was over. All that was left was the clearing up and counting the losses.

Once Tommy and Dana were back at their home, they talked.

"Dad, you need to get the crier," Dana stressed. "We need to get the tribe together now."

"Why? This has happened loads of times, it's always happened. Things go through the forest and we have to count the loss. It's not good, but nothing new. Just hope no one was hurt." He put one large hand on Tommy's shoulder and the other on Dana's. "But to get warning time, to at least hang on, that was really good, it could've saved a lot of lives. Well done, the new roles are already paying off."

The adrenaline had dispersed, the excitement settled, and now the worrying. Tommy thanked his dad for the kind words but was not happy.

"No, you don't understand. Please, please, please listen. You've got to listen, then get the crier. Please." He stamped his foot. "Flax, this's all gonna be flax!" He looked his dad hard in the face, then into his mum's face. "They're all going to Gaul, wherever that is, all our nettles. Please believe us."

After a bit of pleading, the twins managed to convince Jim of the urgency. He called his messenger and sent him off to the crier. "An emergency meeting in the corral, now."

The entire tribe responded to the call of the crier. The auditorium in the Central Corral had been partly flattened by the intrusion, but was still usable and fit for purpose. They all crowded around the theatre.

There was a hubble of anger, frustration and determined grit amongst the crowd, all shouting at the top table but saying nothing in particular. They were annoyed.

The chief stood up. He was quite uninspiring, a typical calendar maker, but on this occasion the crowd were looking for leadership and they climbed up and listened in desperation.

He calmly reported that the direct route taken by the intruders affected only a small area of the forest and no serious damage had been reported, except for the total loss of the Centre Point Pub, and sadly, the much loved barman. Deaths due to accident were very rare in the community and was a shocking piece of news for all. There was a two minute silence, in prayer for their lost colleague.

Once the prayer was over, the Wits went for the chief. "Why we here? What's the emergency? Why take us from our work? Who's got the right call this meeting?" And many, many more calls, chants and unprintable insults. The chief struggled.

He eventually bottled it and handed the chair over to General O'Kief.

Jim stepped up to the table. He caught the eye of Captain Phillips and some of his defence regiment, then nodded to O'Toole. He held his arms out for silence and the crowd responded instantly.

"Quiet please! Quiet, this is a meeting and, just to remind you, I have the right to call this meeting, and believe you me, I have reason for calling it. The damaging intrusion by the farmers was not one of the usual, it was a warning. Now, listen carefully because we could be in big trouble. Please believe me, we have big trouble threatening."

He waited for some grumbling to subside. "This is big, bigger than the threat from the Common Nettles. Bigger than the threat from climate change. Bigger than we've ever known before. Yes, we must prepare. Our agents, who managed to warn of the imminent intrusion, have news of much more. Much worse, more serious, and much, much more damaging." He stopped and thought. "The human farmers have sold the nettles that we so love. They're going to over-plant this forest with flax. Do you understand what that means? It means that our forest is to disappear. Gone!" He hung his head. "I'm sorry to have to say this."

The crowd was numbed. Absolute silence hung over the auditorium like a death sentence, and Jim needed some help. O'Toole knew his place in the CS as the Devils advocate.

"We don't believe you! Never heard of flax."

It allowed Jim's team a bit of time to get to the emergency stash of backpacks and survival blankets. He carefully picked his words.

"Flax is what we believe as a cash crop. They sell it on to other tribes. They make clothing and rope from it. That's about all we know."

Up popped support from Old Murphy Who Knows a Lot Cos He's Old. He cleared his throat and shuffled some pictorial notes. "I've recently heard from my friend from the Cockle Wits. It's all starting to tie in. The humans have built a giant building in the village by the stream and are making things with the flax. He says they're making things called sails, and says they are to drive the long ships along using the wind. He says that lots of ships are coming into the docks for new sails to be fitted, the canvas ones made in the new building, from flax." He looked at his notes. "This ties in. They've got to grow more flax as the ships come in for new canvas sails. That's what's happening. They'll plant all the fields with flax, eventually." He nodded with a solemn face, then sat down.

Jim stood up. "Thank you. It all seems to be making sense. The why's and wherefore's." He looked at Tommy and snapped his head upwards, as if to say 'get up and talk'. He was still waiting for word from his troops about the emergency packs.

Tommy stuttered. "I can tell you a bit about flax. We watched a massive field of it being harvested just last week." He thought carefully. He could feel the power of the communistic culture, and he knew that they would never be led by dictation, but only by agreement. They needed to be gently persuaded. He could feel them willing him on, 'Please tell us what we need to do' was what he could feel and he knew that he was their chosen leader, so, all he had to do was to let them follow. But did he want to lead them? He felt suddenly uneasy.

"Yes, the flax is big, entire fields, and if Mr Murphy Who Knows a Lot Cos He's Old is right, all the fields around here will go to flax. Including our forest. I'm sorry to have to report this." He felt uneasy about making decisions for them. What if he was wrong? "I suppose you're all frightened at what could be happening, but we honestly believe that it will happen. Over the next few days, we believe that the Irish Nettles will be taken to a place called Gaul. I don't know where that is.

"But we lived for a week in the hedges and you know what? I loved it. I didn't want to tell you, but I loved the feeling of freedom out in a place so big that there's room for all of us. The World is bigger than this forest and we may have to learn to love it, as we do this forest. Life can go on despite what it looks like right now and it can go on happily in the hedges around the flax. A new life for all of us." He grinned at the crowd. "What we saw was heaven."

He waited in case there was a response from the shell-shocked tribe. He felt uneasy and began to wish that somebody else would be leader. He needed some help, then he got a response.

Up stepped a young lady and all heads turned as she stood forward from her family. He had seen the girl before, but then she was just another child. What he now looked at was pure beauty. It was the first time in his life that he had noticed, or even seen, a beautiful woman. All girls were just people of the opposite sex, or his mum or his sister. Suddenly one was beautiful and he was struck. After a few long seconds, he was awoken by Dana's eyes drilling and burning into the side of his head. That spike of jealousy? He looked around to her and smiled, then remembered the thoughts that he had suffered over her and Phillips.

Dana quietly reminded him, "I think that young lady has something to say."

He snapped up straight. "Yes, sorry. What's your name?"

She nervously, but clearly, replied, "I'm Ty, from the North Hold, by the walnut tree. I'd like to say something, please."

Tommy agreed.

"Well, you've seen the flax. You've seen the hedges and the outside world and you've come back here with an opinion about that world. But, have you really understood that which Mother Nature has shown you?"

The beautiful girl was getting right inside Tommy's head. His first, his last, his everything. He was falling in love.

She continued. "Mother Nature is always proud to show her ways, and her secrets, and we all know that Mother Nature never lies. She does, though, speak many different languages, most of which we don't understand. So, Tommy O'Kief, have you really seen and understood? After all, we don't understand most of what she shows us, do we?"

He was becoming confused. He was at a meeting to discuss the possible end of a civilization, and here he was, falling in love with what seemed to be the reincarnation of Gayla. He looked sideways at Dana, then at Jim. They both supported him. He was not alone. He quickly realised that the entire tribe, down to the very last man, was waiting and watching, as the girl enchanted him.

He managed to talk. "I know that we don't always

understand her, but please give me an example."

The girl looked back at her family before replying. "I can. I can show just how things can look, but not be. The Robin, our friend who lives amongst us, cheers us on the cold days with his song and is the perfect epitome of peace and love. Robin redbreast. I've learned his language and he sings his heartwarming song, not to us, but to his own type, and this is his song."

She bowed her head to the chief, then to the crowd, then to Tommy, and smiled as she translated the cheerful song of Cock Robin.

"Cock Robins. Cock Robins. I bring, you no cheer.
> I'm the Cock of Cock Robins and my song is your fear.

If you dare to come calling, be clear in your head,
> I'm the Cock of Cock Robins and you'll likely be dead.

For my home is my castle, I'll kill for my crown.
> I'm the Cock of Cock Robins, I'll never step down."

She bowed to the auditorium then moved back with her family.

Poor Tommy, barely a man, found himself standing in front of the entire Nettle Wit population, who all expected much from him, and to make it worst, he had just been hit by his first ever love-lust. He began to sweat. What do I do? What do I do? His conscience gave him just two sensible, clear options; go and hide behind his dad, or support his dad by talking to the tribe. He chose the adult option, to support his dad and talk to the tribe. He had to be both brave and intelligent. He had to be what the chief was not. He had to be an inspiration.

He spoke slowly, deliberately, and with purpose. His normal flowing style of storytelling was not present, but of course this wasn't a story, it was real life and possibly real death.

"Thank you, Ty. True words of wisdom." He looked from Ty to his sister, then to Phillips. "I feel suitably put in my place. I'm a hopeless romantic, who sees the World from high up in the sky through rose coloured glasses. It's just like we see that cute and amiable Robin, who sits high on his favourite perch and thrills us with his pretty melodies of *threats*. We're Nettle Wits, we love to see the beautiful side, and yes, you're right, I haven't seen the World below the surface." He nodded in agreement. "The hedgerows are unknown, but they *are* an option now. The option? What option? Do we need to think of options? The answer is yes. The human farmers are going to take our forest. So what do we do now? I'll tell you my romanticised opinion and perhaps Ty can tell me if I'm wrong."

He waited for Ty to acknowledge. She did with an encouraging smile.

"In Ty's analogy the Nettle Wits were compared to Cock Robin, with an outward face of joy, happiness and contentment, but an inner face of rugged determination. We, like the Robin, will never step down."

He was boosted by the tribes acceptance, a welcome signal and open arms.

"But Cock Robin is a survivor. Only last year he was screaming his threats and challenges from his favourite perch when his challenge was accepted by a caller, Mr Weasel. Cock Robin gathered up his family, and moved them all around the corner. Despite his song, he stepped down to save his family and lived to sing another day. He was proud enough and he was brave enough to put aside his pride and do the right thing. Am I right, Ty?"

She stepped up. Like Tommy she was an equal adult, the same age as all the other adult Wits, but, only having been at that age for a very short while, her credibility was unproven. Sometimes that's the best place to be, with nothing to lose but pride. She spoke carefully.

"I'm sure the tribe will agree that there can be no pride to be enjoyed by fighting an invincible foe. And there is no shame to bear for making the correct decision. Cock Robin is a brave survivor. I think we both know that he was right and, equally important, still alive and happy in his new home." She gave Tommy a smile so deep that he felt he was drowning in love. She stood back with her family.

Jim jumped forward. "Does anybody else have anything to add to the meeting?" Nobody stepped forward, so he looked at the chief and then with the chief's permission, "I would like to make a proposal." He gave the chief a few seconds to respond. "In that case, I propose that we get prepared with immediate effect to leave the forest. We must be ready to go when the farmers start to fell the forest, possibly tomorrow."

He waited for any objections. Some murmuring started out, so O'Toole stepped forward.

"May I ask one question? What if they don't fell the forest?"

"Then we can return the emergency supplies, spend a day rebuilding the Centre Point, and have the biggest celebration ever known. But until then, we prepare and be ready."

The proposal went unopposed.

Between then and sunset, the Nettle Wits went into action. Every adult was issued with one of the new backpacks, complete with bags and ropes, and every individual was given an emergency survival blanket.

They were to collect any tools of their trades, and documents, and would meet at daybreak in the storage caves below the pigsty. The migration had begun.

CHAPTER 23
SNAKE HUNT

They all arrived at the storage caves just before the sun rose, and it was drizzling with rain. The water was running off the pigsty roof, but clearing the base of the wall by about a foot, leaving the wits ample dry area to distribute the salted meat preserves and alcohol.

The loose plan was to be ready to move off as soon as the felling began, and in the meantime, use that waiting time to discuss options. It was a very uncertain time.

The storage caves were about midway along the west wall of the pigsty (the back of the pigsty), so in order to keep early tabs on any movement by the human farmers, a pair of lookouts were placed at each end of the wall. The north, by the walnut tree, was taken by Phillips and his assistant and the other end, the south, by Tommy and Dana.

By the time the sun was up Mr Fuller was in with his pigs. The rain had stopped and the skies cleared, and it looked to be a good forest-felling day.

Tommy and Dana sat high in a sheep's parsley, just a little way from the forest to allow them clear sight of the entire southern part of the farm. When Eileen and the two children left the house, all was quiet, then a handcart arrived from the lane, pulled by Sean Doyle and one of his brothers.

The lookouts gave the call to the tribe, two whoops. It had been agreed that two would mean something is happening while three whoops would be an emergency. The tribe continued with their issuing of rations and alcohol, nervous of what was happening. Everybody was sombre.

Eileen joined Sean Doyle at the lane-end of the Meadow and then Mr Fuller wandered over. They lifted the two cases off the hand-pulled cart and placed them down by the wall of the house, then inspected the contents. Inside were several linen bags, each with a pull-cord closer, and a bundle of birch sticks about three feet long, each with a vee crotch on one end. Then on the handcart were three longer poles that had fine fishing nets on one end. The farmers were equipped for a job, but not nettle felling.

Captain Garibaldi had come to the north-east coast of Ireland via the iron works on Exmoor, and his mission, as always, was to trade. So, while he had his old, heavy, animal skin sails replaced for modern canvas ones, he took the opportunity to do some profitable business with the local wheeler-dealer or Mr Fixit, the man of Jesus, Father Patrick. On his way from Gaul to the Exmoor iron works, the captain had come across an area in the west, now known as the west coast of France, that had been inflicted with plague. But he never failed to spot the business opportunity. The only known protection from the dreaded plague was from the application of snakes blood to certain parts of the body, whilst drinking a potion which contained two drops of adder venom. In the year sixty-nine AD, there was no better way.

So the intrepid Father Patrick, trusted by all parties and paid well by all parties, had put the bundle together for the captain, which included the medical aid for the poor stricken sufferers on the west coast, namely a consignment of live adders and grass snakes. The team of farmers were preparing to capture all the snakes from the Fullers' farm. It was all part of the service, as prescribed by the representative of Jesus Christ, the capitalistic Father Patrick, Amen. God's servants move in mysterious ways, usually profitable ones.

Mr Fuller went into the barn with the two Doyle-boys and returned, each with a scythe. Whilst the three men whetted the scythes, Tommy and Dana panicked. They whooped the warning that something was happening, the three men representing a vision of Death as they honed their blades.

However, they never moved towards the forest, but onto the meadow, the adder country. Tommy whooped a temporary all-clear, and the tribe relaxed, just a little.

A strip of about three feet was scythed right close to the ground, across the entire width of the meadow and the hay taken by Eileen and the children to the pigsties. Nothing was wasted. Four strips were cut, dividing the field into four sections, ready for the beaters to begin. The grass along the strips was cut so short that nothing would be able to hide from the hunters, including the snakes.

As the scything was complete, the rest of the neighbours arrived, men, women and children, the same ones as had helped with the flax harvest, and Eileen organised them into a team.

Eight pairs of adults spread along the first cut strip, each pair with their sticks with a V crotch, and two bags, ready to intercept. Any snake which entered the bare strip would be captured. The snake would be pinned down in the V of the stick, then picked up by the tail and dropped into the bags. The adders and grass snakes were kept separate.

The rest of the team, a mix of all ages, lined up at the headland by the lane and spread out evenly. There were about thirty, so with a bit of a reach they could beat the entire width of the meadow in one sweep. They all had sticks and very, very slowly moved forward, towards the row of men on the strips, and they kicked, poked and bashed the grassland to drive the snakes towards the captors. As a snake entered the short grass of the strip the beaters were called to hold, until the snake was safely assigned to its bag. They then resumed.

It was a slow process. No snake was to remain uncaptured, money was at stake. After each section, the bags were emptied into the two wooden cases, one holding the adders, the other holding the grass snakes.

Tommy and Dana watched silently as the beat moved towards the first strip. It wasn't until the men caught the first snake that they realised what they were actually doing.

"Catching snakes," exclaimed Dana. "What for?"

They watched patiently for clues. Once the beat reached the first strip, they heard a call.

"Peewit."

The call came from down below, from amongst the nettle stalks at the edge of the forest. Tommy replied, revealing their position, with two peewits. It was Jim. He had left the rest of the tribe in the safety of the caves and joined his children.

"What's happening? Why the false alarm? Heard from Phillips, and nothing going on in the north."

The twins explained what they had seen. Dana then went on to say, "They must be catching the snakes so they don't get hurt when they plough the field. Must be relocating them, like we've got to leave, relocated." She felt that she wasn't totally convinced by her own presumptions. "Do you think they'd do that for us?"

Jim huffed. "Don't even know we exist. Probably for the best." He was thoughtful and understandably worried. "Your mum is with Mrs Phillips. They're sorting out what hand tools they can pack. Everyone is doing something, simply to keep their minds occupied."

Tommy, "You know, everyone will be safe in the caves. And anyway, they're gonna be doing this beat all day. They won't get onto our forest before tomorrow, so we could go back to our homes for the night." Jim agreed.

Tommy also suggested they slaughter some fresh meat and make sure no salted meat gets eaten until it was necessary, to conserve the emergency rations.

Jim confirmed. "Yeah, O'Toole's sorting that one." He went very quiet. After a while of watching, he spoke very softly. "Confidentially, I don't know where this will go. I'm scared. Never been scared before."

The twins each put a hand on his shoulder and comforted him silently.

He shook his head. "Chief thinks he's going to lead them to safety, but he hasn't got a clue. Not.... a.... clue."

Tommy looked out at the snake hunt. It was slow going and would certainly last all day. "We've got 'til tomorrow to make any decisions. Something will come up, always does, we're Nettle Wits." He laughed. "We'll never die. Not yet, anyway."

"Let's hope your youthful optimism is rewarded." He again went quiet. He almost said something, then thought better of it. Then, "What was it really like? Out in the hedges? Honestly."

Dana looked at Tommy and nodded, telling him that she was with him whatever he said. So, he answered. "Well, it was beautiful. Everything an adventurer could ever wish for. Beauty, variety, hustle and bustle, open space, food, everything except for Moors caterpillars. Well, we found the last of them. We all loved it, but, no Moors caterpillars. The only thing missing."

Dana thought aloud. "But could we live without them?"

Jim frowned. "Wherever we go we'll *have* to live without them. Wherever we go. The salted meat won't last long. Five months, I reckon. By Spring we'll be out."

Dana nodded. "We think we can live without them. But we don't know."

So, Jim looked them both in the eye. "What's wrong with the hedge life? You love it, but...."

Tommy pointed to the farmers. They had finished the first section. "Only three more to do." Then, he looked back at his dad. "But that really pretty girl, Ty, she knows. She put us in our place. The three of us were on holiday, we all had our holiday glasses on, seeing all the fun things and lovely sights. Once you've looked at a lovely sight for long enough, that becomes the norm. We didn't see past that point. We never saw the norm. We only got a fleeting look at the never-ending battle for survival, which rages below the surface. We never saw the struggle to survive. The winters, we never saw that biting wind, storm and rain, which would hammer those exposed hedges. We never saw the farmers cutting back their hedge growth for their wattle." He stopped, pointed back into the forest. "Ty's right. How could we lead the tribe to a place that we know nothing about? Could be leading them to their death. How could we do it? I don't want to lead them anywhere. Never. I'm not a leader and I think Ty knows it."

Jim and Dana pulled into Tommy for a family hug. They understood.

"We'll let the chief lead. That's what he wants to do, lead his people to the promised land. The chief, the elected leader."

They watched in silence as the farmers beat the second section.

Dana suggested, "They won't get to cut the forest today. We should go and tell them that they must stay in the safety of the caves overnight. Or tell the chief, then it's up to him."

Jim ordered, "Yes, let the chief lead. We'll just advise and my advice is to stay in the caves. But it may be safe at home, as long as we're all back in the caves at first light. They won't cut the forest at night, they're scared of the wolves."

Dana added, before they set off to join the tribe, "We watched three men with their scythes. If those three fell the forest, it'll be over in a couple of hours, maybe less. Anyone in the forest when it happens? Well, they'll fall with the trees."

CHAPTER 24
TY

By the time the three arrived back at the caves, all the issuing was complete. The entire tribe of about three hundred were loitering outside, as leprechauns never enjoy enclosed spaces, and the mood was sombre but noisy. A lot of ifs and buts were flying around.

Jim stood out in front of the group and explained what they had seen in the south and Phillips confirmed that nothing had so far happened in the north. It was, at that point, down to the chief to lead his flock.

The Wits were all loaded up. Every adult and most of the older children had a backpack filled with meat, preserves, alcohol and all sorts of hand tools, and every family had more than enough survival blankets for themselves and their children. Then many adults had a shillelagh and sling across their shoulders, and tool belts, complete with hand tools, around their waists. They were ready to move whenever the order was given.

The chief stood up with Hairy Daniels to his right and Nostradamus to his left. "General O'Kief suggests that the felling won't happen today, but we can't be sure. So I'm ordering that we stay here during daylight hours and if nothing has happened by sundown, we could, if we choose, go back to our homes. But we must all be back here before sunup tomorrow. I'll just say that the safest place to stay overnight would be the caves, but it's your choice. None of us really knows for certain."

It was agreed that the rest of the day would be an ideas studio. Anyone with suggestions or concerns were to give them to the top table for discussion. In the mean time, the tribe felt there should be a lookout at the south border in case things change. Tommy and Dana were the obvious choice.

"Hello."

Tommy swung around. He froze.

"Hello." It was Ty. "Can I come?" She wanted to go on look-out with the twins. "I won't be a nuisance, promise."

Tommy didn't know what to say, so Dana grinned at Ty and nodded. "Of course. We'd love to have you with us."

In the background, Mary smiled her approval.

So, half an hour later, complete with shillelagh and backpacks, Tommy, Dana and Ty were back in the sheep's parsley, observing the snake hunt. The beat was getting very close to the forest, but none of the beating-team were really close to the nettles, as Eileen had warned them not to damage the valuable crop. Even so, the three decided to move from their exposed vantage point to the edge of the forest canopy. They settled high in a nettle head.

"I'm Ty," she said very nervously to Tommy, and then turn to Dana. "from the North Hold."

Dana, who was not love-struck, acknowledged. "We know. You said yesterday, and I'm Dana and this is my brother Tommy."

Ty chuckled, not quite like a schoolgirl's giggle, but more of a dirty one, playful. "I know. Everyone knows you two. You go out the forest, you're famous." She looked Tommy in the face. "You're lucky getting out like that. I've never been allowed. This is about as far as I can go."

Tommy was tongue tied, so Dana had to carry her bashful brother. "This's as far as most Wits want to go."

"Yeah, but we're not all the same. When I get married, I hope it's to someone like us, who wants more than a farming life. Adventure."

Tommy suddenly kicked in. "Like us, we want to get out into the world, Me, Dana and Phillips. You're like us."

Dana leaned forward. "Aaron Phillips. Name is Aaron."

"I know. My dad sometimes works with him. Dad's in the Regiment, like I'm gonna be when I leave school. End of this autumn. Really soon."

Tommy, "I thought you were already an adult. The way you spoke at the meeting, you were really good, really elegant and beautiful. You know, your story." He stopped suddenly but thought all the time, looking at her wonderful features. Then he stated, "You're an adult who's the same as us. A new adult."

"I've got to leave school first."

"You have! You left yesterday if we move, and it looks like we will. There won't be school for ages, so you've left being the big girl, now an adult." He laughed. "You could do what you want from today, even get married."

She took a sharp intake of breath. "You proposing?" Then hid her face in a playful shyness. "Mr O'Kief, you're a fast worker!"

Dana just laughed, but looked at her brother exactly as her brother had looked at her a few times, while they were in the hedges. She pointed to the beaters. "Almost here. We ought to move somewhere safer."

They moved between nettles to a tall one, further inside the forest. They could still see the activities and most of the south meadow.

The courting atmosphere had been quelled, for now.

Dana helped her ailing brother, who was tongue-tied. "Our dad, the big boss of the Regiment. Does he know your situation? Does he know you want to follow your dad into the Regiment?"

"Don't know. Don't know if Dad's told him. Why?"

"Cos I could tell Dad, and tell him about your school situation. He might join you up now, even if it's on trial to see what happens to school."

With a smile from Tommy and a thoughtful nod from Ty, the conversation ended. Everything was quiet, even the snake hunt, which had stopped while the farmers ate and drank in the farmyard. It was early afternoon and the hunt was only about halfway through. Four men stayed in the second strip while the others ate, to ensure no snakes made their way back into the completed section.

Ty was a bit more forward in her chit-chat than both Tommy and Dana. She asked, "Would you really like to take a chance in the hedges? It'd be dangerous and a lot to learn. And what about Moors meat?"

Dana, "Once accustomed to other meat, I think we can live on it. Didn't always eat Moors, so must have eaten other meat a long time ago. Only thing is, we might lose our colour. That's what I think."

Ty nodded and looked to Tommy. "So if I changed colour, would you still fancy me?"

Poor Tommy almost choked, while Dana went into a fit of laughter. It took them right back to the hedge and Phillips, when he asked Dana exactly the same.

Tommy pulled himself together, coughed and with a straight face, told her, "Even more, if that's possible."

At that point she did change colour to bright red, almost the colour of her lips. She shyly looked away.

The two youngsters were saved from the expected ribbing from Dana, by a single peewit call. Somebody was looking for them, so Tommy replied with a location call.

After a few minutes, Jim joined the youngsters.

Dana gave a quick run down on what was happening before Jim explained that the tribe had come up with all sorts of ideas, but none definite. "Trouble is, it all depends on what the farmers do and when. A big feeling that is that the farmers are doing something with the snakes, and that's all. The felling of the forest and the flax are just false alarms. They're almost making each other believe it." He stopped and nodded to Ty. "Ty, can you really talk to Robins?" He waited for an answer, but none came, just a waving of the head. "Can I trust you with Regimental business? I need to know else you may have to leave our meeting."

Dana jumped up. "Ty wants to be in the Regiment, as you probably know from her dad. So sign her up now."

"Not till she's left school."

"Schools finished for now! There won't be school if we move, so she's left, so, sign her up temporary until we know what's happening with school. She's a good look-out, and she likes adventure."

"Do you want to do that, Ty? Is it what you want?"

She nervously confirmed. He shook her hand and welcomed her in as temporary member of the surveillance team. "You'll be working with these two, and Captain Phillips. I'll confirm with your dad later." He turned to Tommy, then Dana. "All right with that?"

The three young ones, each with perhaps a different agenda, nodded and pulled in for a team-building cuddle.

"Right," said Jim, "can you talk to the Robins?"

She carefully replied, "Of course not. I know what they mean when they sing, but no, I can't actually talk to them. Nobody can."

"Never mind. I was just hoping you might be able to help me. Anyway, thanks to Tommy's clever little moral boosting stories at the Holi, the tribe think I can talk to the adders. They want me to ask them what's happening. It might help us decide on what's gonna happen to us." He raised his eyebrows at Tommy.

"Sorry, Dad, I never thought it would matter."

The four sat deeply contemplating the dilemma, in that the tribe was expecting Jim to return with an answer as to what they were doing with the snakes, and that answer was to be straight from the adder's mouth.

Ty eventually broke the silence. "If you can't talk to the snakes, as we *all* know you can't, really, then ask the humans."

Well, the one and only idea that had come up, and it wasn't entirely stupid. Ask the humans. Simple. But it wasn't simple, and it was an idea that had been bandied about since the beginning of time, and the same old answer had always come up. He can't talk to nor trust humans. Leprechauns have never spoken to humans. In the human's minds, leprechauns don't even exists, they're just something to blame when things go missing.

Tommy put his finger in the air. He had had an idea. "Can't talk to humans, but we can go and listen to them. Me and Dana have learned a lot by listening. We could go and see what the talk's about."

So, General O'Kief gave the order for the two girls to remain on look-out while he and Tommy ran to the farm house to check on the snakes in the cases, and see what they could learn from the farmers. Eileen and the Doyles would be the main targets for their eavesdropping.

Before they left, Jim carefully spoke to Ty. "You know, now you're in the Regiment, you must never talk about our work to anybody outside the Regiment. Just like General O'Kief can't really talk to the snakes. Talking about that sort of thing is forbidden. Understand?"

She smiled at Tommy. "It's alright. Everybody knows that it's just a story. A modern legend, that's all. It would be daft to think that anyone can talk to a snake." She shook her head in wonderment. "So much for communal spirit and your tribal secrets, there probably aren't any. And Sir, can I just add that everyone knows about your CS and what you do. We all knew about the secret stash of bags and blankets, everybody knew."

On that note, the men set off towards the farmhouse. The beaters were still resting across the yard.

"I'm very impressed by your confidence out here." He put his hand on Tommy's shoulder. "You and Dana have grown up in front of us a lot more than we've even noticed." After looking up at the towering crates, he resigned himself. "Looks like you're in charge right now. What do you think?"

"Well, all we need to do is find out what they're doing with the snakes and where they'll release them, when they've sown the flax. Then take it from there." He took his backpack off and took out his ropes. One was long enough to reach the top of the case. "I'll climb up between the walls and case, and drop the rope for you."

The young climber was soon sitting on top of the wooden side of the case, and Jim followed up the rope.

They looked down into the prison. Adders, dozens of them, writhed around each other, panicking, frightened, attempting to reach up the wooden walls and then falling back onto each other, silently screaming for help. Tommy quietly said to his dad, "They don't know what's happening to them. They're so frightened. Never seen adders so afraid before." He could not look any longer.

Jim took him by the hand and they went back down to the ground. Once he had rolled his rope up Tommy gently said, "If the snakes do know what's happening to them, then it's not good. Tell the tribe just that."

The youngster led the way round the corner to the yard where the farmers and beaters relaxed. Then, just as they had settled in a crack in the doorstep, the commanding figure of Father Patrick towered above them. He was rattled and shouted at one of the farmers to get Eileen. She came out of the barn.

"Top of the morning, Eileen. Trust the snakes are plentiful." They went around the corner to inspect those in the cases. "How many more do you think?"

She came up with a rough estimate, and the Father grunted.

"About three days and the ship will be ready with its new canvas sails. It'll sail on the first wind after that, so make sure this is all down at the dock before it goes. And the nettles have got to be alive, remember?" He looked around. "Or else we'll have trouble."

As he said that, Sean Doyle's ears popped. He and Mr Fuller decided to join them. There was friction in the air.

Sean firmly told the father that they will keep their end of the deals. "Your other problems aren't anything to do with us. I did try to warn you the other day."

There was a bit of a standoff, so Eileen suggested, "Take a cup of nettle wine." They moved round to the yard, immediately in front of the two Nettle Wits.

Tommy jested, "Last time we were in these cracks Dana sat on my head. The girl stood directly over us with no knickers on." They both laughed.

Then, as the group drank their wine, Eileen's daughter and son approached them. The girl asked Father Patrick, "Will they kill all the snakes?"

The father put his hand on her head and told her, "Yes. And it'll save many lives. They'll do God's work by saving the people from the plague, then the people will eat the bodies with a Stew. They won't go to waste."

The girl turned away, trying not to cry.

Tommy also had to breathe deeply to avert the tears. They had learned the truth, all the snakes would die. He instantly became hostile towards humans and swung his shillelagh around his head, shouting "Murderers. Killers. May Gayla cut you all down." Pure naivety!

Jim led him towards the forest, taking a wide berth to stay clear of the executioners. During the forty minute walk, it was sad for Tommy. He knew so much about life in the world but had never really seen the truth. Ty certainly had a lot to teach him about romance and non-romance and everything in between. The storyteller was finally learning what a true story was all about.

They arrived back at the top of the look-out post, and Jim quickly reported to his staff that the snakes were all to be taken somewhere else, then killed. It seemed for medicinal purposes. The two girls were duly saddened.

"That's why leprechauns never talk to humans." Ty was surprisingly grown up about it. "As long as they don't know we exist, they'll leave us alone."

Tommy at last spoke. "How could they do it? Killing all the snakes in Ireland. Evil."

Jim stood up, making sure that his three staff took proper notice. "Look, this is life. When we go back to our caves we'll enjoy a meal of Moor's caterpillar meat, which was butchered, killed earlier. What's the difference? For one life to come, another has to go. You know what Gayla says about souls? One in, one out. That's life." Straight to the point. "Now, we've got our own issues, and if we don't take them seriously, we'll be joining the snakes in heaven. What do we do now? What do we tell the tribe?"

It was agreed that the truth-and-nothing-but was the best option. Jim did, however, suggest that he took the Heron option. That was, to tell the truth or tell nothing. The bit about talking to the snakes, they wouldn't even mention it.

That was what the tribe was told, that the snakes would be killed for medicinal use and the nettles would be kept alive, somehow, and it would all be delivered to the docks within three days. It left the Wits angry and at odds with their previous respect for humans.

The remainder of the day was spent by the tribe discussing options. Knowing that the snakes were condemned to death put a different atmosphere on the discussions, and some even spoke about burning down the farm house or poisoning the water in the stream and pond, and all sorts of shameful ideas, never before even being contemplated by peaceful Nettle Wits. But moods were changing.

The tribe mostly went home to their platforms overnight, with just a handful of families staying at the caves. In an effort to maintain some communal spirit, the pubs were opened and many attended. It could be the last time they did until the pubs reopened at the new home site. All in all, the evening was a bit of a closing down sale, the idea being to empty the shelves of anything that couldn't be taken with them.

In an effort to show some form of leadership, the O'Kiefs, the O'Tooles and the Phillips stayed in the caves, although they did all visit the pub in the east hold, and they discussed everything but the immediate issues. It was a night off.

Tommy was on edge all night, constantly watching the entrance for the new love of his life, but she had to do whatever her family was doing, and that night they wanted to see out the last evening in their own local, in the north. Whatever they all did, they did go to bed with some pretty intoxicated minds. Not the best, since they needed to be up before the sun.

Despite the intoxication, every Nettle Wit was present at sunrise in the caves. Most remained outside where the early morning light began to filter through, and where they felt more comfortable. The caves were damp and claustrophobic. They were never a popular place to be.

The early plans included lookouts in the north and south, while the rest worked out some form of agenda. The same two look-out teams volunteered.

"I'd much rather be out here," said Dana to Ty. "They don't need us to make plans."

Tommy, however, was not quite so sure. He felt that their experience in the world would at some point be invaluable. "Hope they don't make final decisions without us."

They watched as the Doyles and Fullers families tidied up on the south meadow. The actual snake hunt had been completed the night before, so they were moving to the north meadow, which was only about half the size and was expected to be completed by midday.

The three men cut two strips across the north and suddenly the village had arrived to beat the poor snakes into their clutches.

The big question on the Wits' minds was 'when and how will they cut the nettle forest?'

"Not much is going to happen here today. All in the north now." Tommy was stating the obvious as they looked out onto an empty Meadow. "What shall we talk about?"

The two girls looked at each other. They were beginning to build a relationship and Tommy had noticed and was a little jealous, so he tried to relate to Ty. "What did you do last night? We went to the east pub. I hoped you might turn up."

"Really?" She smiled at him. "I wanted to, but Dad had business to sort. Mum kept saying, 'let's go and see Tommy.' I wanted to."

Well, that was all he needed to hear. She did like him more than a little. Dana also noticed the bond growing.

All the different varieties of leprechaun pair for life, so once the partnership is made it lasts until one or both of the partners die. So, choosing that partner in the first place is very important. Also, due to the small communities, there have never been too many options for the youngsters, so it was important not to let that real opportunity slip. Think very carefully before committing, but don't leave it too long, or you'll live your life alone. Despite the enormity of the decision, there aren't any rules about mating and marriage. When you're big enough, you're old enough, but the general acceptance is that leaving school means three things, adulthood, marriage and babies. The three look-outs looked at each other.

Ty said, "My dad works with Phillips most of the time; he's nice." Ty raised her eyebrows at Dana. "What do you think of him?"

She ummed, then twiddled her fingers. She was very thoughtful. "Yeah, he's nice. We spent all week together in the hedges."

"Really? Tell me about it. Are you married?"

Tommy gaped at the question.

"Course not. We were working. And my chaperone kept an eye on us."

"No, I didn't! You make me sound like a jealous brother. Don't listen to her Ty, I never interfered."

"Did! You said that captains couldn't play with their privates else he'd go blind. And you stood up with your hand on your shillelagh. You were very gallant."

The two girls laughed together while Tommy tried to work out his next move.

Ty helped him out. "That was lovely, looking after your sister. Would you look after your wife so well?" She was teasing him, whilst at the same time giving him the open door. "A strong man like you, bet you'd stand your wife's corner. Always."

He relaxed and smiled at her. She was extremely pretty and sensual, and she was pressing all the right buttons. "I'd do anything for her." A few moments of silent smiles followed.

Dana, "You know, he was first called Tomikins. Dad was drunk when we were born, so Mum had the final say and we were Dana and Tommy. But you can call him Tomikins." They giggled at Tommy.

Ty, "Ain't it weird how dads are always drunk when the baby's born? When I was born, my dad was drunk, so, when I came out, he asked my sister what to call me and she was only a baby herself. She couldn't talk properly and her first ever word was pigsty, because we lived near it, but she could only say 'ty, so my dad laughed and said, 'alright, we'll call her Pigsty', 'cause that's what my sister was trying to say. Luckily, Mum put her foot down and called me Ty. Good job Mum was sober."

Tommy was getting deeper and deeper into the aura of Ty. He suggested, "Dana, why don't you go and look out with Phillips? We could stay here, not much happening."

She jumped. "No chance! You're on duty, so behave. There'll be no weddings today, not with all this going on."

The idea was shelved, but not forgotten.

After a little longer, they heard the peewit. Tommy replied and the caller soon located them. It was Jim and Captain Phillips.

"The work on the north meadow will be completed in about one and a half to two hours, and the tribe are pushing for some decisions. The human farmers could well be in the forest within a couple of hours. We all need some leadership."

Jim then said that the tribe was waiting for them, particularly Tommy, before making decisions as O'Toole had insisted that any decision's had to have his input. The chief was not happy to wait, but the tribe insisted.

"They all see something in you, Tommy." said Phillips.

They left the post and hurriedly made their way back to the caves. Everybody was waiting.

"Right." The chief stood between Nostradamus and Daniels. "We now have a serious option. The farmers all agree that the Moors caterpillars will hang on like limpets. They'll never fall off. So, where the nettles go, the caterpillars will go. General O'Kief says that the farmers are to keep the nettles alive, so if the nettles and caterpillars are going, why don't we go, all of us, with the nettles? Start again with the forest in a different place." He looked around. "Any comments?"

The twins and Ty stood by Phillips as Jim stepped forward. "I have one. Will the soil and the climate be right for the nettles? Could be even wetter than here, and emerging butterflies can't handle rain on them. We could end up with a nettle forest and no caterpillars, or worse. It's a massive risk."

Murphy stepped forward. "The nettles will be taken on a ship, could be for weeks. Now, my Cockle Wits friend has told me about sea water. It'll kill you quicker than thirst, if that's all you've got to drink. So, how would we survive?"

Tommy stepped forward and Dana joined him, holding his hand. "We've seen the hedges, we've seen the beautiful side of life out there and Ty is right, we haven't seen below the surface. And there's no Moors meat out there, but we have seen these things. And we've eaten some of the things and we wouldn't all die just trying to get there. But the Gaul options, who knows? It could be desert, mountainside, swampland, or even worse, city life. Nobody knows, but at least the hedges are right here and we know they have most of what we need."

The chief stood up. "The options are full of dangers, both options. But the Gaul option at least gives us a chance of nettle forests, Moors meat and our civilisation carrying on where we leave off here. It has a promise of paradise."

The man was a dreamer. He should have stuck to making calendars, but he was the chief. He raised his arms in the air. "Now, if we go to Gaul, we need to leave now. It'll take three days of hard walking to get to the docks before the ship leaves. We need to decide now."

Tommy raised his hands. "I don't agree that we should go. It's all or nothing. No second chances, no nine lives, all....or....nothing."

Chief shouted, "Listen to him! He thinks he can challenge the chief, not even out of nappies and is raising his arms to the tribe. Is that a challenge?"

O'Toole grabbed Tommy and pulled him back. He stood forward in his place. "The chief is losing it, as Nettle Wits have never worked like that. Never have, never will. And Tommy is not challenging the chief, but the chief *is* being challenged by true Nettle Wit democracy. You, Chief, have been challenged by the tribe. That's how we work. None of us will follow you to Gaul, we'll only follow the tribe. So tribe, who votes to *not* go to Gaul? Hands up."

The entire Defence Regiment raised their hands, not to go, along with a few of the farmers. After a quick count the vote went sixty-eight percent in favour of going to Gaul. O'Toole ordered the second of the three votes.

"The chance to change your minds."

The second vote returned seventy-one percent in favour of Gaul. Two out of three. For the decision to be made without further discussion, it needed to be three from three. It went sixty-five percent in favour of Gaul.

The chief was smug, an indication of his own insecurities

and probably his inability to lead.

O'Toole stated, "The decision is to go to Gaul! We all go to Gaul, so prepare to leave now."

Tommy stepped up and stood beside O'Toole. "No! The vote was to go to Gaul, but only if we have to, and not until we have to. At the first emergency meeting, it was unanimously agreed that if the forest is *not* cut down, we'll put away the backpacks and party. Well, the forest hasn't gone yet and could never go. What if Captain Garibaldi gets squashed by a carthorse? Or arrested and the order gets cancelled. Anything's possible. So we should do as the chief suggested, go with the nettles, quite literally go with them and *stay* with them." He looked at the chief, who was starting to boil, and nodded. "We've ridden the carts when out in the world. We rode on a cart. We should go on the cart with the nettles, if they go, and we'll be at the docks in one hour instead of three days. And all we have to worry about is not falling off. Wait for the nettles to be cut, then stay with them. Any objections?"

There were none, not even the top table. The tribe was following Tommy without even realising it and it was a real shame that Tommy had to follow the tribe to Gaul, but wherever they went, they all went. Their own God given, unwritten rule. All or none.

The snake hunt in the north was complete by early afternoon. From that point onwards, the tribe were on tender hooks, just like Eileen's woolen cloth, hung out to dry. They were nervous and agitated, snapping at each other, screeching at the children, and pacing and pacing…..

Jim ordered look-outs at both the north and south, so the usual suspects were rounded up. He commanded Captain Phillips and Dana to the north, and Tommy and Ty to the south. He had split the twins.

The human farmers downed tools as soon as the snakes were all captured and moved into the yard. Before the helpers went back to their own farms, Eileen laid on food and drink, the usual formality when their community worked together. One of the Doyles produced a stoneware flagon of alcohol and the party caught alight. The flagon contained alcohol from the farm downhill and was the new local tipple, made by fermenting barley or rye, then stilling to extract the pure alcohol. It was one of the reasons why the local shine had gone off the nettle wine. It was the very early days of the Irish whiskey industry.

It was strange how the humans had taken so long to perfect the art of distilling alcohol, something that the Nettle Wits had been doing for hundreds of years.

Anyway, to the look-out posts. They looked out on empty meadows, and Tommy nervously said to Ty, "Wonder why Dad split me and Dana. Never done that before."

"Because before, I wasn't here." She looked along to the cases by the farm house. "Must be hundreds of snakes in there, all panicking, all waiting to be killed and potioned and then eaten. So sad."

He thought for a while. "It's part of the cycle of life. Mrs Adder told Dad that you can't really save a life, all you can do is move the death. If they didn't use these snakes for their potions, they'd find some others to use. Either way they'll free up a load more souls for the newborn." He nodded. "That's what Mrs Adder told Dad."

She moved her hand over to his and dropped her head a little, looking at him through her eyebrows. "But it's not true, is it?"

"Is. They'd find other adders and kill them instead. Just move the death onto them."

"But it's not true, Mrs Adder never said that, did she?"

He stuttered. "No, not exactly. Not actually her."

"I know. Everyone knows, they all know that it's not true, but they all believe it. That's us, believers. But who did say it?" She inched closer. "You said it. It's all you , and the whole tribe admires your imagination and storytelling, inspiring people and spreading that feelgood thing. It's all good what you say. That's why I love you, amongst other things, and I want to be part of you." She inched really close. "Marry me, now."

His heart missed a beat, then another one and sweat appeared on his brow.

"No." He took a deep breath and hurriedly added. "Yes, yes. Please. Please, please, please. But not now. Dad'd kill us. We're on duty."

She pulled into him and blowed into his ear. "You know, lover, you know lots about this and nothing about that. You need me. We need each other." She stroked his sweating head. "That's why I love you, because you need me. Did you know, I don't just understand what Cock Robin says? I can also understand the howls of the wolves. Our families are just the same as the wolf packs; the bitch is always the boss. That's why your dad sent us here together, Tomikins, because the bitch ordered it, so don't disappoint her, don't disappoint your mum. She's expecting, and she's told your dad what she expects." She pulled on to him and pinned him to the nettle leaf. "Marry me," she growled. "Now!"

The human helpers had all dispersed towards home and the Fullers and Doyles considered their next job, that of felling the nettle forest.

They collected up all the sticks and nets, carefully lifted the two cases onto the hand truck, then pulled it along to the northern edge of the forest. The cases were now quite heavy, but by carefully positioning them over the axle, the cart balanced. They discussed how much more would safely load onto the trucks and weren't very happy with their estimates. "Not enough." Then they went off, out the front and along the lane towards Doyles farm.

Tommy and Ty were visited by Dana and Captain Phillips.

The captain carefully ordered Tommy, "Tommy, I need to show you something over there, in that other nettle."

The two men climbed across the two nettles to the one which Phillips felt was far enough away. Then he shyly said, "Well, brother, you'd better call me Aaron from now. Brother!"

He had married Dana. They both jumped as Tommy reported, "Same here."

Mum had done her magic. All they had to do was to tell the tribe. It's a bit like Cock Robin, shout the good news to the World, whilst instilling that underlying threat, which translates to, "They're ours. Hands off, or else."

Nettle Wits are funny things. Once they know that the pretty girls are married, they look at them through their other glasses, the ugly glasses. It saves a lot of fights.

Then the Doyles and Fullers returned from the lane, pulling a larger, double-axle cart, which was designed to be pulled by four people. They pulled it down past the farmhouse and parked just at the entrance to the pigsty, by the pond. Two hand forks were taken from the back, a bundle of loosely woven linen, and a ball of twine.

Phillips gave three whoops, the emergency call. He ordered Dana and Ty to hurry back to the caves to let the tribe know what was happening, and he then gave the signal again. This time, they had an acknowledgement. Tommy and Philips moved to the ground and headed towards the safety of the base of the pigsty wall. They waited right on the corner, from where they could see towards the cart, as well as into the forest. All they could do was wait.

Eventually, Dana and Ty returned with Jim and two farmers. They all had their packs, belts and shillelaghs on, ready to leave at the signal. First, though, they really needed to do a recci of the cart to determine best access, and travelling positions. Tommy, Phillips and one of the farmers moved off towards the cart along the wall. The wheels were dirty and clogged up with dry mud, making it easy for the three to climb and they soon sat on the low side panel, looking across the platform. It was much larger then they had expected, and a lot, lot bigger than the one they experienced on the field.

The gap between the side panel and the platform was small enough not to be a falling hazard and they were all used to heights and hanging on, so they couldn't see any problems.

They arrived back to the girls just as the Doyles and Eileen arrived, forks in hands. Ty was sent as a runner to warn the tribe to be up and ready at short notice.

The two Doyles stood right on the edge of the forest and inspected the plants. They both held a hand low down and with an upward sweeping movement, grabbed a handful of plants. The upward movement prevented the stinging hairs from sticking into their skin. Eileen tried a couple, no stings.

Then Eileen dug the fork in and loosened the soil, one of the men pulling out a handful of plants. They knocked some of the soil off but left a small amount around the roots, then laid the plants onto a square of linen. The root end was on the linen. They repeated the operation several times until they had a reasonable sized sheaf of nettles and carefully wrapped and tied the cloth around the roots. They agreed that the size of sheaf was about right for handling. They stepped back and looked at the task ahead of them. "It'll take at least the rest of the day, plus all day tomorrow, to bundle up the entire patch." It was a big nettle patch.

The Wits agreed that they would need to get onto the cart later the next day.

As horrible as the situation was, they did at least have a timetable and the inevitable knowledge that the felling had begun. They were no longer in doubt that they were to leave.

Was this the end of an era, or the end of a civilization? It could have even been the start of something good. Nobody knew.

CHAPTER 25
SAILING

By the evening, the team of fellers had worked their way
through about a third of the forest. Most of the South Hold
had gone as well as parts of the East and West. It was the
saddest sight the tribe had ever experienced. They were
stunned. The hundreds of years of management had been
undone in a few hours and they looked out from under the
pigsty across the expanse of lightly dug bare soil, as far as the
blackthorn hedge, and with every pull of the stems, the
wasteland grew.

So, the distraught Wits finally knew for certain! They
would be on the cart by the next evening. They tried to relax
in the late evening, once the farmers had retired to the safety
of their homes, but it was hard. Relax? How does a
civilization of hundreds of years relax as they witness the
destruction of their homes, lands, heritage, food and
everything else? All that was left to prove that the Nettle
Wits' forest had ever existed were the memories, a few
hieroglyphs but not many, and about three-hundred green
leprechauns. That was all, apart from their own resolve.
"We'll never die!" shouted O'Toole.

Another chapter in the history of the world was about to
close, and a new one begin. As with all new chapters, nobody
really knows where it's going apart from The Almighty, but
even she takes it all as it comes, then goes forward
accordingly. She gave the tribe abundant rain to contend
with, and she sent them Common Nettles to steal the lands
from the Irish, and now she sends them the human
bandwagon, which rolls on-and-on, over everything that gets
in its way. "We'll slaughter ten caterpillars to feast on, on this

dreadful evening." The temptation was to curse their beloved Gayla in their grace, but very few were brave enough, so they thanked her.

The next day the human team completed their daily routine tasks before getting back into the felling. The Wits sat around and watched. Then Murphy convinced them that they needed to pack more water bags for the sea journey. They were all hoping that it would rain all the way, after Murphy again reminded them that they would die if they drank sea water, and the chief told them that paradise waited at the other end. It was all a leaderless mess, not surprisingly, as everything that day was plain and simple bad, emotionally hard, unrehearsed, unconsidered and unforgiving. It all seemed to be gone, except for the dejection which accompanied, as the nettles were pulled up, the sheafs wrapped up, the carts loaded up, and the leprechauns fed up. Then, before the sun finally set on the Kingdom of the Wits, they were all up on the platform of the cart, below the sheafs of Irish Nettles and Moors caterpillars.

They spent the night on the cart, wrapped in their survival blankets and all dreaming of various things to pass the time. But it all ended when the sun rose.

"Now, do we have everything? asked the chief.

Whatever they didn't have, they would go without. It was surprising just how much food, salt, alcohol, and equipment they had to leave behind in the caves. They were full, not only with salted and preserved meats, but also stocks which were being built up for trade with the Cockle Wits. They had to leave it all behind because they just could not carry anymore. It is very unusual for a Nettle Wit to cry, but some cried.

The tribe was safely camped along the base of the side-panels, and were cut off from the outside by the cart and the load, the sheafs being quite tightly packed above them. They could see none of the outside as it went by, and even the leading hands were wary of even trying to look. All they could hear was the rattle of the smaller cart and the chatter of the

Doyles boys.

Sean Doyle could be heard criticising Father Patrick. "I hope we don't live to regret getting involved with that wide boy. He's a bad one, to be sure. Just have a nagging wish in my heart that the boy had never hidden his sister's knickers. The bible-basher would have never turned up, and we'd be just as we were a few weeks ago, happy."

His brother replied, "But he did, and we're changing. Too late to gripe!"

The carts were soon rolling into the town, and many other strange noises wafted into the Wits' heads. They could hear chickens and ducks squabbling over their morsels, and dogs barking, and people chattering, then a smithy swung his hammer several times, just as the carts' wheels hit the metalled road surface and rattled. It was all very alien.

Suddenly, as the cart drew to a halt and the rattling wheels silenced, a new noise became dominant; the noise of the waves against the quay. They had arrived.

As the hustle and bustle went on outside, the Wits waited. Nothing happened. They waited. Noise happened, banging happened, chickens and ducks shouted at each other, and humans laughed, some swore, but nothing happened. They waited.

Eventually, Jim sent word along the line of Wits that they would go up and take a look.

Jim, Tommy and O'Toole climbed to the top of the side-flaps and peered over the side. They saw the Doyles pushing their way into a bar, which was heaving with traders, marketeers and sailors, and the beer flowed.

Tickled, Jim grinned, "They're as bad as us."

They looked out from the side of the cart, partly obscured by overhanging nettles, and could see a World that only a handful of Wits had ever seen, the human town. The road was metalled with stones from the beach, and the houses crammed together, some stone built, but mostly daubed and washed with white lime. The air was heavy with the sweet smell of burning peat, which wafted from the buildings. Nice to look at, but not safe for one the size of a leprechaun, crush hazards everywhere. The three of them instantly thought of home.

Close to the cart, which was seemingly parked for the duration, was a stack of wicker baskets. A dog was poking his nose into the base of one of the baskets, but suddenly yelped in disgust and moved away.

"Peewit!" came the sound, a familiar sound.

The three Wits sat up high on their ledge, and stretched their heads around. "What's that?" whispered Tommy. He put his hands to his mouth and replied. "Peewit, peewit."

A single call again came from the basket, then out stepped a strange little man. He was one of the little folk and was bright orange, blending nicely with the wicker ware, but they could definitely see him. It was a Cockle Wit.

O'Toole hung over the inside of the cart and called to the group. "Murphy, get up here. You need to translate!" He looked back at the tiny orange figure amongst the baskets, then swung back to the cart. "The rest stay there. I'll let you know what's happening."

Murphy scrambled up the splintered side and peered towards the Cockle Wit, who was too far away to talk to, so he waved his hands for him to come closer. At that point, a second Cockle Wit stepped out from the wicker, they looked around to ensure that the coast was clear, then rushed towards the cart. A minute or so later, they were standing at the base of the wheel.

Murphy shouted down. "Weaver! How the hell are you?"

Weaver replied, "Top of the morning, Murphy. Been expecting you." He was the older of the two.

The two Cockle Wits waved them down, as they were not prepared to go up, in case the cart left with them inside, so the green folk looked at each other and Jim ordered the descent.

O'Toole poked Murphy on the shoulder. "I heard that.

Thought you said they spoke their own language."

"They do. It's the same as ours. We share." The wily old schoolteacher suggested, "Always remember, knowledge is power." He tapped his nose.

They got to the ground and the Cockles welcomed the Nettles with open arm gestures, then took them under the cart towards the opposite wheel. The pebbled road was slow going, but after a few minutes, they arrived. They warily peered over the rim of the wheel, towards the sea.

Directly in front of them was nothing but ocean. Just a sixty minute walk and they would be over the edge of the quay, and just a ten mile walk and they would be over the edge of the World. They were awe inspired at the endless expanse of ocean and air.

Then to their right, a ship was moored. It was wooden, almost as wide as it was long, with a single mast and a dirty, animal skin sail tied up high, to the single spar. The square-rigged ship was being unloaded. The cargo was packed in sacks, and looked heavy, which was alum from Great Britain and destined for the linen factory where it would be used to fix the natural dyes to the cloth.

Then a little to the left, another ship was moored, and it was even bigger. The wooden hull was quite new and the massive mast had two spars stretching out from it, each with a bright white linen sail tied up to it. They were brand new sails, recently fitted by the linen factory, and the ship was the biggest thing the Wits had ever seen. It was named The Saint Patrick.

Murphy's friend Weaver told them that the giant ship was the one going to Gaul. He asked how the Nettle Wits planned to board the ship.

O'Toole answered, "Our first thought was to climb into the sheafs and go on with the nettles. Stay with them."

Weaver shook his orange head. "Oh no, no, no. Bad idea, to be sure." He shook his head several times. "Real bad idea. Don't let them do it, Murphy."

As they wondered what he meant, Weaver turned back towards the smaller ship. The sailors were carrying the sacks of alum on their shoulders, down the gangplank. They were in a hurry, wanting to get a fast turn around and not miss the tide, and be getting back to Great Britain.

"Look over there." Weaver pointed to a pile of bundles. The bundles looked like bales of woolen material, not very big. There were about twenty. "When they load the wool for their return load, you watch."

Jim and Tommy were keeping quiet, allowing Murphy and O'Toole to handle the locals. They all waited to see what they did with the woolen bales.

As they waited, Weaver told them that they'd heard about the nettles and snakes going abroad, and so guessed that the tribe would be with them. "So we're worrying," he told them, "how the Cockle Wits will suffer by not getting the sugar, alcohol and pelts each year. We'll probably have to steal the alcohol from humans." He was not sure about how to get the sugar, as humans had not yet developed as as far as the leprechauns. "Still like dinosaurs." They all had a strained laugh, then he warned them about drinking sea water, and he told him that when they go right out, over the edge of the World, they would not really fall off. Then, with a frown, he said they hadn't yet worked that one out. "But not to worry."

Then the sailors finished unloading the alum, and the boss ordered the wool to be loaded.

"Watch!" said Weaver. "This'll be like your nettles. They'll load them the same way."

The very first bale was lifted up above the sailors head, taken to the edge of the quay, then tossed through the air onto the ship where it was caught by another sailor, who, in one movement, swung round and threw the bale down into the hold.

That was why. They would never hold on. They would all be in the sea, washed away with the Gods, never to be seen again.

"Good job you're here." Tommy stressed. "We'd all be lost."

They all looked left to their ship, The Saint Patrick. They'd have to go on separately from the nettles. The caterpillars would be able to keep hold, but the Wits would never stand a chance. Only connections between the quay and the ship were the gangplank and four very heavy mooring ropes. At each rope was posted a sailor.

Weaver advised, "The gangplank is always busy. Could be dangerous for so many of you. Now, the ropes. That's the way the rats and mice get on and off the ships, but the sailor is there to keep them off. They eat the cargo, so they'll hit them with their batons. They don't like rats on their ships." He stopped to think, and his mate nodded. "Now, the sailor probably wouldn't notice you lot, too small, but you stand the risk of being tipped off and into the sea if you go at the wrong time."

He had a whispering session with his mate, then he continued. "The main job of the sailor is to loosen or tighten the rope when the tide goes up or down, so if you go just after he has adjusted the rope, you'd have at least half an hour before he needs to touch it. That's the way to go, straight after he's adjusted. And the best one to go up is the one in the middle, nearest the plank, the other end, that's where you'll find the nettles once you're on.

"The walk along the rope will be dangerous, and when the tide his high or low, the gradient of the rope is steep. But you live in trees, off the ground, and I could see no real problem so long as the sailor leaves the rope alone while you're on it." The plan was made.

They left the Cockle Wits on the ground and went back up into the cart to make arrangements. The chief seemed none too pleased that he was not in the driving seat, but he secretly felt a lot easier as a passenger. He would have found more respect if he had admitted that to the Wits. The tribe slowly descended from the cart, all loaded with backpacks, shillelaghs and tools, and carrying the smallest children when required. Most were noticeably afraid of the unknown ahead of them.

The walk to the rope would take at least an hour or so, so they had no time to waste. Weaver and his friend selected a route which took them off the cobbles and along soil and weeds, a longer walk, but much easier to negotiate and away from the feet of humans and animals. There was a feeling of panic amongst the Wits.

They had been on the march for no more than fifteen minutes when the Doyles emerged from the pub and pulled the small handcart to the gangplank. The sailors quickly lifted the two chests onto the ship via the gangplank, then began tossing nettle sheafs up to their comrades. It took only a few minutes to clear small cart. They then moved the big cart a little closer before unloading the nettles and tossing them up onto the ship. Suddenly the Doyles were gone, pulling the two carts away from the quayside.

Weaver urged the Nettle Wits to hurry, to catch up with the nettles, and they all steamed along the dirt and mud. Then Captain Garibaldi appeared. He stood at the gangplank, waiting for something. The Wits were tempted to stop and watch, but Weaver urged them on.

Then Captain Garibaldi shouted out orders to his men, who cleared the way to the gangplank as a group of soldiers entered the quay from the town and they were on official duty. They were smartly dressed in their green tunics, pikes at the ready, and were escorting a prisoner to the ship to be removed from the land and banished to Gaul.

The prisoner was shackled at the ankles and pushed along by the soldiers' pikes, and he had been punished by the locals. His hair had been cut off, his head painted with tar and then covered with white duck feathers. He had been tarred and feathered for his crimes.

Tommy and Dana almost choked when they saw the prisoner. It was Father Patrick!

Nobody will ever know why. It could have been his wheeling-dealing gone wrong, or his constant bashing of the Bible in front of their own Gods, or could have been Gaul who wanted him back for earlier crimes. Nobody will ever know, just that it was, and it did.

Dana whispered to Tommy. "Serves him right. He's destroyed us." Deep down, she knew that it wasn't just him that was guilty.

It was perhaps poetic justice, and being deported on The Saint Patrick suggests that the almighty Gayla may well have played her part. She moves in mysterious ways. It was well worth the 'thank you' at their last grace.

The tribe was about halfway, still at least half an hour away, and the Cockle Wits constantly urged them on. Weaver was beginning to push a little harder and with a little more desperation. They ploughed on.

Captain Garibaldi began shouting. He stood at his gangplank with his first mate and looked at the flag on top of his main mast. It was blowing out towards the horizon. Then the smaller ship began ringing its bell and their sailors rushed around to complete their tasks, and they released the mooring ropes. The smaller vessel's gangplank was pulled in and its oars poked out from the port holes, pushing the small ship away from the quay. It slowly moved out towards the open sea, powered by the oars, before dropping its animal-skin sail. It was away with the tide and wind.

Weaver began to panic some more. Then, as a bell began to ring from The Saint Patrick, he stood with his arms in the air. The tribe stopped in their tracks.

With pure panic in his voice, he shouted. "Stop! No closer."

They all froze as they looked across the cobbled quay at the mooring rope towards which they were marching, and it was released. It slid over the side of the dock and the sailors pulled it up onto the ship. The other three ropes were pulled in and then the gangplank, as the bell continued to ring. Very slowly and very deliberately, The Saint Patrick moved away from the quay, with the tide, and the oars appeared from the port holes. The ship was manoeuvred out, to point towards the open sea, the two new sails were dropped and they filled with the westerly breeze. It was off.

The Nettle Wits were shocked. Nobody said a thing as the giant Saint Patrick left Ireland for the promised land in Gaul, without them. The nettles went, they didn't.

Some of them began wailing. Others cuddled and comforted them. Some began throwing stones across towards what was by then an imaginary ship. None of them knew what else to do.

Weaver was wary of saying anything. He looked at Murphy, who looked at Jim, who looked around at his team. Then they looked at the chief. "Well?" asked O'Toole.

The chief shook his head. He pointed at Murphy. "Why didn't we go with the nettles?"

An angry grumble moved through the tribe. They could all see where most of them would be as soon as the sheafs were tossed. One man shouted to the chief, "You're pointing your finger in the wrong direction. Turn it on yourself, you led us here." He moved towards the chief, but one of the Regiment stood in his way. Things were in danger of turning nasty, they had just waved goodbye to the last of their civilization. It was gone, without them.

An unexpected voice raised. Ensuring that all could hear her, Ty screamed, "Don't start blaming each other! We all know what led us here, the tribe, the vote. So don't any of you start acting like shits, because we *all* decided to come here." She looked around at the shocked faces. "No, we lost our forest when that Bible basher turned up. And it didn't just go today, it went days ago, and all we had to do was to let go. Now we've *got* to let go! Move on. Move on against the world and hope we never see another the likes of Father Patrick. Move on again, but this time, let's be realistic. We belong here in these hills, not in Gaul. I think Gayla has made her point, so now let's take note!" She just stopped.

Right across the group, the faces began to smile. A realisation had hit them, one that they had not properly considered, and it had taken the wisdom of a fifteen-year-old newlywed to show them the way. They lived in the hills, nowhere else, these hills above the sea-level of the township, away from the industry of man, free from fear of salt water, and amongst true friends. They all dreamed of the very first pub to open in their new homeland, not a million miles from their old one.

"We just need one thing now," said did one of the women.

O'Toole humoured her and politely suggested, "Please tell us what that is."

She laughed as she spoke. "Guidance, that's what we need! None of us knows enough to vote for our future, and that's why we're here, because we're guided by ourselves, a committee of pure amateurs. So, guidance from Tommy O'Kief. That's what we need!"

They all nodded in agreement as Tommy shook. Was this his call? Was this the real one?

CHAPTER 26
GAOLERS

All eyes were on Tommy. Ty pulled into him and supported him with every sparkle of her soul, and his family gathered around, including Aaron who held tightly onto Dana. He was not alone, but he was scared.

This was not like the times when he spoke at the meetings. Then he was giving his opinions and they all considered his opinions. But now? Now they were waiting for instruction from their chosen leader. The chief was no longer head of the table, he had been dethroned, and when Tommy looked at him, he dropped his head. Could he accept the role? No, he didn't deserve it.

Dana whispered. "No rush. We're here with all our supplies."

So Tommy took the hint. "Right. We're where we are and have nowhere to go! So no point in hurrying there. We have time to think this time around. So, we need to set up camp somewhere safe and carefully consider our lot." He scanned the attentive faces. "But before we search out a camp, I need to know something. What I need to know, and what you need to tell me, is, 'when The Saint Patrick sailed without us, what did your heart say?" He hesitated. "Because mine said 'yes, yes, yes, saved!'"

They all huddled around in groups, then members moved from group to group, putting their thoughts together. Eventually, the original spokesman, the woman, stood up to speak for the others. She coughed to clear her throat before announcing, "We thanked Gayla. Now we should listen to her, we should stay in our own world." She looked around her. "We think we've had a narrow escape. We think we should count our blessings and go to the hedges, like you suggested. That's what we think." She bowed her head, then sat.

Weaver, the orange Cockle Wit, stood up and held his arms out. "Friends, you've missed your boat. Perhaps for the better, but perhaps not. You need to go back to the hedges, *today*." He looked at his younger friend, who nodded. "Yes, you need to get back to the hills, away from here, and you need to go now." He then turned to face Tommy. "Who's your chief? I've become confused, so tell me please. It's important, so answer wisely."

Reality was starting to bite at Tommy's conscious understanding of life. He felt like clamming up, hiding, running away. He held even more tightly onto Ty's arm, and she winced. Eventually, Ty had to pull him out of it.

She answered "Chief O'Hoolihan, over there. Until there's an election, he's our chief." She looked nervously around at her extended family, who all silently acknowledged. "You need to discuss whatever your concerns are, with Chief O'Hoolihan," She suddenly remembered, "and his committee, his team."

In just a few minutes, the new mood had hit the camp. It is often said that to forget your past disappointments, concentrate on your current concerns. That was a fine attribute in the Nettle Wits' arsenal of defences, and they instantly stopped pining for the forest and began worrying about Weaver and his words of wisdom. Go back to the hedges today, now. Why so urgent?

Weaver asked the chief, "Can we talk?"

They moved sideways, away from the edge of the quayside towards the rough, and found a place to sit; the chief, Weaver and his comrade. Then the rest of the top table joined them, then the Defence Regiment, then the leading hands in the industries, i.e. farming, tanning, butchery, sugar, refining and distilling, and by the time they were settled, about a quarter of the tribe were present.

Weaver frowned. He looked at Murphy and said to his old friend, "Better explain your politics to me. I don't understand." He looked at Chief O'Hoolihan. "Can you speak for your tribe? Are you in charge?"

The chief carefully replied. "I'm the spokesman. I decide what the tribe want me to decide. It's our way, like the ants, one mind in many bodies." The chief looked at his team of about seventy-five Wits. "You can talk to us all."

Weaver acknowledged with a puzzled air. "Then, let's talk." He held his hand sideways to his orange comrade. "My son. I'd trust him with my life, so we can talk in front of him, but please keep your voices as low as you can. They can see us, but not hear us. That's important."

The tribe were feeling that mood change deepening. Little signs raised questions that the peace loving Nettle Wits had never needed to answer before, such as why would he make a point that he would trust his own son with his life, when they would trust any tribe member with theirs, without even a second thought? And why did they need to get away so urgently? And surely all tribes share the responsibility of decisions, and who was watching them and why? This was like an alien world to the naive green folk from the hills. What was happening? And then, why would Weaver think that they may have been better off on the ship?

Tommy, although he had not been elected as chief, took the lead. "We suddenly feel threatened, Weaver. Can you please explain?"

He was pleased to, and spoke with an urgency. "I will. Because of my friendship with Murphy and our annual dealings, you know, salt and alcohol, et cetera, I was ordered by our chief to meet you here and help you get onto the ship." He hesitated, then. "Sorry. I was ordered to make *sure* you got onto the ship, and I failed. Now, you all need to get out of here, now. You're not welcome. You must get out, right away, before it's too late."

Although only a quarter of the tribe sat around their host,

the entire tribe heard the brief statement from the Cockle Wit. Without explanation, Weaver was ordering them out of the town. Fear began to fester.

Weaver added, "You'll never survive here, not for very long. So take what you have in your bags and go back to the hedges in the hills, and I'll look forward to the annual trade in a couple of months time." He stood up as a statement. "Go! I'll stay with you to the edge of the town then...." He put his hands in the air. "Now follow me."

All three-hundred jumped to their feet, fearful of what might happen if they stay. Weaver and his orange son moved ahead of the march, and set off towards the road out, then, almost before they could make a couple of yards, a runner approached Weaver.

The young lad, quite splendid in his yellow tunic against his clear orange skin, warily saluted Weaver, then went to his ear. He had messages from the Cockle Wit camp.

Once the messages had been relayed, the runner stood back, waiting for the reply. Weaver held his hands to his head. He was clearly upset at the messages.

Holding his hands out wide, he announced to the three-hundred refugees, "We're too late! Please don't move. I'm so sorry." He looked at Murphy and those closest to him could see tears appearing in his eyes. Many of them had seldom seen an adult leprechaun cry, so the panic which had rumbled now threatened, as some of the farmers began moving towards Weaver.

Jim jumped in. "Stop! He's our friend. Let the man speak before doing anything stupid. Please."

Weaver, thanked Jim and dried his eyes, then sadly explained. "Chief Running Foot has ordered you to stay right here, until the morning, until he's decided what to do with you and where." His head dropped. "He's changed his mind. He doesn't now want you to go, he wants you all to stay, and anyone who tries to leave will be killed. You must believe me. He'll kill anyone who tries to leave. And the runner says the routes out are all closed with guards. Those guards will kill any of you who tries to leave."

They were prisoners. The tribe was stunned. Of all the stories of their history, legend and even myth, nothing like this had ever been known. They had only ever known peace amongst leprechauns, but this was another world. Was it hell, or just a bit of heaven gone wrong?

Chief O'Hoolihan stepped forward. He was an oldish man, always a pen pusher, never a fighter. He challenged Weaver. "What will you do if we carry on, and leave? Well?"

Weaver just laughed. "It's not me nor my son you need to worry about, it's our tribe. Our tribe would kill you all as soon as you're trouble. Not me. I'll never hurt you, but the tribe will. They're afraid of you, so they'll kill you."

The chief looked around at his friends, family and his kind, and they all waited for a move. It was Tommy who made the move. He had seen an opportunity, not much of one, but a glimmer.

"Chief, we'll stay here as ordered. What now Weaver?" He deliberately spoke as a friend just in case there was a glimmer and that he was it.

Weaver turned to the runner and sent him off with the message 'All safe. Stay here. Await your instruction in the morning. I'll stay to supervise the prisoners.' Weaver stepped over to his son, and they carefully surveyed the area around them, nodding and pointing.

"Yes, this is the place. Nobody can get close enough to hear us without being seen. Perfect." The two Cockle Wits relaxed and waved the tribe around them. They all sat in the large huddle, deliberately in the clear, open area between the quayside and the rough. "Let's talk." He looked around at the chief, who shrugged his shoulders, then at the others. "Well, any questions?"

A young boy put his hand up.

Weaver asked, "Can a child ask?" Tommy fervently nodded. "Okay then, young man."

The boy hesitated as his sudden shyness hit, but he managed to get his question out. "Mr Weaver. Will you eat us?"

Quite strangely, Weaver was set aback. He shook his head. He realised that it wasn't the little boy asking, it was the tribe, who all sat in absolute fear. He cleared his throat. "No, your meat probably wouldn't agree with us. No, we'll never eat you. Promise"

The boy sat down.

Dana asked, "I would like to know what your role in our fate is. The chief can be overridden, can't he?"

"Sorry, Dana, but Murphy and I have spent many years discussing our politics and our politics are quite different. I'm only just now realising just how different they are. In fact, they're the exact opposites. All your decisions are made by all of you, all the time. Us? All our decisions are made by one individual, nobody else, and nobody disobeys or else. What the chief orders, we do. And if we want to question them, he'll listen, or he won't. He's a total dictator, rules by fear rather than love. And it works for us. So I could question his decisions, but if I do anymore than that, he'll kill me." He forced a grin, but it was noticeably false. "That's how it is. Two very different cultures, both very successful until now. Now, you're failing." He looked at the chief.

Suddenly, one of the women snapped. "Someone coming!"

Weaver's son jumped up. There was a soldier marching towards them from the direction of the road. It was a Cockle Wit captain armed with a shillelagh, curved sword and a large sheath knife.

As the man approached, Weaver stood up and the captain stood in front of him and saluted. "Sorry to disturb you, your honour. Just doing a check. Are you alright?"

Weaver confirmed then sternly ordered the captain to put all his men on all the exits. He didn't want any escapees. The captain confirmed that Chief Running Foot would be here at first light, and they should be ready to move when he arrives. Weaver also ordered the captain to ensure full security at all exits and to maintain that level of security all night. The captain took the orders without question, then set off back to his men.

Once he had gone, Weaver relaxed. "Good. That'll keep his men tied up on the exits and out of our way. Gives us some thinking time."

Tommy was still feeling that opportunity, but was not quite sure what it was, or what form it took, but his hunch was beginning to settle on Weaver. He was beginning to get the strong feeling that Weaver was the enemy, but also their friend and their only hope.

Dana could feel her twin's excitement. She stood up for all to hear. "Mr Weaver. You've tied the troops up at all the exits. Does that mean there's another exit, one that's not guarded? Are you leading us somewhere?"

Poor Weaver. He did not really know what he was planning, but felt some sort of obligation to help them, but perhaps deep down, there was another agenda on his mind. He sat and thought for many, many minutes about the situation which had developed. He just sat in thought. They all thought with him.

Eventually, Tommy asked of the two Cockle Wits, "You said earlier that they're afraid of us. Why? What've they got to be afraid of? Is that what this is all about, this fear of us, your fear of us?"

Weaver broke from his thoughts and spoke privately with his son. Once they had agreed on something, he spoke to the tribe. He spoke loudly to all, but directed it towards Tommy. "Yes, fear. This is all about fear. Don't you all feel it? Don't you feel fear for the unknown? Your future, your present? Your fate, your own safety….. don't you all feel that fear? Because we do. We're a civilization of leprechauns, just like you, and we're scared, just like you. Murphy has told me all about the Common Nettle, brought in by somebody, somewhere, and being allowed to settle. Now, what is there? Irish Nettles living happily with Common Nettles? No, never. The Irish Nettle has gone and the Common Nettle rules."

He stood up and walked around. He went into the huddle of families, touching the heads of the young ones, making them feel at home. He looked hard at some of the young women and girls. He finally returned to his place beside his son.

"You are the biggest threat to our culture we've ever known. You're like the Common Nettle, very strong, adaptable, and you work like a thicket, supporting each other, and you'll win. We'll not let you be the Common Nettle here, slowly taking over our land and pushing us out. It'll never happen, and we have to make sure. You have your Spring Holi each year, and Murphy's written me about the lovely stories, particularly young Tommy's tales of legend and pride, and how he brings the tribe out of winter and into the warmth of spring with bolstering myths. He tells me how Tommy will one day rule the World, along with his engine revving him up, Dana, his driving force, and I hear all these things. It's all so strong and powerful. It all frightens us. Our annual event is in the late summer, just two weeks from now. It's not quite a Holi, more of a rut. It's our only chance to become chief. Each year, a contender fights the chief for his position, and the winner takes all, literally. Your Spring Holi, our Autumn Rut." He looked at Dana. "You, Dana, tell me Tommy's reaction to that. Please."

She frowned and thought about what Tommy would say. "The word is mightier than the sword. That's what he would say."

"And that's why we need to get rid of the word, while we have the chance. The sword is not so strong, but it's more fleeting and more final. Kill the word while the sword has the upper hand. Never allow it to fester like the Common Nettle. Kill it now before it kills you." He stopped for effect, and to allow the Nettle Wits to digest his words. "That's where we are, and that's why we don't want you here. The Cockle Wits are scared of you, so kill it off, before there's trouble."

The crowd went silent. Then Tommy's engine revved, and broke the silence. She asked, "My brother, the future ruler of the World, wants to know how the rut is decided, and what happens to the loser?"

Weaver replied, "The chief will be the one who wins a fight. Only one each year. A contender is put forward to challenge the chief in a controlled fight and the winner takes all until the next year's Autumn Rut, while the loser gets a state burial. It's a fight to the death. That's how we select our chief."

Dana, "So things could change for us if the chief loses in two weeks, and the new chief likes us."

"True. But many of you lot won't last until after the Rut. I'll ask you this, if Tommy takes over from your Chief O'Hoolihan, who'll kill the old chief, Chief O'Hoolihan? Tommy, or an executioner?"

Poor Dana scoffed, "No, nobody would kill the chief. We all love him. We've never killed anybody, let alone a friend."

Weaver whispered with his son, then again addressed Dana. "Tell me, Dana, what would Tommy think of his children marrying an orange person? You know a mixed marriage. What would he think?" He sat closer to his son as they awaited the answer to what seemed to be his son's question.

She thought for a while. It was something that Nettle Wits had never before had to even consider, but, "You know, just two weeks ago, I spent time on the edge of the wilderness with Tommy and Aaron and it opened my mind up, as well as Tommy's. Tommy learned that we are Nettle Wits, always will be, and it's within our own mettal to keep it that way. That's what Tommy learned. What opened his mind to the subject? The Moors caterpillar, that's what. We were sent by our general to find the lost forests, but found them gone, and so had to consider the start of the end, but we were inspired by the absolute enormity of the World and our tiny place within that World, and we inspired to realise that the tiny little bit of life that we inhabit is a gift from Gayla. She gave us our life, our farm and our minds, and in return for her generosity, we must look after that which has been given to us. But Gayla would never send us out with such responsibility without providing us with tools and weapons. So, she has given us our identity to hide behind, and our prejudice to blame, for she decreed that we only multiply with our own kind, to protect our form from unwanted mutation. And she decreed that we be driven by our hearts, so she gave us the emotions needed to keep our forms, and one such emotion, attraction to our own kind. At the end of the scale is attraction, while at the other end, repulsion. Now, one of the things considered whilst in the hedges was what happens when we run out of Moors meat. Would the new food kill us, or give us Brady's disease? Or..... What is Brady's disease anyway? We still don't really know, but we did establish that we would lose the colour that came from the nettle and Moors nutrients, and would probably turn grey. And when Aaron asked me if I would still fancy him if he was Grey, mine and Tommy's stomachs turned. We were hit by emotional repulsion. A message from Gayla.

"Anyway, we went to bed worrying about it, but our thoughts shared the sleep space, and we began thinking that skin is just outer, and we would still all be Nettle Wits, and so would still fancy each other even if we were grey. Another message from Gayla. Now, Mr Weaver and son, you are different.... no matter what colour you turn, even nettle green, you'll never be a Nettle Wit. So, purely from a mating perspective, you'll always be repulsive. Sorry, but it's the laws of Gayla. Maintain our form, at all costs."

The group was a little shocked. Nobody expected that and they all sat in awe of what could follow.

Mr Weaver remained seated. He had no readable

expression, and the young Weaver, the son, stood up and shocked the entire tribe, by actually speaking!

"Well. Don't know what to say except *thank you.* Was that Dana or Tommy? However, my brother says thank you. You know, Tommy, the future ruler of the World, will be written into legend. But they'll all forget the real hero, Dana O'Kief, who put him there. But I can relate to you, Dana, as I'm the same. I'm the man behind our new white hope, my big brother. We have the same sort of relationship, like one but in two bodies. And we have similar aspirations. In two weeks time, my brother will contest the Chieftain at the rut. He is this year's contender. The great white hope. He'll fight the strongest chief ever known in our history. My brother will fight the impossible." He waited as his dad whispered a suggestion. "My father has asked me to thank you. The entire tribe is fearful of mixing with you, and nobody has been able to work out why, but Dana has explained beautifully. Gayla gave us our emotional defences, so we can blame her. We only wish our tribe had been here to hear your explanation, it makes perfect sense. Now, Dana, guide me some more. My brother is learning from this exchange."

The young Cockle Wit was firm and strong, but refined. He nodded to, and smiled at, Dana for her to tell more.

She obliged. "So your brother could be chief in two weeks. He could let us go, be friends, carry on trading. We could all maintain our tribal relationship, as we used to, from a distance. Like and admire each other, without any risk of cross contamination. Your brother could be our saviour. Speak to your brother, please."

The young Weaver smiled. "I am my brother, and I am proud to know the Nettle Wits. From a mating point of view, you repulse me." He had a private chuckle. "But I like you and respect you." He whispered to his father. "Now in two weeks time I will, as my brother, fight Chief Running Foot, and he'll kill me. I'll be buried along with all the past contenders. But I hope I'll be remembered in your legends,

Tommy O'Kief, because I'm going to do one final, decent thing before my death. I'm going to let you go. Tonight you'll flee and find happiness away from here, but I hope you won't forget us, as most of us are kind and tolerant. So, I'll let you go tonight, me, my brother, while I still can. God bless."

The tribe was silent as they made sure they were still awake, but one by one they realised it wasn't a dream. Tommy stood up.

Weaver's son asked, "Do you really want to speak for yourself, Tommy? Because Dana is so good at doing it for you. As is my brother."

Tommy never spoke, so Weaver's son announced, "So, tonight, when the sun is down and the watching troops are blinded, you can leave through the wilderness, that one." He dramatically pointed to the sea. "That wilderness."

CHAPTER 27
ALL AT SEA

The mood lifted quickly as the promise of freedom sank in. They all wanted to thank the young Cockle Wit with hugs, but his father asked them to refrain.

"We're being watched. Please put your frightened faces back on and calm down. You can celebrate when you leave tonight." He smiled genuinely at the green faces, all trying to look serious. "Once you've gone, my family will pray for you. Until then, remember, you ain't gone."

Young Weaver, or his brother, seemed to have run out of talk, and he spent the afternoon carefully watching towards the quay. He was looking for something, and as the hunter that he was, he never let his concentration lapse. The many Nettle Wits watched with him, not knowing what for, but they did. Some of the children got together and offered him some elderberry preserve. He took one taste, then spat it out, laughing with the children as he washed the vile, sweetly taste down with some wine. But he never stopped watching.

Then young Weaver ordered, "Chief, whoever that is, come here."

The real chief approached the young warrior.

"Your best two men, young, strong and intelligent. Call them over now."

The chief called Tommy and Aaron. They quickly attended, and lowered their heads to their gaoler.

"You two need to go to the quay and prepare some things. Needs to be done while still light."

He pointed out two posts which rose above the height of the quay but which stood just a few inches away from the edge. They were to go unseen, to the right-hand post. Young

Weaver guided their eyes to a pile of rotten food, which was waiting to be taken away. "Use that for cover. Now go, my brother's waiting."

The two chosen ones set off. Phillips was certainly the one to send on an incognito mission, the man who moves with stealth.

While the men were away, Weaver spoke with the tribe, particularly with his old friend Murphy. The Cockle Wit had great respect for the politics and culture of the Nettle Wits and was quite jealous, with their individual freedom, but also of their ability to all toe the line, even without any form of strong leadership or punishments. It seemed to the orange philosopher that the Nettle Wits were of a different make up to the Cockle Wits, and that their differences went much deeper than mere colour and culture. He spoke with Murphy about their genetic differences, and perhaps despite all being leprechauns, they were two quite separate species. It was an interesting theory which helped to explain the communal behaviour of the Nettle Wits. They were all the chief and all the surf and everything in between. All of them, all of the time. Half jokingly, Weaver suggested that it might be a miscarriage of genetic justice to contaminate either species with the sperm of the other. Pure is how the Almighty made them all. "Dana was right to believe in the divine status of each species. Protection of kind."

Murphy. "Right or wrong, it does make it all virtuous, to allow us to go."

Weaver agreed. "Yes, that's why we did it, if anybody asks." He never spoke of the real reasons for letting them go, and the Wits never even risked asking.

Before the two Regimental members returned, Weaver stressed to the tribe that they must always remember that sea water is poisonous and to keep their bottles filled with rainwater at every opportunity. Apart from that, he had no other advice, except, "Don't talk to any strangers unless you have to. We're a funny lot, us strangers."

Tommy and Captain Phillips returned at teatime, and they all ate very carefully, knowing that their rations would be all they had until reaching their new homes. It was a painful wait for the sun to drop in the west, but it did eventually and they all began fidgeting.

Weaver, maintaining a quiet atmosphere, loudly whispered, "Once it's dark, settle down to bed in your normal huddles and act naturally. When you hear two peewits, be ready to leave quietly. When you do go, there shouldn't be any humans or stock moving on the quay and any sense of danger, a single peewit is the call. If that happens, get deep down into the cobbles where they can't squash you, and wait for the double peewit, for all clear. Now, whatever you see, ignore and be safe, and may the Almighty look after you all."

Weaver was a good man with a good family, but so different in his politics. He was firmly entrenched in a society that was prepared to go to great lengths to go against his own tribe. But who should judge? As he himself had already said, their politics suited them and had been successful for hundreds of years. Each to his own. But it was a deed of sheer connivance that was about to be the saviour of an entire civilization, so, sometimes great things can come out of corruption. Despite this fact, Dana was finding it difficult to understand why the Weavers were prepared to betray their own tribe.

After some stressful waiting by the men, women and children, there arrived a dark figure which stood by Weaver and his son. Tommy and Aaron recognised the man mountain, it was Weaver's oldest son, the contender to the Chieftain. It had been him that met the two at the quayside. He was heavily armed with swords and shillelagh.

"Peewit" called Weaver. The tribe prepared to leave.

Then the oldest son moved to one of the farmers and gently took the shillelagh from the farmers sheath, then, leaving his own shillelagh in its sheath, he used the farmer's to do his work. In a flash he hit Weaver and his own young brother on their heads, just above the eye, and with Aaron's help, tied their hands behind their backs. He left his father and his brother lying beside each other, as the tribe silently set off towards the quayside; a daring and successful breakout by the prisoners, leaving their guards stunned, overpowered and securely bound.

The tribe silently marched through the night for about an hour and arrived, without further incident, at the Quay, overlooking the moonlit seascape. It was still warm and the moon was at half strength, the perfect night for an escape into the unknown.

They all stood at the edge of the quay, looking out onto the silvery seascape, the moon dancing like little fairies on the top of the small waves, and they all momentarily froze. They were standing right on the edge of their known world, peering into the strange new world which would be their future, if they were to have one. This was it. Destiny.

The quay was of wooden construction, with two berths big enough for the trading ships, and in between them, moored to the two mooring posts, was the tiny skip belonging to the harbour master. It was almost invisible in the night, being heavily tarred, but unlike Father Patrick it wasn't feathered. It was big enough for two humans, or thousands of leprechauns. The three-hundred Nettle Wits confidently moved from the quayside, across some long reed-leaves and into the safety of the flat bottomed boat, quickly assembling below the bench seat. The knotted ropes which Aaron and Tommy had fixed up earlier to the sides of the boat, made the descent into the skip easy.

It was a blessing from the Almighty that the tide was very high that night, presenting the top, the gunnel, of the boat almost level with the quay, allowing young Weaver to give out encouragement as well as instruction above the gentle plop of the swell against the quay front. Young Weaver called to Tommy. "Tell Mr Murphy to stay in touch with Dad. Please." Then he told Tommy and Jim to go to the front mooring rope, and Aaron and O'Toole to the rear. Releasing the boat from the slip mooring was essential and urgent. The tide was on the turn and so the boat was not straining on the ropes, leaving them loose. The two teams slipped the loose ends through the loop, and they were free. All they had to do was wait for the tide to turn and take them off into the endless expanse of ocean.

They waited. The four Nettle Wits lay on the top, the gunnel, holding onto a rowlock, while the rest nestled below the bench. It was not long before the inevitable happened, and the tide gently pulled them from the mooring and they waved at the moonlit silhouette of their saviour as he mellowed into the night. All they had to remember young Weaver by, was their freedom. That was enough to keep him right there in their minds, they would never forget him.

The tiny boat drifted with the tide out of the cove and south along the coast. The tribe took the opportunity to sleep as they travelled away from their homeland and away from their aggressors, but they would never forget the bravery of their friends, the Weavers. They'd never understand them, but they would always remember them.

"You'll have to build a legend around our friends." suggested Murphy to the one and only ruler of the World. "You could probably build an entire anthology."

The sun rose, and so did the Wits. Chief O'Hoolihan stood out in the open of the vast flat of the boat, and exercised his authority by ordering the entire population to line up and lay out their survival blankets, to air. Then after a few minutes, ordered them to fold them tightly enough to go back into their backpacks. Not much as far as leadership goes, but important. Their meagre belongings were all they had and were of the utmost importance to their chances of survival. He then demonstrated a typical portion of Moors meat, so small that some groaned, but soon shut up when he reminded them that their only supplies were those in their packs. "So beware of gluttony." He did seem to have some qualities in leadership.

At that point, nobody had climbed up to the gunnel, or the boat sides, to look at their position. The four seemingly leading-hands went up the knotted ropes to the rowlock and looked.

It was amazing. The early morning sky was deep blue and the air absolutely still, and they seemed becalmed in an enormous millpond. To the north, east and south, just sea, nothing else as far as the eye could see, right to the edge of the World, just sea. The grey and blue scene was interrupted by a handful of gulls.

To the west, land. It was quite a way off, but close enough to make out the beach, broken up by rocky outcrops and backed by faint grey silhouettes of hills. They sat for about half an hour watching.

Then they were joined by Murphy.

"What do you know about this Murphy?" Jim asked the teacher. "What's happening? Anything?"

O'Toole interrupted. "I do believe we're moving closer to the land." The boat was sideways onto the land mass and they all sat looking towards it. "Yes, slowly moving that way."

Murphy explained, "The tide doesn't just go up and down, it goes in and out, and according to our good friend Weaver, it goes in then out twice a day. So if we're going towards the land, it's going in and taking us with it."

They suddenly expected to hit land if they continued to move that way.

Murphy added, "If we don't reach land before it turns, the tide will take us out again. We could go in and out forever." He looked around at the four other faces. "Sorry, don't mean to alarm you."

They patiently waited and observed the continued movement towards land. Tommy looked around the boat to give his eyes a rest from the glare of the water, and he noted the mooring ropes hanging each end of the boat, over the edge, where they were left last night. They would be useful for their descent from the gunnel onto the beach. He then noted another rope which was a lot thicker, much thicker. It was several times thicker than their own girth, and it was fixed at one end securely to an eye at the prow, then coiled many times on the floor of the bow, and continued loosely up to a cleat at the top of the prow. It was wound round just twice. From there, it was taught and went over the gunnel, hanging down out of sight.

Several children, all with their backpacks on, played near the coiled rope, looking for adventure, and slowly took an interest in the coil. One boy climbed up onto the coil and stood waving his head and body from side to side. He was the snake's head. Another boy stood on the floor with the other children behind and he spoke to the boy at the top. Tommy then realised that the one on the floor was playing Jim O'Kief, who could talk to adders. He had a glance at Jim and chuckled below his breath. He picked out Ty amongst the other women and waved, and she replied.

Back to the land mass. It was getting closer.

O'Toole said, "If we hit land, we need to get off quickly before we're washed back out." He nodded. "Could be there in less than an hour."

Jim suggested, "After they've all got their packs with them, we'll all need to gather at the ropes. Too many to come up here too soon. But let's not panic them until we get close."

Tommy watched the children at the coil. There were now several children on the coil and one was brave enough to climb the rope up towards the cleat. Then he froze, called to his friends below, and they all jumped from the coil. The boy carefully climbed back down the rope and joined his friends on the ground, then stood in a group and looked up at the rope, pointing.

"What they up to?" Tommy poked Aaron on the shoulder. "Those little ones around the rope."

The two looked at the children and couldn't see anything obvious, but the boy who had been climbing the rope, looked towards Tommy and pointed up at the cleat.

Tommy gasped, "The rope's now wound around the cleat just once, and its moving! The rope's coming loose and slipping. Dad, look!"

All five of them stared at the cleated rope, which was clearly slipping, but very slowly.

Tommy called to Ty, "Get them away from the coil! Quick!"

She and Dana ran frantically across the boat to the children and ordered them well away, and as they moved aside, the rope released from the cleat and rushed over the edge of the gunnel into the sea. The coils unwound as the snake made his getaway, but suddenly stopped. About three coils remained on the floor, the sudden rush over the edge seemed to have stopped, but then the rope again tightened and the coils slowly unwound. Gradually they moved over the gunnel. The three coils unwound and followed the rest of the rope over the edge until it pulled taught on the eye, and stopped moving.

Suddenly, a jolt. They all held on tightly around the rowlock and wondered. The boat slowly began to turn, and it continued to pull round until the side of the boat, which was facing the land, was facing north, along the coast. The boat strained on the rope at the bow, but never turned anymore.

They had dropped anchor.

It took a little while for the five men to realise what had happened.

"We're stuck, all stuck, going nowhere."

As they realised that there would be no more jolts, they relaxed a little.

"Let's not panic," ordered Jim. "Let's think. That's how we get through, by thinking."

They were about three hundred yards from the land, not far for humans, but an impossible swim for tiny leprechauns. So close yet so far.

"About half hour, that was all." groaned O'Toole. "What we gonna do? And why has it happened? What's that rope caught on?"

Murphy explained that it was the anchor that had dropped and it had dug into the sea bed, stopping them from drifting any further.

They advised the tribe down in the floor of the boat that they had temporarily stopped and not to panic.

As they considered their lot, the millpond surface of the sea suddenly took on a swell. It was only slight, but rocked the boat from side to side and the tribe grabbed hold of anything to hand and the men on the gunnel held tightly onto the rowlock. They decided to get down before it became any worse.

Once on the floor, they looked around. It was like being in a walled prison, the only view out being that of the sky. It was scaringly claustrophobic. Then many of them pointed at the anchor rope. It had gone loose.

The first thought was that the anchor had broken loose and they would resume their drift to the land. However, it only remained loose for a few minutes before a sharp jolt hit the boat and the rope tightened back up under the strain.

Once they felt brave enough, the five men climbed up the knotted ropes for a reconnaissance. The side of the boat was now facing south and the land was at the bow end. They had turned around one-hundred and eighty degrees. The tide had turned. It was now going out.

After a while of thought, Murphy said, "Bag of mixed blessings. Once the anchor went down, it stopped us from moving towards land, but we would never have reached land before the tide turned, and now it's only the anchor that's stopping us from drifting further out to sea. So at least we're stuck here and won't be taken out there." He pointed to the horizon in the east. "Not all bad."

Cup half full.

He continued. "This'll run this way for about six hours,

then it'll turn and run to land for six hours. We need to think hard for the next six hours and come up with a plan."

They all moved back to the safety of the boat floor.

Just five days earlier, they had watched the Doyles and the Fullers catching the snakes. At that point, they still had a forest. Now, all their existence was held within the walls of a seven foot rowing boat. It was not surprising that they were quickly turning rancid on each other.

Hairy Daniels told the group that, eventually, they would have to eat the dead. "Perfectly natural survival protocol," he stressed. Then Nostradamus decided to blame the abnormally huge movement of the tides on the Roman navvies, causing one brave lady to say what the others only dared think. "Shut up, Nostradamus. You're going senile!"

So Jim called his team of Regimental members together, along with the chief, and instructed them to delicately police the tribe while under such pressure. He called O'Toole and Murphy to join them for their ideas and O'Toole suggested, "Every backpack has two coils of rope. Get some of them making knotted links to go up the sides and down the other side. Keep them busy. Just like in the Navy, tying knots and scrubbing decks. It'll keep them occupied, and we'll need the ropes when the time comes to disembark."

Tommy pointed at the anchor rope. "Look. The rope is loads thicker than us and tied so tightly into that eye, we'll never undo it. That's a no-go." He sighed. "But we could cut the rope. No other choice. Would take a couple of hours with the butchers' knives, but could be done. If the tide runs for six hours, we could start cutting an hour before it turns, that'll give us about five hours of tide to get to the beach. Do-able?"

Murphy, "Last resort! Once the anchor's gone, we could just drift until we're all dead."

Jim suggested, "We should get the knotted ropes up on the inside in readiness. Look, the prow sticks up higher than the gunnel, so we couldn't move all the way round the gunnel. But at the back.... Put the ropes up at the back, and we could go round to either side when the time comes. No telling which way we'll land on the beach, but gather at the back...."

They sent the chief to organise the ropes.

Murphy suggested going back up top to take stock of the surroundings. He was a good mind, well educated and practical, with an open attitude.

He suggested, as they sat around the rowlock, "We need to have the plan for tomorrow. When the tide goes back in, it'll be getting dark, so we can't do anything on the next tide. That would be suicidal in the dark. Today is for planning."

They looked along the side of the boat towards the land. Murphy noted, "This is like a weathervane. We can tell exactly which way the tide is running by the direction of the boat, and it runs that way." He pointed past the bow of the boat. "It runs right into those rocks there." Even with the millpond-like calm, the waves crashed against the rocks enough to smash the little boat to bits, and when you're less than half an inch tall, you wouldn't last long.

The four men were slowly settling down from their panics and confusions, and becoming more able to look clearly at what was around him. They could see that the route that they would follow on the tide would take them straight onto the rocks, beach to the left, beach to the right, but rocks straight ahead. They would be bashed to pieces if they washed up onto them and they all realised that the anchor had saved them from probable disaster.

After a long thought-break, "So where does that leave us?" asked Aaron.

They all shook their heads. It seemed that their lives were blessed by The Almighty, somehow saving them at every step, but in doing so, creating another insurmountable challenge. They not only had to get to the land, they had to go to the left or to the right, but never straight on.

Then O'Toole spotted something in the water, way up along the coast to the north. It was coming their way. It was a swell and swirl, and the point of a tail, and then they could see several tails. It was a shoal of basking sharks. The initial excitement suddenly turned to panic. They could easily turn the boat over.

"Hang on! Everybody, hang on. Whales coming!"

They moved really slowly, they were feeding, but before the sharks reached the boat, the tide turned, and the boat slowly swung around. The back of the boat now pointed towards the land and the rocks: the tide was going in. After about half an hour, the sharks approached.

Then, an excited farmer shouted. It was Lucky Eddie. He clambered to the rowlock, and with eyes alight with excitement, he stuttered, "M.... M.... Mr Murphy. Remember at school. You told us about the basking sharks. Remember?"

Murphy put his hand on the young man's shoulder and smiled.

They watched in awe as the giants, each many times bigger than their boat, floated by, humps showing and tails gently swilling as their mouths gaped in the sea water, for plankton.

Lucky Eddie gasped. "Their mouths are as big as the pigsty doors, but only eat the tiniest of things."

It was a once in a lifetime for the Nettle Wits. It was a little bit frightening, but exhilarating, never to be missed. Lucky Eddie got so excited that he almost fell back into the boat but Aaron caught hold of him. Then Lucky Eddie pulled out an empty wine pack from his backpack and blew it up. He threw the inflated bag out to where the sharks were passing.

Eddie stressed, "Look. They won't eat that. It's much too big for them. You watch." He danced with excitement. "You watch." They all watched the bag. It was pushed aside, then rolled around, then swished by the tails and eventually, as the last shark floated by, the bag caught back into the tide and resumed its drift towards the land.

"What do you think of that, Mr M.... M...Murphy? That

went perfect, hey Mr Murphy?"

Murphy looked away from Lucky Eddie and back at the inflated bag. Then Tommy moved all the way along the gunnel to the prow and climbed the bulkhead to gain a few more inches of height. He concentrated on the bag. It moved towards the land.

"Can you still see it?" called Jim? "Can you see it?"

Tommy pulled a hook from his bag and banged it into the top of the bulkhead and used it to steady himself as he stood up. He could still see the bag. "It's going straight towards land." He strained. "It's going straight towards the beach. Straight at the beach! Missing the rocks. It's gonna get to the beach!" It had been pushed north by the swirl of the sharks' tails.

They all cheered, then the message was relayed to the tribe and they joined the cheering. It had landed on a sandy beach, north of the rocks. Lucky Eddie beamed with pride. "The sharks swilled it right up that way, away from the rocks!"

The tide was running in and by the time it next turned it would be dark. The men descended into the floor of the boat and considered a plan. They all knew that taking a step to the north or south to ensure a landing on the sand was possible, but....

Jim asked the chief if the knotted ropes were ready. They sent two volunteers up onto the gunnel to securely stake six of the ropes at the back end of the boat to hang down in readiness. The other six were looped and put on the floor by the back, complete with fixing stakes, ready to be dropped over the outside of the boat, when the time came. It was all completed in daylight.

While it was still light, they ate a small amount of their meat, drank a small amount of their water and then, quite ceremoniously, all supped a cup of wine.

Then a young lady stood up in the middle of the huddle and held her arms out for some attention. She made a statement. "I don't really want him to, but my husband wants to save the tribe. He'll tell you how and then we can toast his bravery." She gingerly sat down with her children then her husband stood up. It was Lucky Eddie.

"I have an idea." Lucky Eddie looked lovingly at his wife and children, then across to Murphy. "I can save the tribe. I can. When I was at school, Mr M.... M....Murphy told us all about the basking sharks, and how they're the biggest fish anywhere, and despite their size, only eat things so tiny called plankty." He stopped to recap his plan. "Now, I can get to the land and come back on a raft, big enough to take us all to safety, and we can have paddles to stay away from the rocks. We can do it."

O'Toole asked very gently, "Lucky Eddie, how would you get to the shore? How would you avoid the rocks?"

Lucky Eddie again looked at Murphy. "When I was at school, M.... M.... Mr Murphy told us that basking sharks only eat plankty. So, if one ate me I would get stuck in his filters, and I would wriggle and jiggle and tickle inside him and give him a sore throat. So, they won't eat me." He nodded contently. "So I could do the same as that water bag did, get pushed north by their tails and clear of the rocks. I could land on the beach."

Murphy shook his head, then coughed, then said, "Eddie, what I told you about basking sharks was just a theory. It's never been proven. Just theory."

"Then I'll prove it for you. They didn't eat the water bag, so they won't eat me. Just swish me all the way past the rocks." He bent down and pulled his children up to him. "I can do it. Please let me try, for my children."

The tribe was silent to a man.

To be honest, to say that lucky Eddie had come up with a birdbrain idea would be insulting to the bird. It was quite idiotic.

The chief stood forward and spoke on behalf of all the tribe. "Lucky Eddie.... that's brilliant! The whole tribe is behind you and will give you all the help you need, and be forever grateful."

He thanked the chief and asked, "If I don't make it, I ask just two things. One, look after my wife and children, and two, Tommy, please remember me in your legends. That's all."

Eddie was kitted out with a butchers knife, sheath knife and enough rope to make a reed-raft about twelve inches square, and several survival blankets. If he was to make it to shore, he would make a flag with one of the blankets and wave it from the highest rock, then set about making the raft and paddles. That's all he had to do, if he ever made land. Oh yes, and navigate the raft out on the tide, ensuring not to miss the boat.

It all sounded quite simple, really. Too simple.

CHAPTER 28
THE LEGEND OF LUCKY EDDIE

They were all up and ready, even before the sun appeared in the east. The tide was still flowing out but Murphy was certain that the turn was soon, and so they prepared. Lucky Eddie had to be ready for the floodtide and the sharks. He had a backpack full of ropes, tools and survival blankets, and on each side of the pack was attached an inflated wine bag, for buoyancy. A red jerkin was rapped over the back of his backpack to aid his visibility from the boat. He should be clearly visible on top of the grey waters of the Irish Sea.

They waited deep in the floor of the boat for the tide to turn. Of course, when the tide did turn, they still had to hope that the sharks would come by. They came yesterday so…...

Murphy's theory was that during the flood tide, many tiny creatures such as plankton and krill would wash into the shallows, offering a veritable feast for the giants. That was a theory, or one of them. The other one was that they wouldn't eat lucky Eddie because he's too big and would give them a sore throat. A big day for theories. Everybody had crossed fingers, especially Lucky Eddie's wife and children.

Once the tide had turned the back end of the boat would face the land, so they had laid ropes all along the rear gunnel and pinned them securely with hooks. Eddie's friends and family could then safely go onto the gunnel to see their brave hero off on his gargantuan act.

They all waited quietly in the floor.

Eventually it happened. The anchor rope went limp and the boat bounced in the swell as the water changed direction. The boat swung round and jolted to a stop on the anchor and the rear faced land. The flood tide had begun.

About a third of the tribe went up to the rear gunnel and Tommy took his place on top of the prow, like a figurehead, surveying the waters. He watched for the basking sharks from his elevated post.

O'Toole threw an empty water bottle into the water and noted the speed of the flow. Eddie would need to be directly in front of the shoal when it arrived. It was tense on that gunnel and Eddie kept looking down into the depths of the boat, waving at his family. They had chosen not to watch him die.

Waiting, just waiting. Perhaps Murphy's theories wouldn't hold out. Perhaps the krill had gone elsewhere, followed by the basking sharks. Just *perhaps*, Eddie's bird-brained idea would never be tested. Just *probably*, his idea was the most stupid thing ever even considered by the Nettle Wits. Perhaps their fate lay in that boat, awaiting starvation and dehydration. It all went through many a mind as they waited, but not through Lucky Eddie's; he knew it would work out.

Then, "They're here! Look!" Tommy screamed from his look out post. "They're here."

Way to the north could be seen fins and tails breaking the surface, and swells, as the giants rolled the water aside. They were coming. The mood was electrifying.

"Don't go until I say." ordered O'Toole. He held Eddie's arm to keep him from jumping too soon. The entire tribe was silent, and only the gulls shrilled their encouragement.

Then, "Go. Now go. Go, go!"

O'Toole let his arm go and Eddie took the leap, as the tribe cheered, then silence again hit, as the excitement slowed. The flow was about three or four knots moving Eddie very positively, but slowly, towards the route of the giants.

A few minutes later, the basking sharks reached Eddie. He was in the perfect position, bang in the middle of their path, and the very first shark nudged him aside and the massive displacement of water threw him back, behind the shark. Its tail then washed him northwards. The next shark, then the next, they all rejected him as food and swished him back with their enormous tails. It was working!

He had been passed by about ten of the sharks and was displaced by at least eighty feet to the north, and just two more to come. The ridiculous plan was working. Unbelievable!

"I've lost him!" shouted Tommy. "Hang on.... No, that's not him. Can't see him." They all strained, but the red jerkin was no longer in view. The shoal moved on towards the south and the waters ahead of the boat calmed. Still no sight of Eddie. Everybody prayed.

Tommy maintained his vigil for hours, but he never caught sight of him again.

Modern Nettle Wit legend has it that the basking sharks would never eat a leprechaun for fear of the wriggling and tickling in their filters, giving them sore throats. But just as Eddie was almost clear, the young shark bringing up the rear, noticed him. He'd had a lot of trouble sleeping and found that it helped if he took something with him to bed to suck on, so he snapped Eddie up and put him in his pocket for later. That's how the modern legend goes.

The Tribe gradually began believing that Lucky Eddie had run out of luck and was missing, presumed dead. However, as Tommy pointed out, even if he had made it to land, it could take him a few hours to mount the prominent rock and raise the flag. So, they maintained a vigil right through until dark, then in case he couldn't get to the top before dark, they maintained a vigil for the whole of the following day. Sadly, the flag was never raised.

The mood amongst the tribe had never, in their entire history, been lower. All sorts of talk began going around, such as Hairy Daniels stating if that's our best idea then..... and Nostradamus Who Sees Tomorrow advised that they will soon be eating the dead. It wasn't the first time that eating the dead had been mentioned. It wasn't at all good, but then survival is important....

Jim decided that action was becoming more necessary by the hour and called a meeting of the elders. All the usual, the chief, the O'Tooles, the O'Kiefs, the Phillips, the top table, and a few farmers and industrialists, met at the bow end of the boat.

"We can't just sit here!" bellowed Jim. "Chief, what's the state of food and water?"

Even with a bit of dew scraped from the rowlocks each morning, they had no more than two days of water and four days of food. Creatures so small can only go about one or two days without water before collapsing. That meant that in as little as three days time they would begin to die through thirst. Just three days.

O'Toole mentioned the two small oars which lay up against the side. It was agreed, though, that with all two-hundred and fifty adults beneath them, they would never get them over the side. He hadn't meant to row the boat, but to use one as a raft to drift to the shore. But they would never get one over the side.

"Anything else?"

Hairy Daniels scowled, "If it's no better than Lucky Eddie's ideas, keep it to yourself."

Aaron jumped to his feet. "Shut up, Daniels, or you'll get what you should have got when I was at school!"

That was as hard as they get, regarding anger, but it was enough to kick them all up the arse. Any idea was welcome right then. Eventually, Tommy took the hint from Ty's poke in the ribs. He carefully chose his words whilst also making sure that the rest of the tribe weren't listening.

"Is this our final hour? Are we at the end, or at least close?"

Murphy thought before replying. "I think we are. The start of the end. What you thinking?"

"Well, we should cut the anchor rope. I know it saved us from bashing on the rocks, but do we have any choice but to crash onto the rocks? If we can cut it almost through, then finish it when the tide turns that way, we would be taken into the shore." He hesitated. "Against the rocks."

Murphy added. "If we don't get it right, we'll drift back out to sea. Three days of drifting and we die of thirst."

Tommy forced a smile. "It's the devil or the deep blue sea. Bashed on the rocks or die at sea." He looked at Ty, then at each of his friends and family. "Do we have any real choice? At sea, we die, onto the rocks, many of us could be dead, but not necessarily all. I know what my choice would be. All dead or most of us dead. At least we might keep the species alive. Well?"

On top of the dangers of drowning on the rocks or dying of thirst, they had never really thought about the weather. They were at sea during a rare period of absolute stillness, rare in the Irish Sea, and the boat had begun, just slightly, to roll in a swell which wasn't previously there. It would only get worse as a change of weather slowly moved in from the South. In a tiny rowing boat, built only for sculling around the cove, it would only take one decent wave, and they'd be gone.

O'Toole reminded the group. "The Saint Patrick sailed without us. Do you remember the moment? The wind blew and the waves rolled and broke and chopped. What if we get some of that? How long before we're thrown into the sea? Not long, I wager." He looked around the boat. "We're rolling a bit more today than yesterday. We know what weather is, unpredictable, but always changes. It won't stay calm like this forever."

Murphy replied, "You're right." Their options were narrowing, and the urgency, growing. "Big decision time, or it'll be too late."

They all talked amongst themselves, nodding, umming, tutting and waving heads, then O'Toole raised his hands.

"Well?"

The chief said, "I'm with Tommy, cut the anchor rope at

the floodtide. Take our chances on the rocks and hope. Are you all with us?"

They all agreed.

Murphy spoke. "I think if we go on today's second tide, we'd be hitting the rocks in the dark. We won't stand a chance, so will have to chance the weather holding out, and can go in the morning. As soon as the tide changes in the morning, in the light. I can't see any other way." They all agreed.

The meeting closed and the members dispersed amongst the tribe to explain the plan, and to prepare.

All empty and part empty water and wine bags were blown up and securely fixed inside the backpacks as buoyancy aids. Ropes were fixed securely around the rear of the gunnel from which to hang onto while approaching the landing, and knotted ropes dropped over the edge, ready for the descent. Apart from mental preparation, there was not not much more they could do.

The anchor rope was cut about half way, so they could finish it off as soon as the flood tide began in the morning.

They were ready.

Mary asked about how and when they would leave the boat, but nobody really knew. It would all depend on their approach to the rocks and how hard the swell was driving them. They would just have to suck it and see. It was agreed, however, that once onshore, any survivors would meet up at the prominent rock and take it from there.

CHAPTER 29
THE LEGEND OF THE SPRITES

The wait for the morning's floodtide was tense. They were in a prison, a seven foot, flat bottomed boat with straight walls all around, and only the pair of oars to break the view. They were thankful for the single seat which stretched between the rowlocks, it gave them a little cover from the sun. That was where most of the tribe were camped, below the seat.

Tommy sat with Dana and Ty, below the seat with the bulk of the tribe. Only the chief's top table were missing, as they were busy discussing the state of the World, on top of one of oars.

"That's my old teacher," whispered Ty. She nodded towards a lady who was minding the younger children. They ranged from about five up to about ten, and there were twenty of the little ones. "She was good, taught me everything."

The children were huddled together, but sorted by their family groups and looked somewhat sombre. Perhaps they knew that tomorrow could be their last day in this life, or perhaps they were just bored. Tommy began thinking of their predicament and how they had been put into a position of pending extinction, and he wondered why.

"Why're we here? Is it my fault?" Tommy look sideways at Dana, then the other way at Ty. "They talk about following me. So, is it my fault that we're here?"

Dana took up the lead from the two bitches. "Never! They voted to follow the chief. So it's the fault of the tribe. As always, we all made the decision, the vote. That's what our politics dictate."

"I know, but I could've put the case for the hedges over

much stronger. And the Father.... he only knew Eileen because of our prank. Is all this our fault?" He hung his head. "I'm no leader, I just tell stories, I can't lead. A storyteller, a bungler, that's all."

The girls squeezed up to him as he sulked.

Many of the tribe cast glances towards Tommy, as if waiting for something.

"Perhaps they want you to tell a story, bring one of our legends to life. That's what you do." Dana put her head onto his shoulder. "Forget the knickers, just give them some of our culture and they can take heart from it."

But Tommy was not in the mood.

After a while, the teacher got up from the group of children and walked over to Tommy. She acknowledged Ty and Dana, but spoke directly at Tommy.

"Could you help me? The children are all scared, but I don't know what to say to them for the best. Could you talk to them, please, Tommy?"

After a poke from Ty, he agreed. He moved to sit with the children, Ty on his right arm and Dana a couple of feet to his left. The children all sat cross legged and attentive.

"Well, little ones." He looked around the group of twenty. "I'm hoping we can help each other. We're all scared. So what's bothering you all?"

After a few seconds a girl, probably the oldest at about ten, rose onto her knees. She was the spokesman, and put herself over very well for one so young. "Tommy, Mum says that you will one day rule the World. So, where will you lead us?"

That was not what he had expected, and he was suddenly even more scared. Was this part of his punishment? However, it did wake him up to the notion, and if he was destined for the top job in the World, he could surely manage the fears of the little ones. He thought deeply, then Ty poked him in the ribs.

"Well, if that's what your mum says, then I'd have to be a

brave man to argue it. Mums are always right. But lead you? Okay, tomorrow, we'll be going that way." He pointed towards the prow end of the boat. "As soon as the tide turns in the morning, we'll be going onto the beach."

Before he could say anymore, "Why?"

With a smile, he continued. "We'll all get onto the beach and then go on to our new home."

"Why?"

"Because we've lost the Nettle Forest and must find somewhere new. It'll be dangerous and we'll all need to help and support each other. If we all stay together, we'll all be safe. Look after each other and we'll be safe." He thought. "Once we're on the beach, we can think about our new home, up in the hills, away from the sea."

"Why?"

"Because only Cockle Wits can live on the beach. We'll have to go up the hill into the green world. We'll find a nice hedge, or maybe a copse or spinney. It'll be really nice."

"But…." The spokesman paused, looked around at the frightened faces of the children, then, "But…. the Sprites'll get us….." They all began fidgeting. "The Sprites! They live in the trees and woods and copses."

Sprites are mythical creatures and have been entrenched in Nettle Wit culture since time began, but are pure fairytale. They visit any naughty leprechaun children, taking everything that he owns or loves, and will never give it back. The children know what will happen if they're naughty, the Sprites will come. But they are not real, just fairytales.

"You mustn't worry about the Sprites. Unless of course you're naughty, but they won't be where we're going. Only if you're naughty."

"Why?"

"Because…. they aren't there. That's all. Not where we're going, unless you're naughty."

Shock horror. The teacher stood up and Ty punched Tommy in the ribs, then the little ones sunk into their family huddles and bottom lips dropped. What had the storyteller said which was so bad? A little boy stood up and looked a picture of despair, his red lips almost drooping down to his shoulders.

"Not there?" He took a deep breath. "What about the cakes? Who'll bring us cakes?"

Cakes! Tommy had forgotten about the cakes. They had also been part of Nettle Wit culture since time began and were given once a year to every child during the Holi; the Sprite cakes. Even though chimneys were banned since the great fire, the Sprites delivered each and every child a cake down the imaginary chimney. It was the kind side of the Sprites. Now, what about Holi? No Sprites, no cakes, no Holi?

The boy prompted Tommy. "Won't we get cakes where we're going, even at Holi, or won't there be Holi?"

Tommy was struggling. "Of course you will, and Holi'll always happen each year. The Sprites will always come at Holi and leave cakes. Always."

"Why?"

Why, why, why? Why can't they just accept it? They'll get their bloody cakes, so why keep pushing? The adults don't push and ask 'why' when he tells his stories, they just believe him. So why won't the children believe him?

"Because...." Ty put her mouth to his ear. "they're children. They're different. So, Mr Storyteller, give them what they need, and that's an order." His newly acquired bitch had spoken.

He needed to think. He was tired, as they all were. A couple of months earlier, the Nettle Wit's World was perfect, but now it all nestled in the bottom of that marooned skip, all waiting to die of thirst or die on the rocks. Did any of it matter any more? The entire civilization of the Nettle Wits, all fifteen twenties and eighteen of them, were waiting to follow him onto the rocks with the flood tide, so why worry about the few children's questions? Does any of it matter anymore?

Dana leaned into his ear. "Even more than it *ever* mattered." She pointed to the oars where the top table perched. There was Murphy Who Knows a Lot Cos He's Old, their old teacher and lifelong influence. Just a few weeks earlier, Tommy and Dana were in his class, still children and his mind drifted back to some of the lessons, ones which involved a certain Edna O'Sophical, a right one, and her brother Phil, and those stupid questions like, what came first, the butterfly or the egg, and if Edna O'Sophical is a right one, then who is the left one? All pointless, aimless questions, which probably don't even have answers. Stupid and pointless. Then it began to dawn on him that it was never pointless. He suddenly thought about one of his own stupid questions, and he asked himself, 'are our children so intelligent because they ask the questions, or do our children ask the questions because they're so intelligent?'

Dana pulled into his left arm and Ty clung on to his right. They just smiled.

So, none of it was pointless. Why? Why? Why? He suddenly realised what it was that Murphy strove to teach in those lessons. It doesn't matter about the answer, it's all about the question. Yearn to learn, wonder to perceive, ask to grasp. It was all about the question, and it was all about intelligence. It was about the epitome of intelligent life, the big question, 'why?' The group of children that awaited his story were suddenly the most important Nettle Wits in the World. Why? Because they were the future. So they want to know, they need to know, and they *will* know.

He stood up. The children all looked hard into his eyes and demanded answers. "I'd like to thank you all for teaching me so well. I now know that tomorrow morning the tribe will follow me onto the beach and up to our new world, but not all the tribe will follow. Only fourteen twenties will follow me, but you twenty will *not* follow me. No, you won't follow me, I won't let you because I want you to walk with me, not behind me. I want you twenty children to help me make that new world and we'll make it better than we could ever dream possible. We'll make it as a team, together. Are you with me, into the future? Into our future?"

There were some weak cheers, and a bit of head-nodding, and some shrugged shoulders, before the spokesman stretched high onto her knees. She stamped her tiny knee on the deck, then, "Mr O'Kief," with emphasis on Kief, "Why will we get cakes if the sprites aren't there? Why? And how?"

Just as Tommy was about to burst out laughing, his indiscretion was saved by the very weak voice of a tiny tot. "And my big sister says Sprites aren't even real. She can be very spiteful, my sister."

And that gave him his cue for the next act. He thanked the little one for her input, then spoke loudly to ensure that the entire tribe could hear. Unnoticed by him, most of the tribe had already moved to within earshot. They all awaited the wisdom of the chosen one.

"They are real, not just fairytale to frighten the children, but real! You'd all better believe it. Now, I've spent time around humans just lately, and do you know that many humans, as they grow up, stop believing in leprechauns? They stop believing in *us*. They're so silly, they think we're not real. Are we real? Well?"

The children, and many adults, began pinching each other to prove their own existence. The spokesman shouted, "That's stupid! Of course we're real, we're here, ain't we?"

"And do you know why stupid humans don't believe in us? Well, it's simply because they've never seen us. That's why. How can they be so stupid, just because they haven't seen us? All stupid. Now, what about the Sprites? Do they exist? Are they real? Of course they are, even if we've never seen them. There is no doubt about it, as real a a leprechaun!"

Suddenly, from the back of the adult audience, came a challenge. "What about science?"

Science? The little children all stretched to see who had

shouted, but he was hidden in the crowd, so Tommy looked to the top table who sat on the oars. Nostradamus Who Sees Tomorrow nodded and smiled.

The spokesman shouted. "He's the scientist, ask him!"

So Tommy asked Nostradamus Who Sees Tomorrow, "What is the scientific view on the existence of Sprites?"

"We've never considered the question," he replied. Very diplomatic.

Tommy. "Then it's about time we did! My team and I will now prove the existence of Sprites using your own favourite procedure: scientific logicisation. The case, 'sprites do *not* exist, true or false?' Now, does anybody, anywhere, any age have any proof, of any sort, in any form, that the statement is true?"

The tribe had a few seconds of discussion amongst themselves, but not a shred of evidence was offered.

"So, with no evidence offered, the logical answer is *false*. 'Sprites do not exist' is *false*. Scientific logic decrees that the opposite is true, so Sprites *do* exist. We've proved it beyond doubt, and anyone who doesn't believe it is some sort of fool. What do you say to him?"

"Fools! Idiots!" The children all laughed, pointing at the adults and throwing jeers in that direction. "Numskulls, pea-brains. Stupid, dense, adder poo," and so on.

The laughter and jest carried on for a while and turned the stressful situation into one of happiness, as childrens' laughter echoed through their prison. Then, as quickly as it all started, it ended. Absolute silence, except for the plop of the water and the call of the gulls. The children huddled. They then returned to their sitting positions and the childish glee was replaced by fear. The spokesman rose to her knees.

"So, sprites are definitely real, so they'll definitely get us when we go into a copse or spinney." The children certainly understood the principles of logicisation.

Tommy took a sharp intake of sea air. "Oh no, no, no. Definitely not, no, unless you are naughty. But no."

"So, they're not there?"

"Yes, they're not there."

"Why not?"

"Because they're not there."

"So, they won't get us and nick our stuff when we're naughty? And what about the cakes? Mr O'Kief, you're not making any sense at all. They're either there or they ain't!" The spokesman crossed her arms, a tiny, green ten-year-old with bright red lips, and she huffed. She was definitely a future Nettle Wit bitch; she was the boss!

Poor Tommy, why him? He never wanted to be chosen, to be a figure-head role, nor to lead, he just loved telling stories, legends that inspire. But, despite his wishes and dreams and regrets, he was it, the chosen one, and it was time to put his real skills to the test, telling the legend of the Sprites. All he first had to do was to create the legend, and rule number one, build on what's already there. He looked around the children who all waited, then around the adults, who all waited, then he felt the power from his right and left, from his two alpha bitches who drove, and he felt ready.

"Right, the legend of the Sprites as never told before! But first, what do we already know about the Sprites? What they like?"

A tiny girl, barely old enough for school, opened. She squeaked, "They're even littler than me."

Then, "Yeah, only knee high."

"Yeah, and really ugly."

"Yeah, repulsive."

"Yeah, and evil."

"Yeah, and steal everything from you."

"Yeah, so little it takes three of them to carry my cakes down the chimney."

"Yeah," the spokesman faltered. "Yeah. Apart from that, they're *so horrible*. The ugliest brutes ever known!"

Tommy took over. "Yeah, the most horrible creatures ever. Just knee high, and ugly, with dirty, pasty coloured skin and straggly hair, sometimes ginger, which falls out when they get old and their teeth go black, and some even have warts. Yeah, they're just like little humans! And their behaviour is atrocious. They'll cheat and lie, they'll steal, and are so greedy, wanting everything and more of it. They'll take your food and leave you to starve, take your water and leave you to thirst, take your farm and leave you to wander, even take your beer and leave you to quiver. They'll take everything and give nothing back. Yeah, they're just like little humans! And do you know why they look and behave like little humans? It's because they *are* little humans!"

The children and the adults all sat in shock.

"Yes, they are. The spirit of the humans. When a human dies, his spirit goes into the queue to wait its turn to come back to the living, as a newborn baby, as it does with all the millions of species. One life in, another life out, and a Sprite is a human who is currently dead, just waiting to come back. I think we all know the cycle of life. Anyway, the Sprites are a little different to all other spirits because when Gayla created mankind, She made two really, really, really stupid mistakes."

One of the children shouted, "Stop!" She cowered down with her brother and looked around, then whispered to Tommy, "What if Gayla's listening?"

"Sorry." Tommy smiled. "Yes, you're right, we must never speak ill of The Almighty, especially as She is always listening. But don't fret, She'll never cut me down for telling the truth. But thanks for caring. Anyway, where were we? Yes, the big mistake. The truth.

"It was time for Gayla to create intelligent life, so She began with the human race. They were like Her prototype, a test case, upon which She would eventually base her very own children, us. So She spent a long time working on the recipe, but sadly, when She put the mix together, She found that She'd got some of the ingredients wrong. Too much of this, not enough of that. Once the humans were down here on Earth it was evident that She had given them far too much greed, way too much ambition, and not anywhere enough charity. They turned out to be a selfish, controlling, cunning, determined and uncontrollable species, which sought to own everything it wanted and ride straight over everything it didn't. They are greedy gluttons and will take everything just because they can, and will destroy all that gets in their way, as they strive to take ownership of everything they desire. *Horrible* creatures.

"Well, She was so disappointed by Her creation that She completely redesigned Her own children, us, before creating them, to ensure that they never turned out like the humans. She designed us, the leprechauns, in Her own image. We were given all the right amounts of everything and She thought 'this is good'. So She sent us down to Earth and ordered that we take dominion over the small earth and be kind and good, and represent all that is good in our maker. So here we are, and there are the humans, and somehow we share the same space on Earth, all be it hard work at times, but we all manage to survive. Just as the Creator would expect of intelligent life.

"However, the recipe for mankind wasn't Her only mistake. The Almighty must have had a really bad day when She created mankind, because Her other mistake was so stupid that it came close to wiping out all life on Earth, as we know it. You see, She forgot to make a place for humans in heaven. No place in heaven for humans. What a juvenile mistake to make? Unbelievable. But it meant that when the human dies, its spirit would not wait for reincarnation in the safety of heaven, it would wait on Earth. It would wait on Earth for a new baby to move into, and while waiting it would roam the earth as a Sprite. Well, the spirit of mankind was every bit as evil as its living counterpart, and without the confines of a living body, it just did whatever it wanted. In short, it took everything from the living, leaving the World a dying apocalypse, and the Earth was close to the end.

"Gayla first thought about destroying the humans and everything associated with them, especially their spirit, but Her Conscience reminded Her that She was the Creator, not the Destroyer. She would have to correct her mistakes, not just wipe them out. Mankind would have to continue.

"She realised that the human spirit was the problem, wandering the Earth, and out of control, so, She called a court meeting of all the spirits in heaven. Every single species of life was represented in the massive gallery and they were to consider the case of the Sprites being left to roam the Earth. She called a representative of the Sprites to visit heaven, in defence of the case against the human spirits. Then She asked the spirit of the leprechauns to act as prosecution. The stage was set.

"Gayla laid down the case to the millions of spirits in the court, then stood proud in front of Her bench and addressed the Sprite. She spoke loudly to ensure that all of heaven could hear. 'Well mush, what you gotta say?'

"The Sprite was clever. He was, after all, the spirit of a human. He calmly stated, 'Guilty of doing what you accuse, your honour, but not guilty of doing anything wrong. After all, you're the Almighty, and made us what we are, and placed us where we are. It's all.... your.... fault.'

"After a brief grumble, the Almighty turned to the spirit of the leprechauns, then explained that She was hungover when She made mankind, and now Her Conscience would never allow Her to destroy Her subjects. 'So, I need some suggestions.'

"The spirit of the leprechauns thought very carefully before answering. He was wary of the Sprite's intellect and did not want to risk further bitterness between the leprechauns and mankind, so he needed to be diplomatic, suggesting remedies which would be agreeable to all involved. He stood up very tall on that day and addressed the bench with intelligence. 'Your Almighty, your children have given the situation our most in-depth consideration, and we do not want to pass the blame onto yourself. I choose only to look at moving forward. In no way am I blaming you for this stupid mess.

"She snapped, 'Get on with it. I ain't got all day.' The Almighty sat down on Her throne and waited the prosecution's further input.

"The leprechaun bowed his head and continued. 'Well, the problem is that the spirit of mankind, the Sprites, have to wait on Earth for reincarnation. Now, somebody who shall remain nameless, never made heaven big enough for them to wait up here. So, build an extension onto heaven. Build a dedicated waiting room where the Sprites can queue up and steal from nobody. A waiting room, only for the Sprites, to keep them away from the other nice spirits. Well?'

"The Almighty was impressed. 'Never thought of that.' She looked at the defence. 'What do you think of that, mush?'

"The Sprite was careful with his answer. 'Your Almighty, your honour, it can't be done. After all, you gave us our greedy side and we all love you for it, but if we wait in a heavenly waiting room for too long we'll lose the ability to be greedy and evil. We'll lose what you so generously gave us, our bad side.'

"The Almighty looked to the prosecution, so the spirit of the leprechauns answered. 'I have a proposal, a solution that would suit all parties, your Almighty. When you build the extension in heaven, give the waiting room its own chimney. So, when a child is naughty, the Sprite can come down the chimney to Earth to punish the child by taking his or her favourite toy, and then go immediately back up the chimney to heaven. Then, to make sure they don't lose their *kind* side, make them make cakes for the children and deliver them down the chimney, for every child on Earth. Ensure they practice their good and bad sides. It'll keep the human spirit balanced, good and bad, and keep them away from the living at all other times.'

"The Almighty Gayla was again impressed. She said, 'This

is good. Build an extension with a chimney that goes down to Earth and the spirit of mankind will maintain its different emotions. Punish the children when they misbehave, but reward the children with cakes when they're good. And keep the Sprites well away from life. Now, I think we have a solution to allow the Earth to survive, forever. And I decree that the Sprites will take the cakes and deliver them down the chimney to every child on Earth, once a year, on Holi Eve. Forever. Case closed.'

"So, that's why you'll still get your cakes and your punishment, even though the Sprites aren't here. The end."

Tommy felt a warm glow, with Ty and Dana flanking him and a satisfied group of children looking fondly back at him. He felt like he was ready for the great journey forward. He would rule the World with the children by his side and he would never be alone.

Ty stood up. "Now children, time for bed, and don't forget what comes if you're naughty." She pointed to the top table, "And you too, adults!"

But, as the group began to stir, a very, very tiny boy called out, "Why?" They all laughed and retired. A big day was ahead of them.

CHAPTER 30
BOOM BOOM

Everybody spent an uncomfortable night in their family huddles wrapped in survival blankets and trying to rest. Very few were able to sleep. Tommy and Aaron went up top, to the rear gunnel, just to clear their heads, where a part moon shone, its silver dancers frolicking on top of the ever-increasing waves, but they couldn't see anything apart from the glitter. After a brother-in-law embrace, they rejoined Dana and Ty.

It was just beginning to get light in the east. The tribe had not really slept, so were still under their blankets but talking amongst their family groups, nervous and agitated. Some children began to argue about something or other, then some of the men left their huddles.

A boy shouted, "What's that?" He pulled into his father for support. "What's that? That noise?"

They all strained to hear what his young, sharp ears had picked up. Many began murmuring.

"Quiet all! Be quiet," urged Jim.

Absolute silence.

Yes, there it was, a feint noise, a regular bang, beating about every eight or nine seconds. It was regular and constant, like the distant beat of a drum, muffled in the damp air.

Several men rushed to the stern and climbed to the rear gunnel. The sound continued from the south, and it seemed to be coming closer, very slowly. It was half dark so they could see nothing, but the metronomic bang continued.

As the daylight increased the air hung clear for a couple of hundred yards, then a wall of thick mist blocked everything beyond, but the drumming continued, becoming slightly louder by the minute.

Boom, boom, boom went the drum.

Then it appeared like magic! The small ship emerged from the wall of haze and the drumming was suddenly un-muted, boom, boom, boom every eight or nine seconds. It was a small longship, no sails raised as there was no wind, and powered by eight oarsmen each side and they were orchestrated by the foreman's beat of his kettle drum. With each boom the oars drove the vessel onwards and it moved gently towards the Nettle Wits.

The Wits broke from their trance and flew into a panic.

"Quick, everyone under the seat! Ship coming!"

They rushed to collect their blankets, shillelaghs and backpacks and all huddled as a tight group up one end below the seat. Everybody kept quiet.

The boom was coming closer. The route would have just missed the tiny boat, but shouting began and the boom suddenly stopped. They had seen the abandoned skip.

Very soon the boat rocked violently as the ship pulled closer. Two boat hooks latched onto the gunnel, then a pair of feet stamped onto the floor and a sailor pulled the anchor in, laying the rope and anchor across the floor in front of the Wits.

In no time the boat was tied to the stern of the ship, the sailor rejoined his mates via the scramble net, and the foreman resumed his drumming. The Wits were on their way to somewhere else. Wherever the longship was going, they were going.

CHAPTER 31
REGICIDE

Fortune seemed to be shining on the tribe of endangered leprechauns and the ship was riding the flood tide into the port by the end of that very day. Using the tide to carry them and the skills of the oarsmen to manoeuvre them, they soon tied up on one of the births, and the small boat which had been rescued was moved onto a pair of slip-posts.

The Nettle Wits quietly celebrated below their seat, but decided to wait for the quayside activity to quieten down before making any move.

Eventually it was evening, with the tide still rising, the sun had dropped over the western hills and the quay workers retired for the night, all leaving a very quiet scene. The moonlight dimly lit the arena.

Jim, Tommy and Aaron went up onto the gunnel to survey the area and make some decisions. It was almost high tide and the gunnel was just about level with the top of the quay, so they could easily throw some ropes across to the quay and disembark. They waited a while for the noise of the quay to abate, and the time was right.

So, the tribe took that first opportunity to disembark onto the stony quayside. It was dark, but the silver light from the moon revealed two sailors sitting by the birthed ship. They were on mooring-rope duty. Much chatter and laughter came from the other side of the quay as people drank around the brazier and in the bar, but little else stirred. The tribe hurriedly moved across the stone towards the town and after about three quarters of an hour, found the edge of the cobbles where the weeds and grass grew. They camped amongst the dandelions until daylight, when the entire tribe rose in unison.

They had all slept well and showed signs of getting back to their old ways of hubble, bubble and chatter.

The usual group congregated below a large clump of dock leaves. "Need to work out what's about," suggested O'Toole. "Can't stay here. The humans'll be about soon. We don't know what their business is here, so best stay clear."

Jim, Tommy and Aaron volunteered to make a recce of the area, by going over to, and up, a gorse bush which grew from the wasteland around them. The girls said that they would look along the fringe of the metalled quayside, to see what was there. The gorse was further away than they had realised, almost twenty minutes walk, but once up high in the branches it was worth it. The ship that they had been rescued by was birthed in the right hand mooring, where the smaller ship had been when the Saint Patrick left the birth. Where the Saint Patrick had been, was empty. Then the bar where the Doyles had drunk, was closed Up.

"Oh no! Oh my God." Tommy held his his head in his hands. "Can't be. Please tell me I'm dreaming!" The three of them looked around at the familiar sight. They were right back to where they had escaped from!

Panic set in. "We need to get out of here before they see us."

They scanned the scene for any signs of the enemy, and it all seemed quite clear.

Tommy suggested, "They won't know we're back, so if we can get out of this town now, we'll be safe."

They climbed down, cursing their luck and swearing about their beloved Gayla, their saviour, "Why would She do this to us?" grumbled Jim. "Straight back into the fire."

Captain Phillips led the run back to the tribe. Jim and Tommy struggled to keep up, lagged behind a bit with Jim wheezing and panting, and they lost sight of the young captain. Then Tommy slowed a bit to allow his dad to catch up, but suddenly stopped dead. Aaron was ahead, waving them to get down. They crept up to him and instantly saw why he had stopped.

The tribe was ahead, all massed into a huddle of red and green, and being overseen by four Cockle Wits. They had been found.

The Cockle Wits stood out to the front of the Nettle Wits, talking, but the three were too far away to hear.

"Shit, shit, shit!" Jim stamped his foot. "The bastards. We should kill them. Four of them, fifteen twenties of us! Just kill them all!"

Tommy took his arm. He calmed down.

They were unable to hear, but the big man in the middle was doing the talking. The small group was made up of Weaver, his youngest son, the captain who managed at the exits, and a big man, fully armed and frightening, their chief; yes, Chief Running Foot, the dictator. He stood slightly in front of the other three and was questioning the tribe about where they had been for the past few days. Tommy, Jim nor Aaron knew that the tribe had claimed that everybody was present, and Weaver had not disputed it. As far as Chief Running Foot was aware, the entire tribe was in his custody.

They wondered what to do, stay away or join the tribe. But Jim kept his composure and ordered them to stay until they knew more of what Chief Running Foot's plans were. They watched intently but could not hear the chief talking. They needed to get closer.

Then Tommy heard a cock Robin singing, it reminded him of Ty, his lifelong partner of just a couple of weeks, then he noticed that she was not among the tribe, nor was Dana nor his mum.

"They're not there," he whispered. "Mum, Dana and Ty are not there.

The other two agreed after scanning the huddle.

Then the cock Robin sang again. It was a pretty weak effort, flat, lacking that depth and resonance that they so well knew from the top of the pigsty. Very weak. They looked to a tall milk thistle, quite close to the tribe, where the Robin seemed to be singing from, amongst a group of ladybirds which perched below one of the leaves, but then from amongst the ladybirds rose a green hand and the Robin again sang.

"Ty." Tommy jumped up but was pulled back by Aaron. "It's Ty. Look." He pointed her out and suddenly they could see all three of the girls. "We need to get over there."

The girls waved and indicated that they would come down, and so the boys covertly crept to the base of the thistle as the girls descended. Ty hushed them all. They were much closer to the tribe and did not want to be heard. On the other hand, they were close enough to hear Chief Running Foot as he addressed the Nettle Wits. There seemed to be a lull in the talking.

Dana whispered that Chief Running Foot did not know that they were missing, and nobody had mentioned it, including Weaver and his son, so he must still be on their side, else he would have asked where they were. It was a glimmer of hope.

Dana quickly explained what had been said. "Chief Running Foot was not pleased that they attacked his men when the Nettle Wits escaped, and he would bear that in mind when considering the control of the slaves and the use of the shackles. He stated that any misconduct or defiance would result in severe punishment, possibly starting with the children. There would be separate schools and pubs for the coloured people, that's us, and separate pavements, and the coloured ones would start, with immediate effect, to make the sugar, alcohol and tanned hides that used to be supplied by us as part of the trade agreement. Those not working in the new factories would work in the cockle-boiling plant and in the sewers, and anybody not pulling their weight would be chained and flogged. And any direct association by a coloured with a Cockle Wit would be punishable by death. It was all bleak listening, the sound of hell."

"What can we do?" asked Mary, holding tightly onto Jim's arm. "We couldn't live like that, could we?"

What a predicament. Walk away, find a way out of the town and start again. Just the six of them. In a hundred years, they could have bred a new tribe of Nettle Wits, as probably happened three hundred years earlier. Walk away from their blood and roots?

"Never!" Ty stamped her young authority on her family. "I'll never desert our people and I wouldn't expect any of you five to either. We *must* help them!"

"How? Let them settle into the prison camp and rescue a few at the time?"

Dana said, "No. He also said that if any escape he would punish those who were left, so it would be all or nothing. It would have to be."

They needed to think clearly. Help the tribe from a distance from the outside, or work with them from the inside. They all agreed that Jim should lead on that front, but he was not comfortable with that.

Suddenly, "Look!" Weaver jumped forward and stood ahead of Chief Running Foot and pointed. "Look! It's the missing ones." He had spotted Jim and company. "I thought there was someone missing, and there they are!" He pointed directly at Jim. "Come here, you lot! You're not getting away."

The chief jumped forward and grabbed one of the children. He held his knife to the child's throat.

Weaver again shouted, "Come here!"

They had no choice but to join the tribe. Poor Tommy could not even start to comprehend why Weaver had pulled them in after working so bravely to allow their escape. Tommy felt betrayed, not just by Weaver, but by his own judgement of people. He was devastated. 'Why?' was echoing around his brain as Ty led him and the others to the camp.

Weaver nodded to the six and simply said, "Welcome back. This is your new chief." He held his hand towards

Chief Running Foot. "Say hello to your chief."

Then Chief O'Hoolihan stood up. "I'm still your chief, Chief O'Hoolihan, until I'm replaced by vote. Until then, I.... am.... your.... chief!" He looked around at his tribe. "This man will never rule over you. Never."

The Cockle Wit chief just smiled and reminded him, "I already rule over you all. You're my slaves. But....if I need to tick the right boxes, we'd better fight. Our laws say that my position is won by the shillelagh and defended by the shillelagh. I'll fight you, kill you and your tribe can take that as final." He laughed and looked at the Weavers and the Cockle Wit captain. "As you are my witnesses, I will take this tribe on as part of my Chieftain." He stepped to the clear space in front of him. "Chief O'Hoolihan, defend your Chieftain."

O'Hoolihan's face went grey, facing certain death in a dual which was like a gorilla against child. He bravely stepped forward.

"Stop!" Jim shouted, then moved to the front. "Our chief's a leader, not a fighter. I'm the fighter. I'm his champion, O'Kief Who Fights Adders and Lives."

Running Foot laughed out loud. "Then you're redundant! All the adders went to Gaul, remember? So you've nothing to live for anyway." He bowed his head. "Well, champion. For your tribe, fight."

Dana held Mary into her shoulder. They could not watch Jim die, but they all raised a cheer as their champion stepped up to the lethal challenge.

Jim removed his shillelagh, which was a blackthorn spine, the thick end shaped to a round, suitable for knocking in posts. Running Foot removed his, which was a spine from a baby sea urchin with a nobbled head suitable for crushing bone, and a shaft lined with razor sharp barbs suitable for shredding muscle. It was a foregone conclusion.

As soon as Jim raised his weapon, running for lunged with his and took Jim's arm from under him and Jim's shillelagh flew from his hand, then almost in the same action, swiped sideways, and caught Jim across the head above the ear, and he was down. It took just two seconds. Blood flowed from head wound.

Running Foot raised his weapon, aiming the killer blow….

"Stop! Wait Chief." Weaver carefully stepped in front of the waiting chief. "This is not the one. He's just a decoy, prepared to die for his saviour."

Running Foot frowned, his orange face questioning his right hand man, but also showing great restraint and chivalry, as he placed his shillelagh back in his sheath. "Explain yourself Weaver. It'd better be good."

"Well, the prophecy of the Saviour has re-emerged. Many have been talking about it, and many believe it's true and the time is right for his appearance." He stopped for effect.

"Get to the point, now."

"Well, many are believing that he is here right now, and he'll take you down. You know the legends."

"Your son is a brave warrior, but he'll never beat me. You know that."

"Not my son, the man who will one day rule the World. Murphy has told me about him. He's right here, today. He's just waiting for the right moment and he'll take you down." Again, he stopped for effect. "That's what our people believe."

Running foot looked at his captain. "Is this true?"

The captain bowed his head. "Yes, Sir. That's what they believe, it's what we believe. All of us."

Then Running Foot bellowed, "Murphy, stand up Murphy right now, or I'll come and get you!"

Murphy stood up. He was shaking and pale.

"Tell me, where is the man who will rule the World? Point him out." He hesitated. "Please."

He pointed to Tommy and shook his head in apology. "He's the one who'll one day rule the World, Tommy

O'Kief." He stopped pointing.

"Well, Tommy O'Kief. Is this your father who's prepared to die in your place? He's a brave man." He held his hand down for Jim to take, and helped the concussed man to his feet. Mary and Dana rushed to help him back to his family.

"A brave man indeed. Captain! Remember his name. Jim O'Kief Who Fights Adders and Lives. A brave man, one which we should remember." He scanned the tribe and settled on Tommy. "You Nettle Wits are not as described. You're much braver and more honourable than I thought." He studied Tommy. "You don't look like a man who will rule the World, Tommy O'Kief. You don't look like a man to fear."

Tommy felt encouragement from his sister and his new wife. He felt that the chief was not quite as *he* had been described, and could feel some mutual admiration growing, and could feel similar vibes from his family, in that the chief had shown real compassion towards Jim. Despite his fearsome ability to fight, he clearly had other qualities. Tommy pulled away from Ty and walked forward to Running Foot.

"What should a man who will rule the World look like, Sir? Like you? Like me? Like Weaver? What do you think? Am I a man to fear? Or could I rule with kindness?"

"Well, Tommy.... Do you have a ceremonial name, as your dad has? As Murphy has?" He tensed. "I know! Chief O'Hoolihan, will you take this man to be O'Kief Who Almost Ruled the World? Christen him before he dies, because I have a proposition which, if he really is the one, he'll take up. If he's as great as his father, he'll take me up on my proposition. Otherwise, he's a fraud."

Tommy nodded his acceptance of the proposition. "Whatever it is, I'll take." He looked lovingly at Ty. "What is it?"

"Well, not everybody in my tribe of ten twenties is as honourable as me, but the captain will ensure that my word is good. These are my witnesses and they will witness a fight to the death between the greatest chief the Cockle Wits have ever known, and the Nettle Wit who is destined to rule the World. On paper, it sounds quite even. Will you take me on?"

"What terms?"

"As these men are my witness, if you win, you step into my shoes, then you can decide the fate of your tribe, and fight next week for the Cockle Wit Chieftain. Now, if you lose as you will, your tribe can leave. Free to go home. You have my word." He bowed his large orange head to the young Nettle Wit. "My word is harsh, but always true."

"Why?"

"My people want slaves, but they don't want coloureds. I don't want either, and there can be only one chief, two would never work. But.... I do want our trade agreement to continue. Three hundred years of stability, who would want to spoil it all? So, you have the chance to die for your people, as your father was prepared to die for you. Now fight, if my terms are agreeable, or I can just kill you, Tommy O'Kief Who Almost Ruled the World, then enslave your tribe to satisfy your part of the trade agreement."

Tommy looked around at his folk, his stare ending on Dana, Ty, his mum and dad, and of course Aaron. He took strength from his loved ones, and turned to Running Foot. "Sir, I don't really know what's going on, but I'll fight you. I'll die for my people, but.... there is a condition. My tribe must leave now and I'll fight you once they've gone. Then, I'll give you my word that the trade agreement will continue from the hills. My tribe will always honour our agreement."

A smile and a nod from the chief agreed the deal. He stated, "This is, however, an official event. To make it legal, we need three witnesses from each party. I have mine, name your three. They can remain behind as witnesses. Three from each tribe."

Tommy could see that he was not quite the ruthless dictator that they had made him out to be. He briefly wondered who the real villains were, but then they were all products to their society, kill or be killed. Perhaps their society was just, after all, and he had a sudden desire to learn from it. "May I ask you one question, please. What would you do if somebody did something really stupid, and the act put your entire civilisation at risk?"

Running Foot thought hard before answering, then, "I would raise a court, and if the man was guilty of malice, I would execute him. If, however, he was not found guilty of malice, just stupidity, I would forgive him and support him. Justice is always hard but fair. Why ask?"

Tommy never answered, but simply bowed his head in thanks.

He nominated Aaron, Jim and Murphy as witnesses. "All the others can go, and we'll catch up with them when the fight is over."

"Agreed."

The tribe moved away, including Ty, Dana and Mary, who needed some persuasion from Aaron's parents, but they all eventually went. The eight people who were left nervously watched for the Nettle Wits to go fully out of sight. Then....

The captain saluted both Running Foot and Tommy, and explained to Tommy that during official duals, only the shillelagh, hands and feet could be used as weapons. The two stood facing each other, surrounded by the six witnesses. Jim stepped forward, his head still blooded, and hugged his son. He said nothing.

The fight began with no further ceremony. Running Foot waited for the slightest move from Tommy, then lunged his weapon at Tommy's shoulder. But the youth from the green-corner was too quick, avoiding contact, then as Running Foot swung his club Tommy raised his with great speed to deflect the blow. The chief stood back to regroup his thoughts. He then poked at Tommy's leg but was deflected and swung at his midriff, but a quick step back and he avoided contract. The chief stood back and gently moved around his opponent. He nodded to show his appreciation of Tommy's speed.

The green fighter was fast and could probably dodge the orange man's blows all day, but what then? Kill the chief? How could he bring himself to do it? Kill another leprechaun? He was in a no-win predicament, and his head churned.

The chief suddenly dropped to the ground and swung at Tommy's legs with his foot, which Tommy dodged, but the follow-through of the shillelagh caught his shin, slicing through the flesh and leaving the green one limping and bloody. First blood to the orange corner! The young wit moved backwards to compose himself, but the chief saw his hesitance, perhaps also a bit of shock, and jumped up and forward, club swinging sideways and downwards towards the thigh. He caught Tommy's flesh. More blood, more leg damage and the young Nettle Wit staggered. The chief caught his good leg with his foot and Tommy was down. He lay on his back as Running Foot stood over him, bearing down with the urchin spine. Tommy closed his eyes.

It was just a second later that the sharp end of the shillelagh pierced the body, split the heart open, and broke out the other side. Tommy rolled over as the orange man-mountain fell by his side, stone dead.

The man who would rule the World stared around him, and momentarily choked at the dead chief lying face down right next to him, then he crawled away as Running Foot's blood began to creep from beneath the body.

He had won! How? Why?

Weaver removed the blackthorn shillelagh from the chief's back and laid it across the dead man's shoulders. He had been skewered from behind! The Wits stood in shock as Tommy struggled to his feet.

"You won." Weaver offered Tommy his hand. "Our new chief. Let me help you, Sir." He grabbed Tommy and held him up as Aaron rushed to his assistance.

The victor couldn't comfortably stand up, nor could he comfortably understand quite what had happened. He had won. But he had lost. He had laid waiting to be skewered, but his opponent fell to the ground, dead. He looked at his dad and asked what happened.

Jim wasn't sure what to say, nor was Aaron, nor Murphy. They all looked at Weaver, who stood over the fallen chief. Aaron insisted. "What've you done? Explain, Weaver."

Weaver had stabbed his chief in the bank. The dictator was no more.

"It was a fair fight. We all witnessed it. A fair fight now.... Chief, what should we do with the body?" He bowed his head to Tommy. "We're all at your service."

The man who would rule the World suddenly went weak and heady. He was not only confused but also injured. Weaver's son took some linen from his pouch and applied a tight bandage to the cut on Tommy's thigh, and the bleeding soon stopped.

Once he had recovered his head, Tommy asked the Cockle Wit captain, "What was this all about? Tell me."

The captain stepped in front of him and saluted. "Sir, you've beaten the chief of the Cockle Wits in an official and fair fight, and you are our chief. That's what's happened. You are chief of the Cockle Wits."

"But...."

"No buts!" Weaver raised his hand. "No buts. You know as the teller of legends, or myths, that nobody is interested in the real truth, just the history, the legend. The history shows that you beat Chief Running Foot fairly, and de-throned him. That is the truth, as witnessed by these six responsible adults." He hesitated. "You know, Tommy, we have a saying in our armoury of legends and myths that truth is belief, and we all believe. You should make sure that your legends reflect that, and I do believe that they already do." He looked at Murphy.

The new chief's head was clearing. He was just beginning

to wake up to reality; he was the Cockle Wit chief. The one and only.

He asked the captain to explain why they were all happy to stab their chief in his back, and, "And that's an order. Tell me, captain."

The captain obliged his chief. "Nobody could beat Chief Running Foot and his reign was beginning to damage the tribe. So we had to take the opportunity that you presented. And we did. And besides, we didn't want to see another of our family die at the rut. My nephew can now fight you at the rut." He grinned. "Unless you do the right thing, of course, Chief Tommy."

Chief Tommy, as it turns out, probably could rule the World. He thought carefully about their situation, that bad luck, or perhaps good luck, and how the Cockle Wits had grabbed a fleeting opportunity to take control away from a highly successful, albeit, unpopular dictator, and with the same swipe, save the life of the oldest Weaver boy. And it was all witnessed by six independent, reliable witnesses to make sure that history was only ever told their way. He suddenly admired their cunning, however, that type of cunning was never the Nettle Wit way, and it never would be, and he felt ashamed to be part of it. But he *was* part of it. He was the very centre of it. He had to do the right thing, he had to.

Just as he was about to address his three Cockle Wit subjects, there arrived a group of orange soldiers, led by the big man who had taken them to the boat, Weaver's oldest son. The first thing they all did was pay their respects to the dead chief, and the second thing was pay their respects to the living one. Weaver's son was a general. It seemed that he was the next one down from Tommy in their hierarchy of power, and also the contender for the Chieftain, due to fight the chief at next week's rut. Due to fight Tommy at the rut, and it would be a fair fight. A death sentence for the man who would rule the World.

There were fifteen soldiers with Weaver's son and all offered an opportunity for Tommy to take this dark business outside of the six witnesses, and create a wider case for the Nettle Wits. He was slowly realising that this world in which the Cockle Wits thrived was not for them. It was paramount to Hell. He knew that he couldn't trust Weaver and his two companions, and he also knew that at next week's rut he would die against the contender, who at that moment, was seemingly his loyal servant. If he and his tribe were to live to create a new world of their own, he would have to make it happen. Think like them.

"General Weaver."

The warrior stood in front of his chief and waited. He looked down on Tommy. He was a man of similar stature to Running Foot, but younger. Size and strength was clearly part of the Cockle Wits' status, and as he looked around the soldiers, he could understand that the entire tribe was fearsome. But were they honourable? Well, Running Foot was, but the three witnesses? They never had an ounce of honour in them, back stabbers and social climbers at all cost. But what about the rest of the tribe?

"General, where are my tribe?"

The General looked around at his dad and brother, then asked the captain, "Well, Captain, where are the Chief's tribe?"

The captain did not endear himself to Tommy as he answered the general's question. "Do you mean the Chiefs orange tribe? Or the coloureds?"

General Weaver immediately stepped sideways to face the captain. "Answer the question, Captain! And this time make it a bit more politic. A *lot* more politic!"

Nerves seem to suddenly develop amongst the gang of three, telling Tommy that the general, the contender to the Chieftain, was not part of the plot which killed Running Foot. He was like Tommy, an unwitting pawn.

Before the captain could answer, General Weaver called

one of his men, a slim young man, the runner. He ordered him to get to the exit post and tell them that General Weaver has temporarily overruled the captain. "If any Nettle Wit is harmed, they'll all be pegged out for the crabs. Now go quick. I hope we're not too late, else the crabs'll be well fed tonight." He looked to his father. "You've got some business to discuss with me behind closed doors. I hope you can explain."

But Tommy had learned very quickly about survival. He was proving to himself that his reputation, as unwelcome as it was, had some element of truth. He could see that the general had not just the stature but also the compassion and understanding which had kept Running Foot in his office for fifteen years, and Tommy could see a route out for him and his people. Perhaps the Nettle Wits were not so close to extinction as seemed the case just a little earlier.

"Thank you, General." He studied the orange people. They were leprechauns, but different to them. Different in all ways, including their individualism. Nettle Wits are self disciplined, automatically falling in line with the needs of the tribe. But the Cockle Wits, he could clearly see, needed organising, ordering, controlling and punishing as well as rewarding. They looked for constant leadership from others. They looked to their new chief for leadership, and Jim, Aaron and Murphy could all see evidence of that. Jim called a private meeting with Chief Tommy and the Cockle Wits seemed quite at home with the concept of personal advisors. Weaver looked to his chief as if to ask, 'Do you want me along?' but Tommy shook his head.

Jim whispered. "You've got the power, use it. Get us out of here, Chief." He grinned as he said chief, but was not relaxed. "Use your power."

Murphy added. "I feel ashamed with us all being used by my so-called friend. I hope everybody will forgive me. That's if you can get us out of here, Chief." He also forced a smile at the C word.

Just then, the runner returned and spoke privately to General Weaver. The captain was visibly wilting.

"General." Tommy leaned on Aaron's shoulder to take the weight of his injured leg. "I've spoken to my family. But first, what's the messenger got? Not bad news, we all hope." he looked at the captain.

The general answered. "They're all safe, now. They're being held at the exit post until your orders, Sir. What are your orders?"

Tommy was thinking on his feet. He was, though, realising that the Cockle Wits, or most of them, were honest and loyal to their chief, and like it or not, he was their chief.

"Chief Running Foot must be honoured by the state for his many years of service. Tomorrow, a full state funeral will be held, but before that I need to lay out my own plans. You could call it an inaugural speech." He held his hands out. "Please gather round, as you nineteen Cockle Wits need to convey this to the rest of the tribe, in my absence.

"Cockle Wits live here in the lowlands. You are kings of the coast. The Nettle Wits live in the hills, kings of the moors. Cockle Wits are proud warriors. Nettle Wits are master farmers. Cockle Wits fight, we talk. Cockle Wits are orange, Nettle Wits are green. Cockle Wits relate to their own identity, Nettle Wits to theirs." He paused. "So, as Chief Running Foot said before he died, who would want to spoil it all? Not me, not you. You don't want us here. We don't want to be here. That's the entirety of it all. We are so different.

"If The Almighty had wanted us to be the same, she would have made us the same. So, we're going."

He looked around the group of representatives. "You all need to understand that we are the same as you, but different. With that as the foundation of my decree to my Chieftain, I order both the Cockle Wits and the Nettle Wits to continue the neighbourly relationship that both tribes have enjoyed for over two hundred years, to continue trading and respecting, but from a distance, from our separate lands. Long live our mutual friendship, but may God preserve our identities."

Arrangements were made for General Weaver to be invested as Chief Weaver of the Cockle Wits in the absence of Chief Tommy, and the fifteen soldiers proudly formed a guard of honour to march the Nettle Wits safely to the exit post.

The Nettle Wits went home.

CHAPTER 32
THE MAN WHO RULES THE WORLD.

The tribe walked with slow deliberation away from Tommy's adopted tribe of warriors. They were of a different world, not just in colour but in mental form, in their life-philosophy, in their politics, in fact in everything that mattered. The Almighty never designed the two peoples to consort.

"They're not bad people, just different." Dana took Tommy's arm and smiled at her hero. "That's what Tommy O'Kief Who Rules the World would say, when asked by Young Weaver. Or was it his brother asking?" She had a private giggle. "You know, Chief Weaver was a handsome brute, but repulsive. I think that makes sense."

As the Wits walked positively towards the land which they loved, everybody was thoughtful. Not much was being said, despite their inner discharge from the clutches of the Devil, but they would have plenty of time for talking during the two-day journey home. Tommy noticed how so many were casting glances towards Jim and Mary, then nodding and smiling through their appreciation of what he had risked for the tribe.

Tommy beckoned his sister, wife and brother-in-law to him.

"Everybody is beginning to understand just what Dad did back there. He volunteered his life up for his people, and they're only now taking it into their hearts. The O'Kief Shillelagh was about to deliver true justice, in the defence of its own kind, and Dad's a living legend. We should all do something for him."

Ty, "You're the story-teller. Make a new legend, around the past few days, with him as the king-pin. Remember him while he's still alive."

"Already done it, O'Kief Who Fights Adders and Lives. Remember? I think he's too proud to have another legend in his name, at least while he's still with us."

Dana, "You're right, he's not one who flaunts himself, but the legend still needs to be told. You still need to tell it, it's been a proud experience for the entire tribe, despite being so scary. Just need to work out a starting point, and of course, a moral message."

Aaron eventually made his contribution. "But your dad should still be honoured, even if he does grump about it. So, at the next elections, I'll put him forward for chief. The greatest honour, Chief O'Kief Who Fights Adders and Lives."

They all agreed that it was one to consider, then Dana continued in her role of spokesman to the Saviour. "Me and Tommy both believe that he would never accept the position. He's the Defense Regiment through-and-through and when he stops being the General, he'll retire. Aaron can take over."

Both Ty and Aaron raised their eyebrows at the suggestion that Tommy would not take over from his dad. He and Dana were keeping something from their life-partners, perhaps it was time for Tommy to come clean.

"I'm just about through with leading, so Aaron can lead the Defence Regiment. Look what I've done so far, caused untold damage to the entire civilisation, and it was only through a couple of miraculous pieces of luck that we're still here at all. I'll tell the legend, The Legend of the Girl with no Knickers, but it won't be a story of bravery and pride, but of lessons, ones that must be remembered for eternity and learned from. Serious lessons. And the biggest lesson? Dana? You're my inner force, you tell them what we've done."

Ty and Aaron were respectfully quiet, and waited for many minutes as Dana thought through Tommy's predicament. Eventually she sighed and made the Man Who Rules the World's proclamation.

"The lesson? Never, never, ever interfere or involve with humans. Never! That's what the legend has to reflect, and my brother can lead from the pews, by keeping that simple rule alive through the memory of our trip through the Valley of Death. And you two both know what we're getting at. Ty, you almost said it at the quay when the tribe started to blame the chief. This all started when we threw Father Partick in with the Fullers and Doyles through our reckless prank on the little boy. That's what put that team together, the one that'll get the blame for our sad adventure, but we know where the blame really lies, with us!"

Dana was right, the other two both knew what the catalyst for the disaster was. But, even if the tribe also knew, they would do the Nettle Wit thing, and just get on with life, in support of each other, of the tribe and of the common good. The blame culture had never reached the Nettle Wits, and besides, Chief Running Foot made his point about justice; stupidity should be supported not punished. The entire tribe took in his message.

"Yes, my brother will tell the Legend of the Girl with no Knickers, and he'll make sure everybody knows what caused it. If Father Patrick never had to act as mediator that day, Captain Garibaldi would never have been introduced, and the Nettle Forest would still be there. It was all our fault. We'll make Dad proud, and come clean about our stupidity and pay our penance." She couldn't hold back her grin which stretched right across her green face. "Let's hope they send us all to the hedges as punishment."

The tribe arrived back at the pigsty, full of relief, but as they looked out from the caves below the sty, their sumptuous, green nettle forest was still a tilled field. It would take a long time to wake out of the nightmare, it was real; they still needed to stand to attention.

Mankind was there to stay, at least for a while, and the Wits knew it. They finally believed that the nettles were gone forever and the village was no place for a coloured, so this was their lot, like it or lump it. Snake farm was their paradise, even without the nettles.

But what of mankind? Snake Farm was to become an important player in the wool and linen industries and was about to hit the big time. Mr Fuller and his dad completed their water wheel and automatic fulling hammer, and they took in all the wool from the local weavers to be fulled, tendered and sent down to the quay for export. Then the new linen industry gave the Doyles an opportunity which they jumped at, laying their entire farm down to flax, then leasing the land around Snake Farm to increase their production. It was a lot more than the 'farmers' hovel' that the archaeology expert had suggested to the schoolchildren.

However, mankind is no different to us leprechauns, but at the same time very, very different. He is highly intelligent, but not as intelligent as us, and his God is a jealous God, whereas our God is the only God, so unlike us, mankind struggles to survive through the traumas, refusing to learn the lessons and therefore reliving their nightmares over and over again.

The wool and flax industries boomed for more than ten years, but they weren't so advanced as the leprechauns and couldn't understand that planting the same crop year-after-year would take a lot more than God's will from the soil, and the land soon ran out of nutrients, the crop reducing further each year. On top of that, Gayla sent ample rain until the year AD76, when she ran out of rainclouds in the west, and the area suffered two years of serious drought. The abused soils dried out to dust and much of it blew away with the wind. The Doyles' boom times were short-lived.

But the wool industry thrived. The Fullers took more and more woven cloth in to be fulled and marketed through the dealers down at the quay, and with the flax imported from the fertile Ulster farms, the area continued to boom despite the Almighty's efforts to quell the flow of wealth. But mankind's biggest enemy? Himself. If Tommy really thought about it he would never say that man is his own worst enemy, he would be a little more leprechaun in his outlook and say than man is *everybody's* worst enemy, but let's not get personal. Now, that worst enemy, the one up north in Ulster, had a very strong Tuatha and a massive linen and wool industry of which they were very possessive. When the wool and linen from our own village earned itself such an outstanding reputation, threatening the northern industry, the Ulster Tuatha sent its troops south. They arrived at our village and murdered, raped and pillaged for several days before burning the entire area to the ground, including Snake and Doyle's farms. They then moved further south and wiped out our Tuatha's dynasty home, plundering the royal treasury and in doing so, uniting the Tuathas of north-eastern Ireland; the first steps towards the bloody unification of Ireland (in human terms, that is).

Then there are the Cockle Wits. Well, they have made their own legends, one being when the Cockle Wits chief declared war on the humans and set about teaching them a lesson for destroying their village. The King of Ulster's son was paying a visit to the derelict docks when the Cockle Wits poisoned him with mushrooms and led him in a drunken state onto the beach, then tied him up. They would watch the man who destroyed their village, as the tide engulfed and drowned him. Good riddance to bad humans. But his soldiers noticed him missing and managed to get to him before the tide, and he was saved. But it did get the message across and the humans created their own frightening myth of monsters and ghouls, so never again settled in the area. Heaven for leprechauns!

The story was passed down through many generations until, a thousand years later, the tale was adapted for the stage, and Fergus mac Léti, the King of Ulster, was attacked on the beach by leprechauns. That was the first known writings of leprechauns, just a stage-play, a myth. But we now know that myth is just an adaptation of the long-forgotten truth, and that the Prince of Ulster, in the first century AD, was pegged out on the beech by the Cockle Wits. The truth!

Sadly, no records have survived to tell the absolute true tale of Snake Farm and the trading village, just myths and legends.

Or have any records survived time? Mankind doesn't have any, but....

Snake Farm, AD69, at the base of the pigsty's back wall.

Chief O'Houlihan addressed his people. "We're home! Our forest has gone, but let's not complain! We've seen the options down the road, and even without the nettles, we now know that this is our paradise. We *can* turn this nightmare into a dream, but not overnight, nothing good happens that quickly. Rapid turnrounds are for disasters, and the good things usually take a little longer. So, we can do it, somehow." He held his hand out to Tommy. "We had our first committee meeting this morning, and I can now introduce this man as O'Kief Who Rules the World. It was a unanimous vote in favour. So, I invite the new adult, O'Kief Who Rules the World, to say a few words before we all start future-building."

Tommy stood forward. "Thank you! It's a great honour to receive an adult name, and I'm certain that the real ruler of the World, The Almighty, will not see it as competition."

He looked across the space to Ty and Dana, and they nodded back to him. "Now, before us four go off to the hedges to lay the ground for our main migration, I have a serious issue to clear up, and Chief O'Hoolihan Who Designed the Farming Calendar has given his backing for me to take it up with the tribe, so listen carefully. This morning Ty suggested we go for a walk around the caves, we've never seen them all and they're extensive, reaching much of the pigsty foundations, but we were suddenly quite shocked. As we entered one of the long caverns we couldn't believe our eyes. Graffiti! It was all along a large section of wall. Now....who's responsible? Well? We're Nettle Wits and we don't lie, so step forward....now!"

After an electrifying silence, three young Wits, about thirteen-years-old, stepped out to the front. The two boys and their sister hung their heads low, and Tommy carefully studied their body language. He could see the guilt, as he and Dana had experienced when they pranked the little boy.

"Now, you three put the graffiti on the wall, how long will it take for you to clean it off?"

The three children looked around to their parents, then the mother stepped forward. "I'm so sorry Tommy. It's fungal dye, that we use in the tannery. It'll *never* come off."

Ty and Dana grinned, but Tommy kept a serious face. "Right. Right, never come off. Right. Now this morning at the meeting we discussed the graffiti and spoke about how we could punish the culprits who put it there, and I think it would be proper for the chief to announce the punishment."

Chief O'Hoolihan Who Designed the Farming Callender stepped forward. "You three must be punished for the act of vandalism. The entire committee agrees, but first I need to explain to the tribe what you've done. Ty walked us through to the graffiti, and read the graffiti to us. It was about a tribe of green leprechauns who lost their homeland, and so tried to emigrate to Gaul but missed the ship and then became captives of the Cockle Wits, where they encountered a strange man, Weaver With Many Faces, good, bad and ugly, but he showed us his good face by setting us adrift in a small boat.

"The story tells of how we were marooned on the anchor, and Lucky Eddie gave his life to save the tribe and was swallowed by a Basking Shark, and how we were starving and ready to take the suicidal leap over the top and onto the rocks, when the booming started. The kettle drum boomed with metronomic precision as it moved closer, then stopped when it saw our abandoned boat, and we were towed into port. We were right back to where we started, as captives of the Cockle Wits.

"The story tells of how Chief Running Foot was about to kill our chief, me, to legalise his ownership, when a big man stepped forward and offered his life in place of mine. Jim O'Kief Who Kills Adders and Lives. We all owe him a big debt, as it ultimately saved our entire civilisation. And before the misunderstood Chief Running Foot died, he gave an order to his tribe, of which we were part at the time, to remember this brave man. That is what this beautiful wall art does, forever, remember the bravery of our saviours, Lucky Eddie and Jim O'Kief Who Fights Adders and Lives. They will never be forgotten."

The chief stepped to face the three culprits.

"It is the most beautiful thing we've ever seen. Now, the big man, O'Kief, has a dream, and you three will make his dream a reality during his lifetime. That is your punishment. You will make sure, through your wall art, that our entire history and legends are recorded, never to be forgotten, along with everything about our ways, industries, everything including the mankind with which we share our space around Snake Farm, and the entire tribe can advise, so nothing is missed. That is your punishment, understand? You and your family are the tribe's recorders, a brand new industry."

The three children raised their eyebrows, then one of the boys asked, "How long will it take?"

"The rest of your lives, and your children's lives and your grandchildren's. It's now your family's cast, Wall Scribes. And don't forget....we all need to remember the nightmares, not just the dreams. And don't forget....leave enough room for the next few hundred years."

The three children suddenly had red grins which almost cut their green faces in half. One of them giggled as he asked, "But what about our proper punishment?"

"Don't be silly. We're Nettle Wits!"

CHAPTER 33
LEGACY

Almost 2000 years later, in the year 2015......

The group of schoolchildren had spent five days camped out at the site and had made some digs in-and-around the derelict stone walls, and around the mysterious sandstone slabs which sat a little way from the stone building, but they had, for some reason, been careful not to disturb the foundations nor the flag-stones. The archaeological dig was coming to a close.

"The people that lived in these hills were clearly a very primitive civilization, we believe all living in the only stone building, four families, one in each section." The pigsty! "The two stone flags have worn in such a way that we think they must have had religious relevance, maybe used for sacrifices to their gods." The doorsteps! "They were certainly a civilization with primitive ways, and would have had a hard, desperate existence in these unforgiving hills. There's also evidence of a warring society with the defensive moat which has been cut along the side, there." The clay-pond!

The pupils sat around the fire and marveled at the expert's unfolding story. One of them asked, "What about the walnut trees, Sir? And why is this area called Snake Farm?"

"Well, we know for certain that walnuts were introduced into Great Britain in the third or fourth centuries by the Romans, and much later into Ireland, so these couldn't possibly be anything to do with the primitive farmers who once lived here. Yes, a much later addition, possibly when the peat was being cut in the mediaeval period. And Snake Farm? Don't know, as they've never had snakes here, so, just a name, I guess."

The girl asked, "So, what could have happened to the peasants who lived here?"

"Well, that we can only guess." As if the rest of his twaddle wasn't a guess. "But they clearly moved away, and just disappeared."

Now, that was typical Human Being, don't know anything, so they improvise and guess, and what a stupid thing to teach the innocent young schoolchildren, that anything can just disappear. Ask any good leprechaun and he'll tell you that magic doesn't even exist. It's all fairytale stuff. Disappear? Ridiculous.

On that day, two very distant descendants of The Man Who Ruled the World hid between the slabs, taking in all the bull that the expert handed out. My sister and I enjoyed listening to the 'expertise' of mankind, it was always a good laugh.

Dana said to me, very quietly, "They're almost as intelligent as us, but have some real hangups. They always have to know the answers, even when they don't, and that seems to be what humans do, bullshit their way through life. Dana held onto my arm. "If they had found our wall paintings below the old sty, they'd know the truth."

"Never! They're too small for them to notice, and besides, the only reason they're still there is because mankind *hasn't* found them." Tommy suggested they get back to the others, who were updating the paintings with this year's legend, but held back as the school-children began moving around.

The team of young humans prepared to leave the site, and one decided that she would like a photograph of her, so that she could remember the week. She wanted one with her standing on the 'sacrificial' stones. With the camera focused on her, she stood astride the altar and smiled, one foot on each of the flags.

"Aaaaah!" Dana grabbed my head and shoved my face in the dirt. "Don't look! Don't look up. It'll make you blind."

She laid across me and threatened, "Keep down or else!"

As the schoolgirl stepped away from the door step, we relaxed. Dana whispered, "That was close, you almost saw it." She allowed me up from the dirt, and we watched from the gap as the archaeology group left the site.

I brushed the dirt from my green shoulders and started giggling. "Don't they talk a lot of crap, humans. Hey? Just because everything was wood and was burned, they assume it was never here. That little boy understands, it's not all about hard evidence." I suddenly needed to know. "Why couldn't I look, she probably had her knickers on? And besides, it was only a.... "

"Never! I couldn't take that chance. You've read the legends in the caves, from two thousand years ago? Just imagine what this World would be like if our forebear, Tommy O'Kief Who Rules the World, had looked up and gone blind. Don't bear thinking about. Come on, the Scribes must have finished their paintings by now and'll want to get back to the copse. We can tell them what the old codger thought of Snake Farm. Idiots, all of them!"

It was exactly one hundred-and-twenty generations earlier when the real legend began, the girl with no knickers. "Don't bear thinking about."

And the future legends? Who knows, but I can say that the Copse Wits would go on to live happily, almost forever after. Or is it just myth?

The end.